Some stories can't be contained between the covers of just one book. In Ice Queen, Tyler helped Mistress Marguerite fulfill the mentoring requirement The Zone club imposes on all its Dominant members, to learn about BDSM from the submissive's perspective. Though Marguerite is one of The Zone's most sought-after Mistresses, Tyler is convinced she is a "switch", a closet submissive. But the truth that is revealed is more remarkable than that.

As he begins to unravel the complex and terrible layers of her past, Tyler must do what he's never been willing to do before. Open up his own soul, offering Marguerite his own dark places in order to help them both heal. Only then will they be able to surrender to a force stronger even than The Zone's most powerful Master and Mistress—a force that can bind them together forever.

Mirror of My Soul

Copyright © 2006 Joey W. Hill

Edited by Briana St. James

Cover design by W. Scott Hill

First published in digital format May 2006 by Ellora's Cave Publishing, Inc.

SWP Digital Edition publication July 2015

SWP Print Edition publication March 2016

The following material contains graphic sexual content meant for mature readers. Reader discretion is advised.

ISBN: 978-1-942122-44-9

Mirror of My Soul

A Nature of Desire Series Novel

Joey W. Hill

Preface

Author's Note about *Ice Queen*:

They call her the Ice Queen. At the exclusive BDSM club known as The Zone, Mistress Marguerite is a legend. Tyler Winterman has been fascinated with her since he's known her, though the rules of their world say they shouldn't share more than mutual admiration. He is her male counterpart, one of the most powerful Doms practicing at The Zone.

Due to a computer error, Marguerite lacks the mentoring program stipulation required of all Zone Dominants, which includes spending a number of hours learning about BDSM from the submissive's perspective. Tyler considers it an act of fate that Marguerite chooses him to be the Dom who helps her fulfill that requirement. He is convinced she is a "switch", a closet submissive, but the truth will be even more remarkable than the theory, changing their lives in ways neither of them anticipates.

Ice Queen focused on the weekend that Tyler spent with Marguerite, helping her to fulfill this mentoring requirement. Marguerite found herself overwhelmed by her emotions and strong physical reaction to his Mastering and tried to sever their connection after their weekend together. Tyler, in an attempt to coax her into pursuing a deeper relationship with him, asks for the privilege of serving as her submissive for one night within the walls of The Zone.

Marguerite's desire to prove to Tyler she can top him as naturally as he Mastered her compels her to accept his invitation. But when the nightmares of her dysfunctional past rise during the session, she becomes violent and uncontrolled, breaking every rule a Dominant is supposed to follow to protect the well-being and safety of her submissive.

The fact she beats the hell out of him doesn't turn Tyler away from her. Still restrained and now bleeding, he calls her to him. She responds, ending up at his feet, holding on to him, needing to feel him, to be near the sanctuary of his voice.

She couldn't top him. She didn't want to. She didn't want to be a Mistress to Tyler. The knowledge of it was quietly there, the real battle she'd come in here to fight. What the waiting look in his eyes told her he'd known all along. He'd proven himself her Master even when bound, taking over her senses even without the privilege of touching her.

She was a Mistress who needed a Master. Who needed him.

Mirror of My Soul picks up Tyler and Marguerite's story right after this session, so you haven't missed a single moment between them. Enjoy...

Joey W. Hill

Chapter One

She heard The Zone staff come in but didn't move, simply too numb to do anything. She must have phased out for a bit, just stroking the back of his thigh, for suddenly she was vaguely aware of an employee reaching under her to release the manacles on his ankles.

"Thanks. Darken the ceiling on your way out, will you?"

Tyler's voice, the only thing that registered. There was the whir of the mechanism, shutting out faces that were probably wondering what kind of show they'd just seen. The last performance of the Ice Queen.

"They'll never let me come back. You have no choice but to kick me out now. There isn't a rule I didn't just break."

"Well, I wouldn't count on that. I told Perry we were planning a demonstration of what *not* to do. Like a community service message."

She knew he was free now but he didn't disturb her yet, letting her kneel there, holding him. "Do you always anticipate everything?"

There was a silent moment before he answered. "No. I didn't anticipate that I would fall in love with you from the very first moment I saw you."

She closed her eyes. "No." She ducked her head away as he bent down over her, tried to turn her face. "I can't look at you. I can't."

But his fingers insisted, so at length she did. Tilting her chin up, she saw his beautiful eyes full of something far too perfect for her to see. Then she saw more. Two slashes on his face that were open and seeping blood, the skin around them an angry red. The second one had left a cut across his eyelid and the bridge of his nose. His jaw was swelling, where she well could have broken it with the tawser.

Her fingers were on it before she could stop herself. "Oh God, Tyler. I'm—"

He laid his lips over hers, taking her words, her hitching breath into himself. When he raised his head, she had nothing, he had it all.

"I'll endure anything for you, angel. Anything." He curved that broad back over her, wrapped his arms around her body. Instead of fighting the touch, the intensity, her body recognized it as a safe harbor. Her fingers latched on to his forearm and her nails dug in, cutting as if she were holding on to a cliff edge.

The sobs rolled over her, taking her, her cries of distress that were much too strangled to be called crying. Tyler thought she sounded as if she was being torn apart from the inside.

He'd made it onto the right path at last. But instead of triumph, at her anguish he could only feel the same pain, the pain of a man who loved her desperately, who only wanted to make her feel better, make every nightmare go away.

Her body was shaking as if she had a fever. Another woman's face would be wet with tears but it was as if she didn't know how to cry like that, any more than she'd known how to let herself go, to allow herself physical fulfillment. Her skin was ice cold.

As he comprehended the significance of that, the door beeped, opened.

"Everything under control in here?" It was Mac, his eyes assessing the situation as a cop and a friend. At the moment Tyler was grateful for a person with both to offer. Dan was a quiet shadow at his back, having disengaged the locks for Mac.

"I think she's in a bit of shock. Can you bring me my jacket there?" He nodded toward the corner in the shadows where they'd hung it.

"Her cloak's here too."

"Bring them both over but she needs the jacket first."

Mac nodded to Dan, exchanged a quiet word, closed the

door. He brought the jacket and cape, came over and crouched. Marguerite pressed her head against Tyler's arm, shutting them out. Mac's eyes noted her nails dug deep into Tyler's arm.

"Here, angel." Tyler tenderly pried her loose, slid her hand into the sleeve.

It had been like this a long, long time ago. Marguerite remembered this haze of nothing, where she had thought nothing would ever make sense again. Then there was the social worker reaching through that haze to find her, with the touch of a hand, a doll and a tea set. She resisted his movement of her but he was a lot stronger and simply made her limbs do as he wished, enveloping her in his jacket, his scent. She immediately rewrapped herself around his leg and arm as soon as he was done.

Tyler winced as her nails clamped down into the same spot but he simply stroked her hair, held her close. "She'll be all right in a bit," he said quietly. "Where's Violet?"

Mac reached out, laid a hand on Marguerite's quivering back. Grazed his fingers over her forehead, gauging her temperature.

"She's too pissed off. I talked her into letting me come check on you."

"We're fine," Tyler said.

"Yeah, you look it." A corner of Mac's mouth twitched. "You're going to need some medical attention."

"I've had worse beatings in my life."

"Just wait until Violet gets done with you." Mac stood. "You owe me one. She's going to make my life hell for the next few days for keeping her out of here when she let loose on you."

"Did you sit on her or use a headlock?"

"You laugh now but Mistresses can be meaner than hell when crossed." His gaze lingered on the ugly swellings on Tyler's face. "I expect you know that."

He retreated, closing the door, leaving them alone.

"Angel, let me take you home, put you to bed."

"I can drive myself."

He smiled against her hair but his heart tightened at the rough quality of her voice.

"No, you won't. It's not a request. I'm taking care of you tonight. That's the end of it."

She raised her head and her grip on his arm eased at last. She looked as if everything had been drained away, leaving her skin drawn taut, those blue eyes dominating her face. "And who will take care of you?"

"Well, if you want to rub aloe all over my body, I guess I won't object." As he stroked her hair away from her cheek she sat very still under his touch, staring at him.

"Tyler, you know I can't do this. You need to hear me for once. There's a reason I choose to be the way I am. The alternative is..." Her fingers reached up abruptly, touching his jaw. "This is the alternative for me."

"No, it's not. There's another path. You know it. You accepted it, even if only for a few minutes. That's what scared you so much." He lifted her chin, brought his mouth close to hers as her lips trembled open.

"Say it to me, Marguerite. Say the word that's in your heart, the reason you're on your knees now."

She ducked her head but he caught her chin. Taking her hand, he placed it on the side of his face.

"Your mouth may not be able to say it but every other part of you is."

He knew he shouldn't push right now but the images were in his head. The fierce light in her eyes, the taunt of her body displayed before him, rubbing up against him. The break in her eyes when she knew. Even the energy she put into the beating. Every part of him ached but there was a violent need in him.

"I can't—"

He caught her throat in his hand, kissed her. Not gently this time. Despite her vulnerable condition his intuition told him the moment required hard, brutal demand. His hands running down her arms, over her back, holding her against his bare chest, his tongue invading her mouth, his teeth tasting her. When she made a soft cry that vibrated against his grip, he tangled his other fist in her hair, held it as her nipples hardened against his chest. Reaching down, he put a hand between her legs and shoved the dress up to find her wet and slick, her thighs trembling.

"Say it, angel. Or I fuck you until you do, until you're screaming it every time you climax."

"If I say it, will you let me go home alone?"

"No. I already told you, that's not an option." He brought his hold back to her throat, felt her telltale shudder at the contact while he remembered how she'd constricted his breathing. How he hadn't cared if she strangled him, if only she'd put her lips on his and give him oxygen from the body he craved. "Marguerite."

"I'm not... I can't yet. Please don't do this to me."

"We both know you're mine." *Because every fucking beat of my heart is yours.*

Passing his hand over her shoulder blades, he felt her shiver with a combination of desire and terror both. The former heightened his lust for her, the latter roused his urge to protect. The Dom in him responded to both.

When he laid his palm on the back of her neck he felt the wisps of hair brush his knuckles. Leaning in, he kissed the top of her head. "All right, then. I'll let it go for now. I need to talk to Perry a moment to make sure we're all square but then we'll get you home."

He surprised her, not just with the sudden withdrawal of demand but by simply scooping his arms under her and lifting her, not even giving her the option of rising. He set her in an occasional chair that was in the shadows. The chair was intended for a weak-kneed sub or as a comfortable seat from which a Mistress could contemplate the artistry of her bound submissive. Or she could make him bend over it and place his lips on the cushion where she'd just been while she fucked him with an impressively intimidating dildo. Marguerite had used it for all those reasons. Never because she couldn't stand well enough on her own two feet.

She had to pull herself together. She couldn't let herself believe even for a moment in the fantasy of someone else doing it for her. He kept his profile to her, glancing at her often as he dressed. Socks, underwear, tucking that appealing cock in the snug boxers, pulling up the slacks, belting them. She knew he had to be hurting like hell but not once under her unwavering gaze did he flinch. She knew part of it was male pride but she also suspected it was that chivalry of his that wouldn't let her suffer the full guilt of knowing how much she'd hurt him.

At the height of her frenzy it had even crossed her mind to destroy him, obliterate him entirely, as if the emotional pain he'd drawn from her made him as bad as the source of the pain. At that moment she could no longer distinguish friend from foe and all that mattered was the solitude. Destroying everything so it would be quiet in her head. She wouldn't even care if they took her away and put her in a room by herself forever, her only job to stare at padded walls and wait for the oblivion of the final injection.

Instead, something had changed as those quiet amber eyes had watched her, waited on her. She'd ended up on her knees at his feet, kissing the hurts, a nonverbal plea for forgiveness for drawing him into her nightmare. For not wanting to release him from that nightmare because he made her feel she wasn't alone with it anymore. While she wanted to cringe at the pathetic picture the words painted, her heart brushed that off and simply focused on him, on each look he sent her way. He shrugged into the shirt, left it open, rolled up the cuffs and draped the tie on either side of the collar. His coat was still around her shoulders. She didn't want to take it off, which made her start to do so.

"No." He came and pulled it close around her, enveloping her in the warmth. "You hang on to it awhile. It's steadying you. Your color's getting better. C'mon."

He half lifted her off the chair, his arm going around her waist. She made herself find the strength not to lean so much but her knees were loose, as if the joints had a questionable ability to lock. With the least amount of encouragement he'd carry her and she'd suffered enough humiliation for one night. She allowed the arm, even used a handhold of his shirt and the firm flesh just above his hipbone to help her get out the door of the room she never wanted to see again.

"My... I didn't clean up."

"They'll get it. I'll pay them the extra to do the cleanup, sterilize the whip and tawser. Are they yours or The Zone's?"

"The tawser's mine."

"Okay, then. Don't worry about it."

"They'll charge it to my card. This is my night. I'll pay for it."

The hallway was quiet and she was thankful that The Zone had a side hallway exit that allowed patrons with a code to go straight from the playrooms to the parking lot, rather than having to push through the crowds on the main floor.

"I need to go to the women's changing area. Clean up before we leave," she said. "While you talk to Perry."

"All right." Allowing her to move out from under his arm, he nevertheless took her hand, apparently to steady her and make sure she was standing on her own. He kept his gaze on hers. "Your car keys."

"What?"

"You heard me," he said evenly. "If you force it, I'll just take the whole purse. You're not going home alone."

The marks on his face slapped at her every time she looked at them, making her heart hurt. Jesus, her body and soul hurt. She was so tired and so restless at the same time. Looking at the blows he had taken without complaint, accepting them as he seemed to be accepting her, was too overwhelming. She had to get out of here. Her heart was in anguish and her pussy was throbbing with want.

Before she knew it she'd taken two steps forward. Curling her hands into his lapels, she jerked him to her. She covered his mouth in a way she'd never done in her life, forcing her tongue in past his teeth, snapping at him as she plundered to feel the texture of those firm lips. His strong arms locked around her, held her tight to him. His cock almost instantly stiffened against her as he slid one hand down, covered her ass and squeezed hard, lifting her, rubbing her against him, no restraint now in his actions.

She tore away. Tight-lipped, she reached into her purse, withdrew the keys, slapped them into his open palm. "Perry isn't crazy enough to buy that this was a demonstration. Not after he sees your face up close." The words were raw, forced out of her, but she made the effort to sound defiant. In control. "Anything else, or are you going to send Dan or Ryan in with me to watch me relieve myself?"

His eyes glinted and she thought he would have smiled except the movement would have hurt his swelling jaw. "Your color's definitely coming back. I'll be here in ten minutes, tops. Don't worry about Perry and *don't* make me come in after you. I'll deny Dan and Ryan that pleasure but not myself."

Turning on her heel, she made her way across the hallway and pushed open the locker room door. "Arrogant bastard."

She wished the women's room didn't have a door closer so she could have slammed it. She was splitting into two— no—perhaps three or four entities. Nothing was making sense. She hated him. She needed him, ached for him. Coming face-to-face with herself in the mirror, she couldn't bear what she saw there. The eyes of a frightened child come back to haunt her as they always did if she didn't keep a handle on herself.

"No. No. No." She lashed out, striking the mirror with her fist and watched her knuckles bloom with blood, like the welts she'd put on Tyler. The mirror gave way, fragmented into shards that showed her the many different pieces of herself that were her true reflection, a person who would always be shattered. "No, no, no!"

She dumped the jacket, yanked pen and paper out of her purse. When she'd finished the scrawled note, not caring that she'd stained it with her own blood, she put a paper towel under it, laid it on top of the jacket she folded on the bench. Smoothed it with her hands, once, twice, before she could stop herself, getting blood on it anyway. Then the door opened and she turned to face Violet.

Violet had come down riding on fury, knowing Tyler was occupied and that Marguerite would be here but one look at the woman made her stop in the doorway.

Marguerite straightened, her usual reserved mask falling in place, but Violet took in the mirror, saw the tremor in the bleeding hands, the way they had been smoothing over Tyler's jacket a moment before she burst in the door.

"Please make sure Tyler gets his jacket. I'm leaving."

"I don't think he wants you to do that."

Marguerite's eyes were so fathomless that Violet wondered if the woman ever saw her surroundings in the same reality as everyone else. Her unfocused expression seemed more like a clairvoyant's gaze, seeing auras and heat energy instead of physical form.

"You're a cop, Violet. And his friend. You know what I am. A person like me shouldn't be within a hundred feet of someone like Tyler Winterman. Now please get the hell out of my way."

After a full assessing minute, Violet inclined her head and stepped aside. Marguerite pulled her spare car key out of the inside pocket of her purse. With the elegant scarcity of movement she was known for and that she seemed to have reclaimed, she swept by Violet, carrying her shoes and cape in one hand, the key and purse in the other. Violet watched her take the monitored side exit to the parking area, struggling with her conscience.

She'd give her a two-minute head start, then go tell Tyler, though good sense suggested she should just let Tyler find out for himself.

Coming out of the women's room two minutes later with the jacket and the note, she found Mac sitting on the bottom step, waiting for her. Tyler was just coming down the stairs. Taking in what she was carrying, he swore. Viciously, with a fierce inventiveness that she hadn't known he'd possessed.

"You just fucking let her go?"

Mac rose, his expression cold. Violet moved before the two men got any closer, stepping up next to her husband, putting a hand on his forearm as she extended the bundle. "She left you a note."

Tyler took it, none too gently. His gaze snapped up. "Whose—"

"Hers. She beat a mirror to pieces in there. I didn't see anything that looked too serious. Mostly minor lacerations, though they're going to hurt like hell tomorrow." Much like he would, she thought.

Tyler pushed a hand through his hair. When Violet moved closer, her hand extended to look more closely at the condition of his jaw, he caught her wrist. "Don't touch me right now, Violet."

"You can take your hand off my wife before I decide you need your second ass-kicking of the night."

"Mac." Violet shook her head. She knew her husband understood the code of an alpha male. Lord knew she dealt with his temperament often enough. But he didn't necessarily understand what was going on with Tyler right now. He thought he'd won a key battle only to find his opponent had slipped through his fingers. She suspected his automatic reaction was to shrug off rational thought, go run her to ground and either paddle her ass or fuck her until she couldn't think beyond the climaxes, where all the emotion and pain were drowned in sensation.

But she knew Tyler was a better man than that. So instead of drawing back she pressed forward, meeting his hard gaze with her equally unflinching one until he let her go with an oath and she moved up a stair for better access. A tawser used improperly would break bones, not cut, but she'd caught him with the rough edge during her uncontrolled strikes. A stitch or two likely wouldn't do him harm but she assumed he would heal well enough without them.

"Only luck kept her from knocking out an eye or boxing your ear, bursting your eardrum," she said, an edge to her tone. "Read the note and stop thinking with your dick."

Tyler curled his lip in a half snarl but glanced down at the paper.

Tyler, I need to think. I'm not running from what happened tonight. I know you think you know what it means but I don't. I don't know anything right now. I'm going to go see my brother and then I'll go home. I'll call you tomorrow. Please have Violet or Leila take care of your cuts. I'm sorry. I owe you a formal apology and you will get it whether you want it or not. I'm not your wife. You don't deserve to be beaten down emotionally or physically by my problems.

His hand tightened on the paper, his thumb rubbing

over the bloodstained words. At a moment that surely was agonizing for herself, she had thought of him. It moved him, made his heart cry out for her. As well as drove his fury and frustration to an even higher level. Where had she gone? He needed to be with her.

Also, for your future attempts to bully women, keep in mind that most of us carry a spare car key in our purses.

"Smart-ass." But he folded the paper, put it in his shirt pocket, took a deep breath and struggled for rationality. "I'm going to her house," he decided. "I'll wait there until she gets home and make sure she's all right. If that's okay with you. Or are you planning to cuff me?"

Violet pursed her lips. "In our household, that's considered foreplay. And as tempting as it is to smack you around for being an idiot, I think you've been beaten enough tonight."

"I knew what I was doing."

"Yes, you did. It was still dangerous. She's dangerous. You knew it, you told me about it and it was very clear tonight. She can be pushed to a point of no return."

"She's mine." His expression hardened. "And I'll take care of her."

"I know." After a minute, going on impulse Violet put her arms around his shoulders and hugged him close, though gently. Then, just because he'd pissed her off, she smacked him on the back and made him cringe. "Please just think it through, be careful and know we're here if it doesn't work out. Care about her enough to know if you need to give up, okay?"

He sighed, relenting, his arms closing around her waist and hips as he held her small body close, letting her friendship loosen the tight fingers of tension in his stomach. "I can't do that but I hear you, Violet. Jesus, she has a good arm. I haven't had a beating like that since Afghanistan. The Taliban broke ribs and I swear it didn't hurt as much. Did she seem okay?" He lifted his head abruptly.

"I think she's really rattled and scared, knocked off her foundation, which is why I didn't go ten rounds with her. She knew what she needed at this moment. Space. I think you should give her a little."

The step of a high heel on the landing above them made them turn. Leila stood there, a medical first aid kit in hand. "And before you go anywhere," Violet added, "I think you should let Leila look you over. Or I *will* handcuff you to make sure of it. She's as much as said in her note she's not going straight home. You can get tended and still meet her there in good time."

Tyler reluctantly nodded, glanced up at Leila as she came down the stairs. A professional nurse and the woman he'd trained as a submissive for over a year, she'd become a friend and lover who'd opened his heart again. Now her jade green eyes moved over him, assessing. "Well, you've had an adventurous evening, haven't you, Master?"

She'd never stopped calling him that, even after they'd moved on to other relationships, the title one of affection and shared experiences that could get him hard just remembering. Until Marguerite. He took her hand and Violet's to kiss both. "I'm blessed with the friendship of beautiful, loving women."

Tyler shifted his gaze to Mac's unreadable expression. "And I apologize for abusing our friendship and your Mistress."

Mac nodded, his lips twisting in a rueful smile. "Love can make the best man into a total fucking moron."

When Leila took Tyler's hand in hers and the two went down the stairs toward the coed changing room where she could tend him and examine him more thoroughly, Mac's expression sobered. "Violet, that note said she went to see her brother."

"That's what it said."

"Hmm. You remember when we investigated her for the S&M killer case?"

Violet pulled her attention away as Tyler and Leila disappeared behind the door. "I remember." She would never forget the case that brought Mac into her life and almost took him from her forever. The bullet and lash scars he bore were a permanent reminder of even the strongest man's mortality to a woman's madness. While she wasn't ready to relinquish her anger with Marguerite Perruquet, she realized that a good part of the fury provoked by watching Tyler willingly expose himself to the risk had been galvanized by those terrible memories. She felt like she needed a large cup of wine and a mind-numbing dose of sex.

She knew where to get both fortunately. She wanted to immerse herself in the vibrant life of the man she loved so much, so that the turmoil inside her breast and all the nightmares raised by the evening's events could be laid to uneasy rest again.

"He'll be fine, sugar." Taking her hand, Mac pulled her down the steps to close her in his arms, lifting her off her feet. Violet wrapped her thighs around his waist with a helpful hitch from him.

"More than I can say for you." Cocking her head, she eyed him narrowly. But she couldn't deny the sudden, urgent bite of savage lust that was the body's natural response to threat and survival. "You've been a pain in my ass tonight."

"I won the wrestling match fair and square. Though I think Hank's been showing you some new hand-to-hand tricks." His lips quirked, eyes heating as she rubbed against him, digging her nails into his neck when he would have lowered his grip to her hips. Obeying, he stopped, keeping his hands at her waist. As her lips hovered just over his without moving, he remained motionless even as his cock thickened, hardening.

"Not this one." Her hand went down between them, cupped and kneaded him as he suppressed a groan. "But you'll beg hard tonight before you get to come in my pussy. And I might fuck your ass first to remind you what obeying your Mistress's orders means."

"I love you." His lips parted, showing teeth. "My cock and everything else is all yours, Mistress. Always has been, always will be. I'll serve your pleasure however you want it."

When her fingers passed over the bullet scar at his abdomen and shadows gathered in her blue eyes, his arms tightened around her. "She's not a killer, Violet. She's a very troubled lady but I'll lay good money she's as crazy about him as he is about her. It's going to be okay."

Violet squeezed her eyes shut, nodded. "God, I'm never going to stop wanting you. Loving you. But what..." She shook her head, trying to drive lust back a bit. As much as possible with the muscled, two hundred-pound body of her large husband so close, his cock strong against his snug jeans. "What was that about her brother?"

"Her brother's dead, sugar. Remember? He killed himself at age fourteen. With their mother."

Chapter Two

Get Violet or Leila to tend those cuts.

That had been the hardest sentence of the note to write. She'd never allowed herself to cosset her subs, left that to The Zone staff she'd paid to do so. But she had wanted to do it for Tyler. Had wanted to touch each bruise and cut, every welt. Place her mouth over them like a mother wolf, feel his hands touch her, hold her, exchange comfort.

What was she? Who was she?

She sat down on the concrete block ledge of the roof of the Bank of Florida building, the tallest building in the city, a monolith that overlooked a panorama of glittering lights this late in the evening. Swung her legs over the edge so they dangled, braced her arms and stared down hundreds of feet to the street below.

There would be fewer wind currents on a dive from a building like this versus a jump from a plane. A BASE jumper, those daring skydivers who preferred to do their jumps from a stationary structure such as a building, bridge or cliff, would relish the challenge. Leaping out among a forest of buildings, testing the body's ability to work with the small amount of wind and the chute to find a way safely to the ground.

She was tumbling in such currents now, her chute twisted, tangled, not sure of her heading, unable to prevent herself from smashing into any surrounding structures. Yet she kept thinking about Tyler. Tyler at the bottom, Tyler able to catch her despite terminal velocity. But she'd hit that bottom so long ago and not died. Not technically.

She dreamed of David at least once or twice a week. His

eyes a mirror of her own, their two bodies locked together, rolling end over end toward some unknown conclusion. His end had come but hers had not. And one night not too long ago when she dreamed her dream of falling, it was not David's eyes she'd seen but a tiger's. But the look in them was the same. Unconditional love, the desire to protect. She'd known it in her brother's eyes, knew it was real in the dream as it had been in life, but she didn't know if she was imposing it as dangerous, wishful thinking on Tyler.

Drawing her knees up, she rested her weight just on her buttocks, the soles of her feet over the edge. Forward and back, forward and back like one of those children's toys that once were so popular, the ones that had rounded bottoms and could never fall down, never be knocked over. There had been a punching bag like that, too. No matter how hard it was hit, it came back up for more.

She felt a wind current move over her. It was unimpeded up here where this tallest building had no competition. It tried to lift her, push her. As if that wind knew her natural state was to plunge, to tumble, to finish what had been started so long ago.

Could she survive reinvention? Redefinition of herself? Did she want Tyler that much? Did she even have a choice?

"It would have been so much easier if you'd let me go with you, David." And the ironic thing was, to be with him forever all he'd needed to do was let her go. Her words were soft, spoken to the spirits that still lingered here, that stood by her. "But for the first time in my life, I may not be sorry that you didn't... His pull on me is so strong. I never thought there'd be anything stronger than the call of this place. But he's there...here..." Her fist clutched over her heart, dug into her breast. "And though it makes me hurt so badly, makes me want to hurt him for tearing me apart, tearing me open, I want him there inside me, too. He forced his way in. And every part of me..." She shook her head. "Now I want him so much, I can't breathe. And I'm so afraid he doesn't understand what that means. I'm not sure I do and I've always had to be so sure of everything."

Not just her heart and soul but her body, exhausted as it was, was still throbbing for him. She needed to go home, take care of it the only way she'd ever been able to release herself. Though there was a desolate ache that went along with the thought, she knew she was going to do it, because whatever she did when she next faced him she at least had to have some control over her hormones.

Rising, she stood on the ledge and looked out into the night. Felt the cold touch of nightmares pull at her, whisper their seductive promises. But tonight, instead of her will having to summon the strength to resist them alone, thoughts of Tyler's body, his voice and those eyes invading her dreams coaxed her back from the ledge.

§

She pulled up the alley to her private drive, feeling the exhaustion and desire pushing at her equally. She thought about just locking her doors and sleeping here. The idea of getting out of her car and walking up her front stairs was overwhelming. She would if it wasn't for the heavy ache in her lower extremities she knew she had to assuage to sleep as she needed to sleep. So a bath in her living quarters on the second floor of the shop, a quick few minutes to do what she knew had to be done for that and then a new day would begin. It was a little after midnight. She lived in a rough neighborhood, but tonight she didn't concern herself with checking her surroundings as she got out of her car. Being clubbed to death here in the shadows might merely be a relief. *Never a sociopath around to accommodate you when you really need him.*

She was sensible enough to circle around to the more public front of the house. Holding the handrail in one hand, her door key and soft velvet edge of her cape with the other, she prepared for the daunting task of mounting the five steps to the porch.

There were flower petals on each one. White and pale pink rose petals, leading up to a bouquet of them in a crystal vase by her door. Probably a good three dozen mixed with delicate baby's breath. A classic, the rose never failed to convey its message of devotion and romance. Curled around the base was a nearly life-sized plush stuffed tiger. Lying on his side, massive white paws stretched before him, the tiger's back paws and body formed a protective crescent around the flowers.

Marguerite turned then and saw him across the street leaning against his car, arms crossed, watching her. He had that unreadable, somewhat formidable look. A look which, in her current condition, caused a small gasp to escape her lips at the jolt of desire. Oh, God. It was too soon. She'd refuse him nothing if he came within ten feet of her.

Hell, if he crooked his finger at her across a football field distance she'd be lost. She was probably lost anyway. Sinking down on the top step, she found the tiger's head with one hand, her bare feet curling into the soft silk of the petals as he straightened from the car and came across the street.

Someone had cared for him she saw, noting the cleaned facial lacerations. The tiny bow-shaped pieces of medical tape held the edges of the skin together in several places in lieu of the stitches he probably should have gotten. But she'd committed his aristocratic grace to memory and could tell he was not moving as easily as he usually did. But he moved well enough to tell her he'd be back in form in several days. Even more important to her treacherous and selfish body, it suggested he was up to the physical activity she was imagining.

"It's past your bedtime," she said as he reached her bottom step.

"I've no intention of going to bed alone tonight." His gaze burned into her. She could tell he wanted the cape off where he could see all of her. "Unless you flat out refuse me."

She would refuse him nothing. They both knew it now. Still she cocked her head. "And what if I deny you? Tell you to fuck off, get in your car and leave me alone now and forever?"

He took the next step up, forcing her to tilt her head as he leaned over her. "You know what kind of Master I am. We've covered that before. I don't look for words. What comes out of your mouth most of the time are lies to protect yourself. I look for the pounding of your pulse." His hand circled her neck, nudging up her chin. She nearly moaned as he zeroed in on the most sensitive part of her as if he had supernatural intuition. "Breath. Heat. The smell of your cunt, which I know is soaking that excuse for an outfit you're wearing right now. If those things are saying yes, your lips saying no aren't going to mean two damns to me. I'll just find something to shut you up so we can have an honest conversation between us."

"You're angry." It surprised her to understand it, to be reassured by it.

"I was worried. It's not a crime to have someone care about you. To have that person get pissed off when they're worrying about you. If I hadn't been inside your body, known you weren't a virgin, the way you pull back when I try to penetrate you in any way would make me think you weren't just goading me."

"Goading you about what?"

"That you've never had sex."

"I didn't say that. You asked me if I'd ever had sex. As if any of that was your business. I answered you truthfully." At his furrowed brow, she spat it out. "I have never had sex outside of my family. Until you." She met his look with a hard, unflinching gaze for once, her battle line drawn. "And don't go with the pity or psychotherapy, the sexually abused girl who turns into a Dominatrix because she can only experience sex when she holds all the power. Yes, I am the stereotype, the cliché, but I give my subs pleasure. I'm not a sociopath who causes harm." Then she recalled the past few hours and the incident with Tim. She closed her eyes. "Unless provoked."

"But who gives you pleasure?" Her spat-out revelation didn't appear to cause a hitch in his stride, she gave him that. But Tyler was insightful. It would not surprise her if he'd come to an accurate conclusion about her background some time ago. She was, as she herself had just said, a cliché when it came to the dysfunctional symptoms. "Learning to let go of the control, believing you can trust someone," he continued. "That's key to the pleasure as well as the pain... For some people, it heals old wounds."

A wound inflicted every morning as soon as awareness

hits, as soon as my eyes open? "I can never trust anyone." It was simple, matter of fact.

"Then maybe, Mistress, you need to be one man's sub forever so your Master can spend a lifetime proving that you can trust him, if that's what it takes. One who's willing to start over every morning with you, healing those wounds as often as they need healing. My intuition says you deserve to be happy."

He raised her hand, looked at the ragged cuts on her knuckles she'd blotted with a paper towel until the bleeding had stopped. "I'll pay for the mirror," she said.

"I think it's time for you to stop paying debts that were never yours to begin with."

"I take care of myself."

"Yes, you do." His gaze lifted to the tastefully carved wooden Tea Leaves sign hanging over the porch. "You've created a life for yourself that is as amazing and fascinating as you are. It's a reflection of you. All the puzzle pieces there for the person who wants to put them together. But I'm taking care of you now. And I'm going to take *very* good care of you."

"You couldn't save your wife, so you're going to save me? Like I'm some kind of surrogate, your second chance? I repeat, fuck off, Tyler."

She could tell that hit home, but he recovered more quickly than she expected. He gazed thoughtfully at her face. She could feel the imprint of his assessment on her strained features, the shadows deep under her eyes.

"You're not a second chance, Marguerite. You're an only chance opportunity for a man. For me. What you put in your note, it mattered to me. I appreciated it."

She lifted her shoulder. "I'm not weak and fragile. I'm not incapable of taking responsibility. You have every right to expect my apology." She raised her gaze to him, realized she was getting in the habit of meeting his eyes, something she'd never done with anyone. "It would make me really, really angry if you thought I was so delicate you couldn't demand it."

"I don't believe you're fragile that way. And I don't believe you're a coward," he said quietly. "But sometimes I think when you have to be so extraordinarily courageous for so long, the well runs dry when it comes to facing your own desires, the things you want. So you don't have to be brave about that, or in control."

She looked at him, a tall handsome man with caring in his eyes, strength in his shoulders outlined against darkness. Something in her simply yearned. When she spoke, her voice was soft, no defenses, no games, just the words that were written on her heart.

"I don't know how to let someone take care of me, Tyler. I don't know if I'd be any good at it, if I can ever trust someone that much. And you need that. You deserve it. I see it in your eyes, in all that you are."

He leaned down further, so they were considering each other eye to eye. Cupping her cheek, he rubbed his thumb over her lips in that way he did, that she knew he liked. She liked it, too, the way he did it while gazing so steadily into her eyes.

"And I look in your eyes and see everything I could ever want. Trust in that, angel."

She swallowed, treading into new waters. "I almost didn't get out of the car. Thought I'd sleep there until morning. This is as far as I think I can go."

"I think you can go a lot further." His eyes glinted with a wealth of meanings, none of them unpleasant, all of them capable of setting free nervous frissons of energy through her lower vitals, reinforcing that there were portions of her that still needed attention. "Let's do this. Just put your arms around my neck. I know you're tired."

Tired didn't even begin to describe her drained status. So she did after a brief hesitation. He gathered her in to him, slid his arms under her legs and lifted her off the steps, amazing her as he had before at how easily he did it, as if he could carry her forever. It was a foolish, romantic notion, as was letting her head drop onto his shoulder as he unlocked her door, closed them in, turned the deadbolt.

He took her upstairs where her living quarters were, showing her he had paid close attention on his visits to her place. The stuffed tiger told her he had good ears, too, apparently overhearing Chloe's comments about him spoken through a swinging kitchen door on their very first meeting. He paused at the top of the stairs only a moment, went left.

Tyler found Marguerite's bedroom was a tranquil mixture of Eastern tastes and Western whimsy. The four-poster bed with the carved floral headboard was complemented by the framed Japanese water scene hanging over it, the soft glow of Chinese lanterns she kept lit and strung from each post like a canopy frame. There was a bamboo sea chest in the corner, some photographs arranged on its surface. Somewhat like those in the tearoom, only more personal. Pictures of the little girl whose party she had hosted, all large eyes under one of the big hats, her neck strung with elaborate rhinestone beads. Chloe and Gen conferring over a steaming teapot, Chloe laughing, her eyes alight with whatever dry witticism was falling from Gen's lips. And one that surprised him as he let her feet touch the ground.

It was a photo of him taken in a park in Tampa where he ran when he was staying at his place in the city. He sat on top of a picnic table, his body sweating from the run. His hands dangled loosely between his knees. He had a half smile on his face where he'd apparently seen something in his people-watching that amused him. It was a very intimate picture, his knees splayed in the pose, the curve of his groin visible under the fit of his sweats. The long line of his inner thigh was defined as well as the curve of his biceps as he braced his forearms on his legs. His T-shirt was balled up in one hand. The dampness of the hair at his nape and temple from his exertions had been captured in the photo.

Stepping away from him, she turned her body so she blocked it. "It was chance. I was in the park that day, practicing photography. I saw you, decided to try a shot."

"How long ago?" His voice was soft as he moved toward her, trapping her in that corner unless she made an awkward dodge to avoid it. She stayed still, though her body trembled the closer he got. It heated his blood, made his cock harder, made his heart ache in his chest. "Answer me, Marguerite."

"About two years ago."

Soon after the first time he'd seen her at The Zone, felt that odd connection whenever their gazes met.

"You felt it, even then. As I did."

She tried for a shrug. "Infatuation happens."

"And yet." He placed a hand on her shoulder, nudged her to the side. "The picture is still here. And it appears someone's finger has touched the glass. Often."

"It's a good photograph. And the cleaning service I use probably does that when they dust the frames. I've got to go to the bathroom." She shied away, skirted the bed and disappeared into her bathroom, closing the door.

Tyler let her go with an effort, hoping that it being the second floor and her own house, she wouldn't try to escape again. His gaze returned to the picture. Marguerite had taken care and time with the photograph, capturing the expression she'd wanted, the aspects of his body, his posture. He was aroused and humbled at once by what the picture revealed about the photographer, about the way she might feel for him. He wished he'd been able to handle differently so much of what he'd done with her. No matter that his gut told him he was on the right track, that some fortresses could only be breached by acts of destruction, it hurt him deeply inside to cause her harm or pain in any way.

"I only want to love you, angel," he murmured. "Just let me in. Let's stop making every step into a fight."

His gaze shifted to the shelf of books. Tea, Eastern philosophy. Pain management techniques, mental as well as physical. Interesting choice. His attention slowly covered the simple, sparse elegance of the room. Each item obviously was chosen for its significance to her, which underscored the importance of the photo. At her bedside nightstand there was a book of Haiku, a clock, a lamp. And though he was normally the type of man who accepted the boundaries of common courtesy, when it came to her the boundaries were thin. Especially after tonight. He moved to the nightstand and opened the small drawer, just curious to see if she was as sparse in the contents of what could not be seen as what could.

His gaze narrowed. A black silk scarf. A coiled belt with additional holes punched in its length. Two lengths of nylon rope. He turned, examined the four posts of the bed. He found what he was looking for at the third one, at the foot of the bed. Reaching out, he ran his hand over one hourglass shape where the veneer was rubbed thin. It was not greatly noticeable, particularly if, as he suspected, the only one who entered the room was the one who slept there.

The anger in him which had settled to a simmer after he had seen her arrive safely, after he felt her body safe and sound in his arms, awakened like a dragon from its lair.

Marguerite stepped out of the bathroom. She froze when she saw the open drawer, his hand on the post.

"Tell me this isn't what I think it is."

She tightened her jaw, clenched her fists at her side. Anger flooded her, a reaction to her trepidation at his tone. She couldn't back down from him, wouldn't act like a person that owed him an explanation. Or her submission.

"It isn't what you think it is," she said sarcastically.

She'd not forgotten how fast he could move, just how quickly his temper could motivate him to do so. Abruptly he was in front of her, had her turned and flat on her back on the bed, his body over hers. He yanked open the clasp of her cloak and caught the high neck of the nearly transparent dress beneath, ripped it all the way down, pulling it open so her completely bare body was beneath him. His trousered thigh pressed between her legs.

The moment the hard muscle flexed against her clit, she could not stop the involuntary, almost violent reaction. The arching up of her body as if offering itself to him. She needed so much. She had to have him inside her. He needed to leave, so she could get it under control. She shoved at him and he rolled her over onto her stomach, pinning her wrists behind her back. He used one of the ropes from the drawer, firmly securing them, rendering her helpless.

"Let me go."

"Not now, not ever." His hand was on her bottom now, his fingers clutching her buttocks, squeezing hard, making her want to beg. "Is that what you do? You strangle yourself to make your cunt weep when your subs can't?"

"I get aroused by my slaves. *All* of them," she spat.

"I'm not your slave, angel. Don't even try to be catty with me. And you do get aroused by what you do to them. But the key's been staring you in the face all along, hasn't it? You can't get off without being restrained. Since it's hard to tie yourself up in a way that makes you feel helpless, the way you need to feel to let yourself go, you strangle yourself. You told me you aren't used to touching yourself to bring release, so how do you do it?" His hand tightened on her left buttock, those strong fingers moving more deeply into the crease between. "You'll answer me."

"A pillow...and a towel. Between my legs. I use the other rope...to secure it." She was glad she didn't have to look at him now. His breath was hot on her neck, his body insistent against hers.

"Tell me." His rigid cock beneath the trousers rubbed against her ass where his fingers pressed into her, making her whimper and push herself hard against the mattress, spearing herself with the pressure on her clit. "What do you fantasize about? Who do you imagine is cutting off your air, controlling everything to bring you to climax? Making you come at his command, denying you everything until you give up your cream to his touch, his taste, the pounding of his cock?"

"I hate you." She sank her teeth into the bed linens as he slapped her ass, setting off a ripple of nerve endings, the sensation shooting straight to her core.

"That's what I thought." Leaning over her, he removed the scarf from the drawer. "There's not going to be any more lying."

She opened her mouth to retort and found it filled with the scarf as he gagged her with it like a bit, tied it behind her head. When he shifted, the silken fabric of the tie that had been dangling around his neck slithered against her throat. She closed her eyes as a hard shudder went through her.

"You will never, never engage in autoerotic asphyxiation again. If you want your Master to restrict your air to heighten your pleasure, you'll ask for it. But tonight you're asking for nothing. I'm going for what I know you need, what your body is screaming for."

She wanted his cock. Wanted it deep in her body, filling the emptiness in every part of her. He wouldn't give her that tonight. Somehow she knew he would make her come in ways she'd never experienced but he'd deny her what she most wanted until she begged for it.

He tied her ankles together with the second rope, then took the slack up to her knees and bound those together, confirming his intentions not to put anything between her thighs as large as his cock. The compression of her thighs made the throbbing almost unbearable. She writhed, letting out a short yelp as his palm struck her again.

"Be still, angel. Let it build until it's a fire through every part of you."

She thought it already was but his words made her burn even hotter.

His fingers traveled, knowledgeable and so clever, down the small of her back to caress her fingers, her palms. She didn't try to grip him, far too mesmerized. She'd never been a man's lover. She'd always been a Mistress, so everything was new. It was amazing to her that he knew how to touch her in ways she didn't even know herself. He moved over the rise of her buttocks, then slowly pushed between them, the pad of his thumb finding her anus as it usually did, then he stroked her there, firm caresses with just the right pressure to make her pussy clutch like a fist around the void inside it, the void that wanted one thing. Him. She gnawed on the silk as he kept up the torturous rubbing and then he sank his thumb deep into her there without warning, so easily because of her sensuous writhing, her lack of expectation that he'd planned to do that.

She'd noticed how well manicured his fingers were, the absence of rough cuticles, the precise cutting of the nails just below the end of the fingertip. Now as a result she felt no sharp scrapes that could be so magnified in this area, where a tiny cuticle could feel like a sharp stick, a rough-edged nail like a shard of glass.

Her hips jerked as he curved over her body, his thigh pressing against the side of her bound legs. Putting his lips on the back of her neck, he began to nibble, taking his time even as that finger moved incrementally within her, sending sensations through her stomach like snakes gliding sinuously through a lagoon, leaving unpredictable ripples and patterns in her blood, in the liquid heat that felt as if it were pooling in her lower body.

She was gasping around the gag, her eyes closed as she absorbed the feeling. The heat of his body, the weight pressing on her. Those lips caressing her nape, the occasional nip of teeth. His finger, playing deep inside her. He'd chosen the most forbidden area, a deliberate message that he would not be denied anything. If that was the darkest part of her she would have been relieved but somehow he seemed to know that stimulating that area was a key to unlocking the door to the darkest corners of all. She could feel them rising out of her, lurking around in the shadows, but she couldn't hide them. He'd made her helpless, so she could do nothing but see if they would devour her, tear him limb from limb. Or maybe he would be a white knight, would vanquish them. It was the thought of a child, a little girl, though nothing else running through her mind or body reminded her of a child. Her woman's body desired release, had to have it. He'd made sure it was at his leisure, his Will. As she would do had she been controlling a sub, prolonging his pleasure, knowing he'd be rewarded by the results of denial. But as a Mistress she'd never felt what she sensed drove Tyler in this moment. A desire to bring her to orgasm because he was the only man that could, because it was proof of their connection. Of his claim that her flesh begged for his touch alone, her mind and heart in accord.

When he drew his tie from around his neck and let it caress her cheek, she couldn't stop the moan of need. *Yes. Yes.*

"That's what you like, isn't it, baby?" His voice was a breath against her ear, the new endearment like a different touch, unexpected and welcomed by a sharp jerk of reaction in her body.

He threaded the silk of the tie beneath her throat, out the other side, crossed it in back, twisted it in his fingers so she felt the tension, the pressure on the windpipe. He kept it halfway up her neck, away from the dangers of the lower areas, telling her not only that he'd done it before but that like everything else involving the pleasuring of a woman's body, Tyler was consummately skilled.

When she did it to herself it was a hard, dirty release, something that opened the door within her dungeon where all of her physical reaction to Mastering a sub was imprisoned. In the quiet of her bedroom she could strain against the pull, seeking the explosive wave that would draw it all out in a rush of release so intense sometimes she wasn't sure if it was the constriction of her air flow or the power of it that had her limp and dizzy, too weak to move for the remainder of the dead, lonely hours of the night, the belt and scarf loosened but still lying against her skin as her only company.

This was entirely different. The moment his fingers twisted the tie, caressing the back of her neck and taking command and control of her reaction, something just shattered in her. She couldn't get her hands near herself and all he was providing was the stimulation to her anus and this. Nevertheless, the beast rose in her, violent, dangerous, all-encompassing. She thrashed on the bed like an animal in a trap, seeking to pull against his touch, inviting blackness in before the choice was taken from her.

He shifted, pressing his knee in the area between her shoulder blades, holding her to the bed so she was unable to rise up and put additional pressure on his hold. She sobbed against the gag, his probing fingers deep in her, releasing shudders, more and more shudders, until she was simply shaking everywhere inside and out, moaning senselessly. Her body was attuned to every touch of his upon her but her mind and her soul were focused on one thing. His hand holding the tie, controlling her. Her mind was filled with a screaming desire to simply be his. Always his.

If her mouth had been free, she would have begged him to take her, to fuck her hard, to the point of pain and beyond to drive everything else away. He knew. He understood her in a way no one else did. She didn't know how, only that it made her feel ways she didn't comprehend. She didn't know if that would be her destruction or salvation.

His hand withdrew, found his way between her tied legs, his forearm hard against the curve of her ass. Cupping her mound, his unused fingers now took possession of her clit, his other hand taking another twist in the tie to lift her slightly, a leash drawing taut.

Everything exploded. The orgasm tore through her body, bringing her off the bed, arching into his touch. He moved with her, keeping the tension on the choker as she screamed, so overwhelmed it was too much. She tried to move away but couldn't. He was ruthless, stroking, working, dipping into her. Her wetness flooded his hand, as intense as the reaction of a man. It went on and on, as if the mere handful of days since she'd seen him at her place and the session at the Club tonight had all been foreplay, building and building. He was inside her now in every way but one and that was a formality. A formality she needed like a faith.

She was convulsing, jerking against his hand with aftershocks when he withdrew his touch. He untied her legs and arms and removed the scarf. She curled her arms underneath her, like a bird folding in its wings. When his hand loosened the tie, began to tug it free, she twitched, made an involuntary noise of protest before she could stop herself. His fingers stilled, paused over it, then left it. He tied it so it was snug but with a knot that would prevent any dangerous slippage around her neck, then he had his arms around her, turning her.

She was still hungry, still aching. As he turned her to her back, she gazed up at him in the dim light of her bedroom. His shirt was open partway down his chest, still tucked into the dark slacks. The serious, unsmiling mouth and dangerous eyes that were weighted with desire. She couldn't think beyond the elemental reaction, couldn't edit the thoughts that came to her lips.

"Your cock, in my mouth... Please."

A whispered plea, a desire to sate something hard and burning in her as well as him, something beyond the need of the roaring orgasm he had just given her.

When he put a knee on the bed, she could see the turgid shape of his arousal, proof of his need. For her. But he eased an arm under her, turned her again. Stunned her by stretching out on the bed next to her, curving his body around the back of hers, bringing his heat and hardness against her hips, thighs, her feet tucked between his calves, the linen of the slacks against her soft skin. He pulled her even closer with a hand around her waist, her wetness rubbing against his crotch as he cupped her breast in his hand, his thumb following the line of the tie at her throat. He settled his head just above hers, his breath ragged on her neck.

"Just sleep, angel. I'm here."

§

And she did, in a remarkably short time. Tyler stroked her hair, her slender form. Tracing every rib, the point of her hip and the length of thigh, he called himself a fool for not straddling her neck and shoulders and driving himself between her lips. It was the right of every Master to be served in such a fashion by a willing and eager sub. And she'd been willing, the desire in her eyes unmistakable. But intuition had held him back. That and the way her body had come to orgasm, again that brutal tearing response, as if a monster had to be slain to earn the right to just a small treasured release. And in her case, she'd learned that choking the monster was what worked but he knew it was more than a manipulation stemming from physical response.

She made a sub's every dark fantasy come true, then she came back to this room. Carrying all the arousal she'd stored from the experience, she brought it to fruition by restraining herself the way she restrained subs. The rope was to wrap around her wrists, the belt and scarf for the throat restriction. His gaze rested on the bedpost in the dark. Though he kept stroking her hair, his gaze burned on the place. He wouldn't tolerate it. Couldn't even think past the haze of fury and fear he'd felt when he'd realized it. She was a grown woman. There was nothing he could do to stop her from pursuing a practice that could kill her in a handful of heartbeats if done incorrectly. Except tonight he'd shown her how much more intense it was to be collared by a Master. Experimenting, he plucked at the tie, tugged it against her throat. She murmured in her sleep, moving against his hips in a way that made him stifle a guttural growl.

She sought the restraints for satisfaction but more than that she sought the feel of a collar. The ratcheting up of her desire at his touch on the tie at her throat, the protest she made at it being removed... If it was possible, those two things alone had nearly made him explode.

The idea made him even harder but it was balanced by the fear that if he could not find his way permanently into her heart, he might lose her to life altogether. Every step of her life, every desire appeared to be tormented by demons of her past, demons that took that desire and twisted it into an addictive and hazardous death wish.

It was time to stop relying on pride. In the morning, he would call in some favors. He wanted to know everything there was to know about Marguerite Perruquet.

He pulled the tie away. As she moved restlessly he replaced it with his hand, bringing his warmth and strength over the fragile bones and windpipe, the pulse. She settled in with a soft noise, her hand coming up to lie over his, falling into a deeper sleep with a quiet sigh.

"I'm here, angel," he murmured.

And I'm not going to let hell take you, so whoever the fuck is trying to drag you down into it, you deal with me. Because she's not alone anymore.

He curved more tightly around her, giving her his warmth and all of his protection. Staying awake to watch over her, he waited for the dawn to drive the night from the sky and her nightmares from the corners. And ignored his own that watched from the same hopeful vantage point.

Chapter Three

Marguerite surfaced slowly, disturbed by a hesitant sound. Feet on the staircase.

"Marguerite? Hon?"

She rolled over, her muscles aching from an orgasm that had been an exercise in prolonged isometrics. As she turned, she had a moment of panic when Chloe warily pushed the door open a bit.

She realized quickly she was alone in the bed, no evidence of Tyler in sight and her still naked body was modestly covered with a sheet.

"I'm so sorry to come up in your personal area. I was just worried because you're usually up to let us in when we get here at seven and it's seven-thirty."

Marguerite blinked, shifted and sat up, pressing a hand through her disheveled hair. His scent was still here. She smelled it on her skin, felt surrounded by it. She needed a shower. Needed it now, to clear her brain. To stop her from wondering why there was no note, no...

"How did you get in?"

"Tyler let us in. Talked me into making him *coffee*, the savage." Chloe shook her head. "Startled the heck out of me when he opened the door. And not just because he looked like he'd been a bar fight. Said you'd had a rough night." Her attention moved to the floor. "He wouldn't say he was the cause of it but I'm guessing a big, fat yes."

Marguerite looked over the edge of the bed to find the remains of her dress on the floor. He'd taken the time to leave her bed, cover her, retain her modesty and dignity but he'd left—what were Chloe's words—a big, fat statement of his presence in her bed lying on the floor.

"Nice flowers, by the way. I put them on a pedestal right outside the screen door since it's going to be a pretty day. Thought it'd be a lovely welcome when people come up the stairs. I wasn't sure about the tiger. What do you want to do with him?"

"I'll think about it in a bit. I need to do my yoga first then I'll get a quick shower and we'll be open at our usual time."

"But—"

"Chloe." Marguerite put her hands over her face, laid her head over the side of the bed so all her hair tumbled toward the floor. "I really need a few minutes, okay? Let me do my yoga before I deal with anything else. I need to get on routine, all right?"

She interpreted the girl's startled silence like a judgment. She was always ready to handle everything. She was not being the Marguerite they knew. But if they could give her a frigging half hour and a shower, she could pull it all together. She refused to believe she was as tattered as her dress.

"Okay."

Surprised by the quiet reassurance in Chloe's voice, she stiffened when the girl laid a hand on her shoulder and dropped a quick kiss on the top of her head. "Don't worry about a thing. You do what you need to do. We'll handle the rest."

"I'll be with you in forty-five minutes." Marguerite stated it forcefully into her palms. "Run the new black tea with peppermint and cloves as the Manager's Special."

§

Chloe came back into the kitchen to a curious-eyed Gen. "She's freaking out," Chloe reported calmly. "And my guess is Tiger Man's the reason."

"Is she coming down?"

"She's going to do her yoga first in the back garden."

"Does she know he's still here?"

"I don't know. I didn't tell her." Chloe's eyes were

thoughtful. "Thought I'd give her some time to pull it together. She's seriously off balance, Gen."

"Good way or bad way?"

A spark came back to Chloe's gaze, even as her mouth remained sober. "Look out there at him. Sometimes it can be both, I think."

When Chloe informed him that Marguerite would join him soon, that she was doing her morning yoga in her back garden, Tyler considered giving her privacy, time to regroup. But he wanted to see her. Just wanted, period.

Resolving not to interrupt the work of her staff, he left out the front and slipped through the latched side gate, having little trouble unlocking the mechanism.

He didn't want to disturb her. He wanted to see her at peace among her surroundings. And in accordance with his resolve of the previous night, he wanted to learn more about his Ice Queen.

Her private area was designed like a Japanese garden with the simple designs that the culture preferred. Delicate maples, azaleas and some slow-growing, cool temperature-loving plants that he wouldn't have thought would have had a chance in the Florida heat. He'd thought Robert had a pact with the devil. Marguerite must have made one, too. The garden was beautiful, tranquil and she stood in the midst of it completely naked.

He knew where all her scars were, but illuminated by the early morning sun they were more noticeable. The macabre angel wing arrangement of the cigarette burns. The jagged scars on her shoulder and leg where bones had cracked and punched through her skin. The starburst on her hand.

With her ankles crossed and her slim form straight and tall, Marguerite leaned forward, stretching out her spine one vertebra at a time. As she bent at the waist, her head descended below the line of the rising sun and continued down as she folded her upper body gracefully against the line of her thighs, knees and calves, the pose as much an expression of reverence as an exercise of the body. For a moment she reminded him of a solitary priestess making a low bow toward the Sun God. The light limned her form.

Sinking silently into a patio chair, he continued to watch her perform the stretching move. He could almost feel the vibration of energy coming from her. That stillness he always sensed within her expanded in this obviously sacred morning ritual and reached out to include him. His eyes coursed down her bare back to her thighs and the smooth curves of her buttocks. The soft lips of her sex were revealed by her pose. She was too thin, but then he thought of her with her teas and the way she savored the simplest bite of food. Ascetic. Marguerite maintained the discipline and simplicity of a monastic.

She was creating a place of stillness and peace for herself, like a person in a bubble of light separated from the darkness of hell only by that thin, transparent layer.

He knew from his own experience how blessed that quiet bubble was. But he'd learned it was the same as staying still after taking a painful wound. Moving might hurt worse than anything but if you didn't move and get help you'd bleed to death.

She rose and tilted her head, giving him her profile, though her back was still to him. "Do you ever intend to respect my privacy?"

"It's not looking like it. Not as long as you keep avoiding me for all the wrong reasons."

"Maybe you should tell me the right ones."

He bit back a smile. "What kind of yoga do you practice?"

"Kundalini."

"Tell me about that instead."

Her slender shoulders lifted in a sigh. If she were truly annoyed with his presence, he would have left, slipping away as quietly as he'd come, but he saw the loosening of her fingers, the easing of the tension in her back. Understanding dawned, making his heart lurch. It also made him rise, go and stand just behind her.

"They didn't tell you I was still here. You thought I'd just left without saying anything."

When she folded her arms up against herself defensively, he slid his around her. Crossing his limbs over hers, his palms against her shoulders, he held her in a close embrace, his clothed body against her bare one. "Marguerite, I would never do that to you."

"You shouldn't matter this much to me. Let alone this soon."

"I know. Kind of knocked me on my ass, too. Tell me about this kind of yoga. Stop worrying about it."

Her lips curved and she closed her eyes, shook her head. "It raises the energy coiled at the base of the spine—the serpent power—and draws it up to the crown chakra to connect you to Divinity. There are two forms of energy, Divinity, Shakti and Shiva, male and female. Kundalini is the synergy of them. Their union brings energy and power, peace."

"So the bringing together of the male-female helps open you to divine guidance." He turned her to face him, threaded his hands through each of hers, palm to palm, holding them up on either side of them, a tranquil mutual breathing pose. "Sounds like a wise strategy."

"Do you ever give up?"

"Do you want me to?"

She stared up at him. "No," she said at last. Her cheeks flushed with color. "But it's not about what I want. It can't be, because I'm not what you think I am."

"And what do I think you are?"

"I'm not like Leila, or your others."

His fingers squeezed her, mild reproof. "I know that, angel. You're Marguerite Perruquet, an extraordinary Mistress, a Ka-See-Ka who takes her submissives to unparalleled levels of physical ecstasy and emotional fulfillment. You're also the woman who trembles in my arms, who becomes something entirely different when I dominate you, a woman who craves my touch, my cock. You're not a submissive in the normal sense. You're nothing in the normal sense. You're extraordinary," he repeated.

"You're idealizing me."

"No. I'm telling you that I want you, light or dark, every shade in between. That's the formulation of trust, unconditional acceptance." He locked his gaze with hers. "Remember, I swore it to you. No matter what happens between us, I'll always be there for you."

After she gazed up at him for several moments in silence, with thoughts obviously swirling behind those vivid eyes, he noticed a slight change in her expression. Somewhat more calm, a wary acceptance of his presence.

"Teach me this," he repeated quietly. "Let me do this with you."

She closed her eyes again. He pressed his hands against her palms. "Should I undress?" he asked.

"No." She opened her eyes in alarm.

"It's not necessary?"

"No...it's Chloe and Gen. They might have heart attacks. And good staff is hard to find."

"How about you? Will you have a heart attack?" Reaching out, he caressed her throat with his fingers, his eyes laughing.

She recaptured his hand, put the palm firmly up against hers. "Behave. This is spiritual."

So was touching her throat, he thought. As well as watching the changes that occurred in her body, her eyes. But he let his hand be retained.

"Yoga uses a combination of poses called asanas, breathing techniques and chanting to reach a certain meditation state where the finite self can merge with the infinite, achieving a higher state of consciousness."

"Are we going to chant?"

"No." She appeared amused at his look of male concern. "For me, the breathing and the poses are enough. I like the silence, prefer it. You hold the pose, integrate it with the breathing. As you do so you think about that base power center, the coiled serpent at the bottom of your spine. You imagine the track of the breathing as circular, moving up from the base all the way to the crown chakra and then looping back again. The way of all spirituality is circular, cycles."

"You use this at The Zone. When you had Brendan breathe with you at the first."

She acknowledged his insight with a nod. "Part of that was a method called quantum breathing, which is a way of synchronizing yourself with the energy of the other person, for healing or connection. But there's some of this in it as well. Through this, I can get to the soul and consciousness of the subs I choose, connect with them more easily. It also helps keep me focused. I don't always know when I walk in what my intention is with the sub I'll choose but the ritual of the breathing, the clearing of the mind, that helps reveal that intention. Ready?"

He nodded. "Do what you normally do. I'll follow."

What she normally did would not involve Tyler Winterman standing in close proximity to her, his palms matched to hers, him clothed, her completely not. It was odd how that felt normal, acceptable.

As she started the breathing cycles, Marguerite reflected on something else that was odd. She'd come out here to pull herself together. When she saw him, she thought she'd stay in her flustered, demented state, resigned to that condition until she could figure out a way to get rid of him. But she found that she didn't want to get rid of him. Until he spoke the words himself, she hadn't realized that the bereft feeling she'd had when she woke was because she thought he'd left without a word. As he worked with her now, their palms holding fast against one another, their breathing came together. The tranquility she normally achieved began to steal over her. She transitioned into the meditative state more easily than she ever had, a surprising click of mindless peace with his consciousness moving comfortably around hers, like two cherubic spirits intertwining on the spiritual plane, his presence a balancing force.

The raw edges of the past day began to smooth, the fear and anxiety receding. Her fingers slowly folded in between his, so relaxed that it felt more natural to be laced together. She was alert and aware, yet so calm it was as if she were in a dreamless sleep, just at rest. Being.

At length her internal clock warned her she'd delayed long enough. It was time to get her shower and start helping Gen and Chloe with the pre-opening routine. She opened her eyes. His were closed. Her heart clutched at the bruising and lacerations on his face. In the way of such injuries, the purple and red coloring had gotten deeper and uglier from a night's rest. The compulsion swept over her again even more strongly than before, to cup her palms over the painful areas and brush her lips over each. To take care of him.

At the change in her breathing, his lids rose. His gaze was open, curious. Loving and accepting. For this single second, there was no tension between them, just a clear understanding that them standing here connected to each other was the most natural, desirable place to be.

"That was beautiful," he said.

She nodded. No sense in denying it. "I...I need to help Chloe and Gen."

He turned toward where he'd left his coffee cup, keeping hold of one of her hands. "Would you consider sitting on your front porch with me just another few moments while I finish my coffee? I'd like your company very much. Then I'll go, let you get to work."

"A few minutes. I can do that. Yes."

He picked up her robe off the side chair, held it out while she slipped her arms into it. Reaching around, he belted it in front of her, pulling her back against his body to nuzzle her cheek and neck with his jaw. And remarkably, she let herself lean a moment, reach up to touch him, to receive a kiss on her pulse.

"I could be good for you, Marguerite. If you let me."

"I'm so bad at this, Tyler. I'm...I'm sorry about last night."

He turned her, still holding her hand to lay it over his cheek, over the taped cut from the tawser. She felt the swelling of his jaw under her palm. "There's nothing to forgive. We're working things out. This is just part of it."

"Let's hope I don't kill you in the process," she said.

"I'm tougher than I look, though you can destroy me with a glance, angel, and that's the truth."

He looked tough to her on all sorts of levels with his morning stubble, the eyes narrowed against the sun, the lips half curved in a smile.

"I can't believe you had Chloe make you coffee. I didn't even know we had coffee."

He let her lower her hand but retained it, that sweet

gesture she found she was beginning to anticipate and appreciate, particularly when he idly ran his thumb across her palm.

"She finds me irresistible."

"She's young and hormonal. And she doesn't know what an arrogant pain in the ass you are."

He grinned. "You find me irresistible, even knowing that about me."

She bit back a smile. "Why the front porch? We have chairs in the back."

"So I can see you when I drive away."

She cocked her head as they followed the side pathway past her car and the blooming azalea bushes to the side steps to the front porch. "I think you just want my neighbors to see me sitting in my robe on the front porch with a man and destroy my reputation."

"There's that. And it makes the men realize you're not available."

She came to a stop. "You couldn't possibly be indulging in something so Neanderthal."

She was a step above him. He put his hands to her waist, hooking the robe's sash and turning her so her back was against the rail. Before she could stop him, he opened the front of the robe, worked his hands inside over the soft skin of waist and hip. One hand threaded up behind to cruise up her back and press her into him for a kiss. His lips were not physically demanding but their seductive persuasion was relentless. Her knees went weak, the now almost expected but still amazing sensation of desire curling warmly in her belly, like the question mark of steam over a fragrant cup of tea.

If she had turned a hundred and eighty degrees, she would have faced the street. But in her current position, she was covered, modest. Only the most imaginative neighbor would realize that her fully naked body was pressed against his clothed but quite obviously aroused one. The movement of his hands along her back and over her hips under the robe would be disguised by the fluttering shadows of her magnolia tree on the side of the house.

"You're going to cripple me," he said against her lips, his voice urgent with desire. "You're a drug, Marguerite. I want to keep you near me every moment."

She pulled back, more than a little breathless. "You won't keep my attention that long. I'll get bored of you any day now."

"Ah. You're considering the future. An improvement. You'll find I have a fascinating mind. I'm an exceptional conversationalist. And listener. You haven't gotten bored of me yet, right?"

"Does tedious and irritating count?"

"Keep it up and I'll kiss you again. I'll rely solely on sex appeal to keep your interest."

Hastily, she pulled her robe closed and retreated toward the front porch. She jumped when he caught her hand, settling down when she realized he wanted to do only that.

Her tiger was still there, curled around the base of the pedestal table where Chloe had put the large bouquet. The door was open, the familiar sounds of preparations for the day's first customers drifting out through the screen with the aromas of tea, mixing with the scent of Tyler's flowers. It was an unexpected extension of the peace she'd felt in their yoga session. It wasn't a hardship to be sitting shoulder to shoulder with Tyler on the front steps watching the early morning work traffic go by. As neighbors she knew headed to work, they raised a hand in greeting, eyes alive with curiosity at Tyler's presence. Marguerite turned so her knee was pressed at an angle to his, accepted his coffee cup and took a sip. "So you prefer coffee to my tea?"

"A question with a decidedly female word choice. In the category of 'does this dress make me look fat'." He leaned back, stretching his arm along the top step, which put her inside his arm span. He plucked at the sleeve of her robe, tugging it off her shoulder.

"Tyler Winterman." She shrugged it back up, poked him in the side. "There are children in this neighborhood."

He gave her an unrepentant grin. "Tell me about your neighbors."

She found herself doing so, responding to his questions about them, appreciating his quick mind, his grasp of her affection for her surroundings, his understanding of the unlikely place she'd set up her café. While they spoke, he casually passed the cup back and forth with her, reinforcing the tentative intimacy, the truce in tensions they were sharing. While on one hand she thought of it that way, another part of her wondered if he was trying to prove to her that this was the way a relationship would be. Passion mixed with the beginnings of friendship.

"Another question. There's a locked armoire in your room. What's in it?"

She slanted him a glance. "Tools of the trade. Floggers, plugs, vibrators. D/s magazine subscriptions. Why didn't you just jimmy the lock and find out? It's not like you don't ignore or bypass any other locked door I put up."

"I did. I just wanted to see if you'd lie to me." He grinned, ducked her swat.

"I have a lot to do." *And think about.* She said it reluctantly, handing him back the coffee cup. "Thank you for the flowers and the tiger." Then, because she wouldn't let herself be less than honest in the moment, she added, "And for your understanding. I appreciated this morning. Very much. And, even if it we don't go any further, decide it needs go no further, I've gotten a lot from our interactions...these past few days."

She could tell by his expression she was stumbling into dangerous waters but she didn't know where else to go with this. Where it was going. Or how to direct it.

"Marguerite." He took both of her hands. "I need you to listen to me. Are you listening? Are you paying attention?"

"Of course."

"Good. I'm going to go home, take a shower. Do the things I've planned to do with my day, much as I'm sure you're planning to do. But then I want you to think about last night. What was said, what I meant. And think about what you want." He stood up, still holding one of her hands. "I'm going to try very hard to give you some space. To stay away while you think it through. I'm asking you to think it through. If you accept what we both understood well enough last night, then you come to me. Please come to me."

It was obvious he was struggling with a desire to state his Will more forcefully but he stopped at that. Squeezing her hand, he leaned in and brushed her cheek with his lips. She held on to his touch, not realizing she was squeezing back until he began to pull away and had to wait for her to loosen her grip. Her cheeks pinkened.

"I'm taking that as a good sign." He smiled a smile that did not quite reach his eyes which were warm and intent on her face, spreading that heat on her front the way the sun coming in through the side of the porch was spreading warmth on her back.

Reaching out, he touched his fingers to her throat, a sensual reminder. "No more of that. Remember. I mean it."

She narrowed her eyes. "Go away, Tyler. I'm not fragile 'that way'. Remember?"

"No, you're not. You're strong, so strong you won't bend. You'll snap off like a brittle twig when you finally face up to something you can't handle."

"I can't handle you," she snarled. "And I've bent in twenty different directions trying to shake you off. I haven't broken yet."

She bit her lip, wishing she could have bitten off the words before she said them.

"Why do you think you have to handle me?" he asked after a quiet moment.

"Us. I can't..." She sighed, shook her head. "Tyler, why can't you just leave me alone?"

"You know why I can't. You're inside me. And I'm inside you. If you'd just... Goddamn it, if you'd just open the door so I don't have to pick the lock every fucking time, I promise I won't do anything to abuse your trust." He shook his head, backed off the step, gave her a long, thorough look. "I'm going home. Don't even try to pretend you won't miss me."

"Like a mosquito."

He smiled, for real this time, and went down the walkway. She moved to the top step, her hand falling on the paw of the stuffed tiger. Absently, she stroked the soft plush, watching him walk to his car. He had a fluid stride, a bearing that women would notice and men would respect.

She couldn't pull her eyes off the stretch of the shirt across his shoulders, enhanced by the fact he carried his jacket slung over one shoulder, his fob in his hand to deactivate the security. He was James Bond, she thought with a suppressed amusement, but her gaze lingered on his waist, the fine ass, long legs. He was more than that. He'd just told her he was hers. All she had to do was come to him. The hardest thing in her life she could possibly do.

She glanced over her shoulder to find Chloe and Gen in the doorway, their fascinated attention divided between her and the man leaving. Realizing she was still petting the tiger, she folded her hands together, gave herself a quick, reassuring squeeze—that's that—and rose.

"Give me just five minutes for the shower," she said briskly. "I apologize that I'm behind schedule."

Her employees exchanged glances. Gen folded her arms and tucked her tongue into her cheek. "Should we slap her on principle for that comment and then beat information out of her, or just combine it into one general throwdown?" she asked Chloe.

"If you don't tell us something that explains why he was here this morning, why he looks like he's been in a fight to protect your honor and why your dress is in pieces on the floor, we'll just implode," Chloe added.

Marguerite pushed her hands through her hair. "I suspect it's rather obvious why he's here. I do have a personal life, though it generally doesn't intrude on my routine. Tyler is... We're... I don't know what we are and it..." She stopped, all of the calm she had felt after the yoga drifting away, eluding her desperate grasp before inquisitive eyes that suddenly felt invasive. "I am not a teenager. We are not teenagers. He was here, we fucked." Or something close enough to it that it was not a lie, exactly. They both looked startled at her crudity and that spurred her further. "We had a fight of sorts and I beat the hell out of him. Does that satisfy my staff's curiosity?"

Chloe nodded, hurt written across her features in big letters. Gen, older and more understanding, reached out toward her. "Sweetie, we didn't mean—"

Marguerite stepped back to avoid the contact, forgetting

she was at the top of the stairs. She met air. Falling, the sense of falling. This she knew. And it frightened her as it never had before.

She was jerked to a halt before it actualized. Both women lunged forward and caught her. Chloe her left arm, Gen her right.

She took a deep breath, clutched their arms. They cared about her, she knew that. In the normal world, people who worked together enjoyed a rapport. Would exchange light banter over a romantic interest, women especially. This was yet another reason she couldn't do this. Pain radiated through her chest, but then Chloe wrapped her arms around her in a hug. "I'm sorry, M. I wasn't trying to be nosy. Okay, I was, but not to be mean. We love you, you know? And you looked happy, the way you guys walked up here, holding hands. You don't often look happy. You don't have to tell us anything. We just want you to feel that way. We're glad for you."

Gen put a hand on her shoulder, stilling her, but Marguerite gave her a tentative, stiff squeeze, eased her back. "I know, Chloe. Thank you both. I just don't do...this. And it's hard for me to understand how to handle it. I don't want to hurt either of you, so let's focus on this morning's routine, all right?" Her voice sounded a little desperate, even to herself. "Can we just get back to the morning routine? I'll meet you inside in a minute."

They retreated reluctantly with another of those pregnant exchanged glances, leaving her alone, standing with her back to the edge of the stairs. Turning carefully, she stared down the road after his car. She felt the beat of her heart hitting the wall of her chest, resounding in her stomach like a cavern.

He'd been wrong. It wasn't her that was the drug. It was him, for as he drove down the street, she felt the emptiness, the desire to have him back beside her like a physical pain nothing could assuage, except something she wasn't sure she was capable of doing.

Please, come to me.

Chapter Four

The right connections could get you where you had no business being. Tyler went up the walkway of the modest patio home. It was located in a quiet retirement community designed to appeal to senior citizens of modest income, the type of home that would appeal to a widow who'd spent her career as a social services worker.

She'd opened the door when he drove up, waited for him behind the screen. He felt her assessment of his car, his appearance, even the way he walked as he strode up the paved path. While he made eye contact, determined not to project anything but confidence, he felt like a thief pretending to be the owner of the house he was about to rob.

"You look like you've been mugged." Komal Gupta said as he made her top step. "Since you look like money I assume that's the case, since I also assume that's what greased the wheels that brought you to my door."

"No, actually it was my connections in the government, earned by risking my ass in places where hell would be considered a vacation resort." He met her barb for barb but kept his tone mild. "I know this is wrong, Mrs. Gupta. I know it goes against your ethics and you wouldn't be doing it unless your former boss, a person you greatly respect, hadn't leaned on you hard. But I need to understand some things. I'm hitting a brick wall."

"Walls of brick are built to protect the occupant from the harshest elements. Helping you pull out the foundation so that wall can crumble and leave the occupant vulnerable doesn't seem something I'd be willing to help with. Why would I?"

"Because you care about her. And because I'm in love with her. And sometimes brick walls are a prison, not a protection."

She studied him another long moment. "Come in and we'll see what we can talk about. And I'll choose what that will be. If you can't accept that, get back in your car."

He inclined his head, stepped over the threshold. After a measuring glance, she closed the door and showed him to a small sitting area with couches and chairs comfortable for the frame of a small woman. It suggested that this had become her home since her husband's passing. When Tyler looked at her, he saw a woman with a kind round brown face, her hair in a fat gray-black braid down her back. She emanated the reassurance that he sensed would have comforted a child. Many children.

"I'm sorry for my comment, Mrs. Gupta. I'm sure you've dealt with far worse situations than I have. At least most of mine dealt with adults."

She cocked a brow. "This isn't a contest, Mr. Winterman. You may be right, but I've rarely risked my life. Perhaps my soul, but never my life." She sat down, crossed her legs and pinned him with her dark eyes. "There are times you see things so horrible you become certain that nothing like God could exist. And if there is an All-Powerful Deity, It is a murdering son of a bitch for turning Its back on those who are so helpless to the evil of others. But in time you understand that the comfort of God is a balance to the evil of men. The Deity, whatever Its purpose, is not a warden. It's something you don't understand with the rational mind, correct? It's something you feel with your heart, your instinct. It's faith, for logic and understanding will only send your soul into despair in this human world."

"Is that how Marguerite managed? Or Marie?"

"You did your research. I call her Marguerite. I respected her desire and her need to become a new being." The reproof was in her tone and Tyler found it took effort to keep his expression steady, non-defensive. "Marguerite has managed, has survived. She did it by adopting many of the expected defenses for an extremely abused child and by being gifted with a wholly non-hereditary strength of character. Tell me what you know of her before you try your interrogation techniques on me."

"She..." Tyler, always adept with words, found himself at a sudden loss. The one image that immediately came to mind seemed inappropriate for the company, but he suspected that in order to get what he needed from Komal Gupta he was going to have to answer her questions with brutal honesty.

"This morning I was sitting in her garden, watching her do yoga. The sunlight was touching her hair, her skin. I could have sat there forever, just watching her." He hesitated. "She was completely naked. I could see the burns, every scar. But she turns toward me, so strong and resilient. Looks at me with her blue eyes and it's like I can see down into her soul. She's in mine, I know it, but I can't... I can push hard to get what I want, but I'm afraid the wall holding me back is glass. I wouldn't hurt her if the fate of the world depended on it. She's given enough. But I want her so much, I want to give her anything, everything..." He stopped, closed his eyes, shook his head. "Jesus, if you can pull that out of me just sitting there with that expectant expression, you were a hell of a counselor."

Komal blinked. "I think you had that built up in you and I was just the first recipient you felt acceptable to share it with. I only had moderate success in that area with Marguerite and most of it was deduction, not her opening up." Humor crossed her features. "And what I meant by 'tell me what you know' is what you know of her history."

For perhaps the first time since he was sixteen years old, Tyler felt a flush creep up his neck. She laughed, a sound like bells, reached out and touched his knee. "No, don't be embarrassed. It tells me a great deal about you. It also makes me feel better about our chat. Though you have an intensity that suggests an obsessive stalker."

Tyler snorted. "One of my closest women friends has suggested the same."

"How intuitive of her. I'm regretting not making you tea, as I would an honored guest but to be honest I was planning to boot you back out the driveway, no matter what Henry said. I can tell your feelings for Marguerite are genuine, so I won't do that." She leaned forward, her dark eyes piercing, the humor gone. "But I need to be sure you'll listen and truly hear what I say to you, whatever I choose to give to you."

"That's why I'm here." He locked gazes with her, held it until she nodded. "You introduced her to tea."

"Yes, I did." Komal looked at a set in a hutch behind her, a set similar to ones he'd seen in Marguerite's shop.

"She still has the cups and the doll you gave her."

"I know. I saw them when she opened Tea Leaves."

"So you've stayed in touch."

"I've kept track of her." Komal crossed her ankles, pressed her hands together in her lap. "When she opened the teahouse, I went to see her. I introduced myself to the hostess as an old friend, asked if Marguerite might have a moment to come out and share a cup with me, my treat, to congratulate her on her success. I remember the hostess was so nice, said she was sure Marguerite would be pleased to see me."

Tyler watched the woman recall the situation, a shadow crossing her face. "I was given the best tea on the house, an excellent scone. The hostess was solicitous to my every need. At length she told me that Marguerite was so happy I'd come by but she was very busy today. She apologized on her behalf and said the house would pick up the tab. The hostess was embarrassed I could tell, so I reassured her with my politeness, my understanding and thanks. I sat there for a half hour drinking tea, studied the beautiful haven she'd created, walked the grounds. Then I left her a note on my napkin, that I wished her all the blessings of the world, for she'd earned them all. Throughout my visit, I could sense she was watching me somehow."

"She has a two-way mirror, the Victorian mirror over the mantel. At least it's there now."

She nodded. "It's not unusual for victims of trauma to eschew contact with any memory they have of it. But looking that place told me how carefully she'd constructed her sanctuary, to the point I expect she's obsessive-compulsive about certain aspects of her life, the ones that help keep that brick wall in place."

"And would she be that way about romantic, sexual relationships?"

Komal shook her head. "Mr. Winterman, a serious obsessive-compulsive cannot control the dynamics of a relationship. If I'm correct, I doubt she can sustain any interpersonal relationship, romantic or otherwise. She would compartmentalize any relationship she has.

"Now, on the other hand..." She held up a hand when he would have spoken, protested. "Marguerite is extremely strong. Neither of her parents showed a propensity for handling extreme trauma well. She went through more than either of them, at their hands, and she coped."

"I've seen her interact with her neighbors, her customers. Her staff. They all love her."

"Yes, let's look at that. Where did she build her shop? She built it in a neighborhood where she essentially has no peers, culturally, socio-economically. She can once again keep them at arm's length. The fact she does give to others suggests to me it's a way she can connect without risk. But if a person tries to push past a certain boundary she will retreat, shut them off. I suspect you got in because you were somehow part of the ritualized environment she created, so you were already inside the boundary. She didn't expect you to break out of your role, seek something more personal, so you took her off guard. I also suspect you've been frustrated by the fact that she rejects what she cannot keep within boundaries. And you need to consider carefully that may be the safest thing for her survival."

His expression darkened. "You can't believe that's any way for a person to live."

"That's a very male reaction to a problem." But her voice was kind, softening the accusation. She opened a candy dish, took out a lemon drop, offered him one. Re-covered the dish when he shook his head. "I've done this a long time. Enough to know that people do the best they can. And it's important for those who love them to understand what their best is, because you can break them by forcing them to *your* best, or what you think their best *should* be.

Mental handicaps are no different from physical ones in that regard.

"She's a contributing member of society, but I suspect she's chillingly rational about what she is and isn't capable of. She's created a very carefully crafted environment, which is what people with serious mental issues do. If you start disrupting that, you may think you're breaking through, but she may be literally breaking into pieces, shattering."

Tyler could not ignore the image that rose in his mind of Marguerite's wild eyes, the rage of an animal taking her as she attacked him. The report Dan had given him of what had happened with Tim.

"She's stronger than you think."

"No, Mr. Winterman. I know she's very strong. Strong enough to kill to survive. To destroy herself to protect others."

She turned the lemon drop in her fingers over and over, the powdered sugar coating dusting her fingertips.

"I'm going to tell you about Marguerite's father. Not because I think you should be privy to such information without her consent, but because I believe you when you say you're in love with her. But before I share, you're going to give me something you don't want to offer. An even trade, a surety if you will. Will you agree?"

He inclined his head but even so he wasn't ready for what she asked, a woman old enough to be his mother, surrounded by the trappings of a modest, conservatively lived life.

"You and Marguerite obviously are having a sexual relationship. Based on my knowledge of her, there is almost no way short of a miracle that she can handle sex in a traditional way. Her history makes her a likely candidate to be a Dominatrix. But you don't strike me as a sexual submissive. And I would think that may be one of the strongest conflicts you have physically. Would that be accurate?"

It was difficult, but looking at it through her eyes, Tyler knew it was quid pro quo. He gave a curt nod. "I'm a sexual Dominant. You're right about the way she's chosen to express herself sexually. That's how I met her, through a mutual club membership. But with me...she submits. And it scares the shit...it scares her, very much."

"And you've pushed it." Her attention moved to his cheek. "Pushed it until she lashed out somewhat literally?"

Tyler rose from the chair, moved to the other side of the coffee table. At her assessing look, he gave a short, irritated laugh. "That was a defensive movement, wasn't it?"

"Entirely. You're not comfortable with how you've pushed her." She put down the lemon drop. "And that also makes me feel better about you, Mr. Winterman. You have a conscience that won't let you rationalize your actions, at least not indefinitely. Treasure that. It's a great gift and one that can save your soul in the long term."

He shook his head. "I don't need a lesson in spiritual development."

"You must have God's ear, then." Her eyes glinted. "A pity. Because I'm approaching this my way."

Tyler sat back down across from her, ran a hand over his face. "I didn't mean it that way. I know where my limits are, the lines I can't cross and I've learned them the hard way. But now..." He spread out his hands. "Mrs. Gupta, I don't claim to know everything of the mysteries of the world and certainly not the mysteries of a woman's heart. But I know sometimes the hardest lessons you learn in life will help you to succeed later, in moments where success doesn't seem possible.

"I sensed...I sensed there was something wrong from the first. I know this part is right, that she wants to surrender herself to me during sex and I hope to God as I'm saying this you don't have any moral judgments about it, because you probably will boot my ass out on the street. But I respect and love her, believe in her strength. But when I sense that wrongness... I know I'm in a very dangerous area. What happened earlier this week—" he touched his cheek, "—just underscored it. I don't want to hurt her. I don't," he added fiercely. "And that's why I'm here. I need help. I need to know how to move around in a jungle where I've got no light at all. But I'm not backing out of that jungle. That's not an option. I'm in there now. I know she wants me there. I just have to find her so she won't be frightened by the sound of snapping twigs, thinking it's her nightmares rather than me."

Komal cocked her head, her eyes thoughtful. "Be quiet, Mr. Winterman. I'd like a moment to collect my thoughts." She leaned forward, took the lid off her candy dish again. "Take one this time."

He did after a moment, put it in his mouth automatically, sat back on the edge of the small chair and wished the ache in his chest wasn't adding to the throbbing pain in all other areas of his body.

"Isn't it funny how candy can ease a child's pain for at least a moment through distraction but it's so difficult to find anything to do the same for adults?" Komal spoke at last, when he'd about sucked the candy down to half its size. "As far as I can tell, Marguerite's father was a normal, decent man up until she was eight years old."

Tyler straightened, his attention on her. "There are photographs," she continued. "Photos that were removed from the house that I got to see. There's one of him carrying her on his shoulder, the lights of a carnival behind them. Everything was fine then. It's in their faces, their eyes. But trauma can change people in unexpected ways, uncover weaknesses in character and exploit them to a terrifying degree.

"When Marguerite was seven years old, her paternal grandmother shot and killed her husband, Marguerite's grandfather. No one knows exactly why. There was no hint of infidelity or other disturbance in their relationship. We will never know, because she placed the gun in her mouth and blew out the back of her skull. Our best guess is that perhaps she had early dementia and there was some interaction in the drugs she was taking. The problem was Marguerite's father found them. Or more specifically, his mother called him to come over. She said she was worried about some things she wished to discuss with him. When he got there she was sitting in her favorite chair, knitting. She set her knitting aside when he saw his father lying on the floor in blood. Then she pointed a finger at her son and said, 'You never should have been born. I'm sorry.' She picked up the gun on the side table and killed herself in front of him."

"Good Christ."

"We got this from him in prison. We assume it's true. As you are likely aware, it is difficult to predict, even with all our empirical data and theories, what extreme stress will do to a person; it can act on them in some unexpected ways. Marguerite's father had a complete breakdown of his moral foundation when the tragedy occurred. From eight to fourteen, Marguerite was forced to join him on his psychotic journey, a world where everything to him was violence and pain, punishment. For you see, Marguerite looked very much like her grandmother."

She lifted a binder. It looked as if it had been removed from storage, traces of dust still on the edges of the pages. The spine had been labeled "Peninski". Several folders were inserted in the front pocket but she went to the album pages first.

"Here she is, posing with her grandmother."

Tyler blinked, looked closer. "She's... Her hair and eyes. They're brown." He also noticed the resemblance between Marguerite and her grandmother *was* striking, even to the stance of their bodies. There was a dark-haired boy in the photo. From the sizes of the two children, Tyler made a swift deduction.

"They were twins?"

"Yes."

"What happened to him?"

"Let me take the story in its proper progression, because you need to understand about David. It will make more sense that way. Here's that picture of Marguerite and her father where he's carrying her on his shoulders."

"The brown hair again."

"And you'll notice she tanned easily. She and her father were alike in that regard."

"She dyed her hair white?"

She shook her head, turned the page. "Her class picture at thirteen."

Marguerite had not smiled in this photo, half her face obscured by the fall of brown hair, her eyes already cultivating that distant look he recognized.

"Now, here she is six months later just before the police brought her to me. This was taken in the police station a day or so after her mother and brother committed suicide."

Tyler looked at a teenager sitting in a wheelchair. In a short brown smock dress that had obviously been picked out of a police lost-and-found, she also wore a brace for a collarbone fracture. There was a sling on the affected arm and a cast on her leg. The hand that now bore the sunburst scar had been carefully bandaged. Her hair was snow white, loose on her shoulders.

"Eyes?"

"Blue as the summer sky. Skin pale as a vampire's. I wouldn't have thought it was the same girl except you can see the bone structure of the face. As I said, extreme trauma changes people in ways we still don't totally understand, physically as well as mentally."

"Her father." Tyler ran a knuckle across the face of that young girl for whom hope wasn't even a distant dream. He knew what was coming, had already seen the marks on her, but it didn't make the vicious ache in his gut any less jagged. "She made a joke once. About being from rural Kentucky, so the only sex she'd had was with family members."

He'd read once about a comic book character who gave his soul in exchange for the ability to go out and annihilate those who preyed on the innocent. He knew why a man would be willing to do such a thing if it meant saving only one child, one soul from having this look in her eyes.

"We don't know when he began raping her. We suspect it was age eight, after they'd moved to Tampa to be near his parents and the incident with her grandmother happened. We know the mother knew nothing for a very long time. She'd begun to drink, unable to reach her husband and heal his pain, though to all appearances she continued to care functionally for the children and for him."

"Do you think she was just kidding herself about not knowing?"

Komal shook her head. "It's hard to know. Again it depends on the person, their coping mechanisms. It's one of the most unthinkable things for a wife to contemplate, that her husband is sexually preying on her children, their children. And she was a nurse who worked night shifts."

"Which left Marguerite defenseless to him, night after night." Tyler felt a headache pushing at his temples, a nauseous ache in his gut. "Her brother..."

"Knew. Not just because their bedrooms were side by side, but because of the twin connection."

"Was he molested?"

"No. Not by the father," she said cryptically. "Apparently, his focus was all on the replica of his mother, where somewhere in his twisted, broken mind raping and violating her night after night was her punishment. Oedipus gone psychotic. Every time he sodomized Marie, he placed a burn along her spine, like a mark on a bedpost."

"Jesus. Fucking, bloody monster." Tyler was up again, unable to breathe. He walked to stand at the window. "This bastard is in prison? Still alive?"

Not for long, if he could arrange the proper interaction with the right inmate. And arrange to have him tortured to death.

"Yes."

"How...how do you sodomize an eight-year-old and not have it show up in a medical history?"

"Marguerite's father was a doctor. I assume he took care of any treatments she needed. And the horrifying fact is a man who knows what he's doing can sodomize a child without endangering her life, though there will be repeated trauma to the tissues. Through the rapes, she lost the ability to have children. And we don't know at what age the sodomy began. Perhaps later in adolescence, when she would have been dressing herself without her mother's participation. He only had hospital privileges up until the time she was twelve. Apparently at that time his mental makeup had deteriorated to the point that he stopped practicing, though the official word was a sabbatical."

"So when did it all come to a head? What happened when she was fourteen?"

"Marguerite's mother found out." Komal looked down at

another picture. Tyler came back to see a photo of a woman with some of Marguerite's features. It was a wedding picture, Marguerite's parents before Marguerite was part of their lives. They were obviously in love, likely looking forward to a normal life of ups and downs as a married couple.

"It's odd how fate chooses when to intervene. She had a flu bug, not an unusual thing for a person who drinks too much and has a depressed immune system, though apparently much of her drinking occurred at home, during the day. She went home in the evening, when he was expecting her not to be home until dawn. She walked in on them in Marguerite's bedroom."

Tyler sat down next to her. "What happened then?"

"Marguerite's mother was a good woman who'd tried to honor her wedding vows by standing by her husband through his grief and deterioration, even when he repeatedly refused help, even when she despaired so much she sought solace from a bottle. Finding out he was sexually assaulting their daughter called off all bets. And it was the first time in the story that I developed any sympathy for her." Komal's lips thinned. "She told him to get out, called him probably any name she could think of. When he wouldn't leave she went into her room, pulling both the children with her."

Komal shook her head. "We were able to keep this out of the paper, out of respect for the family. And I was assured all we spoke of would be in confidence."

"It will be."

She inclined her head. "The house got very quiet. She assumed he'd left but she kept packing, knowing she couldn't stay. She had to get her daughter, both of her children, out of there.

"I imagined it, many times," Komal added. At her tone, Tyler looked up from the photo of Marguerite at the police station. In Komal's face he saw the love for the young girl clearly stamped on her features. "The day things could have turned in the right direction for the three of them. David, relieved at last that his mother knew, that his sister would be saved. Marguerite, seeing her mother step forward, be strong as a woman should be to take care of her children, become a warrior if need be to fight and take them to safety. I saw so many cases over the years, cried over them. But this one... I could just imagine that mother packing, stealing glances at her daughter, seeing the things that hadn't made sense now making such horrible sense, things she would have paid better attention to if she hadn't been fogged by drink and despair. The increasing paleness, the weight loss. Wondering, 'when was the last time I saw either of my children smile?' Marguerite's broken eyes. Looking into her eyes and seeing..."

"The distance."

Komal nodded. "You see it in the worst ones. You know somewhere they've shut down. They don't seek escape or affection. You sit them in a corner and they simply wait until the next thing happens. They expect nothing. I suspect her mother probably asked Marguerite some questions in those moments. 'How long has it been going on?' Did she hug her, hold her, try to touch her at all? Or was she numb with shock, focused on getting them out of that house? As I imagine it, I find myself—absurdly—urging her to hurry, get out, don't worry about clothes, just get out, get out now. Trying to impact an event that happened years ago. I do know one of the few personal things I got out of Marguerite about that moment was that David sat next to her on the bed as they watched their mother and held her hand. She remembers him saying softly, 'It's okay now.'

"He was about at the age I expect he would have either absented himself from home as much as possible or tried to intervene. Or both. We have a record of him at eleven coming to an emergency room with a broken arm and injuries to his face and mouth. Two of his teeth knocked out. Supposedly a fight after school. Marguerite confirmed that was a lie, that he'd attacked her father, tried to pull him off her. She knew her father would kill him if he tried to interfere. So after that she told David if he loved her, he'd just stay away as much as possible and not worry about it. That they'd just both try to stay away as much as possible. It's odd they didn't just run away. Though she never said, I think that they wouldn't leave their mother.

"He was devoted to her. School records show they insisted on being in the same classes, spent most of their time together. David had friends. Marguerite was sometimes with him when he spent time in their company but she did not cultivate her own friends. He was her one touchstone to something other than the horror of their home life.

"David was a child's love but perhaps the only pure, untainted love she had where she gave back as well. And I don't think anyone's broken through to her since his death."

Komal shook her head, rose. "I need to get us some tea, Mr. Winterman. This is a story better told in pieces. Would you like to help?"

"Yes." He accompanied her, assisting in silence, respecting her need to reflect and gather her thoughts. She chose a tea that smelled of chamomile, probably seeking the calmness it could offer. When they returned to the main room, he carried the tea tray, set it down where she directed and then watched her pour, the careful balancing, the straining, everything he'd seen Marguerite demonstrate.

"You provided her the way to save herself."

"Isn't that always an odd word? 'Save.'" She handed him a cup, began to pour herself one. "'Save' is what The Lone Ranger does, or Spider-Man. Coming out of nowhere to catch the heroine when the villain shoves her off the cliff, or pull her off the train tracks. No one was around to save Marie Peninski. Marguerite Perruquet picked up the pieces and has been trying to reassemble what was left ever since."

Tyler's brow furrowed. "I don't understand."

"You've seen the popular movies where a personality divides because it can't handle what's happened to it? Marguerite Perruquet is strong enough to face what was done to Marie Peninski. She didn't block it, but she somehow intuitively knew she had to create another name, a person whose shoes she could step into to manage what Marie endured."

"What happened that night?" He put down his cup, afraid that he was going to break it with the rage vibrating through him.

"The mother about had the suitcase packed when he burst back into the room. With a gun." Komal set her own cup back down, added some milk from a small pitcher. "The only way Marguerite could tell this part of the story was by demonstrating it to me with dolls. And because it was in fact that awful, I am going to say it as bluntly as I can, the best to get it over with." Her fingers held on to the pitcher after she replaced it on the tray, her grip tightening.

"Frederick Peninski put the gun to Marguerite's head and told his wife to remove her clothes, to remove her son's clothes. Told Mrs. Peninski over and over that she was no better than him, that if demons were digging into her brain she'd be doing nothing different from him. He then told her to have sex with her son right then and there or he'd blow Marguerite to pieces one shot at a time. Then he'd shoot David as well. To prove it, he lifted Marguerite's hand and shot through it."

The starburst. Tyler closed his eyes but Komal's words kept coming.

"David made a lunge for his father and he shot him in the leg. The boy went down. Even though the boy was bleeding and in pain, Frederick was screaming at her to do it, to show she was just like him. He had the gun cocked, his finger on the trigger, the barrel against Marguerite's temple. So her mother did it. She did the unthinkable, aroused her son with the knowledge of a sexually mature woman and made him ejaculate inside her as Frederick ordered. After, he told her she had nowhere to go. That this was hell and there would be no escape from hell for any of them."

The clock ticked on the wall. Tyler could hear her refrigerator humming in the kitchen they'd just left. Tyler knew that there was sunshine outside and spring flowers, but all he could see were rows of bodies in Panama being bulldozed into a mass grave. The shadows of an interrogation room, a woman screaming, her slender bones breaking.

He jerked at Komal's touch. "Are you all right?" she asked.

"Yes." He cleared his throat. "Finish it."

She gave him a thorough look, nodded. "Frederick left the house then. I suppose he figured he'd made sure there was nowhere they could go to escape the horror. The details of this are sketchy, because I never was able to get Marguerite to speak much of it. Mrs. Peninski must have bandaged up David's leg and Marguerite's hand, got them dressed. They took the car to the tallest building downtown, rode the service elevator to the roof and all three jumped.

"From the estimation of the emergency services team, investigators and eyewitness accounts as well as forensics, the mother fell free but the twins managed to latch on to each other. David landed on the bottom, took the full brunt of the asphalt. Marguerite had a couple broken bones as you see in the picture, but miraculously no head or spinal trauma, the kind of miracle you read about in *Reader's Digest*. The mother and son died instantly."

"And the father?"

Komal looked at him. "It was her testimony that put him away. I could barely get her to talk to me about anything but the sketchiest details, Mr. Winterman. But in court on the stand, she told us exactly what we needed to increase her father's sentence to a twenty-year term. Child molestation, assault and the district attorney did a credible job of showing he contributed significantly to the suicide. I've no doubt that it was the loss of David that did it. Many children are afraid to look at their parents during such a testimony. You know she meets no one's gaze easily. But from the moment she took the stand, she locked eyes with him as if they were standing on a platform over hell and the first one to blink would drop through a hatch in the floor. When she got up from the stand she shocked us all by bolting to his table. She was over it and on him like a wild animal, gouging his eyes, tearing at his face. Screaming at him, wails of such pain and savagery I thought we'd had a breakthrough. But an hour later she was as dispassionate and unreachable as ever."

Komal lifted her cup to her lips with a hand that had a slight tremor. Took a long sip, studied a boy riding by her house on a bicycle. She was apparently lost in memory, a memory so different from that child's innocence, Tyler wondered if she even saw him. Then she raised a hand as the child saw the suggestion of her in the window and waved.

"But a police report I got from some of my friends in Tampa said they never clearly proved the sexual assault."

Komal frowned. "That was an earlier report. We weren't able to prove it because at first the prosecution wouldn't use her. They didn't think she could hold it together to be a credible witness right after it all happened. They were able to put him away on assault for shooting her and David. But several months later when I hadn't gotten hardly a word out of her, she called the district attorney's office from the orphanage and told them how he had abused her. Everything that happened that had led to the jump. They tried him on sexual molestation and the other charges. Your Tampa friends didn't dig very far."

Tyler shrugged. "They were investigating the S&M Killer. She was a suspect for a very short time and they didn't have to dig for long before they found the real perpetrator."

Komal blinked, set down her cup. "Please tell me she never knew that."

"No, she never did."

Komal's lips pressed together firmly. "Good. That child has been through enough. She went into an orphanage, got good grades, conducted herself with absolute decorum. Never responded to anyone we know of except one little boy who was adopted out six months after he got there. I offered to take her to visit him once but she simply shook her head, politely thanked me for my visits as she always did and that was that.

"The moment she turned eighteen, she packed her bags and left. I lost track of her for ten years except for the shock of receiving two postcards from her over that time period, telling me she was learning about the tea trade, traveling through India, Asia. And then as you know, she came back here to open Tea Leaves."

"It's strange, that she would come back here."

And thank God she did. Or I'd never have met her.

"It's not strange at all." She regarded him. "This is where David was. Is. Will always be, in her mind. So now you know.

"Marguerite chose to manage her own emotions. I give her credit for how well she has done. But from what I've observed and learned, she has dealt with that unresolved anger by a combination of the obsessive-compulsive, controlling behavior we discussed and outright suppression, an even more destructive method. And you already know that she has a tendency toward violence when pressed." Her gaze flickered over his damaged face.

Her voice spoke dark truths, truths he didn't want to hear, but she pressed on, ruthless. "When I look at you, I can tell you want to give Marguerite happiness. But I want you to consider carefully that she may have found peace and sacrificed happiness for it. As I said, that may be the best she can do."

Tyler closed his eyes, put his hand on the bridge of his nose to relieve the tension pounding there and winced when he hit the tawser strike. "Mrs. Gupta—"

There was a quiet clink of china as she pushed cup and saucer farther back on the table. His eyes opened, surprised as she reached over and captured both of his hands in hers, linking them in an intimate and almost familial pose. Her dark eyes searched his. "Those are my best theories. Counseling experience, textbook cases, research articles. But here's one more. And this is the *most* important thing I want to say to you.

"I believe that faith and love can heal things science says are impossible. Marguerite Perruquet has haunted me for all these years. She has always been in my prayers as I hoped for her happiness. So hear my words as a counselor and be guided by them. But also be guided by your love for her. For if we can't bring a child out of darkness and save her soul with love, then I'm afraid there's little hope for the world."

Chapter Five

Marguerite threw herself into her routine. If she too often found herself sitting at her desk staring into space, entranced by the way it felt to let her fingers drift over the upper slope of her breast, that was fine. Or tracing her lips, imagining Tyler kissing her there. Passionately, that hard male demand. Coaxing, with seductive persuasion. Casually, with the brief intimacy of committed couples that said "we belong to each other". *I'm yours.*

She hesitated, picked up a pen and drew the letters of his name carefully on her steno pad. T.Y.L.E.R. W.I.N.T.E.R.M.A.N. Winterman and the Ice Queen. An absurd coincidence which meant nothing really, but to a fanciful mind it could. One that still had girlish hopes.

She crushed the paper in her hand, holding it tightly. Brought it to her forehead, closed her eyes and sat that way for some time until she gradually became aware of a hand on her shoulder.

"I don't think—" Gen's voice.

"It's all right. I appreciate you showing me to her office."

Marguerite looked up into the face of Komal Gupta. She looked like one of her Mrs. Allens, her face bearing the lines of wisdom and experience. The tidy hair, the smock shirt and slacks sitting comfortably on her pear-shaped body, a neckline of jade stones around her neck.

"I don't know what to do," Marguerite said. She pressed her face into that soft, motherly midriff under the pendulous breasts and began to shake.

Soft smells, talcum powder. Like her mother, only without the odor of alcohol that would come through her pores. This was simple. Soap, something curry-smelling.

She breathed deep, shuddered. So many new things had happened to her in the past week. This was the most alien of all. Something inside her was simply crumbling away and she didn't know in which direction to scramble before the whole ground slid away, tumbling her into quicksand.

Komal's arms went around her shoulders, her head lying down on top of hers. So much like Tyler, as if she had the right. People who loved you, truly loved you, they could touch you. It was okay. It was good. It had been a long time since she'd remembered that.

"Oh, my sweet little girl," Komal murmured. "I have missed you so very much."

The first sob burst out of her like a hard cough, rough, jarring her lungs, then came another and another. Her fingers sank into the woman's hips as Marguerite held her face tight to her, hiding the hideous folding of all her facial features drawn so taut her head began to pound. But then there was salt on her lips, wetness sliding through those folds, making her lashes soft and wet on her cheeks. She was shuddering, afraid a bone was going to break or a muscle tear, but the seventy-year-old woman was holding her in close, not letting anything break.

"Oh, baby girl," she whispered, over and over, a light rocking that went on forever, the bliss of a mother's womb in a hug. Marguerite remembered how often she'd wished she and David would have always stayed there, that nebulous memory that rare children had, a subconscious prenatal memory of love. Happiness. The touch of her father's hand on her mother's stomach as she'd seen in pictures. So happy. Loving. Not possessed by evil, though she could see in those pictures now the dormant potential, waiting for the events that would release the darkness in him to its true purpose. Her mind went away from him, turned to Tyler's amber eyes. Tyler, who had faced crisis and trauma, had weathered it and offered love and protection instead of hate and punishment.

She didn't know how long she sat there in Komal's comforting hold, letting all the worry, fear and anxiety spill out of her in tears and muffled sobs. She only knew the plump hand never ceased its stroke and the squeezing reassurance of her hold did not ease. Not until she herself felt the compulsion of a lifetime kick back in to make her straighten, ease back, wipe her own eyes and fumble for a napkin beside her half-finished cup of tea.

"I'm sorry." She cleared her throat, heard the hoarseness in her voice. "I didn't...please, have a seat." She pressed the tissue to each of her eyes carefully, wiped her nose, crumpled it and placed it in the wastebasket next to her desk, stared at the surface for long minutes. Inventory records, her blinking computer screen with her financial software, the three tiny teacups holding sample teas sent to her by a company in India.

"India is beautiful, you know. I've been."

"Have you? Is it the first place you went overseas?"

She nodded, still focusing hard on everything before her. "The first time I got off the plane, I thought, 'This is different. Separate.' Somewhere else, where no one knows me, no one ever has to know me."

"For it is through others we know ourselves."

Marguerite closed her eyes. "That's what he's done. He held a mirror up in front of me. It's me, but it's not the me I thought it was. He loves me. I know nothing about love except the pain of losing it."

"You know love, Marguerite. You had it in David, your mother. Even at one time with your father."

"Then it's a temporary, transitory thing, as substantial as standing on water."

"There was once a man who so believed in the power of love that he *did* walk on water. Love is not temporary. It endures everything even if it changes form. Even when it must be put away to handle harsher things, it's always there, ready to be called."

Marguerite made herself turn her head a millimeter at a time, fighting her natural compulsion all the way to avoid looking at Komal. The woman's eyes were wet, cheeks stained with tears. She swallowed, handed Komal an extra napkin. "I'm sorry. I... You don't even know who I'm talking about."

"Tyler Winterman, I suspect." The woman nodded at

Marguerite's surprised expression. "He came to see me."

Marguerite pushed back from the desk, stood up. "He what?"

"He's a very determined man. And very protective when it comes to you. He came out of love, not to harm. And that's why I'm here as well. I feel you have a right to know he talked to me, though I believe he would have told you eventually. For though he's an arrogant, overprotective male—" her mouth was touched by a smile, "he's also an honest one. He was already feeling a little boy's guilt standing on my doorstep. He's quite something. A good match, for so are you."

"He's a pain in the ass. Meddling..."

"Arrogant," Komal supplied again, helpfully.

"It needs to be tattooed on his chest as a warning to all women." Which gave her an interesting picture of him in a cape, particularly the tights. She was losing her mind.

"Oh, God, I'm losing my mind."

"No." Komal laughed. "You're in love."

"What I need to do is chain him to a wall and stripe his interfering ass raw. What did you tell him?" Marguerite paced, stopped to stare out her two-way mirror at her afternoon clients. A frown crossed her face, her eyes narrowing.

"Only what I thought he needed to know, to understand what an incredible woman you are to have achieved so much for yourself. He already knows that about you. But he was afraid of hurting you with a misstep. By pushing too hard. I'm afraid as well. That you'll—"

"Excuse me just a moment," Marguerite said abruptly. She laid a hand on Komal's shoulder before she stepped out of her office. Komal rose from her chair in time to see Marguerite through the large window, moving out into her dining area to a young boy at her front door. He sported a basketball shirt to the knees of his baggy jeans. Speaking very quickly, he made nervous gestures, his eyes wide, an anxious child. Marguerite spoke to him briefly, gave him a reassuring smile, then pivoted toward the kitchen. As she passed her last occupied table, her expression changed from professional pleasantness to a malevolent intent that startled Komal. She was still on her feet when Marguerite stepped back into her office.

"What's going on?"

"Just something I need to address. It will only take a moment, then we can continue our discussion."

She reached around her office door, picked up the baseball bat behind it, hefted it and strode across the kitchen.

"Ah, hell. Marguerite." Chloe dropped a tray to the counter and dashed after her boss, colliding with Komal. Both women recovered, hurrying after the fluttering blonde strands of Marguerite's hair as she slapped her hand against the side screen door and strode down the path toward her community garden and playground.

The man in expensive gangster wear—gold chains, tennis shoes worth three figures and an oversized football jersey—had his back to her. Marguerite assumed he sensed danger in the way that the worst scum of the earth did, for he spun when she was still over two yards away. A tiny strip of children's stickers were in his hand, still half extended to ten-year-old Aleksia, one of the neighbor children who watched her brother while their mother worked two jobs.

"This is private property," Marguerite snapped. "You get your ass out of here."

"You get out of my face, bitch, if you don't want it messed up." The sticker fluttered toward the ground as he reached under his shirt.

Marguerite heard Chloe's scream, but as the gun flashed out, she was already swinging the bat, connecting with his hand hard, sending the firearm clattering into the monkey bars.

"What the fuck—"

She moved in, slammed another stroke on his raised forearm. He howled, she swung again, beating him to his knees, fast, brutal, repeated strikes, no room for mercy or hesitation. He was crawling away, scrambling, stumbling. She got him in the ribs, the kidney. She hoped she was killing the son of a bitch, making his internal organs bleed, giving him a slow death.

"Get the hell off my property. You will never get these children here. Never." It thundered out of her, her scream like the fury of a storm.

He rolled into the street bleeding, struggling to his feet to move as fast as he could away from her park. His eyes were stark white with terror, the knowledge in them that he was staring at death. Marguerite stopped at the fence entrance by a picket gate where she'd planted spring flowers several days ago. There was even a lovely welcome sign that Chloe had stenciled with a teacup and an orchid curling over it. Watching him stagger down the street, she didn't move until he disappeared, until the rage receded and she could feel the eyes of those in the neighborhood who'd come out on their porches to see what was going on.

She turned back to the park. No parents present, not in a neighborhood where the responsible adults often had to work multiple jobs at all hours to make ends meet, trusting their children's street savvy to keep them safe. Tomorrow she'd call a security agency and have a camera installed so she could watch the park area at all times. Shifting her gaze, she registered a white-faced Chloe and a stunned-looking Komal.

She clasped both hands around the bat's fat top and struggled to center herself as Komal took a tentative step toward her.

"Miss M?"

She became cognizant of Aleksia touching her forearm. The child's short brown fingers, the pink skin beneath her nails. In her other hand she held a fistful of the stickers. "I told him I'd give them out to my friends, so's he gave me a bunch. That way he can't give these to nobody. And I picked up the ones he dropped, too."

Her brother, the boy who had come to warn her, was now at her side. "Stupid ass. He shoulda knowed who he's messing with. You don't mess with Miss M's place."

"Jerome." Marguerite reached out to touch his head. "Remember I don't allow cursing in the park. And you need to work a little harder on proper English. 'He should have known with whom he was messing.'" She frowned, going over the grammar herself.

"My way sounds better." He grinned, confirming her discontent with the correction, his twinkling eyes unrepentant. "But sorry about the cussin', Miss M. We did good, though, didn't we?"

"You did very well. So well." She took the stickers, pocketed them and managed a smile for them both. "You were so brave."

He shrugged. "He was hittin' on my sister with his junk. Don't nobody mess with my sister long as I'm around."

His older sibling rolled her eyes but Marguerite saw her elbow his side with affection. "You's all talk. I can kick your butt. We have to get home."

"First, run in and tell Gen you each get a piece of lemon cake. And have her wrap up one for your mother."

"Alll riiight!" The two children ran for the side path entrance to the kitchen, an access Marguerite had always made clear was a door that would open for any of the children or neighbors, the entrance for friends coming through the park. She suspected Jerome had used the front so the drug dealer wouldn't realize he'd gone for help.

She peered into her pocket as Komal approached her with Chloe. "Chloe, remind me I have these when our officers come by this afternoon for their green tea. I'm sure they can use them for training. Or at least dispose of them properly."

"Are you okay?"

Marguerite raised a brow. "I'm fine." She looked at Komal. "I'm sorry you had to see that. It happens occasionally."

Though she'd never gone off on one like that, Chloe had told her. When Komal studied her, Marguerite shifted her glance. "Chloe, will you excuse us a moment?"

Chloe looked between them both, nodded, headed back for the kitchen.

"If you'd hit his skull, you would have killed him."

"If I'd jammed this up his ass, I would have perforated his bowel wall with splinters and he would have died in a couple hours from internal bleeding. Seemed too quick that way. This way I can imagine his kidneys giving him hours of torment just to manage a piss."

Reaching out, Komal put her hands on the bat over Marguerite's hands. "This is the side of you that worries me."

"What? The side that says I won't allow someone to harm the innocent?"

"There are laws."

"Yes. And we both know how well they work to protect the innocent. I'm not afraid of death, imprisonment." She laughed shortly, a harsh, angry sound. "I'm not afraid of having the blood of a drug dealer on my conscience."

"You can lose your soul by making violence your instrument of justice."

"My soul was lost a long time ago, Komal," Marguerite responded bluntly. "And if I still had it, I'd rather lose it to that than have it obliterated by shades of gray."

"A person's actions are not black and white."

"Wrong is wrong. There are extenuating circumstances, but this is a world that takes extenuating circumstances to such extremes that we've turning them into kindling for a sacrificial fire. And we're feeding our innocents into it, one soul at a time. You think his extenuating circumstances make it acceptable to push drugs onto children, turn Aleksia into a crack whore that would perform a blowjob on her own brother for the next fix? You think I of all people have any sympathy for that scum's extenuating circumstances?"

Komal nodded, closed her eyes. "I'm not here to engage in a moral argument with you. I just worry that you think you're like the person standing in front of the tank at Tieneman Square. Except maybe you're not there just for the cause, but for the hope that tank will roll forward and over you. That if people live up to your expectations and are savage, brutal, you have nothing of hope worth staying in the world for."

She took her hands away, touched Marguerite's chin, amazed at how tall her girl had gotten over the years. "And maybe that's why you're so afraid of Tyler. Up until you met him, you could have lived or died any given day and it wouldn't have bothered you. He's made you want to live. You're experiencing the same shock and disorientation as a newborn, only in the very self-aware mind of a strong, determined woman."

"I don't need psychoanalysis." But there was little bite to the words. Marguerite let the bat swing to the ground, leaned on it as she obviously re-marshaled her courtesy. "Let's go in, let me get you a cup of tea."

Komal nodded. "I'd like that. But let me say this, please. It's your soul I care about. You are probably one of the bravest children that came into my care." At Marguerite's startled look, she nodded. "It's not a light compliment, nor a slur on the other children. I see what you've built of your life, what you're giving to others. I also see you standing before the chance of love. You're so very courageous. Believe me when I say that the love of a good man is the very last thing you should be running from. I'm afraid, not that he'll hurt you, but that you won't believe in yourself enough to take the leap."

Marguerite looked toward the ground, an obvious attempt to cover the emotions crossing her face, her beautiful pale hair shadowing her features. Unable to help herself, Komal framed that crown in her brown hands, rose on her toes and pressed a kiss to her forehead. Marguerite did not move. Komal held the kiss there through several breaths before she drew back, touching the woman's hands. Hands now stained with blood from the portion of the bat she held.

"I've left my card on your desk. I'd love that cup of tea, but once I leave today please call me for anything. I would be delighted to have you visit me anytime. As a friend or if you need to talk to me professionally. For you I would hang out my shingle again." She hesitated. "And just for your information, Tyler looked a bit shaken up after he left my house. I'm sure he'd appreciate hearing from you. We forget that sometimes there is something greater than our pain. That's the pain of the person who loves us, who couldn't protect us from that pain. After meeting Tyler Winterman I firmly believe he would sacrifice the world to go back in time and do just that for you."

She nodded at Marguerite's stunned expression. "The gun is still underneath the monkey bars. Don't forget to give that to the police as well."

Chapter Six

She sat out in her private garden that night, long into the early hours of the morning. Listening to the birds, watching the fountain gurgle, hoping it would penetrate the buzzing, the roaring force field around her. But it wasn't the sounds of nature that broke through. Without direction, her mind chose its own compass. It pictured her here with Tyler next to her, his fingers laced with hers, his shoulder handy for her to lay her head.

His smile created a warmth inside her. She recalled the look on his face when she'd exposed her pain, her truths to him. A protective rage. No pity, no revulsion. When he kissed her lips, she felt as though he held her heart in both hands. And she was beginning to believe, just maybe, that there was no safer place for it. That he wanted her, no matter what she could or couldn't give him.

He hadn't shared what memories formed his nightmares yet, but as if they'd shared a secret handshake she knew he'd been places where he watched hell become reality. And he hadn't turned and run. He'd stood, accepting the blame and the responsibility, and done what he could.

He wanted her. Not just because he'd as much as said it to her but because she felt it whenever she thought of him, saw him.

I'm asking you to think it through. If you accept what we both understood well enough last night, then you come to me. Please come to me.

So she thought about it. Thought about it for two weeks. The tears had loosened up some things inside her, given them room to move around and she wondered at them. The way her feelings would dance through her chest when she thought about Tyler, bringing a smile to her lips if she let them. His bare heels treading on the cuffs of those loose drawstring pants as he'd moved around his kitchen. His hair when it was disheveled. The way his gaze focused on her when she spoke. The picture Sarah had painted of him sitting on that landing.

How would it feel to sit there with him, her hand in his, two people avoiding their nightmares as they shared a cup of coffee and watched the sun rise? Maybe together they could stave off the nightmares and the morning would be about nothing more than enjoying the beauty of a sunrise, following a night of making love.

"Chloe." She spoke through the open door of her office before she could lose her nerve. "Could you pack me up a little gift box for a pot's worth of the new Ceylon we just got in and some of those lemon bars? I'm headed for the Gulf tonight."

"Yes!" She jumped as Chloe and Gen did a high five over the counter. Marguerite leaned forward from her desk to study them.

"The two of you should go out and find a social life of your own, instead of meddling in mine."

Gen held up a hand. "Don't encourage Chloe. She's dating a biker now who does tattoos and piercings. She wants me to go on a double date."

"Maybe we could go out with you and Tyler?" Chloe's eyes danced. "Interest Tyler in a Prince Albert, maybe?"

"Oh my God." Marguerite toed her door closed on a burst of their laughter. She felt an answering chuckle in her stomach, mixed up with something lower, coiling tight with her resolve. She'd decided. She wasn't turning back. Now it was time to get dressed.

§

She hadn't spoken to him directly for those two weeks. He'd called her work number after hours to leave her warm, intimate voice mails, telling her his whereabouts, his schedule from day to day. A short trip to New York, his cell phone number. Back to Tampa for a day or so to work on a project. A party tonight at his house at the Gulf for some industry contacts, a favor for a friend. He was respecting his own rule, the one he'd set when he said goodbye to her on her front steps, not forcing direct contact until she made the first step. And despite his resolve, she'd been warmed to hear the edge of male impatience in his voice as the days passed. She wondered how long her knight would have waited before attempting to storm her castle again. She'd kept all the messages, downloaded them so she could hear his voice on her digital recorder as she lay in bed at night. Let them keep her company in the car as she made the drive to his Gulf home.

When she drove up his driveway, there were about twenty cars there, most of them luxury models. All the lights were on, a welcoming, warm vista. She could easily imagine those elegant cars as a group of carriages a hundred years ago, the same welcoming sense of graciousness projecting from the home, that enduring classiness that Tyler complemented with his own style.

As she got out of the car, she heard the warm chatter of voices and laughter that heralded a party where people were enjoying themselves. From the direction of the sound, it seemed they were outside at the pool house. She imagined that the glass doors had been thrown open so people could wander in and out, enjoy the grounds as they made new friends in an industry where success lay largely in who one knew and impressed. She had no doubt that Tyler had guests here that could turn an aspiring actress's or screenwriter's dreams into reality. He'd likely carefully chosen a handful of talents to be here to take advantage of that opportunity. Being invited to such a party would have been enough to make one of those hopefuls spend a month's salary on the right outfit and agonize over accessories days before the event.

Moments like that were turning points. Most of them went unnoticed as such until they passed into hindsight. But sometimes, like now, the significance of the moment was immediately apparent. Something would change forever when the eyes that mattered fell on you. And in that second the aspiring dreamer knew, in order to give the performance of her life, she couldn't perform. She had to give a part of herself to her audience and pull them into who she was.

All of Marguerite's senses were honed for that one person who mattered. As she moved across the lawn, oblivious to the curious looks, the dead physical stop of some of the men she passed, she picked out his voice among the others before she saw him. His polite chuckle. It ran a shiver of pure, hard wanting through her. She actually stopped herself to let her heart rate calm. Goddess, she'd really missed him. She didn't know if he was an obsession or something more, but she didn't care. She just needed to be near him, if it was only to sit across a room from him and stare.

He was sitting just inside one of the pool house doors in a deep man-sized wicker chair. His forearm rested along the curved arm, a drink loosely dangled off the end of it in his hand. One ankle crossed over the opposite knee, his favored pose, his khaki slacks casually adjusted. No coat, just a navy blue silk shirt that only enhanced the breadth of his shoulders, the mixture of the dangerous and the aristocratic in his features. With surprise, she noted that he was wearing his wedding ring on his right hand as a widower would. It made her wonder if he normally wore it but took it off when he was at The Zone or with a female houseguest to avoid questions, or perhaps out of respect for his wife. Respect for the oath he had made even if somewhere along the way the reality of it had become something terrible, unexpected.

Otherwise he was the picture of the relaxed and urbane host, the focal point for many of the women she saw milling around. They watched him with surreptitious glances, gauging their chances for a night or maybe more than a night, or perhaps just fantasizing.

Back off, he's mine. He said so. It startled her, coming so abruptly out of her mind and heart. Spoken with the hope of a submissive as well as the absolute certainty of a Mistress. All of it was rolled together into herself. Her.

Marguerite. What she wanted.

Still, she stayed where she was, taking this moment to study him without his knowledge. Each time he lifted his arm to respond in the conversation, she saw down the short shirt sleeve, the soft hairs under his arm, a three or four-inch length of his bare side. The early evening sunlight shone through the shirt, giving her the outline of his upper body, a simple thing that rendered her motionless, unable to breathe.

He was just...gorgeous. Perfect. She wanted his hands on her, his mouth. She needed him. Now.

He was talking to an intense-looking younger man who'd pulled the ottoman for the chair just beyond the range of Tyler's long legs to sit on it. The man was perhaps in his early thirties with brown and black hair streaked with blond, revealing that he spent a good deal of time in the sun. His gray eyes shifted restlessly. She suspected it wasn't abstract boredom, but because that was his nature. He was not sitting on the ottoman as much as he was perched on it. She also noted that he was dressed more casually than the partygoers, in loose torn jeans and an untucked cotton shirt, only several buttons fastened. Celtic design tattoos were around his wrists and the suggestion of more body art was shadowed within the folds of the almost open shirt.

His wire-rimmed glasses increased the unusual intensity, but made him more boyish and sensually appealing at once. The hair was disheveled, carelessly shoved away from his face. That and his clothing gave the impression of having rolled out of bed to come down and join the party. He was beautiful, the kind of man...

His gaze shifted to her and she picked up on it like the scent of a Darjeeling in the mist-covered foothills of India. Someone she would have snapped up in a heartbeat in The Zone. Perhaps even resorted to throwing elbows to get him if need be. This one knew pain, had the look in his eyes combined with the sweet sensual innocence of his mouth that so strongly appealed to her. But she sensed he was also one who had found peace for his demons. The focus of his eyes was unsettling, the way they examined her not exactly sexual but as if he were devouring every feature. It was obvious that he'd recognized her nature in the same blink of time she'd recognized his.

Jesus Christ. His lips moved in the words, probably said it, but the only voice she could hear was Tyler's as he broke off and turned to see what had drawn his companion's attention so abruptly.

She moved at last, made her way across the thirty feet of lawn left between them. She didn't let herself falter though she was afraid, more so with every step. She was about to go somewhere she'd never thought possible, trusting all her dark corners to someone else.

Tyler had given her that, the awareness that there was a black hole slowly spreading within her that would eventually take away everything she'd built. The things that she'd thought would compensate for the lack of true healing. He wanted her to accept a relationship where she'd have to have the courage to believe the darkest, deepest betrayal would not be lurking around the corner for her again. And there were no guarantees. Remembering her father's eyes—what they'd once reflected, what they'd become—she faltered.

Tyler rose at the same time as his companion. Without taking his eyes off her, he neatly stepped in front of the gray-eyed man, impeding his forward progress. Pressed his drink into the grinning man's hand and came toward her.

Tyler couldn't fault his friend's reaction. Josh was an artist. How else would an artist react to the ultimate challenge to sculpt? How could you capture a tenth of a goddess's beauty in clay or bronze, even with hands as masterful as Josh's?

The people she'd passed when she'd crossed the lawn were openly staring at her. He was sure they were wondering who she was, how she figured into this group.

Men who dealt regularly with beautiful women had gone stock-still when they saw her, probably not even certain what it was about her that made them want to get on their knees. Josh knew and he knew, but it was more than that for him. He'd felt her tremble beneath his touch, just as he'd seen ugly darkness pour out of her. But still she emanated a mysterious feminine power, something that called to the soul as much as the cock. Under her touch, a man could find absolute power, torment, or a lust that knew no civilized constraints.

He could tell she'd come for him with a single-minded purpose and she had no interest or desire to interact with anyone else. The thought made the want that had been branding the inside of his gut for days become raw. He'd missed her to the point there were times he'd felt like a rabid dog. Working out until his muscles were quivering, he'd run along the path by the Gulf until he was so exhausted he could barely make it back home. And still he couldn't keep himself from going back to the guestroom, stretching out on the sheets and pillow linens he hadn't permitted Sarah to change so he could breathe in her lingering scents.

She'd piled her hair up on her head, a twist with a silken tail that fanned out over her shoulder and left breast. She'd done that thing that women knew how to do, soft wisps of hair around her temples. No eye makeup, just a pale pink lipstick.

The dress she wore was a creation of soft cream. Sleeveless, a clinging cotton that hugged her body from breast to thigh, baring the points of her finely boned shoulders. She wasn't wearing a bra beneath it, her small bosom perfectly molded, the posture of her body showing she was entirely unselfconscious by the stretched fabric, the anatomically specific display of the shape of her breasts, the points of her nipples. Those long, shapely calves were bare, tucked into a pair of strappy-heeled sandals, her pale pink painted toenails matching the long nails of her fingers on her elegant hands. No jewelry, no rings. Just Marguerite.

As he made his way toward her, all the sharp desire of the past two weeks throbbed in him like untreated gunshot wounds. She watched him come, certainly read his desire, his intent, but she showed no fear, no compulsion to retreat.

He caught her shoulders. When her body touched his he almost groaned. Maybe he did. All he knew was he needed her in his arms and his mouth on hers before time could move forward.

The strength in his grip, the passion a living thing in his eyes, made Marguerite tremble, though she managed to keep it inside. Barely. It terrified and exhilarated her at once to know he'd wanted and needed her with the same fierceness. How could something be so frightening and reassuring at once?

He stared at her a long moment. The intensity of it was enough to have those around them instinctively giving them space. It didn't surprise her. Tyler had class in every aspect of his life. He'd tolerate no one in his home lacking it.

When he brought his mouth down on hers, she snaked her hands up the inside of his arms and curled her hands around his neck. Burying her fingers into his hair at his nape, she brought her body into his, aching, seeking. His mouth held hers with sure possession, almost savage need.

She was sure it was a good thirty seconds before either of them knew or cared that they were not alone. When he raised his head, she noticed the wounds on his face were healing. Still noticeable, but the tape was gone.

He shifted his glance. "Good Lord, you've absolutely frozen the men here. They're not sure whether they're supposed to worship you or be terrified."

"You don't appear to be terrified."

He smiled, brought her closer. His voice dropped, his lips pressing to her ear. "I'm better at hiding it."

"Not as much as you think." She closed her hands on his forearms. "You're shaking."

"So are you."

His lips were damp with the touch of hers. "You know," he said in a soft rumble. "I've watched you take a sub just over the cliff edge of sanity. Hold him there until I couldn't imagine he wouldn't snap from the mental strain. But you have that uncanny knack of giving him release a second before he'd completely lose his fucking mind for all time. These last couple days I figured you were trying that out on me."

Her lips curved because she heard the wry humor. And

because it honestly felt so...good to be standing here. So incredible.

"Was it working?"

His eyes swept heat through her with their look of dangerous purpose. "One more day and I'd decided to storm your place and drag you home with me by your hair like some kind of barbarian." He wrapped his hand in the tail of hair that fell forward over her shoulder and tugged, his thumb making a discreet caress over her nipple. She emitted a short gasp of reaction before she could stop herself. His eyes darkening, he continued to stroke the hair in his grasp, making that idle pass with his thumb again. "I actually felt it get hard for me," he murmured. "The moment I touched it."

"You wouldn't have gotten past Chloe." She tried to hold onto her sanity. "And I've had the same experience with you. Different body part, though." She flicked her lashes down, back up.

He smiled, a baring of teeth. Spared a glance at the man he'd left who'd resumed his seat and was watching them with avid interest, that amused look still on his attractive face. "I would have brought ammunition to distract Chloe."

"He is quite something." She raised a brow, teasing him, something she'd never contemplated doing before. "I didn't think your taste in submissives ran to the same gender."

Tyler chuckled, slid an arm around her, turned them so they were to all appearances casually strolling back toward his chair, but his fingers played along her hip and the top of her buttock, making her pulse race. "He's a good friend and a tremendous artist. And—I do underscore this several times for the health and well-being of any Mistress who tries to seduce him—completely unavailable. His wife's at a medical conference and he decided to spend a few days here until she gets back because he has a show coming up soon. He's trying to work up a couple additional pieces at the not-so-gentle demand of his dealer. He's done studio time here before. It's quiet and I can keep him from going out of his mind, mostly, without Lauren." Tyler slanted her a glance. "He's got somewhat of an uncertain temperament in her absence, given to falling into artistic melancholy, so she likes having me watch over him.

"The reason I suspect he's staring at you like that and the reason I don't consider beating him up for it is you walked across the grass and his creative wheels started revving like the legs of the Road Runner in a Bugs Bunny cartoon. And of course he recognized you as a Mistress."

"But he's taken."

"Irrevocably. Doesn't mean he doesn't appreciate the qualities when he sees them. He is an artist, after all." Tyler smiled. "Now you know why he's here. Why are you here, Marguerite? And if you're here to tell me you're going to break it off after that kiss, you better slip off those shoes and prepare to outrun me."

She couldn't help it, she did smile this time. When she put up her hand to cover it, he caught it, brought it to his lips, began to nibble on her fingers.

"Tyler, there are people watching us."

"There are people watching you. Thinking what a lucky bastard I am. Tell me why you're here. I want to hear it. I need to hear it."

She closed her hand into a fist, held it there in his grasp and summoned up her courage to look at him. Something in her expression apparently warned him, for he stopped the easy flirting. He let her go, studied her face. "What is it, angel?"

She made it a countdown. She would just count to five and say it. Words. They were just words. Certainly words that could change her life, that changed everything, even though perhaps people said ones like them every day and didn't mean it, just used the phrases as a nicer way of saying what they really wanted to do. But she didn't say what she didn't mean and he knew it.

"I can... I don't want to interrupt your party. But... I can..." She took a breath. Closed her eyes. Felt him waiting. 1...2...3...4...5...

"I want you to make love to me. I want to go to your room, your bed, be under you, feel you inside me, see your eyes, feel your body and know...we're together. I don't know if that's love or just need, but I know I need you. I need that with you. I need what I've never known and I

need it from you. Only you. And it may destroy everything
or build something. I really don't know. I just know...
Please make love to me."

She opened her eyes and she was staring into his, which
had filled with an emotion so strong that she couldn't face
it.

"No. No, damn it, don't you look away." He caught her
face, held her there, brushed his thumbs along the soft skin
under her eyes. "There's nothing on earth I'd rather do,
angel. You know... You understand what I am, who I am.
How I'll make love to you. How I want to make love to you.
As I said before, it doesn't—"

"Turn off at The Zone doors." A shudder ran through
her, her pulse increasing under his touch as the light in his
eyes flared, telling her he felt it, as well as understood the
meaning of her acknowledgement.

She lifted her chin and his hand lowered, collaring her
throat where the pulse beat strong and fast beneath his
palm. She shuddered.

"That's what I want."

He nodded and his lips brushed hers. When she parted
them, inviting, he swore softly. "You're going to destroy
me," he stated. Taking the pins from her hair, he brought it
tumbling down. He spread the silk of it over her shoulders,
an intimate but not indecent gesture that she knew was
just confirming their conversation. She swallowed, aching,
somehow wanting at this moment to do as she had done at
The Zone. Go to her knees, press her body against his
calves, tell him how she needed him. His Dominance, his
care. How much she needed to let go at last. She could sit
here between his knees, at his feet, holding on to him while
he held his court, happy to be quiet and still just under the
touch of his hand.

"I want to feel like I'm yours." *I want to be yours.* She
leaned into his touch, rose upon her toes against his hold
and put her lips against his ear, caressing him with her
breath. Now the words flowed out of her with the ease of
terrifying truth.

"Make love to me, please. Master."

She'd accepted that her wanting him was inseparable

from wanting his Mastery, that undeniable part of himself. Understanding that truth in herself had been as much a source of her fear as simply wanting the man. But now it thrilled her to feel her words ripple through his powerful body, tighten his hand on her throat, his eyes inches from hers, those firm, stern lips. And it brought a wave of energy different in its nature from what she knew as Mistress, but no less potent.

"Damn it," he muttered against her, his fingers digging into her hips as she shifted, rubbed her abdomen discreetly against his groin.

Marguerite felt a flood of ebullience, almost giddiness. When she drew back she knew her eyes were likely sparkling with feverish exhilaration. "I know you have to finish your evening with your guests." She slipped from his grip. "I'll ask your friend to keep me company. Let me know when you're ready to call it a night."

She turned away from him, glanced back. "What's his name?"

Tyler wanted it to be perfect for her. Everything perfect. Which mean he couldn't take her down underneath him here on the grass in front of fifty strangers. Good God, she wasn't wearing underwear. There were no panty lines beneath the formfitting dress, which climbed way too high on those gorgeous thighs. "Josh." He narrowed his eyes at her. "Torture is a two-way street."

She blinked, something almost like a smile playing on her beautiful lips. "I need you. I hope the party is over soon." She turned to Josh, who'd nearly dumped Tyler's drink on the ottoman in his haste to rise at her approach.

"Josh?" She extended her hand. "Tyler tells me you have a beautiful and wonderful Mistress. Your wife. I'd like to hear about her. Let's go sit in the gardens until Tyler finishes with his guests. Would you take me there?"

Josh noted the way her eyes assessed his movements, drifted over him in the way of a Mistress. But he didn't sense her intentions to be improper. He imagined it was just to spike Tyler's blood pressure, which she seemed to be doing admirably well. Her blue eyes as clear and fathomless as a crystal ball, she lowered her hand to his elbow, her fingers playing along his biceps. With Mistresses who were strong Dominants, it was almost second nature to casually touch a man they knew was a submissive. It made the situation even more curious.

As he took her hand, Josh got sensory overload as an artist, as a man and as a submissive. But because he was very much in love with his wife, devoted to her monogamously as his Mistress as well as spouse, he also picked up something through all of that. Vulnerability. This woman was doing a masterful job of covering it, but he sensed that she was hanging on the edge of a cliff in a situation she wasn't entirely sure she could handle. Because of that and because her hand was cold he enfolded it in his, offering warmth and reassurance.

Faint surprise crossed her remarkable features, as well as a bit of relief.

"It would be my pleasure," he said and meant it, already liking the complicated woman who had captured Tyler's interest. "I would love to sketch you."

"I would like to see all your tattoo art."

It startled a laugh out of him. "We'll negotiate it out." He would sketch her and give the result as a gift to Tyler, for it was obvious she was about three steps away from being devoured by the look in his eyes alone.

"Marguerite." In two strides, Tyler caught up with them, took her free arm. Keeping his hand on Josh's shoulder to hold him there, Tyler took her lips in a hard kiss, his hand moving to her nape. When he let her go, his grip on Josh's shoulder eased, but he kept the three-way contact, a message that Josh had his confidence in her care. Marguerite noted Josh had automatically stayed in place at the commanding touch. She lifted her eyes to Tyler's face, the promise there.

"I won't be long. I'll come to you as soon as I'm able. Sooner," he added, with a touch of frustration in his tone that would have made her smile if she weren't so overwhelmed with need. Nodding, she turned and moved away with Josh out of the pool house. Onto the path to a whole new world for herself.

Chapter Seven

Tyler seriously considered fabricating an outbreak of salmonella in the hors d'oeuvres and an impending locust plague, either of which would require everyone to leave now. He hoped he was embroiled in his last conversation of the evening, which he'd strategically arranged to be on the edge of the crowd near the gardens so he could slip away. He'd had to force his mind to stay on the courtesies required of a host to ensure his guests were enjoying themselves and where appropriate, achieving their objectives in attending.

But with every moment that passed a beast stirred within him, growing ever more hungry and ferocious. She'd come to him at last. Was waiting for him. His mind was full of her, every delicious move of her body in that dress that should have been illegal for public consumption. The way her hand had brushed down Josh's arm, the graceful fingers playing on his skin while her eyes challenged him. The damned sorceress.

He'd had submissives that enjoyed flirting and being coy in a pretty way, playfully goading the Dominance from him. Marguerite was a Mistress who demonstrated the tendencies of a submissive only under his touch. Even there she had a Mistress's aggressive way of unsheathing her claws to drive him insane. Well, it worked. He reminded himself the last group he was with right now were all promising talents deserving of his attentiveness and encouragement. He therefore tried not to convey the deadly impatience of a predator coming out of hibernation, ready to tear into whatever stood between him and dinner.

Backing away with a smile and nod, he caught hold of Sarah, passing him with another tray of wine. "Sarah, Michael Atlas is going to take over as host for the rest of the evening. Anything he needs, just help him out. If he wants to line up all the cars and drive a monster truck over them, let everyone run naked across the front lawn or hunt down locals for human sacrifice, I don't care. Just don't disturb me."

"You look disturbed enough as it is." She chuckled. "She's by the Aphrodite statue with Mr. Martin."

"He's probably coaxed her out of her clothes for a modeling session."

"I'm sure he values his life far more than that. Plus, Miss Marguerite has seemed very resistant to your considerable charms. I can't imagine Mr. Martin would succeed where you've had limited success."

"Remind me tomorrow why I don't fire you for your backhanded compliments. And keep in mind it depends on whether the woman in question wants to tempt me to commit homicide."

Sarah laughed as her employer disappeared down the garden path. She wondered if he would break into an undignified sprint and hurdle the hedges once out of her sight. Robert would be sorely aggrieved if a single branch of his rosebushes was snapped. She'd have to put the blame on Mr. Winterman's rowdier guests.

Tyler did take a couple of shortcuts, but avoided the drastic assault on the vegetation that Sarah had feared. He came upon Josh and Marguerite, bathed in the moonlight gleaming off the statue of the goddess. Marguerite sat on the edge of the koi pond, trailing her fingers in the water, letting the fish nibble at them. Josh was lying on the soft grass, hands linked behind his head, staring up at the stars, one bare foot propped up on the fountain wall next to her thigh. She clasped the fold of his jeans at his calf as she leaned over to play with the fish, demonstrating that casual intimacy a Mistress employed so easily. So deliberately. The edge of the mid-thigh skirt had inched up her bare leg. Tyler's mouth nearly watered at the idea of pushing her to her back, spreading those long legs and burying his face in her heat, making her bow up and cries of pleasure break from her sinfully tempting mouth.

"Okay. Here's another one." Josh spoke, still looking up at the stars. "Favorite movie."

"*Armageddon.*"

Josh tilted his head down. "Now that surprises me. I would have expected some artsy foreign chick-flick I'm expected to know about just because I travel in artsy circles."

"Do I look that pretentious?" Her eyes glinted and she made a figure eight over a koi with the pale white color of a phantom. He turned in endless circles, following her impression in the water, apparently happy to please her with the game. Tyler knew just how the graceful beast felt. "Good saves the day. Love is reunited and Bruce Willis proves there are heroes that can make everything all better. I don't believe in any of that of course, but it doesn't mean I don't wish it were true. I love that type of story."

Josh grinned, obviously enjoying her. This was a side of her Tyler had not yet seen, so despite his hunger he stayed still, curious. Whether it was the circumstances, the stress she'd been through coming to this decision, or perhaps it was that Josh was not threatening or a challenge to her, this Marguerite was almost...girlish. And, an added bonus, she was making Josh feel better.

"And how about you?"

Josh studied the sky, a smile still flirting about his sensual lips. "*Attack of the 50 Foot Woman* for such obvious, crass reasons I refuse to discuss it further."

She had never laughed, never that Tyler had heard, and she didn't now but her eyes laughed at Josh. "Of course." Then her gaze shifted. With a flood of heat to his loins, Tyler recognized she was looking for him in the shadows. He stepped out of them, let himself be seen. At the yearning look that flashed through her eyes, he couldn't summon a smile, even a cordial word. He could barely resist the need to fall to his knees.

"Josh." His voice was low.

Josh lifted his head, took in the situation at a glance. Rolling, he rose to his feet and nodded his head, a courtesy to both before he turned and left them. Marguerite blessed his intuitive and discreet withdrawal, for Tyler was advancing across the clearing swiftly.

She was ready for him, had come for this, even if she couldn't say the words. She wanted to be his. All his. Whether it could go any further than tonight, whether her fragile psyche could handle more than this, she didn't know, but she'd wanted it clear that she'd come to him at least this once. She'd met his terms. She had to put herself in his hands, have faith in every moment after that fateful decision. Not because she no longer feared such a decision so deeply she was shaking in places that did not show, but because she couldn't imagine any other action.

He stopped with less than a foot between them. "I want you so much I can't be gentle, angel. Not even close."

Her pulse was high in her throat. At his words, the rate increased. "I didn't ask you to be."

One large hand climbed up her bare thigh which was stretched out as a counterbalance to the position in which she'd been leaning over the pond. The other went to her waist, brought her to her feet, even as the other hand continued its upward advance under the clinging fabric of the skirt to her bare ass beneath. Taking a firm hold, he pressed her hard against him as he brought his lips onto hers. He was making a noise in her mouth, actual growling as he held her tighter, closer, letting her feel every inch of his need for her. She'd never experienced this. Never felt such raw hunger emanating from a man who wanted her, a man with Tyler's finesse who seemed to know her deep inside herself, whose touch could demand and reassure at once.

"I'm going to take you to my room and make love to you," he rasped against her lips, biting them. "The way I've imagined doing it for the past couple of weeks. But first I'm going to fuck you, right here, right now."

He hooked his foot around her ankle, took them both down to the carpet of grass, catching their weight on his forearm. The thud of their impact was jarring, thrilling in its force, but not painful.

"Put your arms over your head." It wasn't a request, his

tone making it easy for her to simply obey, her body trembling, her thighs opened by the press of his thighs between them. He raised his body only to unfasten his trousers and push them far enough down his hips to accomplish his objective. Thrusting his arm under her waist, his large hand palming her bottom to lift her higher, he drove into her. Her pussy was so wet he sank in deeper, faster and harder than he'd expected, causing her to cry out and arch, pain mixed with unbearable pleasure.

"God, I've gone crazy without you," he muttered. Shoving the dress up to her waist, over her breasts, he bared them to his avid gaze, holding the crumpled fabric against her throat and keeping her pinned as he loomed above her. His hips thrust, his cock stroking tissues that were on fire, that were even now rippling with orgasmic response.

"I won't let you stop coming tonight." And he made it sound like the threat it was. "Until I've done every single thing I've thought about doing to you and with you these two interminable weeks."

She moved restlessly against him, her eyes so wide and clear, so full of him he thought he might be seeing his own soul. He hoped she was seeing the same in his. But even that was a garbled thought, for what he needed and wanted in this moment had more to do with things that went beyond words. And she understood his need. His beast roared at the recognition that she kept her hands above her head at his command, because that was the way he'd commanded it and because that was what the desire in her eyes said she wanted as well.

Master. She'd called him Master.

He pulled her legs up higher around his hips. She hooked them at the small of his back, that supple, flexible body undulating beneath him, reminding him of beautiful yoga asanas, of Shakti and Shiva coming together to find peace and balance, passion and joy, everything that made life worth living. The sword that could be raised as a defense against every kind of evil. In this terrible world, there was this gift, this sanctuary. This proof of Divinity.

Gripping her buttocks in both hands, he rose to his

knees and lifted her so he was still driving in hard and steady, watching her breasts spill onto her sternum, wobbling with the force of gravity. The nipples were dark mauve hard points, her cunt slick where he was plunging in, again and again, moving her on the grass. When he thrust two of his fingers deep into her backside she screamed, a full-throated cry he was sure could be heard by his guests, by the stars. He felt a surge of primal pleasure in it, a conqueror's fierce satisfaction, a man's humble gratitude.

"Come, Marguerite." His voice was hoarse. "Come for me, angel. Let me hear you. Let them know who you belong to."

As her body rolled against him like storm waves, she moaned, then cried out again, a long sound of release. He kept thrusting hard, feeling her flesh clamp down on him, unrelenting, telling him she'd missed him as much as he'd missed her. He was inside her, not just her soaked pussy, but in all the complex turbulent and dark mazes that were Marguerite. He wanted to be there forever, wanted to keep her safe and unafraid, give her pleasure and happiness. He could no more consider letting her go now than he would consider severing a vital limb and letting himself bleed out.

She would likely panic and withdraw, run from him again, but he knew the way in now. She'd let him into the deepest room in her heart. He was going to win her as often as he needed to do so, even if it was a quest that took forever, that had to be begun every day. Until death do they part.

Hell. For eternity. No way was she going to get out of this with a flimsy excuse like mortal lifespan.

When they both came down, he lowered himself onto her, breathing hard. Curling his body over hers, his arms around her head, he laced his fingers in her limp ones, nuzzling her cheeks, feeling her legs slide down to hold him in a lower embrace, though he stayed firmly seated in her. He kissed one perfect ear, the tiny hairs at her temple, blew on her eyelashes until she squeezed her eyes closed like a disgruntled cat and made him smile when she pushed against his grip.

"Now that we've taken care of that," he said. "I'm going to make love to you. Slow, soft, long. All night."

She looked up at him. "Carry me. I like it when you carry me." Her body trembled beneath him.

"Ask me."

"Please." The words came out without hesitation or thought. "Would you carry me?"

"Anything you ask for, angel." Though he wondered if he could get her all the way to the bedroom without laying her down three times in between and taking her all over again. "No. It's my right to do it." He stayed her hands, pulled the dress back down over her breasts, down the slope of her abdomen, over her hips, his fingers stroking her damp and still quivering flesh. Reluctantly he withdrew his touch to rearrange his own clothing. But the separation was only for a moment. "Put your arms around my neck," he commanded her quietly.

When he lifted her, he left her shoes tumbled against each other at the base of the statue. He couldn't think of a more appropriate offering to the deity devoted to love and sensuality.

Chapter Eight

When he got to the threshold of his bedroom, Tyler paused. Breathing in, breathing out. Like the woman he was bringing here, he knew the power of a Mastery, the complete surrender of a submissive to the Master or Mistress. When the message was, *"All I am, I offer to you, I give to you. I'm yours."* She'd said this was what she wanted and he was never going to take the gift for granted. He was going to give her the world if she let him. Every beautiful thing he gave her to blot out an ugly piece of her past would tear a hole out of his until they could cast their nightmares like ashes into the Gulf and lay the past to rest. He hadn't realized the key to his own emptiness until she'd had the incredible bravery—so much bravery there was no way to describe it—to open up her soul and shed light on the answer he'd been unable to find until her whispered words had provided it.

He'd never entered a life-threatening situation without a full arsenal of weapons. Marguerite had let her father torture her night after night with nothing to defend her except her fierce love for her twin, the protection of his life the one thing that kept her focused.

Some wounds could only be healed by the touch of a soul mate, two broken pieces coming together to become a whole being again, so simple the jaded world would call it a cliché. The angels would call it one of God's miracles, offered off the tips of His fingers like diamond raindrops, driving and cleaning away all that didn't matter.

That love was worth any torment, every disappointment. It couldn't be explained or described. It simply was, in the same way Marguerite wanted him as her Master, not even understanding what that meant. Just knowing as he'd known all along that she belonged to him. The beautiful, indomitable Mistress Marguerite.

He had perhaps not even comprehended it himself at the beginning, that she could be both. Both aspects were who she was, the sculpted result of her past, the decisions of her present. But there was a newly acknowledged part of her soul. A part that, if she held on to her courage and he didn't let her down, could become the cradle to hold all of her amazing diversity. Protect it, cherish it and let the beauty of her many different flowers become a bouquet of possibilities they could share.

His rational mind knew all that, could analyze it forever while his soul merely rolled its eyes and pushed him toward the path it had always known was the right one. Claiming her fully, making her dark and light his now and forever so there would be no path she had to walk alone ever again. It was what she'd said she wanted in that one word she'd whispered in his ear. The Master in him wasn't waiting to hear it twice.

Putting her down, he guided her in and closed the door. He stopped her at the foot of the bed, the only light coming from the dim strip of hallway light under the door. The house was silent, all the guests occupied outside and Sarah's kitchen on the opposite end of the house. It was just the two of them.

Marguerite watched him move to the dresser. He'd been so quiet since they left the party, but then words didn't feel necessary. Flame illuminated him when he lit a trio of candles that were there, along with an arrangement of fresh flowers, a stack of scripts and a belt he'd apparently discarded earlier in favor of the one he was currently wearing.

"The picture of your wife is gone." The small wooden box with the rings was as well.

"Not gone. Just moved. I had Robert hang it along the stairs with the other family pictures." He turned, began to remove the wedding ring.

"No," she spoke softly. "Don't."

He stopped, a rare look of surprise crossing his face.

"It reminds me who you are."

He put the pieces back together, by himself. And most people couldn't have done that... About eighteen months after she went back to Europe, he went after her... He never divorced her, you see.

Sarah's words echoed in her head, reminded her of the type of man he was. She met his gaze across the room. "I meant what I wrote on that note. If I'm here, it's because I want all of you. You've told me you want me, light and dark. Give me the same trust."

Something painful passed through his expression, his fingers still over the ring. She stepped forward, one step, two steps. Kneeling before him, she took his hands, separated them to press her lips to that ring finger and rub her cheek against his knuckles. When he drew in an unsteady breath, she made a new discovery. The loyalty and devotion of a submissive could be even stronger than the power of a Master.

"Why did you move the picture?"

"I loved her, will always love her, but this room is yours and mine now. I wanted you to know that when you stepped into it."

"When? Not if?" She tried to sound challenging, but her heart was pounding too hard. It increased as he drew her to her feet, took a scarf from a drawer.

"When. Not if. Another day and I would have come for you. And I think you know that."

She put up a hand, uncertainty returning, and halted the scarf's upward advance. "What are you doing?"

"Blindfolding you. Making love to you the way I wish. Trust me, angel. For once I want you to try to relinquish all control to me. Try to trust me as your subs trust you. To give them pleasure, to keep them safe."

She lowered her hand as he tied the scarf around her head, taking away shapes and shadows, leaving only darkness.

"That's an illusion. I can't protect them."

"I've heard about your vengeful streak. I disagree." His lips brushed her forehead. When he moved away, he held on to her hand until the last possible moment.

"Where are you going?"

"I'm right here. I'm just turning on some music."

The rumble of the doors of the heavy armoire, the click of equipment, a remote. The quiet trundle of a CD player opening, closing.

He came back as the first strains of "Unchained Melody", the version done by the Righteous Brothers, poured into the quiet darkness of her mind. His hands stroked through her hair, spreading it out on her shoulders. It soothed, made some of her anxiety recede.

"Every time you see me, you take down my hair. I was thinking of cutting it all off."

His hands curled in, tugged. "You'd kill me, angel. You don't know what your hair does to me when it falls down your body like this. All I can think of is Lady Godiva riding through the village on a palfrey, clothed only in her beautiful hair."

Then his hands moved from her shoulders under her arms. He hooked his thumbs into either side of the sleeveless cream dress, taking it down, baring her breasts, folding it down to her waist. He left it there and cupped her breasts, one in each hand as her hands quivered at her sides, not interfering with his pleasure, their pleasure. Touching the curves, he moved his hands over them slowly, taking his time such that she knew he was watching every change in her body. Not just the tightening of the areola and nipple, but the elevation in her breath, the pulse of her throat, the ripple of gooseflesh in one place, a flush in the other. He kept fondling one breast, but captured one of her hands, lifted it to his mouth, nibbled her fingers. One by one he kissed them, then made his way down her palm to trace her wrist pulse with his tongue as she shivered.

As the poignant, powerful notes of the song continued, she felt them unfold within her like the chapters of her life, mapping her in and out, everything she was there for him to see. It made her tremble in a way she couldn't stop. Halting his sensual nibbling, he dropped to one knee to rub his cheek against her midriff, slide his hands around to her thighs and the base of her buttocks to give her a reassuring squeeze. Her body moved restlessly as the side of his head, his soft hair, brushed the undersides of her breasts with his movements.

"It's okay, angel. I know what this song can do to the soul. It pulls out the magic, makes it easier to give everything to each other. I don't want you to be afraid."

She stiffened, her hands curling into fists. "You haven't played this song... You're not doing something you've done with someone else."

"Marguerite."

Tyler rose, cupping her face in his hands. "No. There's just us in this room. Now and forever." He paused, seeking the right words. He'd never wanted to possess a woman more, to experience the sweet, aching victory of her surrender to him, the willing gift of her faith and trust. And he knew that meant he had to give her the same.

"This... No woman has ever been in this room with me other than my wife. I've lain here in the dark listening to that song, alone after her death. That's how I know."

She raised her hands, closing them over his. His throat closed up at the softer set of her mouth, her sign of forgiveness.

"I'm taking off my clothes," he said. Reluctantly he took his hands away and unbuttoned his shirt, shrugged out of it, unfastened his trousers. He stilled as her fingers found his shoulder and touched it like the brush of an angel's wings in truth, following the line to his neck, then down over the wide plane of his chest. His body rippled with response as she made her way over his pectorals, his nipples, the gathering of soft hair across them. Moving to stand closer to him, she lowered her touch to his trousers. Moved around and under his hands as he withdrew them, letting her take down the zipper of the garment. Her fingers went inside, stroking the surface of the cotton boxers as if she were stroking an animal's soft pelt.

"I thought it wasn't fair for you not to let me see you. But this is even better." Though she was the one blindfolded, surrendering to him, he found himself held motionless by her irresistible whisper, her intimate touch. He wondered now why she even bothered with restraints at

The Zone; if he'd been Brendan, he would have simply lain there and let her burn him alive for the chance of a touch like this.

"I'm going to worship every inch of you," he promised, wondering if she understood that he meant forever, not just tonight. Catching her wrists before her hands could circle him and undo him completely, he set her from him to remove the rest of his clothes. When he moved back to her, the tip of his erection slid against her thigh, the point of her hip. Her tongue touched her lips, nervous anticipation.

Passion rose in him, even harder and more demanding than it had been in the garden when he'd known all the demons in hell and the heavenly hosts could not have prevented him from penetrating her. Nothing but her refusal and she hadn't refused. Had accepted him. Perhaps could even accept his darkness.

He couldn't face that. Tonight was not about that. This was all about her. Taking his belt from the dresser, he looped it around her wrists, behind her back. He knotted the strap through the railings of the footboard so she stood before him blindfolded, her arms restrained.

"Tyler..." It was a soft breath. Dropping to one knee again, he made her spread her legs so he could enjoy the nectar of what lay there.

She moaned, already wet and swollen. His hands came up and anchored her hips more forcefully, his teeth scraping, tongue delving deep, wanting more, wanting her to scream until he'd hear the hoarseness in her voice tomorrow. See in the stiffness of her walk that he'd given her pleasure past the ability of her body to absorb it. He dug his fingers in, wanting to see the bruises that passionate lovemaking could create, the stamp of his presence on her, for they both knew that pain held power and release beyond imagining. His desire for her raged into the dark area of violence as well as the light of ultimate salvation. He wanted her to feel both.

Marguerite felt every touch in a way she knew no other man could emulate. The few touches she'd allowed subs couldn't compare to this and she didn't have to have a legion of past lovers to know it. In her soul she knew this was it, the person who called to her heart, the type of person she'd heard other women talk about, dream about, rarely find. And he had reached out to her, seen it and felt it first. Been persistent enough for both of them.

Having him take her over this way brought a sense of tranquility she couldn't begin to understand, a desire to serve him and worry about nothing else. She wondered if this was what her subs were feeling when she made them reach that elevated state past the point of choice and anxiety. This floating, spiraling...joy.

His mouth left her cunt, whispered down her thigh and across it, up the shallow valley between hipbone and stomach, his fingers touching her navel, touching her waist. Learning her. Registering every tiny mole, plane or curve with mouth and fingers. Every touch was like fanned flame on her skin without her sense of sight. Her thighs remained open to accommodate him so she smelled her scent, felt it wet on her thighs as the petals of flesh still vibrated from the movements of his mouth there.

"Tyler." That soft word again. A plea. A statement. An affirmation.

He straightened, framed her breasts in his hands and began to suckle her, his lower body pressed against her. She moved, feeling the pressure of the footboard against her bound hands, pressed against her buttocks. His tongue played with the nipple of her left breast, drew it in, tugged. He bit down on it more sharply, making her jump, arch into the pain. She wanted him to bite her everywhere, leave his marks on her, even where the belt dug into her straining wrists. She had a sudden, greedy need for him to overpower her. Take her, obliterating everything else. She wanted him to push her past the point where shadows could reach her, to where there was only mindless pleasure, release, fulfillment. Where love was the only thing she felt.

If that was what this was. At this moment, she knew it was. She might doubt it tomorrow when the shadows returned, but if she could believe it tonight, then maybe with the doubt would also be hope. She hungered to feel that, to feel the butterflies when she wasn't with him, when she was thinking about him, the way Chloe and Gen did when they had lovers. Secret smiles, weak knees, chuckling at their own besottedness.

No doubt on that at least. She was most definitely besotted with Tyler Winterman.

And, oh God. That mouth still suckled her nipples, pulling fire into her lower belly, a fire that was spreading even lower so she was writhing sinuously. Rubbing her mound against his hard abdomen, feeling his erection against her inner thigh. She wanted it higher. Wanted it deep inside again.

Abruptly, he released her from the footboard but left her hands bound until he pushed her down on her stomach on the bed. He unstrapped the wrists only to stretch her arms out across the mattress until her hands were clutching the corner seam. He retied and anchored her to the side rail. On the large bed, her feet just went over the edge. When he put a knee on the mattress between her spread legs, there was a quiet, still moment where he simply stood over her, and she felt him looking at her. Her body vibrated, hips moving in alluring, wanton invitation. Then he destroyed her.

Bending over her, he placed his lips on the cigarette scar at the lowest part of her back, his jaw touching her buttocks. He traced the scar with his tongue, kissed and nibbled it, then moved up to the next one, on the opposite side of the valley formed by her spinal cord.

"There's only me, angel," he muttered. "Now and forever. Say it. Mine."

"Mine."

He paused, his lips on her back, and she strained against her bonds, moving against him. "Mine," she repeated.

He bit down not so gently, making her moan. "Yes, angel. I'm all yours. Yours."

He understood. She was grateful because she was beyond the irritating complexity of words. She knew she was already his, had known it deep inside the moment he first came into Tea Leaves and she felt undone by the flash of those amber eyes. But to believe he was something *she* could keep, not a fleeting fantasy or a dream...

"All yours," he breathed as he went up her back, his fingers following, tracing her buttocks, his knee moving forward, pressing against her pussy. She arched up, rubbing against him, making tiny mewls of pleasure and need.

"Please, Tyler... I need you inside me."

He put his arm under her waist, bringing her up higher, her hips into the air, increasing the strain on the restraints on her arms. When his cock slid in deep, his testicles soft against her inner thighs, a secret, intimate caress of contact, he did not even pause in his thorough attention to her scars. Her breath left her on a moan as he worked his way up her spine. The power of the sensation created by his slow swirling of tongue and the brief presence of teeth was matched by each stroke and withdrawal that dragged fire along her slick channel. Her belly clenched for a climax held just out of reach.

"Oh..." She said it softly, trembling on each stroke, each kiss as if her body were frozen, held in the near state of rapture, her skin cognizant of everywhere it was being touched by his. The muscles of his stomach along her buttocks. His hand braced on the bed so close his thumb brushed her side, the outer curve of her breast, increasing the friction of the spread against her nipples, her desire to have him touch her there. His arm around her waist, holding her secure.

Then he withdrew from her despite her cry of protest and turned her over, twisting the belt. She felt him lie down upon her, his chest pressing down on her aching breasts, his cock finding her again and sliding back in, his body pinning her, holding her so their movements became a dance, her undulation against the relentless, steady and slow rhythm of his penetration. He put his hands up on either side of her face, elbows on the bed, forearms pressed against the underside of her arms where she had them stretched above her head.

"My angel," he said in a soft, almost reverent voice. She could imagine his tiger's eyes glowing in the dim light just above her.

She knew he'd chosen this position to seal the intimacy between them. There would be no excuse or rationalizations as escape hatches later. She wished the scarf was gone so that she could meet his gaze, give him that.

"Say it," he said. She felt his body gathering, the power ready to be unleashed with his release. "I need to hear you say it."

"Yours." The words tumbled from her lips. "I'm yours."

"Sweet angel. Sweet Mistress." He nuzzled her ear. Her body was on fire, aching as he drew her higher and higher, both sweating, trembling, him holding back, keeping the pace to deny her release until she made it to a height she'd never known she could reach.

"Beg me, angel. I want to hear you."

She sank her teeth into his shoulder, a growl his answer. Catching her hair in his hand, he wrapped his fingers in it, tightening his hold on her. His strokes became more powerful, demanding. "Making love, fucking you, holding you, it makes no difference. You're mine, angel. I want you in all ways, forever."

She bucked beneath him, violent need taking over, a raging want that she needed him to sate. "Please." She almost screamed it against his skin. "Please let me come for you." The darkness contained him, only him.

"Soon..." He changed his angle again. Gripping him with her inner muscles, she tried to stroke him past the point of control. She strained to lock her legs around him, take him deeper, but he was stronger and kept the pace he wanted.

"Please...Master. Please..." She arched up and he captured one of her nipples, biting down hard on it, even as he surged forward, pounding now, holding her tight.

"Go over, Marguerite. Scream."

The music of it broke from her lips before he finished the thought. She arched beneath him, her cunt sucking on him wildly, her body convulsing from the strength of the orgasm. His own roared through him and he used it, thrusting into her again and again, letting the hot streams bring her own climax to new heights, watching her face as much as he could, every nuance of expression, those beautiful lips that had called him Master, the only woman he wanted to do so again.

Her body was damp and strong beneath him yet he felt her fragility, a woman afraid to call herself his. Even more afraid to claim him as her own, because she'd never had anything she'd loved endure, anything she could keep.

In that brief moment of understanding, he grasped why she'd needed to see his vulnerability, a woman's odd way of knowing a man truly needed her.

If she only knew. He couldn't imagine breathing without her.

He let her hear him as well, giving his release hard and deep in her, wanting to leave no question in her mind, no part of her untouched by himself.

He loved Marguerite Perruquet. All he needed to do was convince her she could love him back and not lose him.

She strained up in the dim light. "Please. Let me see you. Touch you."

He removed the scarf, freed her hands. She touched every feature of his face, light, wondrous touches. "It doesn't really matter, does it?" she asked. "Mistress or Master...slave."

"No. If it's like this, it doesn't matter." He bowed his head down next to her cheek, felt her arms wrap around his damp shoulders. Inhaled the silk of her hair, inhaled her into all of himself.

And remembering Komal, he thanked God for miracles.

§

Marguerite made her way out to the Aphrodite garden, her cup of tea in hand. The statue gleamed in the morning sun, the bronze tresses of hair wound around the manacles on her wrists, face turned up in ecstasy. Freedom found inside the binding of love and pleasure. Trust, commitment. Friendship. They'd always been words belonging to other people, something she watched like television programs about experiences she could never have.

But the way Tyler had left her this morning... With a soft

kiss and regret in his eyes that he had to conduct some business in his home office. He'd promised to join her within an hour. Consideration. The desire to spend time with her.

The grass around the statue was soft. Taking off the slippers he'd provided, she sank her toes in the springy mattress and at the same time set her mug of steaming Earl Grey like an offering at the feet of the Goddess. Next to her sandals from last night, she noted with amusement. After a moment of contemplation, she slipped the belt of the robe and began to slide it off her shoulders.

A discreet cough arrested the motion. She looked over and found the statue was not the only aesthetically pleasing thing in the garden. Josh leaned back on the bench, wearing his jeans of the prior night and an open shirt, carelessly thrown on. His hair was still tousled, the wire rims of his glasses unable to disguise the beauty of his gray eyes.

"I don't wish to stop you in any way, because I'm poised to sketch." He waved the blank pad. "But I find my models usually prefer to have a choice in the matter."

She nodded, her fingers on the lapels of the robe, fingering the silky fabric. The skin beneath still felt sensitized from Tyler's frequent touches throughout the night. "Your wife doesn't mind you sketching a naked woman?"

"It's sort of like the foot on the floor rule." He smiled. "As long as I keep ten feet between us, it's fine."

She noted there was about twelve feet, the bench hugged by the hedge of fragrant honeysuckle behind him. He nodded. "I'm an erotic artist, so of course she knows what my work requires. I'd love to sketch you." A shadow crossed his eyes. "With her gone, it's hard to find inspiration." He lifted a shoulder. "Elements of you remind me of her, so I'm asking you for the honor. Mistress." He gave a little half bow from the waist.

It warmed her like the sun soaking into her shoulders, which was making her drowsy, reminding her of her long night and how little sleep she'd had. Or wanted, at the time. "If I can see the rest of the tattoo work. Fair is fair.

And we'll maintain that ten feet."

Josh chuckled. "While we've discussed women getting naked in front of me, I'm afraid we haven't really covered vice versa. However, I'll show her the sketch when I'm done and see if she thinks it was worth it." His gaze gleamed. "If it wasn't, then it means I didn't do a good enough job of capturing the subject matter and I deserve whatever punishment she deems fitting."

The Mistress who'd snapped up the heart of this beautiful and interesting man had to be quite something. Marguerite thought he'd better make it a very good sketch.

She dropped the tie of the robe, let the garment fall into a pool of satin around her ankles.

Josh was certain she wasn't aware of the correlation between her and the statue behind her, the proud stance, the graceful lines of the body, the smooth, pale skin against the bronze.

"Whatever you were about to do before you knew I was here..." He spoke quietly, too moved by the sheer beauty of the picture to raise his voice above a murmur. "...go ahead and do."

She hesitated, then turned on the ball of one foot, bent her knees. With elegant sensuality, she lay down on her side, her back facing him, her arm curled as a pillow under her head, the other arm lying loosely before her. Her knees drew up, a loose fetal position, the silk of her clipped-back hair spilling perfectly onto the robe's folds. The orchids near the fountain wall flickered shadows over her skin.

The hesitation had startled him, for she'd not struck him as modest in her manner, but when he saw her back, he understood. As she settled, getting comfortable, the air grew still, telling him she was aware he was studying her.

"Will they be there? In your picture?"

Her voice was quiet, smooth, no inflection to betray her thoughts.

"I'm a sculptor, Mistress. The sketch is to help me remember. But..." He paused, starting to move his pencil rapidly over his page, inspiration overtaking him, making it hard to focus on a response. "No," he said at last. "They won't be. They helped make you who you are but they didn't make it all the way to your soul and that's what I try to sculpt."

Her hand curled into the well-tended grass. "Josh, that may be the most lovely lie anyone has ever told me. Thank you. What will you do with it, if it becomes a sculpture?"

"Not if. When." His fingers were already itching to begin, could feel the way she would evolve under his hands. He could visualize how he would handle the different shapes of the orchids in bronze, the contrasting smooth expanses of her skin.

"I'll show it to my art dealer, Marcus. He'll set an exorbitant price on it which Tyler will pay three times over to make sure it becomes part of his private collection and never sees the inside of a gallery. If I wanted to be really terrible, I'd let Marcus know that. Tyler would have to mortgage this palace to acquire it."

Josh assumed a grass blade must have tickled her calf when she lifted a leg to rub at the offending itch. A few moments later her silence and the easing of her shoulders, the rhythmic rise and fall of her upper torso, told him she'd drifted off.

Over the next half hour, he sketched. Rising once or twice to circle her, squat by the base of the Aphrodite and study all the angles. He saw the evidence of her night with Tyler. Faint bruises from passion unleashed in two strong people, the flesh abraded along her fair-skinned breast from a man's rough jaw, even the light impression of teeth on her neck. His nostrils told him she'd not yet showered. He could smell the mesh of their two scents as he chose an angle near her feet to better fill in the slope of her thighs. For Josh, immersion in the sensual elements of his subject matter was all-consuming, so his pencil picked up pace, his eyes flickering quickly, the ideas, the concept forming.

As he moved around her, he kept his bare feet quiet on the grass, but she was sleeping the sleep of the well content, her body relaxed. Not until the sun rose over the statue did she move, shifting so she could lie on her back and turn her face away. When Josh moved so he blocked the light from disturbing her slumber, her brow eased and she returned to her side again.

The loneliness in the pit of his belly, the ache for Lauren that could become unbearable if she was away for too long, became somewhat more manageable as he performed this small act of service for this lovely Mistress. His art reached out to comfort him, a manifestation of the peace he found in Lauren's arms, something so much like it that he knew both were miracles. As he studied the scars, he wondered if Marguerite often slept this deeply, or if she too had finally found her port in a storm. Based on his high regard for Tyler and what he'd seen of her, he hoped so.

He turned to retrieve his sharpener and found Tyler sitting and watching them, his arms stretched out over the back of the bench. His eyes were nearly gold in the full light of the sun. Josh extended the pad and Tyler took it, looked down at it. His finger followed the sketched line of her shoulder down to her waist, over her hip, the shadowing.

After a long moment, he looked back at her. "I held her in my arms last night," he said quietly. "And when I felt her every response, I thought, 'There's nothing else I could ever want.' Whether there's a heaven or not, it doesn't matter. This... Those moments when she gave me everything were more than I ever hoped Heaven could be."

"It's love." Josh nodded. "Once you find her, she's the only way to fill the emptiness. Welcome to the club." He looked over at the sleeping woman. "Will she run?"

"She's been through a lot. She doesn't believe she's capable of feeling the same way, of being brave enough to accept it." Tyler's voice conveyed his conflict over that. "She's braver than any man I've ever met. I just hope I can convince her she can trust me."

Josh tucked the pad under his arm. "I need to call Lauren. Badly. Can you..." He looked over.

"I won't leave her alone."

As Josh stepped past her, Marguerite turned to her back, unselfconscious in her nudity. "Don't you owe me a tattoo viewing?" she asked sleepily.

Josh stopped, glanced over at Tyler. Though his jaw flexed, Tyler imperceptibly nodded his head.

Marguerite lifted her hand to shield her eyes from the sun and saw him there. Warmth flooded her, but then she shifted her attention back to Josh.

He set the sketchbook aside, slipped the shirt off his shoulders as she sat up. Celtic designs manacled his biceps as well as his wrists. There was a dragon pattern on his flat belly just above his navel. He turned so she could see the life-sized sword etched in graphic color down the center of his back, starting at the base of his neck. The hilt was simple, the blade polished silver gray, but from hilt to tip the weapon was wrapped in a barbed vine. Here and there a rose bloomed, perfect in detail, but mostly there were thorns and barbs, stenciled as if pricking his skin in many places, with tiny black drops of blood. In one place, the drop had fallen upon one of the roses, spreading and staining the pure crimson petals. His jeans tightened briefly over his backside as he worked them open. When he dropped them, shoving them down his hips and letting them fall to his ankles, she could see the sword point stopped at the top cleft of his buttocks. He wasn't wearing any underwear, so the loose fit of the jeans had left no skin impressions to mar the artwork.

When he turned, she saw his right calf had a serpent dragon coiled from ankle to knee. From the tender joining crease of pelvis to mid-thigh, another tattoo of a sword had been stenciled. The jeweled hilt was drawn just below his hipbone. A latticework of ivy and pale gold flowers twined around this blade. At its point the greenery wove into a tight vee that curled up into a dime-sized upright pentacle. A symbol of the elements and protection, it anchored the work on the inside of the thigh just below his testicles.

She rose, moved behind him, passing her fingers over the blade where it narrowed to the small of his back, stopping at the tip end, her fingers resting on the upper curve of his buttocks.

"It's beautiful." She looked at his face as he turned his head to look at her, her fingers still on him. "And horrible. They're the same as mine in a way, aren't they?"

His gray eyes warmed, the shadows of past pain still there, still remembered, but without the same power over him anymore. "Yes," he said. "There was never a better tattoo artist than she was."

"And your flesh was a canvas that inspired her like no other," she said softly. "Every needle mark was precise, had to be just so..."

"And you had to be absolutely still, so nothing would ruin its placement." Josh's eyes darkened to storm clouds as he nodded at her shoulder, at what he knew lay behind it. "At least I had a choice."

She stepped back, withdrawing. "We both know sometimes that's not as apparent as it seems in hindsight. Thank you, Josh. For the honor of being your model."

He took her hand, kissed it. It did not have the comfortable flair that Tyler gave it, but it was emotional, sincere. She was glad she was an ethical Mistress, else she would have done her best to steal him.

"The two of you have made me miss Lauren more. And remember why she's my salvation, though I'm not likely to ever forget it." He straightened and held on to Marguerite's hand a moment more, his gray eyes serious. "I wasn't lying, Mistress. The scars aren't soul deep. They only become soul deep if you turn your back on someone who loves you, who's willing to guard your dreams, keep the nightmares at bay. Trust him. Trust yourself."

She swallowed, her gaze shifting to Tyler. Josh also looked toward Tyler, releasing her. "I may drive into Fort Lauderdale and see if I can catch Lauren on a lunch break. Tyler, do you mind if I borrow the Porsche?"

"With your driving skills? Take the BMW sedan in the garage. I'll feel better knowing you have some protection when you wrap it around a tree."

Josh grinned, pulled on his pants. He headed toward the house with eager steps, carrying the sketch pad in his mouth as he shrugged into the shirt.

"Artists," Tyler pronounced as Marguerite turned to face him.

"Is there anything we should do for him?"

"No, he's just missing Lauren. Of course that's often when he'll come up with something brilliant, inspired by his passion for her."

When she bent to pick up the robe, he put out his hand. "Don't. Come here."

Dropping it, she walked toward him across the green grass in her bare feet. She watched his eyes touch every part of her as she came to him. The tightening of her nipples under his regard, her stomach and thighs, the dampening folds of her pussy. She was even cognizant of his eyes on her throat, her knees, feet and flanks. They all reacted as if his gaze alone were capable of caressing her.

When she got to him, he surprised her by sitting down in the grass and tugging her down so she was straddling his legs. He tucked her legs around his hips, his hands loosely linked at the widest part of her buttocks, his fingers playing in the sensitive crevice. "You like him."

"I do. He's something else. If I were Lauren, I'd never leave him alone."

"Once he tells her about you, I'm sure she never will again."

"What? I didn't—"

"I know you didn't. And he loves her to obsession." *Not unlike himself with the woman in his arms.* "I wasn't criticizing. It's something about you. You're more Goddess than Mistress. There's something that makes a submissive feel...overwhelmed in your presence."

She chose to ignore that, as he knew she would. "Did the way I act with him bother you?"

"It's a part of you that fascinates me, but the Master in me does get a bit restive when I see your hands on another man."

Enough that he'd had to take a few steadying breaths when he'd come upon the intriguing tableau of Josh examining his angel naked. He'd had to take a moment to assess it, understand and force himself to appreciate the interaction, rather than break the fingers of a man whose hands created art revered all over the world.

"It's different," she said. She moved her hips over him, a stroke against his already hard cock. His fingers tightened on her buttocks, squeezing so a little breath left her.

"It's like when I drink tea, do the ritual. It satisfies something I need to feel. A balance. Working with subs is like that. But with you, it's different. It's hard to explain."

"I can't describe it either." He touched her hair, lifted it on either side of the comb clip, let it flow out of his hands, brush her bare back. He enjoyed the way she tilted her head back, feeling the sensation. "It's like a vise around my chest, my heart, my mind. It's like if some part of my mind isn't about you, with you, I don't feel whole. I want to be with you. Whether just being with you where you are, making love to you, or watching you make tea. It's obsession, but something so much deeper. It's so deep that I know you feel it, too. It can't all be coming from me."

She considered that. "You know a lot of stalkers feel that way. And terribly arrogant men."

He smiled, a slow, lazy expression. "So they might. You don't mind having me as a stalker, do you?"

"I think I can handle you. I have a bat for your hard head."

"And I hear you know how to use it." He lifted her hand to his lips. At her look, he raised a shoulder. "I regularly bribe Chloe for information."

"I'm going to have to replace that girl with a retired Catholic nun who will see right through your charm, see what a bad man you are."

He shuddered. "I much prefer Chloe." His eyes grew serious. "You terrify me. He had a gun."

"He doesn't anymore. The police have it. I doubt he even has working internal organs."

He framed her face in his hands, commanding her attention with a little shake. "Do you know how it would tear my guts out to lose you?"

She shook her head, looked down, away, uncomfortable. Her body tensed and he knew she was about to pull away. Tyler reined his temper back with effort. *Stop pushing. She was brave enough to come here last night. Don't scare her off sooner than she'll do it on her own.* He reached into a shady corner under the bench.

A wildflower, a delicate star in a shade of pure cream, came into the field of Marguerite's lowered gaze a moment before it was brushing against her lips, the stem of the flower held in Tyler's hand.

"I leave you alone for an hour and you're lying out here naked with another guy. Faithless wench."

She tilted her head, dodging the flower and enjoying looking at him with the sun making the highlights of silver in his dark hair gleam. "Did you like his sketch?"

"I like anything that involves you." He smiled as she reached out spontaneously and touched his throat, caught her fingers in the soft hairs of his chest through the open collar of his shirt. Her deft fingers even slipped one button to play more freely on his skin. "And yes, despite the fact I know his hellhound of a dealer will extort an ungodly amount of money from me to obtain the finished work, I liked it."

"He must be doing well to have a gallery dedicated to him in New York."

"He's had that for a couple years. Josh is getting ready for his second tour of Europe. Milan, Paris, et cetera. That's why Marcus is nagging him for several more pieces. His last one was auctioned off for a quarter of a million dollars."

Her eyes widened. "I thought you were joking...he was joking. Who is he? Oh..." Her hand went to her mouth. "He's the anonymous Zone sculptor."

"Actually, that was done by several of his protégés, under his supervision."

"J. Martin." Her hand reached out, caught his sleeve. "I didn't know... I wouldn't have... It will be all over Europe...the States..."

Tyler burst out laughing at her look of horror. "The only woman I know who blanches at the idea of being immortalized in the art world. What if Mona Lisa had felt that way? Or Michelangelo's David? Don't worry, angel." He stroked back her hair. "I'm going to buy it. The sculpture, the sketch, it will all be mine." *Just like the woman that inspired them.* "I'll enjoy it as privately as you wish." His lips brushed hers. "As privately as I intend to enjoy you, over and over. Just let that be a lesson to you when you let strange men see you naked."

Her grip eased, but something in her face made his eyes narrow. "Marguerite—"

She rose off him before he could tug her back down, reached for the robe. "I wouldn't have let him if I had known. If I knew it would cost you so much money. I can go talk to him, tell him not to...that I withdraw my permission."

He stood, catching up to her in two steps, taking her arm to stop her. "He's in prison."

She jerked free, her expression making that lightning change from malleable woman to hostile wild creature, frustrating him. "And he doesn't know where I am, who I am."

"He hasn't seen you since you were fourteen. It will be a sculpture."

"He'll know. You don't know. You see? I can't do this. I can't..."

"You'll let him put you in a cage, keep you from feeling, loving, because of the fear that it *might* bring him back to you again?" His control broke. "For God's sake, have some faith in us, in me. Stop running from him. Stop being so afraid. You can do better than this."

Something in her went still, frozen. He knew he'd said the wrong thing and instantly wished he could take it back. She lifted her chin, spoke in a voice that was terrible for its low intensity, the enormous feelings that trembled behind the quiet words.

"It's not about fear. It's about never feeling clean, spending years scrubbing your soul raw so you can eat without feeling nauseous, can look in the mirror and meet your own eyes when you put on makeup, brush your hair. To learn to be strong, to run your life and not be a victim of it, knowing in your heart that everything you've built is sitting on a foundation that can sink at any time. And you build it anyway, on faith alone that it won't be shattered, when everything in your life tells you that faith is a fucking joke, but you do it anyway. *You do it anyway.*

"Have you ever been completely helpless while someone is torturing you? Night after night? I should have died on that building that day, but I didn't. I've had to make myself a life, believing I should be dead, wanting to be dead because I couldn't stop him from destroying them. I've done the best I can. The very best I can. And to have the person who says he loves me tell me it's not good enough..."

Her face was strained, white, tearless, which made the brittle brilliance of her blue eyes even more terrible to see.

"Oh, Marguerite." He closed the gap between them and pulled her in his arms despite the fact she stood rigid. "I'm sorry. I'm so sorry. Please forgive me."

She shook in his arms, but the tight fist of fear around his heart eased a fraction as, an eternity of a moment later, her arms crept up, held him back. He stroked her hair, held her fiercely close, whispered to her, but the words were resounding in his head, pounding at him in a way he could not push away.

...to have the person who says he loves me tell me my best is not good enough...

He put his hands to her bare waist, though he felt as if he were the one naked. He even felt a tremor in his hands which he hoped she didn't. Something was shifting between them. He'd hoped to reach the point she would open up to him the way she was starting to do. He hadn't anticipated it would open up things in himself as well, things he'd thought he could keep out of their relationship.

With an effort, he beat it back and lifted her chin. "Your strength humbles me in every way. I'm a stupid bastard and I was taking out my frustration on you. Your fear tears at my heart. I don't want you to have a moment of pain or worry."

Her blue eyes studied his. He was afraid she saw too much of what was moving there. "That is entirely unrealistic," she said at last.

He felt a smile grow in his chest, sweeping the shadows back to their corners and knew Josh had it wrong. It was Marguerite who kept *his* nightmares at bay.

He cleared his throat. "I want to show you a special place on the grounds. Let's go find you some clothes and good walking shoes so I can take you there."

She gave him a long look, which reminded him uncomfortably of how she studied her subs when they were trying to hide something from her, but at length she nodded.

"Okay."

Chapter Nine

She'd brought a loose cotton gauze dress that provided optimal comfort over her assortment of aches and pains from the prior evening's activities. They walked hand in hand to the water's edge and he took her on a path along it, explaining more of the history of the plantation, identifying different birds they saw, flower types she touched as they passed. Marguerite had felt the tremor in his hands when he asked for her forgiveness. As she opened her dark rooms to him, she was making the intriguing discovery that it was providing the key to some of his. She wanted to know this man she'd chosen to call Master down to his soul, in a way she hadn't tried to do even with the submissives who had offered her everything.

However, she wasn't as ruthless as her reputation. She suspected the past twelve hours had drained him as emotionally and physically as they had drained her, so for now they walked quietly, talking of easy things. At his prompting, she described the trips she'd made to South America, India and other parts of Asia for different tea auctions and plantation visits, the people she'd met there. His arm slid around her waist, bringing her closer as the day became cloudier and a breeze started to build in strength off the water. "We're going to get a storm." He eyed the sky. "We're about halfway to where I wanted to take you. You want to keep going or turn back?"

She looked up at him. "Keep going. I'll risk the storm."

He tightened his hold on her and they resumed walking. "Marguerite," he said after a bit, his voice more serious. "I am sorry, about before. I'm an ogre like that, you know. I get impatient when the people I care about are threatened. When I feel helpless to make them feel better, safer."

"A very male reaction. Men get angry and aggressive when things don't go their way." She stopped, gave him honesty. "And you do make me feel better, safer."

He half smiled, but something deadly moved into his expression, something that startled her, though she had sensed it was in him from the first time they'd met. "I can have him killed. There are men who owe me favors, who wouldn't even blink at ridding the world of a piece of garbage like him."

"I thought about it, several times," she responded softly. "Even went so far as to make an inquiry or two. But...it's not the right path. Not for either of us." She tilted her head. "But thank you for asking. For offering."

It was a remarkable exchange, Tyler reflected as they walked on, both of them now content not to say anything further on the subject. The first fat drops of rain began to fall and he grinned. "I told you. It's going to get here faster than I thought. Can you sprint like that day at the tennis courts?"

"I almost beat you," she reminded him.

Even with that, in the way of Southern storms the full force of the shower was on them in twenty more steps, a heavy rain that made the winding asphalt path slick and dark like a raven's wing. Steam rose from the tarred surface, disrupted by the raindrops. She stopped, pulling her hand free to push her wet hair she'd left down for him from her face. He saw her eyes were laughing, her mouth quivering against the real thing.

"It's like music," she said, her voice rising over the wind. Lightning flashed over her, followed by the roar of thunder. His angel spread her arms and began to twirl, her hair spinning with her, the wet skirt fluttering with the wind, grabbing for slick purchase on her legs.

As it grew wetter, the dress's white cotton fabric began to cling to her. When she twirled, she stepped into a puddle, splattering water on her ankles and the glistening curves of her calves. Gathering up her hair in her hands, she held it to the top of her head as she swayed with the movement of the wind, her eyes closing, her mind obviously concentrating on the presence of the storm on her body. She undulated her upper torso with that rhythm, began to perform a sensuous dance with the elements. Turning and jumping as lightly as a dancer, then stomping in the puddle with both feet with the abandon of a child. She opened her eyes, stretched out a hand and he took it, moving with her in a spinning dance across the path and back. Taking both her hands, he swung with her in a wide circle, mesmerized by the way the water rolled down her face and the top curves of her breasts, revealed by the scooped neckline of the dress. He brought her into him, a turn that put her back against his body. He held her there, nudging her head to the side to suck beads of water off the side of her throat. When his hand came up to catch a cold wet nipple through the cloth, her back arched, rubbing her bottom against him. She broke away, headed down the path as her laughter—*her laughter*—called him to give pursuit.

Kicking off the comfortable slides, she ran from him in bare feet, her arms wide like wings, ropes of hair spilling down her back wildly like a glossy cape. His heart had wings of its own, as if he were a young man again with no weights on his heart, but with the wisdom of his present age to know what a tremendous gift this moment was. He caught up with her, seized her hand. They kept running, both running from shadows but running together, throwing off a light that he reflected might keep those shadows cowering in the past where they belonged.

Thunder rolled across the sky, punctuating the heat lightning over the horizon of the Gulf. They stopped to watch it, breathing hard from the physical exertion and the sheer pleasure of arousal, of being in love. It was in her eyes. For once, out here with nature, he believed nothing would interfere with it. He wanted to stay out forever but he saw her shivering. Unrealistic or not, he didn't want her to experience a moment of discomfort, not when he could help it.

"The church." He nodded to the small white clapboard building in the distance, about a quarter mile down the road. "That's where I'm taking you." Then he jumped, both feet coming down in the puddle next to her, splashed her good. Grinning at her, he put one toe in the water and lifted the loafer to sprinkle individual drops on her feet, as well as the hem of her now soaked dress.

"You—" She kicked a foot through the deep puddle, sloshing it along his wet jeans all the way up to his thighs. She took off again with him in hot pursuit.

When they arrived at the double doors breathless, Tyler pushed open one door for her. She hesitated, looking down at her clothes. The dress was practically transparent when wet and of course he hadn't allowed her to wear any underwear. Putting a hand to the small of her back, he urged her forward. "There's no one here. It's all right. This is on my property."

He closed the door behind her and they stood dripping in the narthex. Marguerite smelled old wood and peace. A great, hushed peace.

"This was the church that the plantation owner built for his family and his slaves." When Tyler's gaze ran over the deep wood paneling, the vaulted ceiling, his approval of the workmanship was reflected in his gaze. "I'd planned to donate it to the community nearby when we finished restoring it. It seems a shame for it not to be used by the living, but sometimes it feels like those long-ago spirits are still here. I imagine them attending on Sunday, finding answers to their various worries, comfort for things that seemed unsolvable. Coming to find tranquility."

"Like us." She moved into the main worship area where there were a dozen wooden pews lined up in two columns facing the front altar. Above it was a beautiful round stained glass window depicting a dove taking flight. The bird clutched a red rose with bright green leaves in her beak and a circle of cobalt blue framed the diamond-etched glass. Below, embedded in the wood floor of the raised altar area, was a wooden cross. A minister's pulpit was located just to the left with a small table for candles waiting to be lit. Since a handful of them already were, she wondered if Tyler had come here earlier. Three phrases were embroidered on the linen tablecloth.

In memory. In prayer. In comfort.

"You restored this for your wife. To honor your love for her."

When he looked unsure of her reaction, Marguerite rose on her toes and brushed his lips with her own, tasting the rain between them, the heat of the storm. "Tyler," she murmured softly, "you are such an idiot."

A light flashed in her eye that Tyler would have recognized as teasing in any other woman, but he'd never seen her do it before. Not with him.

"A man devoted and faithful to his wife, who cared for her to the very end, even after she left him." She shook her head, her lips pursed. "And I find myself with such a horrible man. Stalking me, by his own admission."

Holding on to his hands, she leaned back from him on her bare heels. Swayed back and forth, the prominent display of her nipples as arousing as her sudden mischief.

"I can't think why so many women would find a man like you invaluable. It's probably just pity," she decided. "A man with so few brain cells needs a woman to watch out for him."

Tyler shook his head, smiling despite himself. She squeezed his hands. "Did she get a chance to come here?"

He nodded. "When we first came in here, she did a dance, an impromptu ballet up the aisle, along the pews." He remembered it with warmth. "She loved to dance. Used it to express her every mood the way the rest of us use our voices or our faces. She brought her whole body into it. That day was a dance of joy, of reverence. You reminded me of her a little, just now. Out there. Your spontaneity."

Seeing he was flustering her, he changed the subject. "You seem to enjoy the peace in here. I guess I expected you might have some issues, some anger with God."

Marguerite shrugged. "I'm not sure I believe in the idea of a deity that micromanages our lives."

She considered the cross. "In almost every country I've visited, there are pictures of a Goddess specific to that culture. Mother, lover, friend. Many different faces. The first time I looked out over a tea plantation, it was an overcast day, but it was so incredibly awesome, beautiful. It filled my heart. At that very moment, the sun came out." Her gaze shifted to him. "It felt like She saw it through my eyes, felt how amazed I was by it and that made Her smile.

"I feel sometimes the same way when I'm being a Mistress, like I understand it all without words. The way you do when you're in a church like this and it all gets quiet. Everything gets so clear in my head, so peaceful. I'm part of Her at that moment, as it was always intended and everything makes sense. I can see and feel inside my submissive's soul, know what he best needs, give him that.

"You can think all sorts of nonsense when you're crazy." Her lips curved a little. "I guess what I'm saying is that God or Goddess, They have a plan. I believe that. There's too much wonder for there not to be. Just because I don't understand it doesn't mean it's not there. I have to believe my mother and brother are somewhere, happy." She added the last, softly. "And so that keeps me from hating. So you finished it after she died?"

Here in this place, he couldn't evade a question from her. Not with the spell she had just woven, the sacred presence she'd invited to fill the air between them. "Yes. It took a little longer, because I took over doing a lot of the work myself. When I...there was a time things didn't make sense to me."

"When you came back from Panama."

He shook his head. "I'd fire that woman if I knew how to operate a vacuum."

"Maybe she thinks you should be as honest with me as you're demanding that I be with you. Or do you think I can't take it?" She arched a brow.

He lifted a shoulder, moved down the aisle toward the wooden cross hung there. Marguerite followed, trailing her fingers over the silken wood of the pews, watching him. When they got to the cross, Tyler lifted his fingers, pressed them into a gouge in the wood. "I did that, when I came back."

She stepped up next to him, pressing her shoulder to his, and put her fingers in the same spot. It looked to have been caused by a tool, perhaps a chisel. "While you were working in here?"

"Yes. I'm not a great craftsman, but I wanted to... I needed to do something. And the more I hammered and sanded in here, the more the silence... It's as you said, God is in the silence. And sometimes it's hard to be in the same room with Him.

"After I did it, I brought the local minister here, showed it to him and asked him if there was a way he could bless it, purify it. I felt like I'd somehow desecrated it. He told me, 'The cross is supposed to bear pain and sorrow, betrayal and anger, so that it may help you forgive yourself.'"

Marguerite felt the emotions emanating from him. The strain of keeping the rest under careful control was evident from the tension in his face, his shoulders. He was trying to give her more of himself, just as she'd asked, but now she didn't know if that had been a wise request. She was already too absorbed in him already.

"I was raised Baptist," he said, his fingers remaining just below the gouge, his attention on it. "I was taught that you're always a child and God is the father. That we're weak, unable to help ourselves if we're bad. That there are so many things out of our control we just have to do good where we can and leave the rest up to Him. When I did this, I was reacting as a child would, angry because the parent had let me down. And then as I sat here, quietly spent, the teachings went away and there was only Presence." His gaze flicked to her. "Somewhat like you described. And I knew that I was an adult, responsible for my actions, as responsible for protecting the weak and innocent and for fighting evil as He is. And while there's so much wisdom that I don't know, I know that evil doesn't happen for a cosmic reason, a 'balance of good' bullshit. Evil happens because it can, because circumstances allow it to take place. And you build your own sanctuary against it to keep yourself sane, to keep yourself fighting it."

He turned to face her fully then, his amber eyes bathed in the colored light of the stained glass. When he reached out, threaded fingers through her hair and watched it ripple across his knuckles like pale wheat, she couldn't move. She was held still by all the memories she felt pulsing from him, intertwining with her own. "Sometimes,

I think it's like a fable," he said. "One powerful god released all the evil things on the world. Another god, a god of light, could not undo what the other god had done, but he could give us something to make life worth living. So he gave us love.

"I'm working on it." He met her gaze. "Working on sharing with you. But I've been places where there are too many dead and I helped increase the body count. Each of those lives meant something to someone. And to the person themselves. But whatever lies beyond... You've helped me remember why it's worth fighting. Living. Even when the lines get so confusing you think you're losing your mind."

She reached up, touched him at last. "I need you, Tyler. More than I've ever let myself need anything. I'm so messed up at times, but I look at you and everything eases."

He smiled. "For me, too. Maybe that's the simplest definition of love there is, angel."

Cupping her face in his large palm, he kissed her deep, slow until she was leaning into him, holding on to his wet polo shirt. Laying her palms on either pectoral, she thought about how much bigger, broader he was than herself. Though she'd dominated subs, the experience of touching a man and feeling the gift of his strength and protectiveness, his masculine self, was something Tyler had specifically given her. She traced the outline of him, the way the cloth fit over his body and felt her breath catch in her throat at the wonder of it.

He could feel her knees weakening, just as she felt his heart increase its pounding beneath her hand. Tightening his hands around her waist, he lifted her, carried her to the space of floor between the altar area and front pews where a deep blue rug had been laid, a tapestry of birds and angels.

"Tyler." She looked up at him. "This is blasphemous."

He couldn't resist the heat of his desire, not with her mouth wet with rain and his kiss. Her neck and breasts were beaded with drops while the soft pinkness of her flesh showed through the cotton dress. Lovely, natural.

"This isn't sin." He managed the words in a voice thick with want. "It's sacred. Everything I do with you, every touch, every kiss, every word murmured in reverence against your flesh, is sacred. And you're cold. I want to warm you."

Standing above her, he toed off his loafers and removed his clothes. He came down to her naked, kneeling between her legs. Sliding the wet fabric of the dress up her body, over her stomach, he bent to kiss her navel, took a sloping track to one hipbone, then the other. He pulled the dress off her, laying it aside to look at her, pale, wet and naked under his gaze.

Marguerite was helpless not to do the same. His tanned shoulders gleamed with the light of the stained glass window and the dampness of the storm outside. His chest expanded as he breathed deep and long, breathing her in, his eyes locking with hers. At length, she lifted her arms and he lowered his body to her, guiding himself. She tilted up, aching to find him, letting out a soft moan as he eased into her, bringing her his heat and life. When she wound her arms around his neck, her legs twined around his hard, muscular body. She realized then there were ways to cleanse her soul she'd never known existed. Like immersing it in the loving embrace of another. The candles flickered on the altar and she counted. One...David. Two...her mother. Three... Perhaps even the long-dead spirit of what had been her father. There was a fourth, making her wonder if Nina's spirit danced here still, touching Tyler, being a part of him forever.

The clouds shifted and the shadows of the dove's wings covered her face, broken by pieces of sunlight now coming through the clear planes of glass. The jeweled blue of the design joined the mix, coloring his skin, making his eyes glow in the church's dim light. He stroked her inside with his cock, the length of him deep in her channel and against her quivering clit. Because she wanted to do it, she released his shoulders, let her hands fall above her and offered her throat.

"Ah, angel." He covered her jugular with his mouth. Bit. Her body tightened, surrendering with a soft sigh of relief, wanting to give him anything he asked, wanting him to ask for it all.

Her cries came easily, echoing off the vaulted ceiling, cries of fulfillment, of desire and peace at once. Of triumph, when he let go and poured himself into her, reinforcing the promise that had begun less than a handful of weeks before. He'd said she was his. Now she couldn't imagine having ever wanted anything different for herself in her whole life.

"Tyler…" She reached up and touched his face, closed her eyes as he turned into her palm and kissed it, bit gently.

"Yes, sweet Mistress?"

It made her chest hurt, how much she felt in this moment. She knew she should not say anything impetuously. But under the light of the stained glass window, the flickering candlelight of their shared memories, it felt like simple, unexamined honesty. No matter what the darkness brought back to her tomorrow.

"I'm in love with you."

Framing her face with his hands, he brought his lips down on hers in answer. His body moved upon her again, renewing their passion. As he took her up, she was flying again, higher and higher. Wanting nothing more than to keep this soaring peace with him inside her forever.

Chapter Ten

"So, you're going to go home and forget all about me."

"Pretty much." She watched him put her bag in her BMW and rested her arm on the top of the car door as he closed the trunk. When he came around the car, approaching her with an intent look in his eye, anticipation flooded her. As if they hadn't made love less than two hours ago when he woke her for a Sunday morning breakfast. And several times during the night.

Pressing her up against the car's frame, he delved into her mouth with his own, his hands wandering down to fondle her ass, squeeze, press her hard against his cock in a way that made her knees tremble, loosen.

"No..." Marguerite murmured, a smile on her lips. She wiggled, squirmed, managed to drop and fold herself into the driver's seat, quickly slamming the door before Tyler could push his suit further. Bracing his palms on the frame of the open window, he grinned at her, though his eyes were hot, demanding she get out of the car, stay.

She couldn't get this much off track. The past thirty-six hours had been fantastic, in the literal sense of the word. She needed some time to think about the changes he'd brought forth in her in such a short time.

"Don't do that." He cupped her face, brought her startled eyes up to him. "Don't retreat from me again."

She swallowed, reached up and closed her hand over his wrist, the strength of it. "I'm not. Not that way, I promise. I know the type of man you are. You're impatient, sure of your feelings. I've been alone a long time. I just need a few days of normalcy. To get my balance."

"Every time you get your balance, I get shut out." He squatted, going eye to eye with her. "Just remember, angel, there's not a drawbridge you can raise that I won't scale. But it would be a hell of a lot nicer for both of us to conserve my energy for better things."

"Don't you think of anything else?" But her own body was vibrating with need just at the sweep of his possessive glance over it. "I'm trying. Just trust me. Please. I don't..." She sighed, closed her eyes. "How does last night change things? Do I tell you where I'm going, who I'm with, my schedule? Do you tell me yours? Is that how this works?"

"Is that how you want it to work?"

She studied him a long moment. "All I know is every moment I've been without you, it feels...wrong. Does that get better or worse with proximity? Will your insufferable arrogance make me want to slap you around?"

He flashed a grin. "As much as your haughty tone will make me want to turn you over my knee."

Her smile faded at the corners, her expression becoming even more thoughtful. "And that's something else. What about The Zone? You're a Master, I'm a Mistress. I know with you it's different, but there are times... I want, I still feel the desire..." She flushed. "It hasn't gone away, and I don't know how you feel about that. Is that unfaithful? I don't want to make you angry, or jealous."

"Tell me how you imagine that part of your life, now." Tyler kept his face carefully impassive, somewhat encouraging, wanting her to be honest, though his gut was clutching in a tense knot, waiting to see where she was going with this.

"I don't know how to do this. I mean..."

"Marguerite." He tightened his fingers on her face, an unmistakable command he intended to focus her. "Without thinking about it, tell me right now how you feel. Everything."

"I miss you," she said softly. "From the moment you leave or I leave, I think about you. I wish you were sleeping beside me. I have this insane notion to call you to tell you to come over, right then. But it also feels good sitting there at my desk, holding on to the thought of you, reliving everything we've said and done." She pushed her hand through her hair, tugging at her own scalp in a frustrated move he'd never seen her make.

"How do we do this?" she asked. "I know I'm like a silly teenager, but I never had a boyfriend in school. There was no possible way I could have anything, with my home situation, with the way...he made me feel... Boys seemed to know. Like animals know when another animal is sick, to keep their distance." She lifted a shoulder. "And those boys who didn't... I knew what the look in their eye was about. So I don't know the right way to do this. I feel like I'm standing in the doorway of a room and everyone's staring at me, waiting for me to say and do the right thing and I don't know..."

He felt the fist around his gut ease at the stream of words. Relief that her struggle was not in how to pull away, but how to become closer.

Despite the amazing breakthrough of the past day and a half, he knew that Marguerite's past would not let go of her without further struggle. Perhaps full-pitched battle.

"Angel." He pressed a kiss on the lid of each of those confused blue eyes. "Since the time I've met you, you've set your own style, your own way of doing things. You can call me anytime you want. *Anytime.* Every second, every hour. And every time, I'll answer the phone with the same eagerness to hear your voice as I did a second before. I'm here. I told you that last night. I'm not going anywhere.

"Now." He wrapped a hand in her hair, played in the strands as she tilted toward him, moving her head in that way that she'd started to do, telling him she liked to be stroked. "I've always loved watching you be a Mistress. Come stay with me at my Tampa house next weekend and we'll talk about it some more. We'll figure it out. Mac and Violet are staying with me that weekend and I want you to come." He traced the shell of her ear. "Maybe she'll let you play with Mac some. Or maybe we'll cover that Zone requirement we missed. The one where you submit to a Master's desire to share you with another Dominant."

She jerked back from his touch, her eyes narrowing. "Do snowballs and hell mean anything to you?"

He burst out laughing. It caught her breath, the rich, sexy sound of it. Marguerite realized suddenly how rarely Tyler laughed like that. Almost as rarely as she smiled. And it made her realize that perhaps she was changing his life as he was changing hers. It was a startling thought, one that made her reflect ruefully that love could cloud your perspective so you could be surprised with the obvious. "You were teasing me."

"While the idea of you and Violet together would be every man's fantasy, I do recognize it's a safer bet as one of my and Mac's prurient dreams." His eyes sobered and he twined her hair back around one of his fingers.

"They're good friends of mine. I'd like you to see the side of them I've seen. Will you come?"

She nodded, started the car, gave him her look of practiced diffidence. "Now leave me alone this week. I have a business to run."

The corner of his mouth turned up. "I was just thinking I'll be in Tampa most of the week. Since they're doing some work on the house, I may just have to come and do some paperwork in a corner of Tea Leaves. It's a wonderful venue for working. The service is topnotch, the waitstaff very solicitous and the owner... Well, one glimpse of her is enough to get me through the day."

"Ass," she said, shaking her head, hitting the up button to her window, forcing him to back out of it. He did with easy elegance and a grin, sliding his hands into the pockets of his slacks and keeping his gaze on her while she backed the car, put it in drive. Marguerite kept both hands firmly on the wheel, knowing that otherwise she'd be tempted to leap out and snatch one more taste of his lips.

§

Unfortunately, the renovations at the Tampa home and the lackadaisical attitude of the overpaid coastal contractors who preferred to fish during the warmer days required him to stay on the premises Monday and part of Tuesday. Then a problem came up with the actress he'd wanted for a production Michael Atlas was handling.

Persuading her to change her schedule required a quick flight out of town to her home in Cape Cod.

Tyler had to be satisfied with daily calls to the woman whose very existence now burned in him like a fever. He made a habit of calling the main number of Tea Leaves to talk to Gen and Chloe first, before they transferred him into Marguerite's office. While he didn't pry or ask any questions about Marguerite he did not ask her when she came on the line, he knew Gen and Chloe would convey any problems just by the tones of their voices. And it was that which caused him concern on when he called Wednesday late afternoon, for there was definitely a hesitation in Chloe's voice when she picked up.

"Are things going okay, Chloe?"

"Oh, sure, fine. Um...let me get Marguerite."

"Chloe."

"Well..."

There was a sharp comment in the background and Tyler was put on hold. Marguerite picked up in her office a moment later, and he heard the snick of the office door as she closed it.

"Good morning from New England," he said. "Are you all right?"

"You know, babysitters get at least five dollars an hour now," she said caustically. "And Gen and Chloe are putting in overtime for you."

"I'm not..." He closed his eyes, massaged the bridge of his nose. "Yes, I check with them about you. I care about you. And I know you get down sometimes. I just want to make sure you're all right."

"Why wouldn't I be all right?" Marguerite stared down at her day calendar. At the date marked with a red X. Somehow the past few weeks had allowed her to push to the back of her mind the last thing that ever should have been relegated there.

Everything had been about Tyler lately. Each day since she'd seen him, without his touch or his smile, things inside her had gotten progressively darker. Knowing the danger of opening her heart, now she faced the reality of an addict deprived of her daily fix. Each day the doubts crowded in that much more. Such that when she woke this morning, the first thing she'd done was remember that date. And she'd moved the tea samples and stack of invoices off of the calendar with deliberate care, as if removing the casing of a bomb, and stared at it. A reminder that she shouldn't be letting down her guard, shouldn't be allowing herself to be swept away so incautiously on a wave of infatuation. She had to stay centered, focused. She could enjoy Tyler, but she couldn't lose herself in him. She couldn't depend on anyone but herself.

"I'm fine." She struggled for a lighter tone. "I hope you're having a good trip. It's just been a stressful day. You don't need to call me every day, you know." *Though I count the minutes between the times I hear your voice.*

"You're still coming this weekend."

"I said I was. But there are some things that have come in, a new tea shipment, and—"

"Marguerite, don't make me have this conversation with you again."

"About dungeons and drawbridges, white knights who think they can make the world a better place?" Her attempt at control exploded. Goaded by his tone, the darkness surged up in her. "I'm not a damsel in distress and I don't appreciate being treated like one. In case you, my staff and the whole fucking world hadn't noticed—"

As she raised her voice, Tyler could almost see Chloe and Gen shrinking into the recesses of the kitchen. "I don't need to be babied. I've taken care of myself for a long time."

"You need all the babying you can get, angel. And something's bothering you. Are you going to tell me what's going on?"

"Go to hell." She slammed down the phone.

He snapped his cell phone closed, held it in his hand for several moments, thinking. He turned as Michael, carrying an open longneck, approached him on the outside balcony. "Megan's completely sold on the project now." He grinned, tapping Tyler's beer sitting on the railing. As he took a swig, he studied Tyler's expression. "Okay, your reaction was supposed to be jubilation, not murderous fury. Have I missed something?"

"I go home tonight," Tyler said grimly. "I've had something come up."

§

Nobody was going to run her life but her. It was that simple. If she lost the reins, she'd never get them back. The horses of Hades would simply break free and drag her over the edge of the chariot, scrape every protective layer off her until she was nothing but an incoherent chaos of vulnerable internal organs and exposed nerve endings. She'd even thought about going to The Zone last night, as she'd always done before when the fear and anxiety, the darkness swept in. Find someone to help her balance. Pick a submissive, as usual one that she'd never touched, that would never touch her, even as she found the secret to his soul and used it to retrieve her own from perilous waters.

But then she remembered the last two times she'd been there and didn't know if she would be allowed. She couldn't face the humiliation of being turned away at the door. Not to mention, her traitorous body wanted Tyler. Not just her body, but her mind, her heart, her soul. She could only calm the scream of her body and even that was a temporary, empty fix that did not assuage the yearning within her.

Chloe and Gen kept a low profile, their tones quiet in the kitchen area as they performed the morning routine. She picked up the napkins and moved out to the main floor. She was going to shape them into lotus flowers today, practice some of the origami tricks she'd recently seen in her tea industry magazine, a nice touch her clients would appreciate.

The moment she stepped onto the floor, before she saw him, she knew he was there. He sat at his preferred table, the one he'd chosen when he responded to her call for a meeting a handful of weeks ago. A meeting she never should have initiated.

But, oh, he looked so good sitting there. He was dressed

more casually than she'd ever seen him in Tea Leaves. Well-fitted jeans, dark T-shirt, a day's worth of stubble. In order to be in her tearoom when she'd talked to him on the phone less than ten hours before, he must have taken a red eye home. He looked dangerous, all the more because he didn't move when he saw her, just pinned her with that tiger's gaze.

She tightened her chin and her resolve. "I didn't expect to see you so soon."

"I was told to go to hell. My connecting flight was delayed so I thought I'd drop in."

She raised a brow. Stopping at station four, she laid out the stack of napkins. She took up one by the two corners and did the first fold, though it took all her concentration to keep her hands from shaking. He had to get out of here. Didn't he know she couldn't do this, couldn't want anyone this much? She knew just how his hands would feel on her, his mouth.

"You've never paid any attention to anything I've told you to do before. Why would you start now?"

He stayed quiet. He was probably trying to figure out how to manipulate this situation, get her to be as absurd as he always seemed to make her. Insane was a better word than absurd. But not this time. This was her territory, her fortress, where she could best keep the nightmares at bay, and she was not leaving it again. Resentfully, she wished fairy tales were true, specifically the one about unwary knights being turned into toads when they ventured uninvited into a sorceress's palace.

She was messing up the design. Picking it back up, she shook it out and started over again. Her fingers kept twitching involuntarily, more and more as the silence grew.

Or a herd of swine. She'd keep him as a pet and let him wallow in a mud puddle in her private garden. Feed him scraps.

Even as she dwelled with satisfaction on the image, her radar picked up on a different quality to the quiet. A dangerous shift. She glanced up. His gaze had settled on her throat, the decorative scarf she wore around it, tucked into the neckline of the sleeveless button-down blouse she wore loose over the pleated broomstick skirt. She quickly turned away, but spun around as she heard his chair scrape back. In a flash, she moved to put a table between them. "Stop," she warned, gesturing with the napkin. Thinking better of it, she put it down to keep both hands free.

She resisted the urge to put her hand over the scarf, over whatever part of her neck might be exposed. Last night, she'd done it in angry defiance and fear, but now, looking at his face, she thought she'd lost her mind. Proving that even when he wasn't around, he was making her do insane things. A century or two of advances in women's rights meant very little to a man like Tyler, who felt it was his job to protect a woman and give her hell when she didn't follow his orders to do so.

"I told you what would happen if you did that again."

"Chloe and Gen are here." It was a desperate statement and she cursed herself for making it, for showing him that he'd unnerved her.

"You think that will protect you? You take one step back from me, I'll throw that table through the wall and haul you up the stairs over my shoulder. Or you can lead me up there now and we'll have this discussion in your room. Your choice."

"I don't owe you a conver—"

His hand caught the edge of the table and she quickly sat on it. "Gen," she called out, pulling back her lip in a snarl at him. "I'm going upstairs a moment. Will you watch over things?"

"Sure," came the reply from the kitchen. "Take as long as you need." A chuckle wafted out from Chloe, indicating they'd seen who their first customer of the day was, but Marguerite wasn't seeing the humor of the situation. Not faced with a man of Tyler's imposing stature who was obviously, genuinely furious with her. He made a gesture, a clear command for her to precede him up the stairs. She didn't have to do so. She could scream her lungs out, even stand in cold defiance and call his bluff...except she knew it wasn't a bluff. She was trembling at the look in his eyes. And what was more terrifying to her was that all of her reaction was not fear. Any more than all of his was anger.

Chloe peered out, her smile vanishing as she looked between the two of them. "Everything all right?"

"Fine." Marguerite forced the words past her lips. Tyler moved. One step, two, to come around the table and take her arm. He brought her to her feet with a firm lift, drawing her hips off the table. Marguerite nodded to Chloe with a reassurance she did not feel as he guided her up the narrow staircase, down the hallway toward her room, away from the safety of an audience.

"Are you finished being overbearing and obnoxious?" She said it between gritted teeth because if she loosened her jaw she was sure they would chatter with nerves, the way her arm was vibrating under his touch.

"Is there anything you do that isn't designed to take you a step closer to the other side?"

"I have no idea what you're talking about."

"No? The rituals, the ceremonies you surround yourself with. The way you cut yourself off from everything and everyone, only allowing us so close. You're a ghost. You act like you died at fourteen and you've been conducting the damn funeral for your whole life, figuring out the most likely way to get yourself in the coffin in just the right way. So what is this?" In the privacy of her room, he let her go, gestured at her throat with an accusing finger. "A hope that one day something will go wrong so you can be a corpse stinking up your bedroom with your post-mortem bowel release?"

She drew herself up. "I won't have this discussion. You've no right to make demands on this part of my life."

She'd always thought great levels of anger were like conflagrations. With Tyler, it was an arctic wasteland that frosted his gaze, living up to his surname and making her realize instantly she'd just said the worst thing possible.

"I'm in all parts of your life. If you're determined to be in that coffin, you're going to have to make it a bigger size as part of your 'preparations'."

He closed the bedroom door with a snap. "I made a promise never to strike you with anything other than my hand. I'm going to break that promise, because you broke one to me."

"I never told you I wouldn't do it again. I didn't promise." She backed away. "You don't own me, Tyler. I'm not a child."

"No, you're not. But you know one of the reasons a child tests her parents, asks for punishment by being bad? Because it tells her that someone loves her enough to keep her safe. I'm not your father or your brother, but I'm your lover. You didn't protect your neck under the belt so the strap would mark you. So you'd have to wear this." He lashed out with a long arm and flicked the edge of the pale blue print scarf she'd worn, making her jump and despise her cowardice more. "You did it to test me in exactly this way."

"I didn't even know you were going to be here."

"You knew I'd be here sooner than later. Take it off. Now."

When she didn't move, he stepped forward and her heart leaped, though she tried to maintain an indifferent outward appearance. "Marguerite." His every syllable was carefully pronounced, underscoring the threat. "You won't do this anymore because I'm telling you that you won't. You belong to someone now. Me. And I take care of you, even if your greatest danger comes from yourself. *Take the goddamned scarf off.*"

She raised her chin defiantly, but her cold fingers rose, unknotted it, let it fall away. Let him see the red mark of the belt, the light bruising.

His eyes coursed over it. His gaze rose, pinning her with a look she'd never seen before. A look that gave her chest wall jagged edges which stabbed her heart with every painful beat.

"I told you who I am, what I am," she managed. "You can leave. No one's holding you here."

Though I'm afraid I won't survive if you turn your back on me now. Which makes no sense. I don't need anyone.

Clenching her fists, she stared at him with as much disdain as she could manage, trying to reclaim her aloofness, her protective isolation in a room where she was almost overcome by his heat, his presence.

"Go away, Tyler. Just go the hell away."

"Did you get the fucking orgasm you sought from it?" He loosened his belt, stripped it off him with one quick, deliberate movement. "Take hold of the bedpost."

"Wh-what?"

"I'm going to spank you with my belt and then I'm going to fuck you hard and strong with your ass still smarting to remind you not to defy me. Not about this. Not if you know what's good for you."

She stood staring at him, their expressions clashing for a solid minute. Her gaze shifted to the door.

"Don't try it," he warned, low. When he closed the last gap between them, it took all she had not to step back for she was afraid of the swirl of emotions roused in her by the implacable resolve in his eyes. He took her arm and turned her, wrapping her fingers around the post. Reaching under her skirt, he caught the elastic of her panties and pulled them down to her feet. He left them at her ankles, the lace draping the straps of her heeled sandals. His hand went to the small of her back, pushing her lower, and the other moved under her waist to cant her ass upward. Folding the skirt into the small of her back, he pulled her back a couple awkward steps with her ankles manacled in her underwear.

"Stand just like that," he said, his voice thick with arousal and other things she didn't want to face. "Ten licks. They're going to hurt."

She heard the snap of his belt as he doubled it, tightened her fingers on the post. His hand moved down her waist over the curve of one flank, caressing the whiteness of her skin, making her even more aware of what he was about to do to that delicate flesh.

"You will never, never choke yourself again, Marguerite. Not ever. Do you understand?" His tone sharpened. "Answer me."

"I understand." Her voice shook. Though she tried to infuse it with anger, it was lost in the nerves.

"Tell me you'll obey. You're right. You didn't promise before. But you will now. Tell me you won't do it ever again. Once you say it, I know I can trust your word."

And trust him to take care of her demons. She shut her eyes, thinned her lips, fighting a compulsion she didn't understand. Tears wanted to swell into her eyes, but not because he was hurting her physically. In a way she couldn't explain, barely understood, she wanted to say yes to him. To say that she would obey, that she was sorry, as if the apology was to herself as much as to him. But punishment...she wanted, needed the punishment first.

The belt slapped her buttocks with exceptional accuracy and strength, though she'd had no doubt it would. She found for all that Tyler supposedly didn't flog his submissives much, he knew exactly how to do so. What he was doing wouldn't break the skin, but he intended to leave welts, a way for her to remember the lesson for several days afterward. Maybe a week, she thought, as the next stripe came. Her breath expelled sharply on the third as real pain sang through her nerve endings. But another reaction was occurring at the same time. Her cunt was dripping her response onto her legs. Between the third and fourth stroke he reached down and fondled her, running his fingers through the slickness. She moaned, raising herself higher for him. At the fifth and sixth, she cried out.

"Tell me you're not going to do this again. Now. Or I swear to God I'll give you ten more."

"I'll... I won't do it again."

"Promise me."

She bit down on her own arm to keep from screaming as seventh, eighth and ninth cut into her tender flesh.

"I promise."

The tenth blow landed. Even as she was gasping for breath from the throbbing pain, he had her arm and pulled her up to hold her against him. The skin of his arms pressed hot and demanding against her back. When he dropped his grip down, caressed her hips with rough, demanding hands, she thought the ache was going to explode in her chest like a wound as he deliberately squeezed her raw buttocks hard. She struggled against him and he turned, pushed her down on her stomach on the bed, holding her there a moment to keep her still, his hand running over her sore ass, quivering under his touch. "Christ, I'm so furious with you."

When she closed her eyes, the tears burned. He was

right. Since she was seven years old, no one had punished her because they loved her. Because they cared if she lived or died. Because they wanted her to stay safe. Or were scared of losing her. She should hate him, be angry at him for humiliating her, but she didn't feel humiliated. She yearned for something, another way to punish her, a way to take her, invade every part of her, make his claim one that could not be denied.

"You haven't..." Her voice was thready, such that the words almost weren't coherent to her own ears. "Taken me there yet. Put your cock there."

His fingers stilled on the crease of her buttocks, his other hand resting on her back, over her scars. His reaction made her wonder if Komal had told him that one shameful thing.

"No." The roughness of his voice hadn't abated, but the tone gave her the answer to the question. Her heart was shattering and only he could pick up the pieces. "I won't punish you that way. No."

She pushed against her hands and rolled to her back to stare up at him. He was standing over her looking angry and anguished all at once. And so terribly dangerous and sexy.

"I need you to. I want to feel you've been everywhere in me, that your come has scalded his away. It's an illusion, but if you do it once, I can make it real." She caught the waistband of his jeans, pulled herself up so her chin was resting on his hard flat stomach, her fingers digging into his thighs. "Don't ask. Don't ever ask me for anything again. Take me. Your slave is begging you. Punish me when I need it, never make me doubt whose Will I have to obey. Whose love will protect me from the darkest shadows, especially the ones I carry inside myself."

As if the hands of conscious time had stopped, Tyler stared back down into those wide, frightened eyes and knew that this was that moment Komal had warned him about. The moment of triumph and greatest vulnerability. She'd cracked open, everything ugly as well as beautiful there for him to see. She was offering it all to him and there was no going back.

He didn't want to go back. He wanted her. Every tragic, beautiful, amazing, dysfunctional, exceptional, infuriating inch of her.

"Open my jeans," he ordered, closing his hands into fists to keep him from cradling her face in his palms, kissing away each tear. She needed to know he did care enough to be angry. He needed to impress upon her in an irrevocable fashion that she answered to someone in her life. He told himself she needed that more than he needed to relieve the aching pain in his heart that felt as if it were infecting his soul.

Her fingers moved over him, took the zipper down. Stepping back from her, he shoved them down his thighs. "Take off the rest of your clothes," he said gruffly. "Turn around on the bed and get on all fours, on your knees and elbows. I want your ass in the air so I can more easily fuck it, see how I've strapped it."

She obeyed, tossing her white hair forward in a way that had his mouth watering, the well-toned, lithe body stretching out in the position he proscribed like a fabled white she-tiger, her back arched, head down on her elbows. She was shaking. So was he. He'd believed she was his submissive, his slave, from the beginning, this great Mistress and strong woman who had been through so much, but until the moment of this reality there'd always been the possibility he'd been wrong. This was the turning point, even more than the night at his Gulf home had been.

"Lubricant."

"In the armoire in the corner. Where I keep all my Zone things. It's unlocked."

He discarded the rest of his clothes and strode across the room. Marguerite watched him, a pure, virile male animal completely in control of the situation and of her. A deep quaking was going on in the pit of her belly. She needed him to ease it. To assuage the hunger and the pain. She needed to bite and claw and fight him and have him win. Needed to know he would claim her, make her submit to him, not because it was a game or Zone requirement, but because they were mated together. Belonged to each other as he said.

So when he came back she tried to roll to her back. He caught her elbows, flipped her, held her down with a hand on her neck and a growl, bringing her back onto her knees with her hips in the air. She was so slick that he rubbed his fingers in her cunt and used that to initially oil her rim.

He also used the lubricant, slid his slicked-down fingers into her ass with deliberate efficiency. No hesitation, firm, not brutal but not gentle, underscoring his right to use her body, take and give pleasure to it as he chose. She moaned softly, rocking against his touch. At his growl to be still, she hissed a challenge, struggled for her way, but at his hard slap on her abused buttocks, she went still again.

From his vantage point Tyler could see her night drawer. A portion of the black scarf she normally would have used under the belt was not tucked all the way in, goading him further. Though he recognized it as the same type of anger a wolf would show toward his mate for endangering herself, he did not deny the animal drive to it. When he'd seen the mark on her neck, he'd known she'd deliberately defied him. She'd thrown down the gauntlet, perhaps not knowing why herself. Within Marguerite the woman, the abused child still sought answers and peace. He wanted to give her both. Give her everything. And paddle her until she cried for scaring him so badly. And fuck her until she couldn't imagine any day without him.

As he slid his fingers in her tight rear passage he spoke, commanding the answer he'd not gotten from her earlier. "Did you climax when you did it?"

"I... Yes."

"What were you thinking about?"

"You." Her head was pressed to her forearms now. Reaching forward, he caught her hair in his hand, tugged it back so he could see her face. The desperate arousal, the need. And it was that which gentled his touch at last, made him ease his hold into a stroke.

"I won't do this rough." Pressing her head back down to her arms, he let his fingertips drift along the nape of her neck, back over the scars and her reddened cheeks. Welts were already rising on the pale, delicate skin. She wouldn't sit easily for a week. While that gave him lustful satisfaction, the idea of rubbing healing salve into them stirred him as well.

He straightened, guided himself into the lubricated passage and went deep as the muscle released, letting him in. She moaned as he dropped to all fours over her, covering her. Her cheek pressed against his forearm, her lips to his hand. "Everywhere he's been, I'm there now, driving him out. I won't let him come back. I'm inside you, in every part of you." He started to move his hips, slow, incremental friction that made his cock even harder and thicker, made his desire to thrust more violently grow.

"This is still a punishment, so I'm not going to let you come. You're just going to have to walk around all day today with your ass too sore to sit, your cunt swollen and wet, your nipples hard and pressed against your dress, knowing that tonight, I'll come back to your bed. I'll make you come then, hard and often, until you're so exhausted you'll beg me to stop, but I won't. Not until you call me Master over and over and I know you'll never forget it."

When she shuddered, he kissed her between her shoulder blades. Pressed his hard thighs against the back of her lovely ones and the rise of her pale buttocks to drive into her more deeply. Balancing his weight with one arm, he collared her throat, lifted her so her back was against his chest, her head against his shoulder. "By my hand only. By my cock and mouth only, unless I command otherwise. Say it and mean it."

"By your hand only," she whispered hoarsely around the pressure of that grip. "By your cock and mouth only, unless you command it. Master. I'm sorry."

He closed his eyes, pressed his temple to hers and began to thrust home. Harder, as she needed, as he needed. Holding her throat, her life pulsing strong under his touch, he accepted responsibility for it. She was so strong the only thing that could shatter her was the thing she'd never been offered, that had never nourished her long enough to count.

Love.

He felt his testicles draw up, snarled low in her ear and let himself go, flooding her, feeling the slap of their bodies together, his thighs against her striped buttocks, his cock stroking that tight passage over and over. He didn't want to stop, groaning his release hard and fierce as she whispered his name in frantic arousal.

Oh, hell. He couldn't bear to make her wait. His hand moved down between that perfect meshing of their hips and found her clit. It was as much for him as for her. He wanted to hear her full-throated cries as she came at his touch. Two, maybe three adamant manipulations and she went over, rolling hard against him, her head turning into his shoulder, even with the collaring of his hand. He used the movement to dip his head and fasten his teeth in her flesh, holding her as he continued to smack against her ass with his body, play with her swollen folds, feeling her juices in his palm, her cunt against his fingers.

His.

They shuddered into quiet, becoming aware of the turn of her ceiling fan, the dim light of her room with the sheer panels at the windows. The world outside continued going by, oblivious to their struggle, their passion, the moment of fulfillment and change.

He eased out of her as she remained still, obeying his Will by staying in the same position, her ass raised high in the air. It made his drained cock stir, telling him she could well nigh kill him with lust. He eased her to her side so he could lean over her, stroke the hair from her face.

"Where is it, Marguerite?"

He knew, but he wanted her to actively participate. Shifting her head, she looked toward the nightstand. He reached across the mattress, pulled open the drawer and removed the dark scarf, the ropes, the belt itself. His hand traced the smooth interior of the strap. A long blonde hair was caught in the buckle. "Have you ever lost consciousness from doing this?"

Her answer was slow in coming and he shifted his gaze back to her. "Once," she said. "Only once."

He nodded. "It was this week, wasn't it?"

She began to rise from the bed.

"You leave that bed and I won't hesitate to beat your ass ten times worse than I just did."

She froze in the act of sitting up, but after a moment, she nodded. "Yes. I was angry. I wasn't careful. I didn't use the scarf. I thought I was trying to drive you out of my head and I tugged harder than I intended." Her eyes shifted away. "When I woke, I was off the bed. It broke free because I guess I hadn't hooked it around the post as securely as usual. When I lost consciousness my body weight went left, pulled it loose, I think. Tumbled me to the floor."

He rose, his expression such that Marguerite wanted to sink her backside a little lower into the mattress to protect her more recently aching parts. The man had an arm, and she was sure he'd held back. She'd seen him put a mugger through auto glass, after all.

"And how did you feel when you woke up?"

She swallowed. Trust him to dig right to the most difficult point. "I was... I can't."

Unexpectedly, his tone softened. "Tell me, angel. I need to hear it, because you're destroying me here."

Her gaze snapped up to him, to the harsh planes of his face, the tautly held mouth, the belt clutched in his hand with her scarf. Pain lanced through her heart at what she felt from him. She moved toward him on her knees, to the edge of the bed where he stood, staring at her. She bowed her head.

"I was ashamed," she whispered. "And afraid. Afraid that if I'd died you would have been hurt beyond what you could bear. Because I told you I'm not her."

"No, you're not. You have a strength she never had, a strength so terrifying you have no regard for your own life. And you're right." He dropped the belt, turned toward the window, turned his back to her. "If I lost you, I don't know if I'd ever find myself again. Please..."

She raised her lashes, astounded to see his head bow to his own breast. "Promise me you'll never hate me that much."

"Oh, Tyler." A thousand punishments with his belt could not have struck her harder than those few words. She stumbled off the bed, went to him and wrapped herself against his back. Held him so that her fingers dug into the

144

skin across his bare chest. "No...please." She kissed the nape of his neck, moving along his shoulder, across his spine, holding him closer, tighter, her heart breaking as he stayed motionless.

"My wife stood on a chair *en pointe* until she tired and hung herself. That's how she committed suicide."

Cold gripped her vitals as he turned toward her, stepped back out of her embrace. "Tyler, you never said...oh my God, I'm so sorry. I was so angry with you, I just..."

"Didn't think?" He snapped it out like a whip and she flinched. "Didn't think about your life, about its value? I didn't tell you that to feel worried or guilty about me, damn it. Her manager found her. He's been in love with her for years, worshipped her. Her personal assistant of fifteen years saw her too. Something they'd found so beautiful and precious, hanging there, face black, bowels expressed, stinking up the room like a cesspool. Do you want that for Gen and Chloe? If you're going to take yourself out, do it with flame. Burn it all away, so there's nothing left but ashes, so we can still imagine everything we valued and loved..."

He swung before she anticipated him. His fist went through her sheetrock as if it wasn't there, shattering paint and substance. He followed it with the other, a hole right next to it. She realized he was venting fury he could not take out physically on her. The pain from him radiated onto her. Before she knew it she was sitting on her knees on the floor, her arms wrapped around his legs, whispering to him, pleading.

"Forgive me. Please. Please. Please, forgive me. I'm so sorry, Tyler. I'm so sorry."

She was crying. Bending down, he caught her face in his hands to lift her up, make her stand on her knees. The strength in his hands could crush her skull and she wondered a moment if he would do just that but he didn't. He just held her there, made her face the blazing rage in his eyes like the fires of hell. It was a heat that burned her soul and made her see in full light the terrible darkness he kept in himself, a violence not so very different from her own.

"You'll promise me. And you'll never betray that promise, or I swear to God it will kill me. Do you understand that? Do you know how much you mean to me? Even if you don't want me, you have to give me this."

"I promise. I promise." She reached up, gathered him to her. He came inch by resisting inch until his face was against her neck. Suddenly he gave, dropping to his knees, his arms surrounding her so they were pressed against each other thigh to thigh, heart to heart. He pulled her in so tightly against him she couldn't breathe, but that didn't matter. Suddenly the world was about more than herself, more than about her pain and it was easier to let go of it to hold him in her arms, to give him comfort.

His charm and arrogance were his shields, such that she'd not comprehended until this moment the depth to which she could hurt him. She'd been frightened, thinking she'd crossed a line where she couldn't survive without him anymore. It had never occurred to her that his feelings would be a mirror of hers.

Only the strength of a Master like Tyler could reassure her, could force her to believe in his love by reinforcing the same lessons over and over. She wanted the Master in him, needed it. But she realized she also loved the man himself beyond comprehension.

When he started to rise, rather than letting him draw her up with him she stayed down, rubbed her head over his right hand held in both of hers and pressed her lips to his bare hip, his thigh. Holding her cheek to his leg, she spoke against the coarse hair and muscle. "I... It's only been me, for a long time. I've never had to answer to anyone else. Be responsible or a part of someone else's happiness. And I don't know how to handle any of it. I'm afraid I'm going to hurt you over and over, until I drive you away. And that would kill *me*."

His hands clasped her upper arms. He brought her to her feet, tilted her chin to look at him, his expression full of emotion.

"Tell me just once," he said. "And after that, not heaven or hell or even you will take me from your side. Not ever." His voice was harsh with tears he wouldn't, couldn't apparently shed. She began to cry again for them both, reaching up to touch his face.

"I love you, Tyler. I love you."

§

He took a few minutes to clean up in the bathroom. When he came back to her, she was waiting for him on the bed, her blue eyes like soft jewels in the semi-darkness of a room where the curtains were drawn, her hair floating around her body. He made love to her then, tenderly, the both of them nested in her quilts. His body stretched out on hers, moving slow, easy strokes into her heat and wetness. Her body clasped his with arms and legs and she buried her face into his shoulder as they finished together, shuddering.

Tyler suspected it might be the first time in her life that she was unconcerned about anything outside her bedroom door. He could feel her worry, though. Knew she was afraid her darkness made her incapable of living up to the expectations of the words she'd spoken to him. So with every touch, every softly murmured word of love and admiration, he let her know she was already everything he wanted, everything he needed. He put away his own dark fears where they could not touch this moment. And when she slept, at last he felt her relax into a world where there might finally be no dreams at all.

He watched her doze and held her close, his breath on her temple. Inhaled that familiar scent of tea tree oil, lavender and woman until he too succumbed to slumber, his feet over and under hers beneath the covers, an intimacy he'd not allowed himself with any woman since his wife. The simple joy of it after the past hour of intensity made him reflect that Marguerite was right. She wasn't the only one who'd kept herself closed off.

But now it didn't matter if she ripped his chest from his heart every day. If she was the eagle come to disembowel Prometheus and he was chained to that rock, he'd raise his face in welcome the moment he felt the breeze off her moonlight-colored feathers touch his brow.

Chapter Eleven

Perhaps because of jet lag he fell asleep more deeply than he would normally. When he opened one eye, he found it was nearly eleven. While Marguerite was no longer beside him, her scent was on the pillow and a tray with a small carafe and coffee cup was on the nightstand. A spray of daisies and wildflowers tied in one of her ribbons rested beneath the tented note.

I'll be back this afternoon. Had a class at eleven. If you can't stay, I'll be at your house tonight as planned.

She'd drawn... He drew back, squinting. Not for the first time, he acknowledged that eventually he was going to have to give in and admit that standard middle-aged farsightedness was about to overcome forty-plus years of twenty-twenty vision. XXs and OOs. OOs with smiley faces in them. He smiled, picked it up. She was never going to stop surprising him. Of course, she might have dictated the note to Chloe and the hostess had added the little flourish. Since he was lying in the bed with one length of leg from sole to buttock stretched bare over the cover, he hoped it was Marguerite who'd left the note, regardless of who had written it.

He took a quick shower, enjoying the intimacy of being surrounded by her razor, shampoos and soaps, though possessing the usual manly distaste of the floral aromas on his own skin. Pulling on his jeans and T-shirt, he courteously decided to wait on a shave so he didn't wear out her blade with his rough jaw. Those were things he didn't know about her. If she'd be annoyed by a man borrowing her razor. If she preferred her shower in the morning or evening. He looked forward to finding out.

It was an astounding nine in the morning. He found himself grateful that he could follow the corridor at the base of the staircase past the café's restrooms and take a detour into the kitchen that didn't take him across the public floor. A quick glimpse showed him at least ten of the fifteen tables were occupied with morning tea drinkers.

"There you are." Chloe beamed as he came in. "Was the coffee to your liking?" At his alarmed look, she added hastily, "Marguerite took it up." His instant relief produced a snort of laughter. "Though from your expression, I'm sure I missed a morning perk by not offering to do it myself."

"You are incorrigible," he said reprovingly. Her grin broadened.

"Hey, you got to enjoy it while you're young enough to do more than just look."

"That's what worries me. Particularly when I'm unconscious from jet lag."

She giggled, gestured. "We've got scones and a really excellent coffee cake. In the boss's absence, I won't even charge you."

Tyler sat down on a stool in a corner of the kitchen and willingly filched a piece of the cake, gesturing with the full mug of coffee he'd brought down. "Marguerite said she had a class. What class is she attending?" There were so many things he didn't know about her. He did make a mental note to pay Chloe for the cake. He didn't want to give Marguerite an excuse to throw him out on her next mood swing. He suppressed a smile at the image. He wouldn't put it past her to do it.

"Oh, she's an instructor."

"So the note was true. I figured she was just avoiding me."

Chloe chuckled, putting down a sampler next to the coffee mug, thinking no woman in her right mind would leave her bed with something that looked like Tyler in it. "Try this. It's a new green tea. No, if M wanted you out, I suspect she'd just kick you out."

"My thoughts exactly."

And wouldn't she like to be the fly on the wall for that one, Chloe mused. She had a tremendous amount of faith in her employer, but she thought this one might be more than a handful when crossed. She liked him, though. Not only liked the way he looked at M, but how he looked after her. And how M acted around him. So she figured she'd take the risk of getting fired, play dumb if M asked her why she spilled the scoop over something very few other than her staff knew about her Thursdays.

"Today's her jump day."

"Excuse me?"

"M's a serious skydiver. Has a standing appointment on Thursday of every other week."

Tyler put down the sampler, having stopped it two inches from his lips. "She jumps out of airplanes."

"Yes. Hey." Chloe was concerned at the look in his eye as he rose, tossed some bills on the table. "I told you that you don't have to pay for that. Seriously. And she's really good. There's nothing to worry about. In fact, she does it every other Thursday because they use her video stream to help teach the classes they hold that day."

"Where?"

When she hesitated, Tyler's expression changed and her mouth opened before she could stop herself, a reflex of self-preservation. "Oconee Airfield."

As he nodded and left, she shook her head. "M's going to kill me. Kill me, then fire me."

§

She was already in the air. The staff at the front desk encouraged him to go sit in on the advanced class that would be watching her video stream live.

Tyler took a seat, nodding to the class instructor who looked as if he had served in the military. His class of six or seven students ranged in age from twenty to forty. They were mostly men, adrenaline-seekers he guessed. Only one woman, a thirty-something who looked like she was doing it to break her out of the mediocrity track. In the back near Tyler two men sat in flight suits with the airfield's logo, indicating they were also instructors assisting in some manner with the class.

"Marguerite is truly one of our exceptional jumpers," the instructor was saying. "She'll be demonstrating the Atmonauti method we've been going over today. In a few minutes, you'll watch her exit."

Tyler's gaze turned to the wide-screen television behind them. At that moment, the screen flickered and they had a picture of the inside of the plane, the camera holder obviously moving to the open doorway.

The camera tilted and Tyler blinked, his stomach dropping at the free-fall effect of seeing the ground thousands of feet below and the tips of the cameraman's shoes as he stepped on the small platform just outside the door.

"Now the difference with Atmonauti is you're flying at about a thirty degree angle to the horizon and you can vary that about fifteen degrees in either direction. You're looking for a certain zone and wanting to hold it. You control the speed with your legs, move them wider to slow down, arrow them together to go faster. You can fly more efficiently and do more things because you're working with the airflow." The instructor went to the chalkboard where he'd diagrammed stick figures, angles and figures on velocity and ground covered. "She'll be going a hundred miles an hour in the right heading. You can go slower with this method, prolong your dive. She'll go about 1.5 miles out and then use her chute to bring her back to the DZ, the Drop Zone." He glanced toward Tyler, acknowledging his presence and apparently taking him for a potential new diver auditing the class.

When hell freezes over, Tyler thought with grim humor. On several missions he'd been forced to jump out of plane, in such less than ideal circumstances that it had been added to the list of things he would never do if he had any kind of choice. Jump out of an airplane, cut off his genitals with a rusty knife...

Marguerite was at the opening in a white diving suit that covered her from head to toe, her body clearly defined, smooth and sleek as a seal. Her goggles were down, but he'd know those soft lips anywhere, the way she tilted her head, apparently listening to something the cameraman was saying to her. She nodded, reached out, clasped his hand. Drew back, adjusted her goggles and then leaped.

Tyler's chair scraped as he stood up, unable to stop himself. Fortunately, the instructor and class were too riveted on the screen to notice his involuntary response.

"She chose a forward exit. Notice how quickly she orients herself, finds that angle we talked about. You can do a head down or a backward jump as well. In fact, she's likely to roll in a few moments...there she goes...now she's on her back, which is an outstanding view. Just blue sky, folks, nothing up there but you and God. The beauty of the Atmonauti jump is, because you're at that angle, you find silence. No noise, no air rush, no disruption..."

"Well, except for John and his camera," an instructor near Tyler quipped.

"God, she commands the air," one of the students said, awe in his voice.

"You don't command the air," the teacher reproved. "You learn to work with it, respect it. She does, on all levels. She's part of it."

Tyler noted the man did not take his gaze from the screen as he added, "Marguerite is poetry up there. She's the best of Walt Whitman with some of the darkness of Edgar Allan Poe thrown in."

"Yep." The staffer who'd made the original quip gave the class a wink. "For a lot of guys, it's a beautiful girl carrying a six-pack of Budweiser, but to Kyle here, it's a woman who looks like that and is a hell of a diver. What more could he want?"

How about jaw replacement surgery if he doesn't stop salivating over her? Tyler quelled the territorial surge. She WAS beautiful. Even the woman in the audience was riveted, as if they were all watching an angel, something not quite one of them and capable of marvelous feats.

"All right, she and John will break now and she'll pull her chute and come back in." The instructor turned back to his class. "Let's go over the head down jump..."

Tyler watched the full jump, his eyes trained on the

television even as John got farther from Marguerite and his camera at times was swinging to capture the scenery, above and below. But eventually the camera would swing back to her and it was for that Tyler waited, leaning forward in his chair to watch the now small figure. The chute pull, her body drifting up with it gracefully, then her arms moving as she used the cords to take her in the direction she wanted to go.

Did she go there for the stillness? For the weightless feeling? For the memory of her last moments with David, spinning through the air, knowing that it was when they hit the ground that everything would change?

When the class was complete and the students were headed out to practice landing techniques, he stepped outside, standing in the shade of the hangar, simply waiting for her. He wasn't sure how he felt. He'd come, driven by anxiety, but now he just needed to see her, touch her, reassure himself that the endearment he used for her was not in fact what she aspired to be, to fly away from him, from all of them.

The Jeep that pulled into the parking lot was driven by a kid who he assumed was John. An eighteen-year-old geek type with a surfer's physique who looked at her as if she was everything he could ever want in life. There was an older man in the second seat who called out as she left the Jeep, "Be sure and put something on that scrape."

Tyler's eyes coursed over her, saw the rip in the knee of her suit, the stain of blood. It was superficial, something probably caused by a stumble on landing, but it still made him take a deep steadying breath before he stepped forward.

She'd already seen him, even as she lifted her hand in acknowledgement of her companion's comment. Carrying her gear in her arms, she came toward him, her expression unreadable. Not welcoming or unwelcoming, just neutral.

"You know, certain royal personages used to cut the tongues out of their servants' heads to ensure their secrets weren't revealed," she said when she was within earshot.

"As devoted to you as she is, I'm not sure Chloe would stand still while you got the butcher knife," he commented.

"Unless you presented papers proving you were related to Prince William and could arrange a date with him."

She stopped a few feet away, studying him. He raised a brow. "What?"

"I'm wondering if I need to run. You have that look like you did the other night."

"I was angry at first," he admitted. "I thought this was more of the same. Your constant flirtation with death. But—"

"It was." She stated it quietly, met his startled gaze. "At first." She glanced around. "Let me put my gear down and maybe we can walk down to the duck pond, there at the end of the runway."

She dropped her equipment in her car, shoving it into the second seat to repack later, and pushed back the hood of the jumpsuit. Her hair was wound in a crown of braids tightly pinned against her skull. When she released the pins and let the braids drop, she tied them together with one of the braids, making the tail look like a flogger of multiple blonde strands. After a hesitation, she reached out. Bemused, he took her hand. She started down the runway linked to him in that fashion.

"I like holding hands," she said, with a shy nod that he found charming.

"I like holding yours." He cocked his head. "You're different every day, you know that? I can't keep up with you. A week ago, I'd have had to take you through an interrogation to understand something like this. And now you're initiating the conversation, taking me somewhere we won't be interrupted."

"Or I could be taking you somewhere to take advantage of you," she pointed out. "The duck pond is rather private. Though if we have a plane come in to land, or the students go up, they'd get an eyeful."

"Or you could be taking me there to drown me. I never know."

"Well, you said like you liked my unpredictability." She sobered. "You want me to explain this to you. I promised, last night..." She swallowed, met his gaze with an obvious effort. "To be open to you as Master. And as a lover. And I understand that answering your questions is part of that. It's not easy for me. I'm just trying to do it right."

"You're doing fine." He found it difficult to speak, too overcome by the urge to simply kiss her.

The duck pond was inhabited by cattails, lily pads with white blooms and a wooden bench. A group of ducks that were gathered companionably on the banks waddled away at sauntering speed, proving their wary acceptance of human companionship, though quacking their mild displeasure at being disturbed. When she sat down on the bench, he took a seat next to her, stretching out his arm behind. He felt her tension rise, so before she could start speaking he put two fingers under her chin and turned her face to him. Parting her lips with his, he tasted her, then groaned as she opened for him further, taking him in. Her arms came up around his neck, pressing her body against him in the formfitting suit, letting him feel her pleasure at seeing him, being with him. When he eased back, he didn't know whose heart was beating faster.

"Thank you," she said softly. "That made it easier."

"Any sacrifice to help." He tugged on her tail of braids, but she didn't smile.

"When I first started jumping, it was to make me feel like I was back with David, in those last moments. You know how my brother died."

Tyler nodded, ran a hand up her arm. "I won't press, but one day, any day you're ready, angel, I'd like to know more about him. I know he was important to you."

She wasn't ready to tell him. Marguerite couldn't tell him that before she'd shared her bed, which meant before she'd met him, she'd had to tie her arm loosely to the bedpost. That way when she tried to sleepwalk, to fly, she'd wake half slumped on the floor, her arm pulled taut. During those quietly despondent hours of the night, she'd sit crumpled on the floor and blearily look up into the night sky, at the stars or various phases of the moon. She'd think how their light was like the promise of a heaven she could never reach, because for some inexplicable reason she wouldn't free herself to go there. To go to David.

She closed her eyes. "Not today. Today's too good." She

opened them, looked at him. "But something changed, as of this week. For the first time, it was about joy. True freedom. The first freedom I think I've ever felt. And I shouldn't be telling you these things, because you're arrogant enough as it is..."

"Tell me anyway."

She reached out, trailed her fingers along his forearm, let her hand be captured and held on his thigh. "I felt like there'd be someone to care, to catch me if I fell."

"Next time you might mention when you're going out, so I'll know to arrange for that."

She gave him a tiny smile. "I know it's not realistic. It's just a feeling." She bent, unlaced her shoes, removed them and pushed up the fabric of the bodysuit covering her calves. Rising, she moved to the water's edge.

"So how long have you done this?" He looked up as a Piper Cub buzzed over for a landing.

"About ten years. I could take you up one day. I'm a trained instructor."

"Not happening."

Her attention flicked over to him. "It's really wonderful. Falling at over a hundred miles an hour, just you. Sometimes it's nice with others, too, because you don't talk. You're just up there together, feeling the same thing, not having to explain or understand anything." She sloshed her feet in the water and shivered, enjoying the coolness. He enjoyed watching her indulge in the almost childish whimsy and wondered how often she'd had moments like this by herself, these many faces she revealed when no one was there to see.

"I'm afraid I'm just going to have to watch you fly, angel."

Her brows lifted. "Surely you're not one of those people who are afraid of flying? You know they're safer than cars."

"So I've heard. And I think that argument is more effective for someone who's never crashed in a plane. I have. Twice. I totaled a car once. I'm here to tell you that the car crash, as scary as it was, was nothing next to the plane."

"Twice?"

"Both in small surveillance planes, bad weather conditions. Both times we went down where we'd have been executed if we were caught. If we were lucky."

"Well, it makes it hard to argue, putting it that way. But..." She slanted him a glance beneath those silky lashes. "Did you know there's such a thing as nude skydiving? A growing chapter."

He chuckled. "You think the overwhelming male desire to see a woman naked can overcome any fear?"

"Just about."

He grinned. "As long as I can see you naked down here, angel, I'd prefer to enjoy the pleasure on the ground. But I'll think about it." He surveyed the planes lined up on the tarmac. "You know there's very little I'd refuse you. You just have to ask me."

"Always conditions..." He heard the humor in her voice and smiled.

When Marguerite came back to him, wet clay from the banks of the pond was between her toes, across her feet, even up her ankles. She shook her head over them. "I'm afraid you're seeing one of my private rituals. A balancing thing. Coming from the sky, I always like to do this grounding in the earth."

When he didn't reply, she raised her gaze. Marguerite found him staring at her feet, his expression distant, almost empty. "Tyler? Tyler." She said it sharply when he didn't respond at all. Reaching out, she touched him, seeking a response.

He started. His gaze jerked up to meet hers. "I'll get some water."

He dumped the water cup he'd brought with him from the classroom water cooler, rose and strode down to the water's edge.

Her brow furrowed. "I keep a towel and some towelettes in the trunk of the car. And there's a hose back there. It's okay."

Again, he acted like he didn't hear her. Genuinely concerned now, Marguerite started after him, but he'd already turned. Drawing her by the hand to the bench, he pushed her firmly down to the seat. He knelt there before her, poured the water over her toes, rubbed his hand over them, trying to remove the sticky clay. He went back to the pond several times. There was something in his face, something about the determined way he scrubbed at her feet that kept her silent, watching him. There was nothing left on her feet that she could tell, but he poured a fourth cup of water over them, lifting her foot to check the soles, parting each toe to ensure each one was completely clean.

When he started to rise again, she'd had enough. She caught his hand, held on firmly. "Tyler, quit it. They're clean. Tell me what's happening. And don't tell me nothing." She increased her grip, alarmed to see his face was growing paler by the minute, his eyes unfocused as they moved in the direction of her voice. "Sit. Now."

She was familiar with the signs of an impending faint. Fortunately she had a bottle of drinking water she'd brought with her to replenish her own fluids. When she practically shoved him into a sitting position on the bench, she used the head cover of her jumpsuit as a towel, dampened and pressed it to his forehead. He pushed her away after a second, leaned forward to put his head between his knees, taking deep breaths. When she tried to close in, he shook his head, lifted his hand, warding her off.

"Give me a moment."

She couldn't stop herself from easing onto the bench next to him, reaching out and touching his hair lightly, tentative, one stroke, then another. Sweat was beaded on the back of his neck, staining his shirt, the man she'd never seen truly out of control, the passion of sex notwithstanding.

"The watch. Don't take it. Leave it all alone."

"I will," she assured him. "Tyler, it's Marguerite. I need you to be here, with me." Pressing her knuckles against his temple, his jaw, she leaned down and put her lips over his.

He bolted up off the bench, startling her so that he knocked her backwards, made her land hard on her hip on the ground. Lifting his hand to his lips, he pressed where her mouth had been. He shook his head as if clearing the confusion, reminding her of a horse she'd seen run into a barn once, trying to get his bearings back. His attention moved to the planes, down the runway, then to the bench, to her on the ground.

"Oh, Jesus. Angel, are you okay?" He was by her side in two strides, his arms under her, lifting her, putting her on the bench, checking her arms and legs, cupping her face. "I didn't...please tell me I didn't hit you."

"Not recently." At his look of horror, she caught his hands, held them. "Yesterday, the spanking. I was teasing. No, you didn't hit me. You're fine. You just made me lose my balance when you got up so abruptly. Ssshhh...it's okay. I'm fine. I'm *fine*."

He stared at her and Marguerite squeezed his hands. "Tyler, are you all right? Can I do something for you? What's going on?"

"Your feet..."

"They're all clean. You took care of them. They're fine." She guided his face away from the pond and back to her, not wanting to set him off again by letting him see the pond's banks, the muddy footprints she'd left.

Tyler pressed his forehead to hers, drew in a deep shuddering breath. Let it out after a long moment. "Jesus, that was embarrassing. I haven't done that in a long time."

"Yes. I'm disappointed to find you're human. I was arranging to have a big 'S' tattooed on your chest for your birthday and now I'll have to come up with another gift."

His jaw flexed and he drew back. "I'm sorry. That was inexcusable. And you don't have to make jokes to make it less awkward." He rose. "I should go."

"Pardon me?"

He shook his head. "I shouldn't be subjecting you to this."

"What?" She rose and slapped a palm on his chest as he began to stride away. "Could you please stop for a moment?"

He laid his hand over hers, cupped her cheek. "It's all right. I just need a few moments and I'll be fine."

"You're sure? I mean, I need to know this for certain."

He straightened at the temper in her voice. "Yes, I'll be fine. It won't happen again. I just need to go." He started to step around her and she moved with him, this time catching hold of his shirt with both hands, making it clear if he wanted to escape he was going to have to drag her. His eyes narrowed dangerously, his hands latching on to her wrists. "Marguerite—"

"Of course it won't happen again. I mean, it was obviously planned this time. I'm sure you can control it in the future."

"Marguerite—"

"Tyler, shut up. I mean it." She dug her fingers into him. "We've been to this doorway before and you keep leaving me in the cold. I've beaten the hell out of you, tried to stab you, tried every conceivable way to shut you out and yet that's okay. But you won't even tell me what's going on in this one moment, where you're obviously a greater danger to yourself than me."

"I'm fine," he snapped. "I just have to get away from it."

"No, you're trying to get away from me." She walked in to him, surprised him by putting her head down and bracing her arms, backing him like a tug pushing a freighter many times its size toward dockside, only she was pushing him back toward the bench.

"Marguerite, what are you—"

"Sit." She sat down next to him, took his hand, put her shoulder against his. "Tyler, I need you to tell me what just happened."

He started to rise. Seizing his shirt collar, she jerked so that he lost his balance and sat back down, not expecting the rough movement. She put her hands on either side of his neck, drew his gaze to her fiery one. "I'm not going to run because you're not invincible every moment of every fucking day. And guess what? I'm a pretty smart woman. I know what post-traumatic stress syndrome is. So why don't you tell me what triggered it."

She swore at his indecision and cupped his face, pressed her lips to his, opened his mouth, explored him, tangled with his tongue until his hands were at her hips, gripping her with strength, his lust rising as she deliberately stoked it, drawing the animal up in him, giving him back his pride. She drew back, not surprised when his hands tightened, holding her fast, his amber eyes roused. "Any sacrifice to help," she repeated his own words, gently teasing now. "You're frightening me. You're shutting me out, not trusting me to be strong enough to take it. To help. To listen."

Relief, sudden and strong, flooded her chest at the rueful curve of his lips.

"Marguerite, I think of the two of us, I'm the least courageous."

"Hush," she reproved. "Tell me about clay."

He turned, leaned forward to run a hand behind his neck. She caught it there, tangling their fingers together on the back of his shoulder. She heard him sigh.

"We were in Panama with the right intentions, but so many things went wrong. And then there was this day... You find yourself doing so many things you never think of doing. Standing there, watching bodies be bulldozed into a mass grave because there are so many of them that they can't be properly buried before they'll rot, creating disease.

"Then I see this boy walking through a pile of bodies that hasn't yet been scooped up. Looking for something he could barter. He'd been in blood so long he didn't notice it dried on his feet. Over his toes, his ankles..." He reached down, passed his hand over her foot, as if reassuring himself it was clean and pale, cool to his touch. "This kid was wearing a Led Zeppelin T-shirt. We surround ourselves with all these things that are civilized to make us feel safe. A rock band T-shirt, linoleum for our kitchens...and yet we're not civilized. Just like you said that very first night at Tea Leaves. We never have been.

"I had to chase him off from stealing a watch. I don't know why it mattered. But I looked at his feet and remembered walking on the banks of the river in Georgia, near where I was born." The shadows moved behind his eyes and he turned his gaze back to the pond. "Now I have these dreams of it, walking in Georgia, but the mud becomes blood and the bodies come out of the river toward me like some horrific zombie film, only so real."

A quiver ran through the muscles under her fingers. "Sometimes Nina is dancing among them, on top of the bodies, standing on their backs, walking on her toes. Tears

of blood are running down her face. She tries to kiss me
and I smell all those corpses on her breath. When I have
that dream, it makes me never want to sleep again."

"What happened, Tyler?" She trailed her fingers on his
nape, soothing, stroking, keeping her other hand linked
with his. "Why did you leave the CIA? You said you
couldn't refuse me anything. I need to know."

Tyler knew he was going to have to answer her, to say
the words. The pregnant silence, the strength of what lay
between them now demanded it. He could not turn away
from it unless he wished to turn away from her. But it
might turn her from him.

He rose, squeezed her hand and took two steps away.
She didn't stop him this time.

"There are things you do to keep your country safe that
no one wants to talk about. That we all know happen, deep
in the shadows of our soul. Those of us that do it know that
people are not all basically good, as many sheltered souls
like to believe. That there are places where there are not
shades of gray, where it comes down to good and evil,
places that are so far from our idealism that those who
spout about political correctness and peace can't even
comprehend the high price of having the freedom to speak
their opinions. And those of us who are immersed in
violence for that high price, who try to do the right thing in
such an immoral world, know that they're right about one
thing. Violence eats your soul. Eventually you become what
you fight in order to destroy it, in order that there may be
people and places untouched by either your filth or your
enemy's. All those movies about the soldiers being taken to
another planet, where their barbaric natures, which
protected the people, can't be turned against them..."

"Tyler." There was love in her soft voice, so much he just
wanted to fall on his knees and let it cover him like a
blanket tucked around a child's shoulders by his mother's
hands. A shudder ran through him.

"Information." He spat out the word harshly. "When
you know lives are on the line, information is extracted, no
matter the cost. You learn to detach, to watch every subtle
nuance of your enemy's psyche, to know just how much

they can take. And I was very good at it. I've been a sexual Dominant since I was twenty-one years old and the same talents that can be applied to pleasure can be applied to torture."

When he turned to face her, Marguerite saw his expression was hard, almost monstrous, the darkness there for her to see.

"Torture is about psychological regression. You break the subject down until they lose their grasp on all their learned personality traits. They can't handle complex tasks, deal with complicated or stressful situations. It's all about stripping away the shields. Sensory deprivation, unbalancing them with the unexpected, over and over, removing their anchor on reality by confusing them, making them think it's night when it should be day, day when it should be night. Sound familiar?"

"Tyler." She said it again, pain in her voice. Pain for him. He turned away from it, stared at the ducks.

"During the Gulf War, we knew a bomb had been planted and we needed to know where. We caught the lover of the bomber. She was on the inside and knew what we needed to know. And we had to know fast. We didn't have time for those types of methods." He crumpled her head covering in his fist and Marguerite saw the muscles bunch in his shoulders as if he were preparing for a physical fight. "Ten years of intense, pretty much back-to-back operations, yet somehow I'd never had to use severe interrogation techniques on a woman. I removed nine of her nails, broke seven of her fingers before she told us. Fingers are one of the worst pains there are because the nerves are so dense there, even though people are more psychologically cowed by threats to genitalia, nipples. She was small-boned, like my wife. Delicate hands, like yours.

"It's funny." He drew a breath. "That's not the worst thing I've done. I've taken a lot of lives, buried them where their families will never know what happened to them. For causes I believed in. Even her... We got the information, we saved lives. But when I touched my wife... Even later, when I'd touch Leila's hands or her face, or you... When I see Violet's delicate fingers reach out toward Mac, see how large his hand is over hers... Sometimes I can't help but remember that woman. I couldn't do it anymore. Everyone has their threshold. I did the job that day, but that was the end. I was sick, inside and out. All I knew was I had to come home."

To the arms of a woman who didn't have the strength to heal you. Marguerite felt the tears rise in her throat.

He sat down on a stump, still facing away from her. "In this *civilized* world..." The word came out like a curse through his teeth. "I don't abuse women. I'd never strike one in violence, would lay my life on the line for any of them in danger. But somewhere, if she's still alive, there's a woman who dreams of me only when she's in the grip of a nightmare."

The breeze moved over the pond, creating ripples, making the cattails dance, the lilies drift slowly back and forth. A duck entered the waters, paddling, her tail waddling, dipping her beak.

At length, Marguerite stood up, moved to stand before him. For once it was he who was reluctant to meet her eyes. She watched the lashes raise, the golden brown gaze climb to her face. When he got there, she thought there was nothing that could tear at a woman's heart like fear in a strong man's eyes. Not fear of violence or danger. Fear of loss. Fear of rejection, fear of not being loved when he didn't meet expectations.

Reaching out her hand, she grazed her fingertips over his face and then moved in, nudging until he parted his knees. The position compelled him to wrap his arms around her waist and hips, hold her in close to him. His jaw pressed into her soft breasts, the tips of her braided hair whispering along his neck as she bent her head over his.

"You don't have to be the one who always takes care of someone else, you know. In a real relationship, so I've heard, people take care of each other."

He drew back and touched her face. "Is that what we have, you and me? A relationship?"

"That's a frightening term for me. But I think...we have something."

He nodded, laid his forehead on her shoulder. "I don't deserve you. I'm not sure I deserve anyone."

"Maybe I'm your penance." She lifted his chin, gave him an arch look. "And that's why I put you through hell every several days or so. I'm a punishment sent to you by God."

He chuckled at last. The sound of it released the worry around her heart, made her arms close around his shoulders and hold him tightly to her. After a moment he returned the embrace, burrowing his nose in the tender pocket of her collarbone, breathing her in.

"You're my salvation, angel." His grip tightened. "I loved her. But she never got into my soul as deeply as you did the first time I touched you."

It took a moment for her to register the significance of that statement. When she did, she couldn't speak. "I felt lonely without you this morning," he continued. "That's the main reason I followed you out here."

"I didn't want to go, thinking you might have to leave and I wouldn't see you until Friday night." She shook her head. "What are we going to do about that? The whole desolate-without-each-other thing."

"That's easy. Marry me."

Her eyes widened in shock. She didn't ask if he was serious, since she could well see by his expression that he was.

"A reasonable engagement, followed by a marriage ceremony, as quiet or elaborate as you like, anything you want. You want big and opulent, we'll do it, or something small and lovely, maybe at my house."

"Tyler." She simply couldn't think of anything to say or do to such a proposition. "I barely know you... Okay, yes we know each other." She rolled her eyes at his raised brow. "But I don't even know... Do you shave up or down, are you a morning or night person? Do you spend your spare time watching reality TV?"

"Would that be a deal breaker?"

"Absolutely." She threw up her hands, tried to struggle away, but he held her securely. "You're moving too fast."

"That's why I said engaged."

"What if I want to get married in an airplane? Jumping

out of an airplane?"

He lifted a shoulder and rose. "I said I'd do anything for you, angel." Closing his hand over hers, he captured her in his gaze. "It's soon, if we're thinking of time, but I love you, Marguerite. That's not going to stop today, tomorrow, or in a thousand years from now. And I think you need to know that."

"I need to think about this."

"Think as long as you need. I shave upward, I'm a night person and no, I don't watch garbage that insults the hard work and struggles of talented scriptwriters. You think of any other questions, you let me know. Now, let me tell you about this deli nearby that I think we should check out for lunch..."

She resisted the urge to scream as he closed his arms around her in a hug, lifting her off her feet. With his face pressed hard against her hair, he held on to her in a way she knew made it impossible for her to refuse him anything.

In that, they were entirely too alike.

Chapter Twelve

A couple busy hours finishing up the day at Tea Leaves kept her from dwelling too much on all the revelations from the airport. But the scent of Tyler in her room as she packed for the weekend and changed clothes brought it all back, along with other distracting thoughts. If she knew him, he was figuring sexual deprivation would force her to capitulate much more quickly to his absurd offer of marriage. He was relentless. It almost made her smile.

As Marguerite drove up to the gate of Tyler's "city house" late Friday afternoon, she noted it had many of the same qualities as his Gulf home. Acreage, privacy and lovely, tended grounds that suggested Robert either had a twin or divided his attention between both places. The house had a Caribbean flare, with tall front columns, wide vistas of windows and charming touches like the center fountain in the front drive. Sculptures of two children frolicking in the water reminded her of their puddle stomping, the laughter that had bubbled out of her, his playful grin.

He was sitting on the front steps in khakis and an open-collared white shirt, the sleeves rolled up, his back comfortably leaned up against a column.

She got out, shouldered her overnight bag with a casualness she was far from feeling when he looked at her out of those half-lidded, direct tiger eyes.

"How much money *do* you have?" she asked waspishly.

"You after me for my money now?"

"I have never been after you, Tyler Winterman. You've chased me from the beginning. Shamelessly and tiresomely."

"Really? That embarrassing, am I?"

"Like a slavering hound." She walked up to him, making the mental correction that he was more like a bloodhound. He tilted his head, surveying her from the tips of her sandals, her bare knees, the hem of her sleeveless linen sundress, up to her breasts and face, lingering on the hair she'd caught in a banana clip and which spilled over one shoulder.

"You look like a beautiful island sprite." He ran his hands up her calves, under the skirt. Before she could back away, he had a firm grip on her thighs. "Drop the bag and come down here. Give Fido a break and let me drool on you a bit."

She knew there was nothing joking about the underlying command as his strength pulled her inexorably forward. She only had a moment to drop the bag before he had her stepping over him. Bringing her down to straddle his lap, his hands comfortable under the short skirt, he found the front of her thin panties with his thumbs while his fingers took a firm grip on her bare cheeks. He looked at her eye to eye as she felt the delicious pressure of his cock.

"Did you miss me?"

"A little. When I was bored and had nothing else to think about."

He caught the back of her head with one hand and took a nip at her bottom lip, made them part, his breath stroking her face. "Liar. Your cunt was wet for me all the way here. Your panties are soaked."

"I was thinking about someone else."

"Mm-hmm." He covered her mouth with his, plunged deep. His hand held her nape while his other slid farther into that wet area, fingering her, making her shudder. "Tell me his name then. Say who you're thinking about, who's getting your pussy so slick. Say it."

"Tyler," she whispered softly in his mouth. He made a satisfied growl, moving his grip to her waist and pulling her further onto him, his fingers digging into her hips.

They'd made love, said the word "relationship". She couldn't help feeling sensual delight in the easy banter, the passion of newfound romance, the wild addictive quality it had. She'd never experienced anything like it before, knew she couldn't trust or absorb it this fast, but he took over as he seemed to know how to do with her, leaving her with no footing and no anchor but him.

He pushed the skirt up to her waist, baring her lower body to the sunlight. Finding her bra strap, he unhooked it, his hands coming around to capture her breasts beneath the loosened cups. When he surged up, working his mouth down the side of her throat, the upward pressure on her breasts made them all the more visible to him in the scooped neck. He was going to have sex with her right here on his front porch. While the winding drive and high brick fence hid them from public view, it still added to her arousal to feel his desire to take her here, wherever he wished, on his territory.

She didn't push him away as his mouth descended, took hold of her nipple through the cotton, suckled as he squeezed her buttocks. Her hips moved on him, wanting. Wanting him now.

"Please..."

"Please what?" He nipped her sharply.

She gasped, tightening her hands on his shoulders. "Please, Master. Take me here. On the stairs. I need you. Now."

Tyler realized he hadn't meant to make the demand, but her immediate response punched him low in the gut as he saw she hadn't expected herself to respond as naturally as she had. Or as immediately.

"Soon." He cradled her face, kissed her mouth hard again. "I'll fuck you, angel, make love to you, make you scream when you come. But first I have a gift for you. I've been counting the minutes until you got here so I could give it to you."

He refastened her bra for her, lifted her off him and straightened her skirt, as if unaware of her mutinous look. As he got to his feet, Marguerite deliberately trailed her fingers over him, a light scrape of her nails on his turgid cock, straining against his pants. Catching her hand, he pulled her to him. "Behave," he reproved. But he gave her a tender kiss on her nose that surprised her, though it barely distracted her from the throb of her body.

What had happened to her infamous control? But she knew. A sub didn't have to have control around her Master. Only within his demands. She was quite literally a switch when she was with him, all of her compulsions commensurate with a submissive's behavior, as strong in her as the Mistress when she stood over a different type of man.

"So how was your day? What did you do?"

He opened the door for her, guided her in with a hand at the small of her back. Behaving like the perfect gentleman while she had to clench her fingers into fists to keep from slapping him. Or jumping him.

"We had a large afternoon crowd," she said at last. "Chloe tried her hand at a poppy seed cake that was gone in no time."

"I assume you brought me a piece."

"With paying customers willing to put down six dollars a slice? You're going to have charm her into baking you one. On her own time."

Her tone was cool and Tyler knew she was getting back at him. He grinned, recognizing the challenging light in her eye. The sexy pout of those soft lips had his lust rising to the point he had to stifle a groan.

"Mercenary."

"Fiscally responsible," she returned. He saw he'd restored her good humor with his teasing. He squeezed her hand.

"I love it when you do that."

"Do what?"

"Really smile."

She raised her hand to her lips, startled. It amazed him that she wasn't aware of it, that she needed tactile experience to believe it. He touched her face, hurting for her and loving her at once. To keep it from becoming too serious, he curled a lock of her hair around his fingers. "And what if I have to offer Chloe sexual favors to wrest a cake out of her?"

Marguerite raised a brow. "Are you trying to make me

jealous?"

"Are you jealous at the thought?"

She considered it. "I don't... I guess I haven't gotten as far as to think I have the right to be possessive with you."

Raising her hand, he kissed it and bit her knuckles with sharp pressure, watching her eyes focus on the mark of his teeth into her skin, pain offered as a pleasure. "You have every right to be possessive. Because I sure as hell consider you mine."

"Well, there goes the affair I'd planned with half the men in the neighborhood. Tyler..."

"I'll ease up," he promised. "Come on out to the back. Your present is there."

"Where are Mac and Violet?"

"Out back as well. I have a pool here, too. They're taking a swim before dinner."

He took her down the hallway, past an opulent dining room set for seven, through the sunroom and out a covered walkway flanked by blooming gardenia bushes. The walkway led to the enclosed pool area which currently had all the windows open to allow the fresh air.

As they stepped in, a man was coming out of the pool. She registered that there were three other people in there with him, but could not immediately focus on anyone else as her senses were abruptly inundated with him. He was the type of submissive that always called to her. In his late twenties, with green eyes like sea glass, his streaked chestnut hair to mid-shoulders, his lips soft, curved pleasantly. The upper torso was well-muscled, a lean, taut body. He was completely naked, obvious as he walked up the steps at the shallow end, hand on the rail, water sluicing down his flat stomach over the groin area and long thighs.

"Marguerite." Tyler nodded as the man approached. "This is Roland. It's his pleasure to serve you this weekend in whatever manner you wish. He works at True Blue, but volunteered to spend the weekend with us because he enjoys the company of strong Mistresses." He looked into her amazed face. "I give him to you, as your Master. You have my permission to enjoy him fully in my company."

171

She met his gaze. "Not alone."

He shook his head. "I am possessive," he reminded her, his gaze sweeping over her. "And I love watching you as a Mistress."

He moved his touch up to her neck, caressing her, murmured in her ear so only she could hear him. "As your Master, I'd like to see you top him. Indulge yourself as you desire and let's see how it goes. I never shared Nina with another man, wouldn't countenance it. But this is different. I know the compulsion that drives you to be a Mistress, just as I know that your soul is mine. As mine is yours," he added quietly.

Marguerite reflected that it felt odd to be here as Mistress and slave both, primarily because it did not feel odd at all. Her mind was swirling with ideas already. Only this time, it was with the things she would do to bring Roland pleasure while Tyler watched. She imagined his eyes on her as she moved her hands over another man's flesh, as her fingers closed over Roland's even now thickening cock.

Tyler wrapped his hands in her hair, drew her head back to suckle her throat as she studied her gift. Reaching out to Roland, she drew him to her, desire sweeping her hard at the feel of one man possessing her while she sought to possess another herself. Roland stepped closer, his green eyes respectful but avid. She could feel his desire to serve, to be commanded, emanating off him like heat.

She'd heard wives lament their husband's inability to pick out just the right gift, even when signs and clues were practically mapped out in front of them. Tyler had known exactly what she most appreciated. The beautiful purity of Roland's features, the eyes that had that seeking quality, the quality a Mistress cherished. While she could tell this man did not have as many personal demons as the type of submissive she usually chose, the very fact he seemed more balanced complemented the social tone of this weekend. As always, Tyler had chosen thoughtfully.

When Tyler released her, she remained very cognizant of his whereabouts as he withdrew to take a seat in one of the pool side chairs, his hands on the arms, long legs stretched out before him. She ran a hand down Roland's chest and his eyes lowered, acknowledging her acceptance, submitting to her authority. She felt the surge of power and stillness at once, a drug she always harvested for such interactions, but now there was a new ingredient, one that made heat climb up inside her and set her imagination on fire.

"Roland, the first thing I want to do is take my afternoon tea. You will be my table. Do you understand?"

"Yes, Mistress. It would be my honor."

"I'm not very graceful. I may spill a drop or two, here or there." She moved around him, trailing her fingertips along his back, down to the upper curve of his buttocks. And wondrous buttocks they were. "Can you be still and not upset my cup? I'd like to use my fine china, but if I must I will use a plastic set."

"I'll not move a muscle, Mistress," he promised.

"Oh, I'd like to see your muscles move. I'd like them to hold a plug while I take my tea. Vibrate deep inside you, massage you until you're fit to burst. Can you come without upsetting my tea?"

"I won't come." He smiled, confident, but his eyes were shifting, thinking. Not as certain. "Unless Mistress commands it."

"We'll see about that."

As she circled Roland, she examined her immediate surroundings. There was a comfortable wicker arrangement near the pool, wingback seats with deep cushions, a style of chair where it would be comfortable to perch, ladylike, while she enjoyed tea on her "table". She suspected that the chairs were for Tyler's female guests, while the nearby loungers would attract the more sprawling nature of the males. With his propensity and preference for being outside near his gardens, she could well imagine him there, one long leg braced on the ground on either side of the lounger as he studied a script or did paperwork.

She remembered then that there were three others in the pool and got the second shock of the evening when she turned to make the appropriate courtesies. Violet was sitting on the edge of the pool, Mac still in the water, his arms crossed and propped on the edge. Her foot and calf rested on his shoulder as they watched the goings-on.

The other person in the pool was Leila.

The surge of emotion she felt at the sight of her, naked like Roland as befitted a submissive's status, gave her an answer to Tyler's earlier question. She *could* feel jealousy. Why on earth was she here? Certainly he wasn't going to entertain himself with Leila while she exercised her Mistress craving on Roland. While she recognized it logically as a double standard, emotionally it wasn't. Tyler was acting as her Master, facilitating her interaction with Roland, a submissive. Roland was like the other subs she'd taken. Two hours of play, no commitment beyond that. Tyler and Leila had a history, a genuine bond of affection based in sex and shared experiences. And as Leila came out of the end of the pool to take a seat near Violet, Marguerite further observed that no woman should be that well-endowed.

Did that mean he preferred women with bigger breasts? Come to think of it, many of the women he'd chosen as submissives had been blessed in that regard.

Stop it. She was appalled at herself and gathered her dignity up with both hands. She wasn't like any of the women he'd chosen in the past. Any more than he was like the men she'd chosen. But they'd chosen each other.

Marguerite forced her attention back to Roland. "Move the center table to the side of the sofa," she ordered. When he complied, his muscles shifted along his back, buttocks flexing as he turned.

"Now on all fours," she said softly. "Where the table was."

He moved to obey, those same well-toned muscles rippling in his thighs and across his obliques as he knelt before her, then went to all fours. He surprised her by making an unexpected dip, brushing her foot with his lips.

"It is an honor to serve you, Mistress. Your reputation precedes you."

She moved to the sofa, bade him lift up and put a cushion under his knees and another under his hands, leveling the surface appropriately and giving him comfort for a prolonged position.

"I'm going to go change," she said, caressing the back of one thigh. Reaching up, she fondled the free-hanging testicles, easing a hand between his buttocks and earning a slight shift, a further hardening of his cock. "And I'll find the appropriate plug to keep you struggling not to come while I take my tea. While I'm gone, I want you to practice holding my table steady." She picked up a flower basket arrangement from the side table and put it in the center of his back. Watched him get still, focused.

She moved her attention to Tyler, decided to grab the awkward bull by the horns. "May I make use of your slave, Master Tyler?"

Tyler looked startled. The sound of footsteps approaching made Marguerite look away from him to see a handsome man of Latino descent with dark eyes and sleek hair enter the pool area from the garden. When his attention went immediately to Leila, the woman lowered her gaze, cheeks pinkening at the attention.

"You think I'd..." Tyler shook his head, stopped what he'd been about to say, turned toward the other man. "Master Joseph, Mistress Marguerite would like to make use of your slave for her purposes. I believe she wants Leila to help Roland practice keeping her table steady under stimulation. Would you consent?"

Marguerite remembered now that the dining room table was being set for seven, not six. The relief that flooded her chest was as surprisingly intense as the jealousy had been.

Before Joseph could respond, Tyler stepped up to her, drew her to him with his hand caressing her neck, immediately catching her attention, of course. His calf was pressed to Roland's forearm, so there was no way he would miss their conversation.

"Marguerite." Tyler brushed his lips over hers, her cheek, her ear, dwelled there. "Despite the different twist that BDSM brings to our relationship, when I set my heart on someone I'm monogamous. And I damn well expect her to be as well." He glanced down at Roland. "I know your heart, what you enjoy. And what you need. I'm not confused. And I don't want you to be, either. For your sake. Or Roland's well-being."

It was the arrogance that brought back her confidence. "I didn't bring high enough heels for that level of testosterone."

"Then strip off your clothes and you can swim in a vat of it." He pressed his cheek to hers, whispered in her ear. "You remember the night I spilled my come all over your back and you begged me to leave it, to mark my claim on you?"

Stepping back, she tossed her head with irritated petulance. He gave her a satisfied look, moving away. She decided she would try integrating the feelings he stirred up with her normal inspiration with a willing sub and see where it took her. There was an excitement low in her vitals roused by the unique situation, spurred by the changes that had happened over the past week. With a shock, she realized some part of her confidence came from the fact that she trusted Tyler to guide her, that she could do as she wished and he would set the boundaries, as a Master would. Boundaries that would likely only heighten the spiraling sense of arousal she felt with Roland's breath on her calf, waiting. Waiting for her Will.

"Master Joseph." She courteously nodded her head to him.

The man sketched her a bow in return, appraising her with a warm look. "It would be my pleasure for you to enjoy the talents of my Leila. Leila, please follow Mistress Marguerite's direction as you would my own. You may advise her of your boundaries as necessary."

Leila stepped to Marguerite's side at her beckoning, keeping her eyes down as a sub would, but Marguerite could feel her tension.

She raised Leila's chin so she would look at her. "You are very fortunate, Master Joseph," she said. "And I thank you for the gift."

This was a woman who had brought light to Tyler's life when he desperately needed it, who had offered him friendship and physical comfort. Though they'd released their claim on each other, Marguerite could not deny lingering jealousy. But at this moment, Mistress to sub, she was able to move beyond that and convey respect in her touch. Leila relaxed slightly, acknowledging it.

"Leila, while I go change and pick out some things I'll need for my tea, I want you to lie on your back, here." She guided Leila down to the floor, enabling her to slide her head between Roland's spread legs until her head was propped on another small pillow under his lower abdomen, his stiff cock at a perfect angle to be taken by her lips. "I want you to take your pleasure." Marguerite's finger whispered down his back. "But you're not allowed to come, Roland. No matter how long I take. If you think you're going to lose control, you will tell her so she can ease off, but only until you regain control. Then she should start again."

She turned her gaze to Joseph who was apparently absorbed by the sight of Leila's smooth pussy, the clit jewelry she wore in the piercing there, her body stretched out beneath Roland's. "And while I change, I expect your Master might devise ways to make you come, Leila, to reward your service to me." For they all knew that her cries and arousal would further torture Roland, prohibited from releasing his own desire even when Leila sucked him harder. Caught in the throes of her own passion, she would scream against his hardened flesh as she came at her Master's touch.

Joseph nodded, his dark eyes wickedly gleaming in anticipation.

Marguerite turned to address the only two members of the party that she had not yet. She found Violet watching her closely while Mac massaged the calf resting on his shoulder, pressing his mouth along her skin. Her lips had parted, showing her distraction, but her gaze stayed on Marguerite nonetheless.

"Mistress Violet, would you be willing to join me for a cup of tea when I return?"

Violet's Caribbean blue eyes were alert, cool. "Yes I would."

They still had a score to settle, obviously. Marguerite inclined her head in just as reserved a fashion. On that challenging note, she let Tyler show her out of the pool house.

Chapter Thirteen

He followed her up to the second level and took her hand, guiding her to his room. From the shirt casually thrown over a chair and the hairbrush and cufflinks sitting out on the dresser, Marguerite was certain it was his room this time. She also noted that her overnight bag had been brought here.

"I'd like to choose a plug for him, after I change clothes. I assume you have some that are sterile?"

"Mmm-hmm." He drew her to him, began to unbutton the front of the dress, peel it off her shoulders.

"Tyler." Her breath escaped her as he bit her neck, took the dress off. "What are you doing?"

"Exercising a Master's right to dress and undress his slave. I've gotten you another gift."

"Your most recent one was more than I could ask. I don't need to be spoiled."

"On that, we'll have to disagree." He dropped her dress over his shirt on the chair, a curiously domestic, intimate picture that absorbed her attention for a moment. "Take off the rest of your clothes. I want you to stand before me naked."

Leaning against the closet, he crossed his arms, his attention focused solely on her in a way that made her body grow even more full and heavy with need. His command of her while a willing, beautiful slave awaited her on his hands and knees downstairs released a dichotomy of reaction in Marguerite that was as overwhelming for a moment as a physical climax. She savored it, wondering at the way it spread heat over her skin, drew her nipples to hard points and made moisture gather at the gateway between her thighs.

She put her hands back to unfasten the bra he'd readjusted before she met Roland. His gaze dropped as it came free and she eased the straps down her arms, entranced by how he watched her. She employed the same deceptively passive methods she employed to rouse a sub, only this time she did it to tantalize the man she chose to call her Master.

She'd worn thong panties. For him. Enjoyed putting them on, easily imagining his hands as sensuous a touch as the light nylon. Pivoting on her toe, she reached back, hooked her hands in the side straps and took the panties down slowly, bending fully as her yoga practice allowed her to do. Once she had her head to her knees, she came up halfway, just enough to step out of them and loosen her hair. She straightened, tossing it back so it spilled down her bare back. Turning, she dropped the panties and stood before him naked, her clothes littering the floor, discarded with the casual indifference a Mistress would show.

His expression was one of complete absorption, his body tense, erection visible. He might very well decide to fuck her here and now before she went to Roland so the scent of his come would be on her. Primitive and direct, the leader of the pack making it clear to other males his claim on the alpha female. When more response trickled down her thigh, he moved, coming to her. Removing a handkerchief from his trouser pocket, he widened her stance with a nudge which caused her to grip his shoulder for balance. He put the cloth full against her, making her hold tighter, her lips part as she stared into his face, not wanting to look anywhere else.

"You're ready to come already, aren't you, angel?"

She nodded, lowered her gaze, her lashes fanning her cheeks as she reached forward, stroked her knuckles over the hard length of him. "But I would go to my knees and give you pleasure first." She wanted to, her mouth watering for it.

"You will, but not now. I want to watch you with Roland. Watch you handle him, bring him to screaming climax, begging to serve you."

"So you know you can make me do the same?" A smile curved her lips. "That stereotypical alpha male need to Dom the Domme?"

"Perhaps." His lips were firm with sensual intent. "I want to watch that magic you do. That place you go and take a sub with you, bringing him a Nirvana he never knew was possible. And know that what's getting you hotter and hotter is feeling me watching, that later tonight all that excitement and arousal you have will explode around my cock, my mouth, my hands. And when you do suck on my cock, I'm going to put a vibrator in you. Each time you rock forward it will drive into you so you'll climax again as my come explodes in your mouth, over your breasts."

She swallowed and wondered if he knew what power he could wield over her with only words. Her fingers itched to touch him, but she curled them into her palms, trying to maintain some semblance of control.

"Let me show you my gift. You can decide if it's what you want to wear to dominate Roland."

At her curious look, he shook his head. "I won't command your actions as a Mistress. I told you, I love watching you. I love your sheer artistry." He picked up a blindfold from the bed and came to her, fixing it around her eyes, bringing his body close so he was pressed against her bare skin, his fingers whispering down over her hair, her shoulder blades. "I want to put my gift on you now for your own pleasure, to get the full effect. But if it doesn't suit your purpose with Roland you can change."

A moment later, he directed her to hold his shoulder and had her step into what felt like a pair of loose pants. He drew them up just to her hipbones and asked her to hold the edge of the waistband so they would not tumble back down her thighs.

"Either you're a poor judge of sizes or I've lost a lot of weight since you last saw me."

His chuckle came from below, as he had apparently knelt to her left. "I've been around long enough to know there is no safe conversation for a man to have with a woman about her weight, good or bad. I'm not that gullible."

His hand was at her hip. Feeling the pants tighten their hold on her there, she realized the pants laced all the way up the leg. He made a similar adjustment on the other side, getting the seams set where he wished before he began to draw the laces snug from hip to ankle. The seams for the back molded into the crease of her buttocks tightly enough that the cheeks would be clearly separated and defined as if she wore no clothes at all. The fabric felt like a wet latex. Her breath got a little shallow, not from the constriction but because of how it felt to have him dressing her, on one knee to her left, then her right, then behind her. He didn't prohibit her from touching him, so she kept her fingers grazing over his shoulders, his hair, feeling his shoulders move under her touch as he worked the laces to adjust the pants.

He was dressing her as she might command a sub to do, though she'd never commanded one to do something so intimate to her person. Yet he was also dressing her as was a Master's right. She was already shaking as she did when he touched her this way, compelling her submission. It made her realize how much overlap there was in serving and being served, the needs that were met not so far distant from each other. The important element apparently being the focus, the absolute attention and devotion demonstrated by either Master or slave. The way his hands arranged the clothing, cared for her appearance, the comfort of the fit, the way he knew she needed to touch him as he did it. So much he'd given her in a short time. Though her mind was still fairly certain that he could be gone from her life tomorrow, he was so strongly insisting the opposite that some part of her was beginning to hear him, to believe.

When the pants were in place, they were low on her hips and she felt the light brush of the tied strings at her ankles, the tiny chatter of beads decorating the ends. She felt him stand and she turned, finding his chest with her hands. He stilled at her unexpected move and she took a step back from him, her hand flat on his chest. Slowly, gracefully, she went to her knees, bent and touched her forehead to his feet, then straightened enough to offer the same homage with her lips to his knees, his groin, his stomach, upper abdomen. Rose to touch her mouth to his heart, throat, brow. At last, rising on her toes, her hands on his head to bring it down to her, she kissed the crown chakra. Then she sank to her knees again, her hands drifting back down his body.

"Thank you," she said quietly.

Tyler looked down at the woman kneeling before him and could not speak. He knew the spiritual significance of what she had just done, knew she would never do such a thing lightly. But even more than the spiritual impact was the emotional one, the fact she'd just offered him an act of love, of respect and honor. Of trust. Lifting her to her feet with hands that were not quite steady, he laid his lips over hers. Not moving, not taking, simply connecting, trying to feel and give everything at once in that light touch. Her hands came up again, framed his face. When her lips parted he groaned and dove in, feeling consumed by the shape of her lips, her teeth, her tongue, the brush of her cheek. He'd missed having a woman in his soul. He found himself wondering if Nina had ever fully gotten in, for with Marguerite he felt there were so many chambers in himself he'd never noticed before. Somehow she was in them all. Perhaps a part of him had known Nina couldn't take all of what lay in those chambers, that she was only so strong. The woman before him needed his protection and love, but... He remembered yesterday by the pond, how she'd turned him toward her, would not permit him to hide his pain. Her face caring, supportive. Not afraid or uncertain because of his moment of weakness. She'd offered compassion. Strength.

"Hold still, angel. One more piece, the top. You'll find you can sit and stand in the pants relatively easily. They have enough stretch built into them so they fit like a second skin, but give you freedom of movement. Raise your arms for me."

Marguerite complied. Something like slender chains drifted down her arms, fell lightly against her breasts and back. He had her lower her arms and moved around her, again making the garment fit to her upper torso. Only it didn't feel like fabric. It felt like...jewelry. Jewelry that snugged under her breasts, crisscrossed between them, lapped around her neck erotically to dangle down her back like the ends of a scarf. He pulled her hair back in gentle hands, secured it up, surprising her. Small beads brushed the rounded part of her shoulders.

Then his hands moved to her eyes and he took the blindfold off, letting her open her eyes to see herself in the full-length mirror toward which he turned her.

The pants did fit her like a second skin. They rode low on her hips and laced down either side, showing an inch of her bare body from waist to ankle. The garment he placed on her upper body was a creation of sapphires, pearls and onyx that fastened around her upper body beneath her breasts, then crossed between them and doubled around her throat. The two ends, ropes of the precious gems, made a delicate double strand down the column of her spine, explaining why he'd deviated from his usual preference of leaving her hair down. There was a separate scalloped piece that he'd draped from the points of her shoulders so the crescents of the sparkling gems hung low along the top of the breasts and fastened in the back.

She looked like a primitive tribal queen, her breasts bare but adorned opulently. A Mistress who would make a sub froth at the mouth to touch her. And yet it was more than that. It was a harness, a collar of sorts he'd given her, the snug fastening of it reminding her when she moved that she belonged to another.

Tyler stood behind her, and his hands came up, cupped her breasts, teased her nipples as she arched, rubbing her snugly held backside against his crotch. He suppressed a groan, dipped his head and nuzzled her bare shoulder, biting. "They had another pair of pants. Instead of opening at the legs, it laced up over the ass, and you leave the lacings loose enough so you can see the crease between the buttocks, can reach your fingers through the crisscross of the ties to play, bury them deep. Rip them open and fuck your lover's ass when she needs it. But I thought these would do for a Mistress."

"So you didn't get the other pair?"

"One in white and one in pale blue. You got a better discount if you bought three."

She almost smiled, but looking in the mirror, she lifted her hand, fingered the scar at her collarbone, a frown crossing her face as she thought about how the beautiful garment bared her upper body.

"Hey." Tyler bent his head, kissed the top of her hand, nudged it aside and laid his lip on the scar itself. "Don't worry about that. They're not going to ask. All right? I already took care of that."

Before she could respond, he caught her nipple, pinched as she gasped. "I need to get you out of this room," he rasped. "I'm going to explode if I can't have you. My plan to torment you all night will be for naught."

She leaned back into him, sliding her buttocks this time deliberately against him, reaching up her arms to wind them around his neck. "We have at least another five minutes before Roland is in true agony."

She was in agony right now, her body screaming for his, intensified by his anticipation of her fears, her needs. *I already took care of that.*

Catching her by the throat, he drew her to her toes, pinning her against him to cup his other hand over her mound. She made a sound of desperate pleasure, but he held her still with his greater strength.

"No, angel." He breathed hoarsely into her ear. Let her feel the rock-hard presence of him. "When I take you tonight, it will be when you're screaming for my cock, wherever I want to put it. When you don't care who hears you call me Master."

He'd never been this demanding with her. Something had shifted between them. She realized the significance of that, wondered if it had to do with their current situation, the fact he'd likely never had a woman who was submissive to him but Mistress to others. He was making his territorial claims clear. Or perhaps it was all that they had experienced in the past few days together. It should have offended or even frightened her, but some odd shifting of her own had happened over the past couple of days. Her mind was still exploring all the meanings, not judging so much as experiencing the way that felt to her. And it was not unpleasant, especially with him now nibbling his way down the line of her shoulder.

"I can't keep up with your shifts between charm and testosterone," she managed. Closed her eyes as his hands kept up their kneading at her breasts. Testing him, she reopened them, lowered her hands to her pussy, watched him watch as she rubbed herself there, building her sensation under his intense golden gaze.

"You get the whole package, angel." He caught her hand, pulled it back behind her while he anchored her against him by maintaining his hold on her throat, jutting out her breasts in their beautiful jewels. He laid her hand on him, on his enormous need. "All of it."

§

Marguerite kept the outfit on. When she came back to the pool Tyler left her side, but with a lingering kiss to the sensitive inside of her wrist and a thorough look over her body, the breasts only adorned in jewels. It was a look that made the nipples tighten again, showing her arousal to the others.

Fortunately, it was difficult to be self-conscious given what else was going on around the pool.

Mac was supine in a lounge chair as Violet sat upon him backwards, straddling his upper abdomen, her fingers playing up and down his fully erect cock while she watched Roland and Leila. Mac's fingers were locked to the top slat of the chair, his wrists held there by straps. His feet were on the ground just on either side of the end of the chair due to his height, his ankles attached to the legs with the same type of straps, keeping his thighs open to everyone's view, the sizeable testicles, thick cock. The upper part of the chair was raised to a shallow angle so he could clearly see and be stimulated by Leila and Roland as well.

Leila was where Marguerite had left her, on her back, her head on a pillow, straddled by Roland's knees and spread thighs. She had her chin tilted up to give her better ability to take him more deeply down her throat and was currently doing so with enthusiasm. Her clit and labia were slick with excitement, her legs spread, obviously at Joseph's behest, since he reclined on a chair just between her feet, one hand dangled off the chair to caress her ankle. Roland's thighs were trembling, his body gleaming with sweat, suggesting Leila had followed Marguerite's direction faithfully.

"She's very well trained," Marguerite complimented Tyler. He inclined his head. He slipped on a pair of sunglasses and sat down several yards away from the tableau. Something about the way he looked, the sensual mouth still, the jawline emphasized by the concealment of his eyes, made her own state of arousal in the moment more intense.

"How many times has she had to stop?" she asked Joseph.

The man glanced up, his eyes moving from her face down her body and back up. He had to forcibly snap his jaw closed, but did so quickly when Tyler made a quiet noise and shifted to cross his ankle over his opposite knee. "Three times."

Marguerite tilted her head, taking Tyler into her peripheral vision. Another strange situation. As a Mistress at The Zone, she was used to the admiring but respectful glances of other Masters, the line clearly drawn in the sand, enforced by their known preferences. In this situation, Tyler's obvious claim on her as a Master had blurred those lines. Joseph had stepped over it with his more thorough regard. He had looked at her as he might a submissive. Tyler's subtle though clear message had redrawn the line firmly. His submissive she might be, but to all other men she was to be treated as a Mistress. She stood a moment, absorbing that interesting change in her status, wondering if she should feel insulted by his championing. But then she drew in her breath, inhaling the environment of sex and power, control and trust and knew that in their world, lines had to be made clear. They walked close to the primitive line of conquering, taking, the civilized posturings of consent just shadows at their backs, easily forgotten if those lines got confusing.

"Good. He's well aroused then. Master Joseph, would you please ask Leila to keep Roland in her mouth, but she should no longer suck or lick him. I want her to hold him without moving."

He gave the order and Leila stopped while Roland's breath rasped erratically.

"I would like to reward your slave by making her come. May I have the pleasure?"

Whatever the assembled had been expecting, it was not that. She could tell by the surprise on Joseph's face, the slight lifting of Tyler's brow, the interest in Mac's expression. Only Violet's unwavering attention was unaffected, but with respect to that one, Marguerite knew she was being judged and measured. From Mac's occasional concerned glance in his Mistress's direction, she knew she wasn't the only one noticing it.

"It will be our pleasure to watch. A gift to us all." Joseph nodded.

Because of her request, all the men in the room were now riveted by the tableau, even Roland putting his head at an angle where he could try his best to see as much as possible. She felt the male power wash over her like magical energy, an energy increased by the connection she felt with Violet in this moment despite their differences. Two Mistresses in full command of the subs there. And, in a peculiar way, in command of the two Masters, with the power a woman fully encompassed in her sexual self could hold over anything male within distance. After all, there were not many myths about powerful Queens being brought to their knees by the sexual charisma of an island sorcerer, or male sirens singing a female captain to her doom.

Marguerite squatted next to Leila's thigh and Roland's hips. When she spread out her knees to balance herself, she knew the position would tighten the fabric over her ass in a seductive way. Tyler's angle of vision was behind her though she'd settled far enough to the right he could easily see Leila's wet pussy between her body and Joseph. It was new, being conscious of where he was, wanting to be sure everything she did was at an angle where he could see her actions and be stimulated by them.

Leila watched her, her mouth stretched and still over Roland's stiff cock. His flat stomach moved erratically above her forehead, reflecting how stimulated he was. There was power in this moment as well. While not objecting to it, if Leila had her druthers Marguerite suspected she would prefer not to have Marguerite bringing her to orgasm. Marguerite respected her and what she had done for Tyler. But this moment wasn't about civility. Tyler was hers now.

She'd selected a vibrating plug as well as a standard vibrator from Tyler's well-stocked toy room. Even then she'd been very conscious of the way he watched her. As she'd picked up the different ones, run her fingers along the smooth flared heads to gauge the width of the base she wanted and chosen an oil lubricant that had an exotic scent like sex, his attention had been as tactile as his caresses.

Leila's eyes shifted as she set both aside. Marguerite reached forward, laid one hand on the small of Roland's back, the upper curve of his muscular buttock. "How are you, Roland?"

"Ready to serve you, Mistress." His voice was hoarse.

"She sucked your cock well for me, didn't she?"

"Christ, yes. Mistress," he added hastily.

Laying her hand on Leila's breast, she cupped it, rubbed the nipple, her gaze going to its fullness, its perfection. "I'm going to make her come. You won't come, though. That will be your gift to me, when I allow it. You will listen to her come, feel her hot breath panting against the head of your cock, feel the back of her throat tremble against you when she lets go, the scrape of her teeth as she fights not to bite down and you will wait. Wait until I'm ready for you to explode at my command."

"Yes, Mistress," he groaned.

"Good." Leila's body was lifting to her touch, her back curving as Marguerite skillfully pinched the nipple, squeezed the hard tip. At the same time, her fingers curled around Roland's left buttock, nails tickling the fine hairs in the crease. Watching the muscles ripple along his back, bunched and restrained, trying not to upset the flower arrangement, was as much of a pleasure as seeing Leila's hips press down and then lift up, an involuntary plea to be touched between her legs.

"God, but you do have beautiful tits." Marguerite used the crude male word, her voice sensual and soft. "I remember one night when Tyler made you slip off the straps of your top and sit bare-breasted in the booth next to him, allowing all the Masters and Mistresses walking by the opportunity to enjoy looking at them. He made you cup them in your hands, play with the nipples until you were arched back in the booth, gasping. At long last he put his hand beneath the table and just a moment later you came. Moaning, unable to stop your cries, orgasm and embarrassment both coloring your fair skin. You'd been apprehensive about submitting to a Master's desire to exhibit you publicly for His pleasure, and he was quite ruthlessly helping you get past that fear. Helping you discover the heightened pleasure of having others watch you submit to him.

"I won't ask you if you want me to touch your pussy, Leila." She dug her nails into the plump curve, just a little, to heighten sensation. "Because I want to do so and this isn't about your choice. It is mine and Master Joseph's. He wants to see a woman's hand on his slave's cunt, bringing her gushing forth."

Leila's throat worked on a swallow of desperate arousal. Roland made a noise of equal need at the involuntary pressure. Walking her fingers down Leila's stomach, Marguerite caressed her navel piercing, tugged on it and earned another writhing of pleasure from the woman. When she moved down to stroke her mound, she parted two fingers so they bypassed the clit and followed the labia, played around the opening, catching in the piercing there as Leila's legs jerked.

Joseph extended his long legs and planted his feet inside of her knees, his dress shoes nudging, pushing her open even wider, holding her as Marguerite worked the wetness, dipped there, drew through it, using her nails on the sensitive outer edges here as well. Another strangled sound of desire caught her attention and she deliberately stilled her touch to watch, teasing Leila.

Violet was stroking Mac's cock with stronger intent, forefinger and thumb tight on him, moving up and down the velvety rock-hard shaft as the powerful upper body strained, arched. He obviously could have reduced the lounger to matchsticks, but it was his Mistress's bonds that held him. His jaw was held tight, his eyes riveted on Marguerite and Leila, as Violet commanded.

"Don't take your eyes from them, Mackenzie. Feel my soaked pussy against your stomach, know you'll come in front of them all to earn the right to fuck it."

And then there was Tyler. Marguerite turned her head for just a moment and found he was now leaned forward on his lounger, a foot on either side of the footrest, his fingers loosely dangled between his knees. The sunglasses hid his eyes, but his very posture suggested she had his full attention. At her regard, he removed the glasses, let her see the warm gold color that coated her in his heat, reminding her of that night he had referenced earlier, when the heat of his come had coated her back, his pleasure her only garment. "Make her come for me, angel," he murmured. "Make her come for all of us."

Her own cunt tightened like a fist around a hard shudder of response. It was the first command he'd given her, Master to Mistress. Despite his stated intention not to command her as Mistress, he was pure Master, after all. The shudder was so strong her knees trembled and she had to take one to the ground. He saw it all, his eyes coursing down, lingering on her breasts and her ass in a way that made no attempt to disguise his pure lust for her. To take her, to have her. Everything in his expression made it clear that no matter what began the evening's entertainment or what happened during, it would end with him buried to the hilt in her. She could imagine him thrusting into her in his big bed, her body pushed deep into the mattress, sinking beneath his while everything inside her rose up to meet him, give him her response, her screams. She'd never been a screamer until she met Tyler. Never made more than a gasp of sound when she had an orgasm. He pulled it all from deep within her, let her speak her pleasure and pain where always before it had been expressed in frustrated silence. As he had brought forth her cries of pleasure, so she offered Leila's to him now.

Looking back down, she moved her touch directly over Leila's clit, snugged her knuckles down on either side of it and began to manipulate it in slow motions, working the piercing even as she allowed her thumb to continue to play in the opening, rub the lips. Leila's mouth had opened wide, her body surging up, which put Roland's cock deeper into her, her breaths coming more harshly. Marguerite could see her tongue flicking against the underside of his cock, not intentionally or with any rhythm, just as a function of her gasping breaths. Marguerite lifted her other hand from Roland's ass, picked up the anal plug and switched hands on Leila to deftly insert the thick plug into her soaked pussy. Leila bucked, moaning. Now Joseph let out a low growl of appreciation. Marguerite flicked her attention over him briefly to see him nicely prominent against his slacks. She was sure Leila would be on her knees sucking that cock before the night was over. He'd build her up again in no time, then lay her over the bed and fuck her from behind while she bit down on the bedcovers, crying out her need. The glitter of his eyes, the way his eyes lingered on her movements, told Marguerite he was the kind of Dominant that enjoyed it most that way. That sense of total control, the helpless pleasure of his sub being on her knees or taken from behind, completely at his mercy. She felt the sexual Latino energy pouring off him and imagined him crooning to her in his native language. Urging her to suck him with her mouth, draw him deeper into her pussy, take all of him as Marguerite had taken Tyler in the kitchen on her knees. Holding on to his thighs, savoring every drop of him, wishing he could be buried in all of her empty spaces at once.

She thrust in and out as Leila's muscles clamped on the plug, stroking it. Marguerite slid it from her on a downward stroke, replaced it smoothly with two of her fingers. Plunged deep into her, deeper than the plug could go, watching her angle so her nails would not cause the woman any discomfort. There was a delicate art to it, one that took practice, particularly with an aroused body. Leila gasped in pleasurable shock at the invasion. Marguerite ruthlessly brought her thumb back into play on her clit. "You're going to come for me, Leila," she said low, an inexorable demand. "Make these men's cocks so hard, all of them thinking about fucking you, using you, making you come again and again."

Roland was twitching, unable to stop his movements against Leila since she could not stop the inadvertent stimulation of her mouth on him. Taking the now well-lubricated plug, Marguerite pushed it against his ass.

It sunk into him, into an ass conditioned to take a Mistress's Will. There were many advantages to a seasoned slave. Not that she didn't intend to break in a virgin sub eventually, for Tyler had opened her eyes to the potential pleasure. In fact, he'd made her wonder since then what it would have been like to have been Brendan's first.

However, she had a deep appreciation for the Mistress who trained a sub so well for the pleasure of her successors. Or Master, she thought, thinking of the great pleasure the woman beneath her hand was offering to them all, a result of Tyler's tutelage. Leila's insides were slick and hot and Marguerite liked the feel of the pussy lips, the hardness of her mound pushing insistently against her knuckles.

"Oh, Jesus..." Roland's guttural growl, indicating that he was near breaking, was music to her as she felt Leila's pussy rippling, rippling... "Mistress—"

"Now, both of you." Marguerite's voice was strong and sure, commanding. "Come for us. Roland, pour yourself into Leila's mouth. And you." She rubbed the clit in circles, fast now, ruthless. "Let me feel that sweet pussy clamp down on a woman's fingers. Come, both of you."

Roland's hips lifted and dropped, lifted and dropped, shoving Leila's head back into the pillow, the vibrating plug working its magic in his ass, his movements so forceful his testicles flailed against Leila's chin, the upper part of her neck. Her back bowed up, the weight of her breasts quivering forward as her mouth opened wider, taking him deep as a scream erupted around him, vibrated on him the way her pussy was violently vibrating against Marguerite's touch, the fingers deep within her.

Another sound of release joined theirs and Marguerite divided her attention to see Violet cover Mac with a hand towel as his cock pulsed, his powerful body bowed up, the muscles in his thighs knotting as she whispered the command.

"Come for me, Mackenzie."

His eyes had become almost glassy in the effort to keep his gaze on Leila, Marguerite and Roland as she'd commanded. Their visual stimulation obviously had intensified the impending climax, but now in willful disobedience, he shifted his gaze to his Mistress, his eyes on the line of her back, bared in the bikini she wore so that his gaze coursed over her spine, the nape of her neck, her swept-up hair. The chair lifted, thudded back against the concrete in a rhythm that bucked Violet against him as if she were riding a bronc. Her thighs tightening accordingly, attuned completely to the big male animal beneath her, his strength and savagery all hers to command.

As Leila slowly came down, shuddering, Marguerite withdrew her fingers, cupped her palm over the quivering clit and mound, making Leila writhe with the sealing in of the aftershocks under her Master's avid gaze. Roland's head was down, his sides shuddering like a horse after a long run. The plug still vibrated in his ass, making him jerk periodically in short convulsions.

In the corner, Violet turned her body in a lithe movement to face her husband and discover his eyes on her. Her lips twisting in a smile, she leaned forward and kissed him, biting his lips in reproof at his disobedience. Her hands went up to his bound ones, lacing her fingers with his. Her lips moved, whispering to him as his large body trembled. Catching her bottom lip in a flash of teeth, he tried to shove his cock up against her, but she laughed, though the laugh was more like breathlessness. Slapping his organ playfully, she rose off him, giving his bound body a thorough appraisal. "You lie right there and get that cock hard for me again," she purred. "Let Mistress Marguerite look at you. She's invited me to a cup of tea."

Joseph rose, his dark eyes like coal fire, skin drawn taut over his expressive features. "*Jesu Christo, Maria Madre.*" He laid a hand over his heart, nodding to Marguerite. "I am overwhelmed and honored to have witnessed such expertise."

As Marguerite politely withdrew, Joseph bent and guided Leila's hands onto his shoulders to pull her with fierce tenderness from beneath Roland. Holding her naked body against him, he filled his hands with her generous bottom. "Come, *querida*. You'll be fucked by my cock now. On your hands and knees by the water, while I watch the sunset." He caught her chin, pulled her face out of his neck. "Thank Mistress Marguerite for the pleasure of serving her."

Leila flushed. Marguerite waited until Leila raised her head, brilliant green eyes meeting hers. There was a wealth of meaning in the air between them in that moment. Not bad or hostile, simply full of the mystery of their world of bondage and submission and the complex relationships it created. "My thanks, Mistress, for the great privilege of serving you."

"The privilege was mine and I thank your kind Master. You serve him well." She watched Joseph leave them, stopping at the door to lift Leila in his arms to carry her.

"Marguerite." It was Tyler who spoke, whose voice commanded a warm shiver down her spine.

Marguerite turned and saw him extend a hand to her. Every movement toward him felt heavy, sensual. The swing of her hips, the sway of her breasts were all stroked by his gaze, making her react by swinging out her hips further. She drew back her shoulders so her breasts were even more prominently displayed, wanting the pleasure and desire in his gaze stoked to raging by her deliberate provocation.

Take me if you dare, it said, and she knew it. She couldn't divide the Mistress from the sub with him. She didn't know if she needed to, or even wanted to do so.

When she got to him, he caught her hand by the wrist, the one that had brought Leila to climax. Putting those fingers to his lips, he began to lick them. One by one, drawing each finger in, he sucked on her, taking Leila's scent off her hand while she stood aching and wanting his mouth all over her.

When he was done, he kissed the back of her hand. "You please me very much, angel."

"I want to please you even more, Master." She said it softly, without thinking of the words. From the flare in his eyes, she realized it was the first time she'd spoken it before others. When she would have drawn away, he held her fast, held her gaze with his own, steadying her.

"Then go have your tea with Mistress Violet. And I'll be pleased just to be near you, for now." The look he gave her had all sorts of images coming to mind. As if he knew it his gaze caressed her body again, moving over her jewel-encrusted bosom, the nipples hard and erect, her navel, the low cut of the tight pants, their firm fit at her crotch. "I should have put you in the kind that lace up the back, so I could see the lovely crease of your ass, imagine driving into it deep and hot later tonight." His attention lifted. "But perhaps I'll just rip that seam down the middle, take care of it myself."

"I'm yours to command," she whispered, lost in the visual. Just lost, adrift as only he could make her feel, now that he'd somehow managed to open a fortress she thought she'd reinforced past invasion.

With the thought, the uncertainty came in, the worries. How real could this be, happening so quickly, so powerfully? Then she remembered his head against her breast at the pond as she drew his pain into her. The desire between them was powerful, but it was powerful because it rested on something else, something against which she feared the lust was merely a shadow.

Violet had taken a seat on the wicker sofa, her knees pressing against Roland's side, her arm along the back of the sofa in a deceptively casual position which allowed her to keep her peripheral vision on her husband. But it was obvious that her main focus at this moment was Marguerite.

Despite the rapport of the past few moments, Marguerite knew things were far from friendly between her and the other Mistress. Tyler's love had apparently won Violet's forgiveness, but not her trust. Marguerite didn't blame her. She didn't trust herself either. But it was time to clear the air with the person she knew Tyler considered his best friend.

"Mistress, with your permission..." Roland interrupted her thoughts. "I need to be excused for a few moments. The call of nature and all."

Marguerite nodded, removed the plug and helped steady him to his knees, though male pride kicked in and he made it the rest of the way to his feet despite a stifled groan as she closed her hand on his cock. It moved eagerly beneath her touch, telling her he would be ready for whatever she had in mind next in little time.

"You may take fifteen minutes. Drink a glass of water to re-hydrate. Come back soon. I want my tea."

A tremor ran through his body and he dared a glance at her. The expression in his eyes was somewhat dazed and she felt that familiar tightening in her body, a Mistress's recognition that she had successfully swept the rug from beneath his reality, taken complete command of him in a way he had not expected. She passed her fingertip just along the edge of his lashes, a whimsical, ticklish touch, and he swept them down.

"Yes, Mistress." He inclined his head. "Thank you, Mistress. It's...it's a pleasure to serve you."

"You're a pleasure, Roland. Hurry back."

When he nodded, she watched the virile body as he strode toward the end of the poolhouse, exercising the haste that respect for her command required. He disappeared through a door she assumed held a bathroom. Knowing Tyler, probably communal showers and a hot tub as well. The thought conjured some interesting scenarios that heated her blood further.

Sarah appeared at the entrance to the pool house, tea tray in hand as if Tyler had a way of telepathically summoning her. Again, Marguerite wouldn't put it past him. He rose and met her at the door, took the tray so she did not have to come all the way in. Marguerite noted the way Sarah studiously kept her eyes only on Tyler's face, though when she turned, her gaze inadvertently swept over Mac. She tripped on the threshold. Tyler steadied her, murmured his thanks.

Marguerite's amusement gave way to surprise when Sarah postponed her retreat until she'd found Marguerite and inclined her head, a courteous acknowledgement that might have been offered the lady of the house. Marguerite nodded in return, somewhat amazed and warmed. The woman smiled, retreated up the walkway to the house.

Tyler brought the tea tray over to the two women and gave Marguerite a wink. "She's tough to impress. I think she might decide to keep you and throw me out."

"Probably a wise decision on her part," Violet observed dryly, but Marguerite noted her eyes were thoughtful at the exchange. She herself felt absurdly bolstered by Sarah's vote of confidence.

As Tyler settled the tea tray on the side table next to Violet, Marguerite reached out, touched his arm. "I'd like to ask you to give us some privacy for a bit. I want time with Mistress Violet."

Violet looked surprised that Marguerite herself had initiated the confrontation, but she quickly recovered. "A good idea. Go play over there." Violet nodded across the pool, to a grouping of lounge chairs. "Read one of your tedious industry magazines. Marguerite and I want time for girl talk without your busy nose in the middle of it."

Tyler raised a brow. "Last time I checked, this was my home."

"Last time I checked, I could probably kick your ass."

He snorted, straightened as Violet regarded him with dancing eyes, but there was a firm determination to her mouth that made his eyes narrow in return.

"Do you promise to play nice?"

"Tyler, there's nothing here I can't handle." Marguerite interjected it before she could respond. She locked gazes with Violet in direct challenge. Violet dipped her head, a grudging smile tugging at her lips.

Tyler at length nodded, passed a caressing knuckle over Marguerite's cheek. He did in fact circle to the other side of the pool, but once he was there, he apparently decided he preferred a more active use of his time than Violet had suggested. Stripping off his shirts and slacks, he revealed that he wore a pair of thin swimming shorts underneath them. The movements of his body lithe and male, he dove cleanly in the pool to begin a series of laps.

Violet cleared her throat. Marguerite pulled her gaze back to her, saw a flash of humor in the woman's eyes. "Men shouldn't be that beautiful, should they?" She tilted her head toward her husband, not looking directly at him, but from the gleam in the Caribbean blue eyes, Marguerite was certain Violet had perfected the art of perusing him at her leisure while driving him mad with the feigned indifference. An indifference she was sure Mac knew was illusion, driving up the sexual tension between them. His attention was riveted on her every movement. Even as his head rested back on the lounger, his fingers gripped the straps holding him with tension. Marguerite noted his cock was rising again, noted that Violet had not completely cleaned him. Apparently she preferred to leave the stain of his semen dampening the trimmed thatch of dark pubic hair beneath the stiffening shaft, the thin point of dark hair running down his hard lower abdomen.

She was right. Men should not be that beautiful. Marguerite forced herself not to look back at the pool, at the sight of Tyler completing a turn, his lean body swift and powerful, the water gleaming on the length of his arms and breadth of shoulders as he stroked across it. She took a seat in a chair, crossed one leg over the other, folded her hands in her lap as if she were in her tearoom. "We have our privacy. Cut to the chase, Mistress Violet. Say what you've been wanting to say since the night at The Zone."

Violet sized her up with that measuring gaze, a cop's eyes. "All right then, I will. You know how his wife died."

With those few words, she'd effectively narrowed the room to just the two of them. Violet kept her voice low, obviously not intending Tyler to catch a snippet of the conversation, which Marguerite was certain would have ended it abruptly.

"I do. She should have been there for him, as much as he was there for her."

Violet inclined her head. "Amen to that. I know it, you know it, but guys like Tyler and Mac, they don't believe in therapy sessions and psychoses. They come from this medieval age bullshit that says if they aren't a hundred percent together for their women, they aren't men. So if I hadn't known him as well as I do, I'd have said he went to Europe to prove something, not because he loved her and truly wanted her back. But he *did* love her."

She paused. "He was going to surprise her. He bought a ticket to her performance, but was too late to get the good seat he wanted. He hoped to let her see him, let her know he was there."

Marguerite's hands tightened together as she realized what she was hearing was firsthand, what Violet had learned from Tyler himself and now interpreted with the love and outrage of a close friend. She leaned forward so Violet would not have to raise her voice further, wanting to hear all of it.

"He bought her flowers, planned to go to her hotel that night. He walked in about ten minutes after they found her. That, like nothing else, nearly killed him." Violet's eyes were vibrant. "Because he genuinely believes if she had seen him there that night, known he was there, she wouldn't have done it. And the bitch of it is, he's probably right. She couldn't handle being without him, but she also couldn't handle being with him when he had to break down and be fucking human."

"And you think I'm like her?"

"No." Violet surprised her with the immediate answer. "You're like Tyler. Whatever happened to you, you pulled it together on your own, kept on going. That's a point in your favor and why I'm telling you this. When he came back from Europe, he stopped writing, producing, stopped going to The Zone. Got drunk a lot. I was the officer who arrested him after he went looking for a bar fight and fortunately was too blind drunk to kill anyone." A grim smile touched her lips. "It's funny how friendships get started. But then he pulled it together one more time. I don't know how often a person can do that before he's got nothing left."

You'd be surprised, Marguerite thought.

"He loves you, Marguerite. With all of him. It's so plain that it hurts me to see it, to worry that it might not be enough for you, because he has so much to give."

Marguerite held Violet's penetrating gaze. "I never wanted to hurt him. I've tried to say no in every way I could."

"He doesn't know the word no." Violet sighed, considered Marguerite. "You're not who I would have chosen for him."

"I know that. I wouldn't have chosen myself for him, either. I know a relationship with me is likely to bring any man irreparable harm." She turned toward the teapot, intending to use the ritual she knew to cover the misery that Violet's words provoked in her own heart, disquieting her mind. It made the jewels chafe, made her feel suddenly like she was playing dress up in someone else's clothes.

Violet's hand touched hers. "You love him, too."

Marguerite raised her lashes to find the woman looking at her, not with distrust and dislike as she expected, but compassion. Even kindness. She tried to find an answer, failed. The emotions filled her chest, making it hard to breathe.

Violet blew out a breath. "Don't answer such an obvious question. Despite the worries of my husband and Tyler, I do know when to stop being a hard-assed bitch." Her gaze shifted to her husband who was watching them closely, as if he knew what being discussed. This time she met his gaze directly, let him know she was looking at him. Marguerite saw something soft come into those vivid blue eyes. "There's nothing irreparable when it comes to love. If you want him, you love him and he loves you, you don't have any choice. You fix it, you figure it out or it kills you." She shot Marguerite a sideways glance. "And here comes our very tasty table."

Violet withdrew her hand as Roland returned to them. Marguerite had to recover quickly from the flood of reaction that the sincerity in Violet's eyes had caused in her. As she bade Roland return to his position as their table, she had no idea where Violet would go from this point, only that she was intrigued to find out. And Violet did not disappoint her.

"Let's get down to the really important things. How do you get your hair to stay that smooth and silky in Florida's humidity?"

Tyler pulled himself from the water, toweled off and took a seat in the chair where he'd left his clothes. Though he couldn't hear what they were saying except for the occasional word out of context, he'd followed the gradual transfer from serious discussion to girl chatter. It intrigued him to watch Marguerite ease her toe into that end of the pool, the way her eyes widened in surprise when Violet gestured her forward so she could fix a section of the jeweled top that had gotten twisted. Then she touched a lock of Marguerite's hair, let it flow through her fingers as she obviously complimented it.

He also watched with amusement, sympathy and admiration as the women managed to integrate their idle chatter with highly effective torture of poor Roland.

Violet moved to the chair opposite Marguerite. With a quiet command, Marguerite bade Roland prop his chin on that chair, putting his nose and mouth no more than an inch or so from Violet's pussy, readily outlined and visible in her Brazilian bikini bottoms. Marguerite idly played with the plug, caressing Roland with her fingertips as they discussed things any women might discuss over tea. Though they took pains to appear indifferent to the two men they were teasing, Marguerite knew both of them were aware of every shift from Mac, every rasping breath from Roland. And she was hyperaware of Tyler, of his regard. Of the desire she could feel emanating from him.

With occasional sweeps of her lashes, the posture of her body, the upward curve of her breasts with the pink nipples framed by the jewelry, she conveyed the body language of a woman who was stimulated though she was not being physically touched in any way. And through all of those things, she wanted to let him know it was his regard that was causing it.

Marguerite had played so little with others, staying one-on-one for so long, she was amazed at how enjoyable this was, the many different dynamics to arouse them all. So her next question surprised herself as much as her tea companion.

"May I touch your piercing?"

At Violet's smile and nod, Marguerite reached forward to touch the woman's recent navel adornment. Conveniently, she had to lean forward so her knee insinuated itself between Roland's thighs, pressing on his testicles. She brushed her fingertips over the tiny pair of handcuffs dangling from Violet's navel, taunting Roland as much as the position taunted her husband, who looked as if he was going to erupt from the lounge chair any second.

"It hurt like hell for the first few moments," Violet offered. "But it's worth it. God, all Mac has to do is touch it and I practically go off. It doesn't make sense, really, because my navel wasn't the least bit sensitive before then. Leila says it does the same thing to the clit and nipples. This is good. What did you say it was?"

"Ti Kwan Yin, tea of the iron goddess of mercy."

Violet's eyes gleamed, appreciating the subtlety, and shifted her legs, producing a frustrated noise from Roland.

Marguerite noted that her sub kept swallowing, suggesting that he was having a difficult time keeping the saliva from pooling in his mouth, but she knew he would not disobey either Mistress, even to steal a single kiss against Violet's skin. Not only because he would risk punishment from one of them, but he might lose a limb to the territorial ire of a husband who outweighed him by fifty pounds at least.

Marguerite knew it all to be purely teasing on Violet's part, however. She did soft play with other male subs to rouse her husband's unexpectedly strong alpha nature, or as part and parcel of the intimate atmosphere of The Zone, but male subs did not touch her except in the most restrained of ways. They definitely did not engage in serious play with her. The smell of her pussy was as close as Roland was going to get to it, but of course that was more than enough from Mac's perspective, if the tense line of his body in the lounger and the narrowed, intent focus of his silver gaze was any indication.

Marguerite poured another cup for herself and set the

pot back down on the small of Roland's back, just above the curve of his buttocks. It was a small teapot, easy to take with her on overnight visits and she was fond of it, the rounded base and sturdy balance perfectly appropriate for her needs at this moment. She put it down directly on Roland's skin this time rather than the tea cozy, for it was hot enough to be uncomfortable, but not dangerous. She ratcheted up the vibration level of the plug, noting his cock was stiff as steel with his nose inches away from Violet's crotch and her own hands stroking his flanks. Scraping him occasionally with her nails, she fondled his testicles, ran a nail down to the base of his cock or rocked the plug as the mood took her. Compounded with the psychological impact of using him so functionally, she suspected he was on the knife edge of climax. Ready for the release of pain. "Would you like another cup?"

When Violet nodded, Marguerite placed the cup in the small of Roland's back. "Stay very still, Roland, no matter what. Mistress Violet will be very displeased if you spill her tea."

"Yes, Mistress." Roland's voice was hoarse. The head of his cock glistened with pre-come. Marguerite noted that Violet's body was obviously being well aroused by the heat of his breath stroking her, which in turn was likely making him insane with the scent of her desire. The woman's hand feathered up her belly, playing with that piercing and then went farther, her fingertips whispering up to her breast, over the nipple that had peaked beneath the brief bikini top as she watched Marguerite pour. Mac made a noise that could only be called a growl as his tiny Mistress leaned forward to take the cup from Marguerite, which pressed Roland's face into her thighs, his nose practically buried in her cunt.

"You're torturing him," Marguerite observed. "He's enormous now."

"Mmm." Violet swept her lashes down. "He's amazing that way. And I'm afraid I'm too easily overwhelmed by it." A smile crept onto her face. "Sometimes I think falling in love makes you lose an edge as a Mistress. Other times I think it makes it easier to stay on that edge, to have the confidence to explore it more deeply than you would otherwise. It makes you even more adventurous."

Marguerite was fighting against her amusement and Violet suddenly picked up on it.

"You were talking about Roland, weren't you?"

"Yes, I was." Marguerite sighed. "Roland, I suppose you'll just have to make do with my attentions. Mistress Violet is a bit distracted. Though I think—" she raised her voice, her eyes meeting Violet's in perfect accord, "that you've done an admirable job of making her pussy wet, just with your warm breath. Perhaps she'd pay more attention to you if you blew on her a bit to cool her down."

She ran her bare toes along the back of his muscular arm, braced out next to the leg of Violet's chair.

"You're a troublemaker." Violet's laughter was a little breathless, ratcheting up as Roland apparently followed Marguerite's direction. "Both of you."

When he shifted his head, Marguerite caught a glint in Roland's eyes. She allowed him a tiny smile of approval. Since she had his attention, she lifted the pot and very precisely poured a teaspoonful of it onto his skin, watched the steam curl up. Roland quivered hard, but did not move.

"Again, Mistress," he begged, his voice muffled against Violet's skin.

She obliged him, in several places, until he was panting with the exertion of staying so still, his cock leaking its need onto the pillow. Violet was making short, taunting rubs against his mouth, a mouth not allowed to move against her without a command from his Mistress for the evening.

"Violet." Tyler called to them across the pool. Marguerite could tell he was trying to keep the humor out of his voice and sound reproving. "That chair Mac is going to turn into kindling in about twelve seconds is imported from Egypt. It probably constitutes three months of his laughable salary, which I will not hesitate to take out on your cute ass if he breaks it."

Violet cast a look of feline satisfaction at her husband, then gave Marguerite a genuine smile, a steady look.

"Thank you for the tea, Mistress," she said formally.

"Perhaps you'd like to try the furniture at my home some time." Her eyes danced and she sent Tyler a wink, then bent and placed a light kiss between Roland's shoulder blades. She gave him a light swat as he returned the favor, a stolen kiss across her crotch as she rose. "Now Mistress Marguerite will have to punish you for that, Roland."

"Yes, Mistress. I'll take it gladly." There was a smile in Roland's voice as well as desire. Marguerite was amazed to discover that a D/s session could be about fun as well as intense release. Though from the size of Roland's erection, she thought it might be about time to reward Roland with the latter. For the moment though, she let his arousal build watching the scenario playing out before them.

Violet sauntered toward Mac. As she did, Marguerite saw the playfulness shed off her shoulders like a cloak, her walk becoming almost predatory, a woman on the hunt for sex, her expression becoming one of hunger. The game she'd been playing was ready to close into something that was not a game at all.

Marguerite had to catch her breath herself at the sight of the furious man. Of Mac's body, all the impressive musculature drawn up in tense readiness, every smooth, powerful curve defined as he resisted the desire to shatter the bindings which were psychological only. He was not resisting the raging need to be with his Mistress, however. His silver eyes were focused only on Violet as she met that intimidating gaze with one of her own, one that challenged him, that told Marguerite clearly that Violet had been aware of every degree of frustration she'd been causing her husband.

"I can smell you from here, sugar," he said, his voice a low rumble. "You value his life, you better come here."

Violet was wearing stilettos with her brief bikini and she used the combination to good effect now, swinging her hips, untying the top as she came toward him, dropping it without self-consciousness in front of her audience. It dropped to the concrete, exposed her small perfect breasts to her husband's avid gaze. In a graceful move she straddled his face, clamping her hand down on his throat to hold his head as she slowly, slowly lowered her hips until her crotch was right over his mouth. "Can you eat me out better than that young stud over there, Mackenzie?"

"He should take notes."

Violet smiled then, a softer expression. Resigned humor entered Mac's gaze as well, tempered with a mutual heat and energy that made Marguerite feel they were no longer aware of anyone else. "You're making me fucking crazy, Mistress."

"Can you serve your Mistress so she desires no others?"

"I'll do my best." There was a raw quality to his voice now. Violet's touch on his neck eased, became a caress.

"Make me come with your mouth. You know I love that."

Marguerite found herself riveted by them, the slide of Violet's body over that strong jaw, his body still stretched out and bound as he served her, made her body sinuously dance upon him. She threw her head back, the auburn curls tumbling, her hands rising to caress her breasts before his gaze. She moaned at the first touch of his lips, a sound of coming home as much as it was of sexual pleasure. Roland's body quivered and Marguerite had a sudden urge, an urge so strong she couldn't deny the image in her head. She wondered if she could trust as Violet had suggested she could trust, to explore the many things that love could be, ways it could be expressed.

She removed the teacup and pot, set them aside. "Roll to your back, Roland." He obeyed, adjusting himself on his back on the row of cushions. His green eyes were sparkling jade with anticipation for what he obviously hoped she was about to demand of him. When he moistened his lips, she was riveted by that soft, clever mouth. Bending, she reached under him and made sure the plug was turned back up to its highest setting, made more potent since the pool deck floor beneath his pillow pressed it deep and steady into him now. His eyes widened and his body quivered, his cock jumping in response.

"Not until you make me come," she told him. "Only then."

"Yes, Mistress. Oh...Jesus..." Roland strangled on a moan as her fingers caressed his cock before she straightened.

Marguerite rose, as aware of Tyler's attention as Violet had been of Mac's. As such, she took her time, teasing both the man across the pool and the man at her feet as she loosened the lacings on either side of the pants, easing their hold on her sufficiently. Picking up a large navy blue towel, she brought the pants even lower on her hips, knotted the towel around her waist and slid the garment off her legs with only a brief glimpse of her upper thighs, the crease of thigh and hip, curve of buttock. She moved the knotted side of the towel to her hip, keeping that side bare so her flank was exposed, but nothing else was. Then she stepped deliberately over Roland's face and sank down onto the young man's eagerly waiting mouth, as Violet had done with Mac. She kept her eyes on Tyler as she did so, even as the sub's clever lips and tongue immediately went to skillful work on her beneath the dark concealment of the terrycloth, making her rock, reach behind her to brace herself on his flat abdomen for balance. Because of the towel, her sinuous, seductive dance of pleasure did not reveal what was being done beneath the skirt, the way her cunt was shoving against his mouth, surging sensitive skin against the rasp of his jaw, spreading her moisture over his lips, chin, cheeks. But her upper body shuddered at the sounds of his pleasure, at the hardness of his cock when she manacled it with her fingers, held tightly onto it, letting him feel the power in her grip, the command she still held of the situation.

But when she looked into Tyler's eyes she was lost in the pleasure of performing for him, a pleasure that had heightened her tea during the past hour, just as Violet's teasing of Mac had heightened it for her.

Whereas Violet had been teasing her slave, Marguerite had been teasing her Master, feeling his eyes on her throughout. His increasing heat as she brought Roland and Leila to climax together, talked to Violet, stroked Roland to fever pitch. She was rocking, so close, but even as she reached that pinnacle, she knew she wouldn't go over. She'd never been able to do it this way, always hitting that wall, the slammed door, only able to push through it with the destructive restraint of a scarf and belt on her throat.

But she had another way now, the consent of her Master. That reassurance that his restraint was upon her, ironically giving her the safety, the freedom, to take that leap. She looked toward him, the realization in her eyes, communicating her desperate need to him.

"Come for me, angel." He understood, was ready with the harsh command, his face alive with a hunger as if he had ordered her to sit on Roland's mouth himself. Her body exploded, her body arching back, quivering against Roland, the tissues throbbing with the orgasm as she cried out, driven higher by his order, by his eyes upon her, by Violet's mating cries as Mac brought her to the same pinnacle.

Roland gasped against her vibrating pussy. "Mistress, please..."

"Let go, Roland. Let us hear you."

His strong body bucked under her, moist mouth opening wide on a groan of release that vibrated against her, increasing the aftershocks as his come jetted out of him like a fountain, bathing her hand gripping him, her wrist and forearm above in liquid heat.

When she flicked her gaze briefly across the pool, she saw Violet had moved back, impaled herself on Mac's cock, lowering herself inch by inch onto it. She began to move, riding it, his great body surging up into hers as she milked him, drew him out with her whispered demand.

"Fuck me, Mackenzie. Fuck me hard, baby."

It made Marguerite's own pussy contract again to hear the words, to have it match so closely her own need, even so close on the heels of the orgasm she had just had. She wanted, needed...

She gave Roland a full measure of satisfaction from her hand, taking him down slowly, sitting back to ease the plug from him, turn it off. Then she bent down, brushed her lips over his jaw, tasting the mark of her scent. "Thank you," she murmured.

He gave her a lethargic smile, managed to turn his head and press his lips to her hand. "My pleasure, Mistress."

She rose, felt his eyes follow her as she dropped the

towel and walked down the steps into the pool, moving through the water, across it to her Master.

Tyler still sat in his chair, watching her approach. She wanted his firm lips on her, the hard cock she could see under his wet shorts deep inside her, his body all around her, holding her, caring for her, bringing her pleasure.

He rose as she stroked across. Unfastening those shorts, he kicked them off so when she reached the pool's edge he met her naked. Taking her hands, he lifted her out in one powerful motion that took her breath from her. He kissed both her hands, then kissed her mouth, gathering her in close, his hands wandering down her back, caressing her ass in front of the others. Turning her so her back was to him, he took a seat in his chair again, guiding her hips down, down, so she sat in the chair on him, facing outward. His cock slowly slid into her tight wetness while she shuddered, rocked upon him, made a keening sound she could not control.

When she was fully seated on him, he put a hand over her throat, brought her back with his hand there and the other flat on her belly, snugging her hips deep into the crook of his. As he held her head back so she was staring at the sky through the solar panels in the ceiling, she felt every eye on her exposed body, especially at his next whispered command.

"Spread your thighs wide, angel. Let them see how beautiful you are, my cock deep inside of your cunt."

Never would she have believed in this moment. That she would be held in a man's arms who made her feel safe, loved. Who was the release valve for the sexual pressure that built so high inside her when she Mastered a sub, a valve she couldn't release herself. That she would take warm pleasure the way a submissive did in being displayed by her Master, knowing she was his, all his.

And when she did spread her knees, his fingers were there, playing with her stretched lips, her clit, pinching and stroking as he moved inside her. Tiny but wondrously effective movements stimulating her, his strong thighs moving her in a position she could do little to nothing to control. And always that hand a firm collar on her throat, her breasts bouncing hard as the strength of his movement increased. His intent was clear. A rough quick fuck to spill his seed in her, to show her how the past hour had teased him to raging for her. It was what she wanted. The proof of his possession, his desire to be Master of her as a Mistress and watch her do what she did so well, took such pleasure in. To know emotionally and physically he would control the release it built in her.

He took her up, up...and then he took his fingers to other territory. Her breasts, the delicate skin under her arms, playing in the shallow indentation of her navel. She wondered what it would be like to be pierced there like Violet. She gasped his name as he prolonged the torture, returning to her clit and pussy enough to keep her on the precipice, but drawing back each time she was close. Her breasts and nipples began to tingle painfully at the jolting, pleasure-pain that wanted his mouth, his touch. But he withheld it, teasing, rousing, bringing her almost there, retreating. She wanted to feel him come inside her, needed it.

"Watch them," he said, directing her glazed gaze to Violet and Mac. They were being roused anew by watching the two of them, such that Violet was kissing her husband, riding him again, his hands now free, hard on her hips, driving the pace this time.

Tyler's words were ragged, indicating his control might be as frayed as hers. She squeezed down on him, turned her head against his grip to speak, her breath hot and wet against his neck.

"Master, please. Please come inside of me."

With a groan, his control broke, telling her he'd been waiting for that gift, the gift of submission only she could offer his soul. When the hot streams of seed brought her to orgasm, she cried out, rising up even as his hands tightened, holding her steady on his cock as their bodies pounded together.

Moving like they were meant to be so fused, now and forever, she knew the complex give and take of dominance and submission between them no longer needed explanation or apology. The answer could be no clearer than it was in a moment such as this.

Chapter Fourteen

After the intensity of the earlier part of the evening, the rest of the night was quite mellow, social. Clothes were changed or donned as appropriate, and the seven of them reconnected to eat an elegant dinner, play card games in a screened gazebo by a manmade lake, drink wine and watch the moonlight play on the water. They discussed life and politics, and the philosophy of BDSM, as people of similar interests would who enjoyed one another's company.

At length, it was time for Roland to head for home. Marguerite walked him to the door, allowed him to bid her an affectionate farewell, his lips brushing either cheek. There was a slight hesitation as he hovered over her lips, giving her the choice. She drew back, softening the refusal of that privilege with a warm look, a press of his hands. He gave her a rueful smile, a wink and retreated down the steps, lifting his hand in a parting goodbye.

She sensed the goodness in him, but also sensed he was still at that age he wasn't ready to find one woman. He was having too much fun in the sampling. And that made her smile inside, reminding her of Chloe's joy for life. She found herself wishing him a good life and a good love, a permanent woman to claim him when he was ready for it.

As she came back into the house, Mac was heading to his and Violet's guestroom. He was wearing a pair of jeans now that the tone of the evening had changed, though his Mistress hadn't been inclined to allow him a shirt. Marguerite certainly didn't object. However, he still nodded his head respectfully, murmuring "Mistress" as he went by her.

Marguerite watched him go up the stairs, the broad back marked by lash scars, the jagged bullet scar that had nearly ended his life.

"Mac?"

She realized at that moment she'd never directly addressed Mac Nighthorse, such that his name almost sounded odd on her tongue.

He stopped, turned. "Yes, Mistress?"

The tone of his voice distracted her, as she realized it was more gentle, softer than when he spoke to a man. Thinking about their conversations tonight at dinner, when he spoke to Leila versus Roland, or Tyler versus herself, she realized he'd done it consistently. And now that she thought about it, so did Tyler.

She crossed her arms over the banister, considered him with a frown. "Earlier tonight, Violet suggested that men like you and Tyler don't see a woman as capable of taking care of herself."

He smiled, apparently not the least offended. "Maybe we don't believe a woman's ability to take care of herself should relieve a man of the responsibility of looking after her."

She opened her mouth, shut it as his grin deepened. "Was that what you were intending to ask me, Mistress?"

"No. You distracted me. Your tone of voice," she amended quickly at the twinkle in those silver eyes. "I'm sorry. I don't think it's a question I have a right to ask. I'm not even sure why I want to know."

"Mistress Marguerite, you can ask me anything."

"Do your scars still bother you?"

He cocked his head, came down a couple steps. "Not the ones on the outside. The ones on the inside, sometimes. But I've figured out if you can't heal them, you need someone to help you accept them."

"Is that what Violet is to you?"

"She's everything to me," he said simply. "Without her, there isn't a me. Not a me I'd want to live with, anyway."

"And that loss of identity doesn't worry you?"

Now his smile got broader. "It's not a loss of identity, Mistress. It's called finding yourself."

When his gaze shifted, Marguerite turned to discover Violet standing at the opposite end of the foyer.

Marguerite could think of no other word than reverent to describe how Mac looked at his Mistress. Not in the sense of overlooking her flaws, but of seeing everything in her he could ever need for emotional fulfillment. "When I'm with her," he said quietly, "I see who I really am, the mirror of my soul."

"Mac and I are going for a walk on the grounds." Violet pulled her gaze with obvious reluctance from her husband. "So I know Tyler would appreciate your company. Leila and Joseph have already gone to bed. He's back at the pool house."

"I'll head that way." Marguerite nodded to them both, left them with that energy pulsing between them. She wondered what it would be like to feel like that on a daily basis, to be inside one another so deeply that there were no doubts, even when you were at one another's throats.

She took the long way, wandering through the living area, disturbed by Mac's words. No, disturbed was not the right word, but she didn't know what was. She just knew she had an unexpected desire to simply lie down here on Tyler's sofa, become part of his furniture, of his daily life, and never leave again.

He rose the moment she came into the pool house. When she got close, he reached out and she automatically put her hand in his to let him lead her outside behind the pool area. There was a sloping lawn here and she could see Mac and Violet as hand-in-hand silhouettes walking along the pathway by the small manmade pond, a dotting of solar lights guiding them. The water glittered in the moonlight.

Tyler could tell her thoughts were bothering her, so he coaxed her to lie down with him on the soft grass in front of the bench. It was an earthy, sweet-smelling mattress, almost as sweet as the woman who lowered herself to the ground with easy elegance. He raised one foot up to remove his loafer, then the other, then curled his bare toes into the sod.

"If there are better moments than this, I don't know what they are." He looked up at the starry sky, listening to

215

the music he'd turned on inside the pool house, a classical piece. "This is my favorite time of day, when it starts getting dark and everyone around becomes a silhouette. We're like the stars, aware of the other celestial bodies but undisturbed by them, surrounded by our own quiet world of darkness."

"You're composing again. And you're right. The spirit is in space, not matter." The smile in her voice came to him, as perfect as the music. He kept his eyes closed, letting it wash over him as he reached out and found her hand.

"Tell me what that means."

"It means the power isn't in the matter. It's not the people or the music that give this moment its special quality. It's the space between them where everything important is, where it appears nothing resides. It defines the people, the music. If you meditate on that space, you find whatever it is that you call God. Do you have a faith? You never told me."

"I believe in this." He tightened his grip. "More than that, it gets too complicated. I don't think it's supposed to be complicated."

"You remind me of David."

It was a quiet statement, a bare murmur of sound. Tyler waited several heartbeats, not wanting to push. "How so?"

"When I needed to do it, I could go into his head, surround myself with his thoughts like a protective blanket." She tilted her head, closed her eyes and he increased the pressure of his hand on hers, letting her know he was there. Quiet. Listening.

"I'd be on the bed...with my father. I'd thread my hands through the slats of the headboard and press my fingertips to the wall. I knew David was there, lying on his side of the wall, his palms pressed right where my fingertips were. So I wasn't alone. And though I could still feel the pain, hear what my father was saying to me, part of me was inside David. I told him that, a lot of times. I think it helped him to know it. He was a good person. Would have been a good man." She turned her head, met his gaze with those blue eyes that were like looking into the vast expanse of the sky. "I like to think he's an angel. Not the fluffy way people talk about, but one of the spirits who go out and guard the innocent, intervene on their behalf. Helping them survive the long cold hours of the deadliest time of night, when you're sure pain is all you're ever going to know. When I lost him it was like my heart stopped beating, but I could still breathe."

"Marguerite..."

She moved to her hip, rested her fingers on his face. "He was like you," she repeated. "You've been ankle-deep in it like David, unable to protect, and now you're determined that the person you love will be protected in every way. I guess I understand that when you push so hard. You know the difference between force driven by love and force driven by hate and evil. But can you rescue a damsel after the dragon's already eaten her, spit out the bones?" She considered it, her hair rippling over her shoulder. "Do you pity me? Knowing what you know now, would you have treated me any differently?"

"Yes and yes." He needed to touch more of her suddenly, intensely. He sat up, putting his back against the bench seat and pulled her over onto his lap, held her in the cradle of his arms. She settled in with surprisingly little resistance, twining her arms around his neck, pressing her face to it. "Even knowing you wouldn't want me to do either. But I love you, Marguerite. That encompasses everything. Pity, respect, a whole oceanful of admiration. Desire. I couldn't have pushed certain things so hard if I had known about your life before but I would still have tried to make you surrender to me. Because to me that's about trust, not violence, and I think you deserve someone in your life you can trust. Though I admit the passion I have for you is so strong that sometimes it's close to violence."

"I like the fact you never lie to me," she said after a moment. "And I wanted what you did that weekend. What you've done to me since. It's hard to admit I understand a submissive's mind so well now from their side of it. You didn't give me the option of maintaining shields. And for the first time that I can remember..." Her voice lowered to a whisper against his skin. "I feel loved. And I don't know if

I'm strong enough for that."

"I'll be strong enough for both of us, angel," he promised.

Rolling her head back on his shoulder, she gazed at him, a tiny smile at the corner of her mouth. "Arrogant man." She parted her lips when he touched his fingers to them. Bit him. He smiled, though his body was rousing at the lazy heat in her expression. But when she tilted her head back to look at the stars and became quiet again, he let her be at peace, content just to hold her.

Tyler's gaze drifted down the lawn to where Mac and Violet were. The two of them were just defined shadows. When they stopped and turned to face each other, something about their posture suggested the conversation had gotten more serious. Violet's gestures were even a bit nervous. Mac was still, as if he'd become a statue. Then he reached out, his fingers touching her face, slow, almost reverent. While Tyler watched, he went to one knee, framed her hips with his large hands, leaned in and pressed a kiss in the center of her stomach, bowing his head.

"Is she... Did she just..."

He glanced down, saw Marguerite was watching them, too.

A moment later, they heard the wind bring a snippet of the conversation. Violet's quick joyous laughter, tinged with a sob. Mac rose, taking her hands, leaning down to meet her mouth in a sweet, chaste kiss. A kiss that became less chaste very quickly.

"Yes," Tyler said. "I think so."

Marguerite rose, leaving the warmth of Tyler's lap to watch the couple. They resumed walking, only now they were like one person, Mac's arm around her shoulders, both of Violet's arms around him as they moved through the night. Together. Now not just a safeguard for each other, but for the life they'd created.

When Tyler's arms slid around her from behind, she pushed away, but of course he caught her hand, pulled her back, this time holding her so she couldn't get away. "Let me go," she said.

"Do you always want to live with this death grip on the past? It doesn't define who you are."

"Hypocrite," she said, bitterness burning her lungs. "When you see blood instead of wet earth between my toes, do you think it didn't define who you are now?"

He threaded his hands through her hair, which he'd taken down with his fingers when they sat with the others having after-dinner drinks. Teasing, flirting, gentle romance that seemed diametrically opposite to this moment of pain.

"You can honor what your past has made you without enshrining it, worshipping at its feet, dedicating yourself to it for life like a monastic taking vows to serve a cruel god. What do you want, Marguerite?"

He asked it in a voice that sounded to her as relentless as time and power. Not the power of man, but the power of the wind, the sun's heat, the determination of flowers to push up through the earth every year and prove that beauty could rise from the rich earth of the grave. The power of water, cycling through tide after tide, like the power rising in her now. For dinner she'd changed into a strapless top that hugged her hips and a soft gauze skirt that floated around her calves. His hands moved to her shoulders, her neck, his warm strength touching her bare skin.

"What do *you* want?" She tossed it back at him. "Children, I'm sure. I can't give you those. I can't give you anything, be anything remotely close to normal for you."

"What do you want, Marguerite?" He tipped her chin up.

"Don't touch me. I don't want to be touched right now."

That was no more true than for a figurine of porcelain, too thin to be handled. She did want to be touched, she was just deeply terrified, deep in a part of her that knew only fear, that his touch would break her into pieces, an explosion of shards small and thin as confetti, lost to the wind as if she'd never been.

"Tell me what you want." His mouth whispered it, those lips close to hers. Her own parted, letting out a breath that was a near sob.

"I want to be whole. Feel it just once more." She raised

her palms before her face. "I remember lying there with David beneath me, feeling his heart stop beating. I tried to cup his head in my hands and it was wet...so soft. Softer than a baby's skull.

"And there were these people around. Staring at us. But I felt so alone, because David was gone. His heart was no longer my heart, his voice in my head was gone. And they didn't know me, didn't know us. And I wondered, 'Will anyone ever share my soul again? Get inside me and know my thoughts?' No. Surely not. And yet, I didn't die. That's the most intolerable cruelty, that you can realize that truth and not die. It seems a revelation like that should simply pluck your soul right out of you, cast it into the earth. And I think it did. I *am* a vampire. Sitting in the shadows, sucking in everyone else's light and life to feed my own, but it's false, because there's only darkness within me."

When Tyler took her hands from her face, he was alarmed to feel her cold skin had gotten even colder.

"I don't believe that. Sshhh..." He soothed her, touching his lips to the juncture of her neck with her shoulder.

His hair brushed her jawline and she tilted her head despite the scream of resistance in her head. Easing one arm around her back, he brought her a step closer. Turned her to face him. "Let me in," he said softly. "And I'll light a candle."

He didn't threaten a roaring blaze, as if he knew a being that had lived in darkness as long as her soul would be agonized by bright light. She raised her hands to touch his back, closed her fingers into handfuls of his shirt.

Keeping his eyes on hers the whole time, Tyler leaned in and pressed his mouth over hers. Over her bottom lip only. A brush of that fullness, tasting the flavor of a moist lip gloss, finding the source of the scent of raspberry he'd occasionally caught when she spoke tonight at dinner.

He moved his kiss to the upper lip, nibbled there, nuzzled her cheek with his nose.

Sliding both arms around her shoulders, he wrapped them across her back so she was folded in toward him, her elbows bending to maintain her grip on his back. He took her into a deeper kiss, one where both of her soft lips were covered by his mouth. Caressed her tongue with his own. When she made a curious noise, somewhere beyond a whimper into the realm of a sigh, he kept exploring her mouth with his own, cognizant that her body was rigid against his, but he realized it wasn't conscious resistance. She had a death grip on his shirt. She was simply, totally petrified, rendered to catatonia by something as simple as a kiss.

Following instincts that had been honed from nearly twenty years of enjoying, mentoring and training submissives and Dominants alike, awakening them to their natures and how to accept and exercise their desires to bring them and their partners pleasure, Tyler increased the power of the kiss, the demand level to it. Gave her heat.

"Do whatever you want, dear heart," he murmured. "But I won't go away. I'm all yours. I'll be your Master, if you surrender to me."

He didn't know if the compulsion was intuition or the poor judgment of a man too much in love to exercise good timing or sense but he shifted one hand from her, dipped in his pocket to retrieve the object he'd been carrying most of the night and drew her left hand from around his waist.

Marguerite's eyes flitted down and shock captured her features as he slid a ring over her finger, fitting it snugly past the knuckle. "And I'll be your husband. I'll do my best to keep you whole. To catch you when you fall. You're the only woman I want. And I knew it the first time I saw you."

The ring was a platinum band with a marquise diamond framed by metal work. There were Japanese characters etched in the band on either side of the gem. They looked like elegant decorative scroll, if the person wearing the ring hadn't known what the characters meant.

"Trust. Faith." She murmured the words.

"On the inside of the band right beneath the diamond is one more. Love."

Simple concepts and the most precious in life. Marguerite closed her fingers over the metal.

"You've lost your mind."

"I'll say. Do you know there's at least three ways to write Japanese and some words have ten different characters, depending on how you mean to say them?"

"No, that's not what I... Tyler, I can't..."

"You can think about it. That's all I want you to do for now, angel. Wear it and think about it." He brought her around the bench, turned her so she was watching Mac and Violet again. "Put your hands on the bench. Obey me."

She did, her emotions scrambled. Her already stimulated body was suddenly more so as it became obvious what he was intending to do. He did it without ceremony. Caressing her cunt beneath the skirt to confirm she was wet, he unfastened his jeans and eased his thick cock into her, filling that aching void that was threatening to close in on her mind, as if he knew exactly what she needed at this moment. The ring pressed into her skin as she gripped the top of the bench. Her eyes clung to the band the same way, to the promise of it, as immediate and verifiable as the man's body covering her now, driving into her.

"Tyler..." she gasped his name, her fingers clutching the bench edge as he pushed down the strapless top, freeing her breasts to grip them in his hands, kneading as he stroked her inside.

"Watch Mac and Violet," he ordered in a firm tone that had a ragged edge, betraying his own desire at this moment. "And believe in fairy tales. In happy ever afters. In the fact that I will never stop loving you, no matter how often you pull away. No matter how many times you get lost in the shadows, I'll find you. Because you're my light and salvation, angel. I have to have you to have light in *my* life."

He put his teeth to her shoulder then, his cock working her, bending her further over the bench. When he took command of her pussy with his fingers on her clit, he shoved her over the edge of the climax, leaving her writhing and crying out. The two figures stilled on the opposite end of the small pond and she knew they were listening to her pleasure, her pain, her fear, her fulfillment. It seemed all the different reactions were inseparable.

"Tyler, I can't..."

"Come for me, angel. That's all you have to do right

now. Come for me."

Chapter Fifteen

But demons preyed on happiness, she knew that. She lay in her bed and heard him coming, knew that it was one more night to get through. She'd stopped wondering how long it would last. Just like an abused dog, she simply had to endure this moment and then there would be a void of nothingness. Nothingness was good, undemanding.

"Time for your punishment."

After he raped her, he turned her over. This hurt even more than the other way, but she'd learned not to resist. She smelled the cigarette, felt his organ penetrate her backside, heard his guttural command to her to stay still as he pressed the tip of the cigarette to her skin. Her flesh burned, but she didn't move. She'd learned never to move.

"This is all there is. All there will ever be. This is your hell and mine."

She hoped it would not be one of those odd nights when he turned her over, held her and cried. Called her "Mother" while her insides burned with agonizing pain and blood stained her thighs, her small buttocks.

When she fell from great heights the sky became white feathers. There was the sense of tearing as well as floating, as if there were two parts of her, her soul fighting to get loose of her body.

It's because the soul is weightless, little sister. David's voice seemed to whisper to her in her dreams. *You just have to let go...*

Only the voice wasn't David's. It was her father's. His hands bruised, took, demanded, invaded.

She jerked out of the dream, her body tense, motionless,

afraid to move. Blinking several times, Marguerite told herself it was a dream, that the nightmare was no longer a reality. She used a simple one-syllable Kundalini chant to balance herself, the one she usually did to make the lie a workable rationalization so she could get up and face the day. But her reality had changed. The bed she was in was Tyler's. There was a rose on the pillow next to her, a note from him to come join them for breakfast. When she reached for the note, she saw the ring on her finger. She looked at it for a while, her gaze shifting between it and his bold script on the note. As she touched the stem of the rose his fingers had touched, it occurred to her she was using the things he had left for her in the same way she had used the chant.

At length she rose, washed, put on her slacks and blouse, fixed her hair. It was when she was packing her bag she realized she had made a decision to leave. Suddenly needed to leave desperately. Shouldering her overnight bag, she walked down to the main floor to the foyer and heard them in the kitchen area. Mac and Violet. Joseph and Leila. Tyler. Talking, laughing, the relaxed atmosphere that friends could enjoy. That she'd enjoyed last night. Why couldn't she hold on to it? Why did the darkness always come?

Because you're always running from it. The answer is to stop running, to simply let the darkness have you. She shuddered at the insidious whisper which always sounded so simple, so truthful.

Hands coming at her out of the dark.

She yelped, spun, striking out at the touch. When everything came back into focus, Tyler had her hand, his brow furrowed in concern, his stance non-threatening and reassuring.

"Angel? Where are you going?"

"Home. I have to go home."

"Come have some breakfast." His eyes got that firm look, the determined set of his mouth that said he understood what was going on with her and he would help bring her out of it.

Only it wouldn't matter. It always came back.

"Marguerite." He took her other hand, caressed her palms with his fingers. "It's all right." His gaze took in the shadows under her eyes and he cursed himself for leaving her alone. "You had a bad dream. It was just a dream."

"No." She shook her head. "It's a warning."

"Stay here and talk to me."

"No." She snapped it, yanked her hands away. "I have to go home."

"Marguerite, I'm not going to let you—"

"You can't make me do anything, Tyler Winterman. Not marry you, not stay with you. Give me some room to make my own goddamned decisions."

She spun on her heel, left the house and tried to ignore the absurd twist of pain in her heart when he didn't reach out, use that greater strength and arrogant male chauvinism of his to haul her back, make her stay. It didn't make any sense to say one thing and want another so much.

When she got in her car and turned it to leave the driveway, he was on the porch, watching her. There was pain in his expression and anger, but something else, too. Something she chose not to acknowledge. She hit the gas and fled.

§

It mesmerized her. She didn't want it to, but it did.

All the way home the light of the sun caught the diamond, made it sparkle, distracting her so a motorist had to honk to get her moving at one of the intersections. Damn him, why was he rushing her? Why couldn't he just let it be for a while?

I will never stop loving you. She was at loose ends, uncertain of what to do or be and he'd picked up on it, given her the anchor. Forever. For better or worse.

Well, he'd seen some of her worst. Particularly a few minutes ago. She'd hurt him she knew, but he didn't let go. And she hadn't given back the ring. Her lips curved wryly and she almost laughed in the quiet solitude of her car. *That* had been the emotion in his eyes, damn him.

Satisfaction. She'd ranted, stalled, lashed out. But she'd kept it. And she hadn't said no.

Pulling into the alley by her house, she got out and locked the car. She was going to do something very unlike herself. She was going to go show the ring to Chloe and ask her what she thought of it, listen to her giggle and squeal. Gen was picking up a tea shipment in Miami, so when she got back she'd have another opportunity to go through it again. She liked the idea. They would talk about Tyler, Chloe making suggestive comments that would warm her insides because Marguerite knew the comments to be true and then some. The hold of the dream loosened further. She had the fleeting thought that maybe Tyler was right. If she'd just given herself some time the dream would have faded, and she could have enjoyed breakfast with them.

"Rich, handsome, great in bed and he loves me." She said it out loud. Wasn't that the fairy tale? Well, maybe they left out the "good in bed" part in the children's version, but it was implied for adult ears to hear.

It was at the side door she remembered. Understood what had driven her from Tyler's house. Understood why she had known when she fled that she was right and he was wrong.

She wasn't allowed fairy tales or fantasies. She wasn't allowed anything good, anything that attracted excessive amounts of happiness, because it attracted the attention of darkness.

She remembered because the pane of glass in the door had been broken out and the door was not fully closed.

Chloe. Chloe was in Tea Leaves. Knowing she should call the police, knowing all the things she was not supposed to do, she went in because Chloe was inside.

The kitchen had been destroyed. Every dish was on the floor broken. Cakes and cookies had been tossed on top of them and smashed with clear boot prints. She came quietly around the corner of her office, every part of her going still, watchful, pushing out everything that did not have to do with protecting Chloe. The instincts she'd kept honed for over twenty years, though time might have laid a veneer of false peace over them, came thrusting to the surface.

Her desk had been turned over. From the aroma, someone had urinated on it and perhaps done something more among her papers. Squatted, took his time and defecated on her life. Her stomach muscles were tight, her throat thick. She would not allow herself to think, hypothesize, speculate. There was only now, the moment of hell come to claim her and she had to do what was necessary. Her bat was not behind her door. She bent and picked up two shards of a broken cup that had wicked points, closed one in each hand where they wouldn't be readily seen and eased into the main dining area.

A similar scenario. Tables and chairs overturned. One had been used to smash her wall display. Crockery from her XiYing original lay in pieces. Her eyes rested on the doll, the ceramic set that had been stomped into tiny pieces next to it. The doll's face had been gouged out with a bloody screwdriver that was still in it, the porcelain shattered, twisted and stained with that blood.

He'd spent extra time on it. Knowing. The cold sickness in her stomach increased.

Her gaze covered the area. Found Chloe, her body stretched out on her side, blood on her face and a wet fist-sized circle of it staining her cotton shirt, the one that had a gold and black depiction of Buddha against a field of pale green. Her arm and right leg were bent back in a way that suggested they'd both been broken.

Marguerite quelled the immediate urge to run to her side, continuing her examination of the room. Above the entry door a message had been smeared in what appeared to be blood. Chloe's blood.

Let's finish it.

Not at any moment had she considered the invader was a disgruntled drug dealer she'd driven from her park or someone seeking drug money, though the neighborhood had enough of both elements. She'd always known if anyone came for her, it would be him.

But the message told her he wasn't here. Spell broken, she lunged to Chloe's side, knelt and felt for her pulse. Felt like weeping at the faint flutter and when Chloe's eyes opened. Her lips parted and Marguerite saw more blood, two teeth broken, dislodged. Took in all the bruises on her arms and at her throat.

"Oh, Chloe." She stroked back the girl's hair, pulling out her cell phone to hit 911. "Why did you fight him? You should have run, damn it. Yes, 400 Carolton Avenue. I've got an employee who's been attacked and needs emergency medical attention. Yes, yes." She answered the few questions, clicked off as Chloe fumbled for her hand.

Thank God Gen had gone to Miami to get the shipment. Marguerite had no illusions that the two women here together would have made things better. Neither woman would have anticipated the insidious evil coming at them. They would have fought that much harder and likely both been dead. Chloe had lost so much blood, her mischievous face so pale, so strained as she tried to speak.

"Sshhh...Chloe. Please just rest. The ambulance is coming."

Chloe made a noise of protest, so insistent that Marguerite felt the dread creep up in her shoulder blades. She bent down as Chloe pulled, so the girl could force out a whisper.

"Tina...Natalie. Asked if Natalie could help me while she...ran an errand."

Ice gripped every part of Marguerite, rising up in her, taking over. It stopped all human functions, giving her only cold clarity. Focus.

"He has Natalie."

She looked at the message over the door. Nodded. Looked back down at Chloe and molded the girl's bloody fingers around the cell phone. "They're on their way, love. You just stay put." She could already hear the sirens. She had to go.

But a thought crossed her mind, making a crack in the frigid wasteland of her soul. It didn't surprise her that the only thing that could get through at this moment was Tyler. He'd been able to break through the constraints of her past time and time again, where no one else had.

She bent back down. "Chloe, can you remember something for me? It's important."

Chloe looked up at her through a haze of pain.

"Tell Tyler I loved him enough to live for him. Can you remember? It's incredibly important."

"Marguerite...don't."

She brushed a kiss over her friend's forehead. Her friend. For the first time she realized that you didn't have to believe someone was your friend for that person to be one. But she couldn't look back and didn't as she snatched up what she needed and sprinted for the car.

When she roared out of the neighborhood, she passed the ambulance. The red lights glinted briefly across her vision, washing crimson over the pale skin of her hands, tight on the wheel.

Let's finish it.

Chapter Sixteen

The damn roses sensed his mood, knew to be defensive. That was the only reason Tyler could figure he had pricked his fingers three times in less than fifteen minutes. He never wore gloves, preferring to woo his thorny ladies with careful touches. He had his ear tuned to the phone, the portable and cell within easy reach. He was no better than her assessment of herself, acting like a lovestruck teenager.

She wouldn't call tonight, he was fairly certain of it, for all that. He knew her well enough to know she needed to think. Needed space. But she had kept the ring.

Violet and Mac had left only an hour before, headed for home, Violet had been scheduled for a weekend work shift, so the sound of a motorcycle pulling up in the driveway surprised him. Mac was the only friend he knew who regularly used one. The ring of the cell phone jerked his attention away from that puzzle in a blink. Snatching up the phone, he recognized Violet's cell number, squashed his disappointment.

"Tyler, where are you? Are you still in the city?"

"Yeah." Mac, apparently having gotten his whereabouts from Sarah, came through the backyard, a grim set to his mouth. "Mac just got here. What's going on?"

"Tyler, someone broke into Tea Leaves. They beat up Chloe pretty badly. She's on the way to the hospital. Marguerite—"

Her next words came as quickly as the first, but for Tyler there was an abyss between her name and that moment, as if he was teetering on the edge, straining for that opposite side but knowing that eternal darkness yawned beneath him. He was cognizant of Mac at his shoulder, the look in his eyes. "—wasn't there when it happened. She called it in, though. Mac picked it up on the dispatch radio at home."

"All right, I'll head right over there—"

"There's more. The perp kidnapped a little girl Chloe was watching named Natalie Moorefield. Chloe's a tough kid. She wouldn't let them put her in the ambulance until she told them all she knew. Marguerite's gone after him."

"What? How the hell does she know—"

"Chloe said he wrote something over the doorway. 'Let's finish it.' Marguerite took one look at it, left Chloe her cell phone and was gone. Mac called me. I sent him to you right away but I went with a hunch and called the prison where her father was. They've released him, time served."

"But she would have—" Tyler broke off, remembering Marguerite's behavior when he'd called her from Cape Cod that day. How she'd been so standoffish and prickly, then suddenly desperate in the dim quiet of her bedroom.

He doesn't know where I am.

How many women had said that? Believed it? Died believing it.

"Bank of Florida building. I'll bet my life on it. We can be there in two minutes from my place."

It was ten miles from his house but Violet wasn't going to argue it. "I'll call it in."

Tyler broke the connection, headed into the house. Going to his office, he unlocked the gun safe, pulled on the dual shoulder holster and fitted it with his nine millimeter and his Desert Eagle. He slipped the licenses to carry the guns and extra clips into his jeans' pockets. "Don't say a fucking word to me about being a civilian."

"Wasn't going to."

Rage and fear mixed together became hard, cold resolve. "He's intending to take all three of them over. He's sick as they come, Mac. The only thing he's living for is to finish the equation. The child's just a bonus, the bait to get Marguerite there."

The two men left the house, hit the bottom step of the front porch together. "I gave her an engagement ring last night," he said.

Mac glanced at him, understanding in his expression. "Then I hope you're asking Violet to give you away, or she'll be pissed."

"Marguerite hasn't said yes yet. She actually was kind of ticked off at me about it. We have to protect her, Mac. At any cost. She doesn't deserve this."

Tyler strode out into the driveway. Mac didn't reply, knew he didn't need to. From the set of Tyler's shoulders his mind had only one track now.

Mac's VTX was parked next to Tyler's Ferrari. "I *can* make it there in two minutes on this," Mac said. "Where will they be?"

"The roof." Tyler got in the car, slammed the door, fired the engine. "And you won't beat me there." The car spun out of the driveway.

Mac had feared for the life of his woman before, knew what it was to find that icy center of control and do things that no person under ordinary circumstances would survive. So he was not at all surprised when Tyler ran through stoplights at busy intersections without pausing, ran up on the shoulder to get past a garbage truck, took turns at velocities only an experienced driver and a car with the Ferrari's engineering could successfully manage. He just hoped they wouldn't be too late. If they were...

He leaped onto the sidewalk through the next intersection and then shot back out behind Tyler's taillights, hearing the scream of brakes as motorists tried to avoid hitting them both.

...he was going to make damn sure Tyler didn't get there before him.

§

A light drizzle was falling and it was always colder on top of the building. Natalie might need her coat. Turning up the collar of her rain gear, Marguerite stepped into the foyer of the Bank of Florida building, thinking that everything around her had a surreal quality. All the colors turned up to high volume yet coated with a dull patina that made the world ugly, not vibrant.

Over the years, she had visited this building often enough that the indifferent security detail had accepted her as one of the corporate types. She'd even manufactured herself an ID that passed at a distance as one of those assigned to the major banking office housed in the building. Today her elegant London Fog rain cape worn against the outside drizzle and her determined step made her look as if she was just an employee coming in to do weekend work.

She needn't have worried. The security officer was not there and the lock on the glass door that had to be deactivated with a buzzer after hours was not engaged. She peered over the edge of the horseshoe desk. Spots of blood were on the visitor's log, marks that would have passed as ink stains to the unsuspecting mind. She hoped he was knocked out, dragged to a closet somewhere, but then she leaned farther over the counter, saw his body curled under the desk, his eyes staring. He clutched a note in stiff fingers, the print large enough to read, as if the guard had been turned into a macabre form of sign post.

Come on up.

She looked at the guard a full minute, reached down, closed his eyes. "I'm sorry," she said softly. To him. To his family. To the children whose photos were on the desk, who wouldn't have him as they grew up. For them, it would be a tragedy, a loss. For her, it would have been a gift from God.

She straightened, went to the elevator, set it to go to the top floor. If she had died that day, a guard wouldn't be dead. Natalie wouldn't be in his hands now.

Do you know how it would tear my guts out to lose you?

Tyler's voice. Rough with need and love, desire.

Some things just weren't meant to be. But she really wished it had been.

When she got to the top floor, she took the service staircase up to the roof, stepped out into the mist that had become a light rain, the clouds and gathering darkness dulling the earlier promise of a sunny morning. She was watchful, looking before she stepped out, but he came into view almost immediately, directly across from her. He stood at the roof's edge, not up on the ledge, but next to it. He had Natalie standing on it, though, his hand holding on to the collar of her shirt, the nape of her neck. Her body was trembling, cheeks wet with tears, eyes round with terror. Her hair was frizzy with the humidity, streaked with the rain.

"Miss M—"

When he yanked on her collar to keep her still, her arms flailed and latched on to his side. He shook her off. "Shut up and be still."

There were bruises on her arm where he'd handled her. She was wearing a pale pink cotton shirt and a pair of jeans on her tiny hips. Sneakers that looked no longer than half the length of Marguerite's hand. The new earrings winked at her. She took in every detail of Natalie's appearance and used it to steady herself before she turned her attention to her father.

Prison had changed him of course, but it surprised her nonetheless because he had lost so much weight and become lean, burning up with his hatred, far beyond that fateful turning point when she was fourteen. His hair had thinned. The lines of his face were as deep as wounds, the mouth thin and harsh. Evil had completely taken him so there was no way he could live among the world and normal people not see it, recognize the danger and shun him. She thought about the way she had described herself to Tyler, the teenager who could not be close to others, not only because of her own desires and problems, but because of what the others sensed about her. The evil had stamped them all, but it could end here. She wouldn't, couldn't let it take Natalie though.

"Marie."

She inclined her head. "I'm here. And I'll do what you want. Just let her go back down the stairs."

"She's special to you. I know that." Marguerite wondered if it was fanciful imagining, the red tint that seemed to glitter like blood in the once rich golden brown eyes. His voice was a chain smoker's voice, the vocal cords scalded by nicotine. "I know everything about you. You thought changing your name would do it, didn't you? You've been my only focus for twenty years, Marie. There wasn't a single moment I didn't know where you were. Did you think you could carry her face, her soul and I wouldn't come after you?"

"No. I knew you would come one day." And she realized it was true. She'd lived every day of her life holding herself back from love and friendships, knowing it. But love and friendship had been given to her anyway, offered freely. In Tyler's case, insistently. She knew that even if Natalie hadn't been involved, Chloe would have fought him because he was attacking and destroying what belonged to Marguerite. Just things. Ceramic cups, dolls, even the ring on her hand now... But those things symbolized something far more important. The only thing that mattered. Love. It was more important than survival.

Which is why she was glad she'd left her message with Chloe. That Tyler would know she hadn't intended to leave him. Hadn't wanted to, ever.

"I always knew you'd come back," she said evenly.

She walked across the roof toward him, feeling the breeze lift her hair. Thought of Tyler's fingers threading through it, loosening it. He loved her hair. Had loved making it tumble down. Natalie's eyes, the irises the color of dark chocolate, watched her approach. The child's lips quivered, the involuntary flow of terrified tears making her upper lip wet.

"Do you ever think about Mom? David?"

His fingers tightened on Natalie and she whimpered. "Don't talk about them."

"Me too. I miss them every day, Dad. It hurts to be without them. Like a burning inside that never stops."

Their eyes were locked. In that one brief moment, she sensed he was unable to look away, her words reestablishing their bond. It made her think of all the submissives whose minds she'd plumbed, tearing past the curtains to find their souls and hold them against her heart. The outpouring of emotions had been a bath for her own soul which she'd thought was forbidden the same experiences, forbidden to come out into the light and love. Like a Goddess of the Underworld, she'd pulled those souls to her. Now she kept moving across the tarred roof, all vestiges of civilization far below and prepared to take the plunge into her father's blackness.

"You..." He shook his head, breaking the contact, denying with his body language the words she'd spoken. "You always were her. You look like her, spoke like her. You were my little girl, but then you took her over, possessed her." Natalie yelped as he thrust her forward, as if he was using her as an extension of his hand, pointed in accusation at Marguerite. "So you could infect me with your poison."

Marguerite forced herself not to look at Natalie, clumsily scrambling for solid ground. His yanking had taken one foot off the ledge, unbalancing her. At least he'd pulled her toward the roof and not away from it. "You didn't matter enough to Grandma, did you, Daddy? How do you ever get over the betrayal of a parent?" Bile rose up in her. Her focus slipped as his face, the thin cruelty of his lips, the curl of his chest hair in the open collar of his shirt all seemed to expand and fill her vision. Parts of him she knew in a way no daughter should, sickening her. "How do you ever forget him coming to you in the night, raping you, teaching you how gray the line between pain and pleasure is? Knowing I had to take it night after night, or you'd hurt the only person in the world who loved me?"

She remembered the nights he'd collapsed on her body, sobbing, calling her "Mother" when the pain was so intense she hadn't been able to do more than dumbly stroke his hair with trembling fingers.

His lips drew back in a snarl. "Don't pretend to be my child. Your face. Her face...you're the same. I could see her in the things you did, said. The way you turned your head or laughed, the way you touched me. I see it even now. Had to punish her. And you stop your sniffling and squirming!" It was a hoarse scream, making Natalie's face fold into itself as if he had blasted a dragon's heat across her tender skin.

"Miss M..."

It was the wail of sheer panic that recalled Marguerite. She shoved her anger and memories out of the way and was lunging forward when he put one foot on the ledge and thrust the child out into space.

"No!"

"*Stop.*" He roared it. Whether he meant Natalie to stop crying or Marguerite to stop moving she didn't know, but he accomplished at least one, for she came to a tense halt when she saw he had his hand screwed up in the cloth of the shirt. It gathered like a tight sling under her armpits, baring her midriff. While the sight of the child dangling over thin air was enough to stop her heart, his hold told her he didn't intend to drop her. Not yet.

"Dad." She brought his attention back to her, compelling him with just the tone of her voice. She had to raise it to be heard over Natalie's cries of distress and tried to keep her heart from tearing in two from the sound. Calling on the same discipline that had made her lie still when this man pressed a cigarette into her spine while sodomizing her, she sought that stillness inside, the ability to block everything out. "It's time for it to be over. That's why you came for me, called me here, remember? It never could have ended any way other than this. But we need to go together, all three of us."

"Damn right. We'll all three go." He abruptly jerked the child back onto the ledge, taking his own foot back off to pull a bandana from his pocket. Natalie's tiny hands came up, ineffectively trying to block him. Holding her head with a brutal grip on her hair, he roughly forced the wadded cloth all the way in until her mouth was unable to close, silencing her cries. He kept his gaze on Marguerite throughout so she had to hold her ground while Natalie's eyes pleaded with her for rescue, filled with bewildered terror. The past hour of the child's life was rapidly becoming a decade of nightmares to overcome.

No. It wasn't going to happen like that. "Yes. We'll go together, like we should have that day. Mom should have waited, so we could have all gone together."

With the sun obscured by even more gray clouds, she could see the brown eyes they'd once shared. And they were thinking. When he focused on her, she drew in a painful breath. For just an instant she saw him, a glimpse of something remembered in the way he looked at her now.

"M-Marie. We have to do it. You understand, don't you? It's the only way she'll be truly dead. She won't hurt either of us anymore. She won't make me hurt you to get at her."

"Daddy," she said softly. "That's why I survived, so you wouldn't have to go alone. So we could go together."

His hand dug into Natalie's collarbone beneath the shirt and the girl's lips pressed down on the cloth, registering pain.

"You weren't with us that day, but you've been with me ever since." She took another step forward. While his grip didn't ease, he watched her, his eyes searching her face so hard she thought he might be seeking the soul he'd lost, hearing it somehow in the words she spoke to him. "Are you tired, Daddy? Are you tired of hurting?" She pulled it deep from inside herself, remembered the years of loneliness. Of wishing, time and again, that David's body had not turned at that last moment, that she'd not been left alone in the world with no one. No bulwark against the nightmares. She'd survived, built her life. And Tyler had come and given it all a purpose in a handful of days. If there was such a thing as last wishes, she hoped he would somehow know that the joy he'd given her was timeless, eternal. And if she could do it over, she would have embraced every second they were given, not fought it with such fear. She embraced every moment she'd had with him now.

"I'm tired," she admitted. "I have been for so long, until recently."

She saw the man who had lifted her on his shoulders at the fair and told her he'd ride the Ferris wheel with her, that he'd take care of her, always. In whose arms she'd fallen asleep, never thinking she'd have any reason to fear him.

Natalie coughed against the gag, strangling on the phlegm that was also coming from her nose.

"You—" The memory was gone, driven away by the fury rising in the red-tinted eyes.

"Let me help," Marguerite said quickly. "I know her crying is upsetting you. Let me make her understand, the way Mom made us understand."

He lifted Natalie to her toes and the child's eyes grew even wider, the coughing worse.

"Dad." Marguerite's tone became more firm, steady, a voice she'd used to good effect when subs started to panic. The sound of someone who was in control, who would make sure everything worked out. "Let me help."

As she held his gaze, she stepped up to the child.

"Stop there."

When Marguerite stopped just out of reach, a muffled sob made it past the cloth.

"Shut—"

"Natalie." Marguerite reached out then, caught the child's hands before her father could stop her. In the same movement she went to one knee, a non-threatening posture incapable of taking the child from his grasp. "Natalie, honey. Look at me." Glancing at her father, she carefully reached forward, removed the gag, easing it out of the small mouth, the saliva wetting her knuckles. "I'm going to help, Dad. Breathe, sweetheart. Just breathe. Deep breaths. Watch my eyes."

She held both her hands, watched the little girl try hard to follow her direction, fighting the natural flight instinct of a young defenseless creature that could easily become fatal panic.

"M-Miss M...I...I'm s-so sc-scared. I wanna go h-home."

"We're going to go home, sweetheart. I promise." She cupped her hand over the side of her head, the small ear, fingering the new piercing, drawing Natalie's attention to something other than the man at her side.

"She's not going home. We're not going home."

"Yes, we are." Marguerite looked toward him. "Don't you think so? Isn't that what this is about? Bringing an end to it? Peace to it? Let me tell her, Dad. Let me tell you both what Mom said to David and me that day. And it will all be clear. Do you want to know what Mom said? Her very last words?"

He blinked several times, his mouth forming a tight line.

His eyes glistened. "She didn't understand the evil. The danger."

"It will all be clear to her shortly. Because you'll see her and tell her. But first, I want to tell you both this."

Marguerite pulled her gaze back to Natalie, saw she had successfully acquired the attention of both of them.

"Did you know that I was once up here with my mother? And she told me and my brother something very special, something that made us not afraid of anything. Not even of being up so high, or the possibility of falling. I want to tell you what she said, but I need you to stop crying and be a very, very brave girl. Look just at me, honey. Just at me." She squeezed the girl's hands, rubbed her cold fingers, willing her to be calm. The child began to hiccup. Trying for Miss M, making Marguerite's throat hurt with burning tears. "Remember how I told you I'd always love you, no matter what? And that I'd always tell you the truth. Remember?"

She could feel her father's growing tension enveloping her and Natalie like a suffocating stench. She concentrated on locking Natalie's attention in the cool blue of her gaze, visualized drawing her into peace, tranquility.

"Would you like to know what my mother said?"

Natalie shook her head. "I want to g-go home."

"I know, sweetie." Marguerite stood up, let go of her hand and stepped onto the ledge in one motion, again arresting her father in mid-lunge as she proved to him that she was trying to move herself closer to the ledge, not take Natalie farther from it. He held on to Natalie's shirt as Marguerite turned, faced him over her head.

"Are you ready?" She gestured at the ledge on the opposite side of Natalie, inviting him to join them. The child was staring up at her, quieted to strangled sobs of breath. Marguerite did not know if it was her words that had brought the sudden stillness or if the little girl was retreating into the blissful numbness of shock. Her capacity for terror had to be long past overload despite the continuing dangerous menace of the man holding her.

A man who looked baffled, even deceptively docile as at last he put one foot up on the ledge, then the other, lifting himself up to stand across from her. Marguerite realized age and the hard life of prison had warped his bones to match his soul so that they were almost eye to eye. She was perhaps even a little taller.

His expression was uncertain, the aggressiveness broken for the moment as he sought the trick, not knowing where to look for it. Marguerite dared to glance down at Natalie for one precious moment, met the brown eyes.

"My mother said, 'Don't worry. The angels will catch us. And then we'll learn to fly with them.'"

Ripping open the neckline of the cape, she sent the garment into open space. "You didn't know everything about me, Daddy."

His gaze jerked away from the fluttering cape to her, but that second of distraction was the only one she'd counted on.

Darting down, she seized Natalie under the arms, breaking his grip. As he howled and snatched at them, she shoved off the ledge. He latched on to Marguerite's left hand and she tumbled all three of them over the edge.

§

Skydiving off most manmade structures was illegal, for valid reasons. The proximity of buildings changed the expected air patterns, made them fluky, hard to predict the right heading for the chute gear when it opened. She'd had only a couple opportunities to practice it, and both times it was off bridges, one in India, one in Malaysia. Never in close quarters with other buildings like this. And never with less than fifteen minutes in her car to repack one chute for the type of jump that typically demanded a careful half hour of gear preparation.

Her father's weight on her arm flipped Marguerite forward, ruined the twisting dive that would have set her up better.

When she practiced Atmonauti maneuvers, she focused on the number of flips and turns and calculated their speed so she could release the chute at the right moment. Jumping from a plane at ten thousand feet, she would deploy her chute around three thousand feet to handle any unexpected incidents. From the top of this building, she had eight hundred feet, which meant she needed to deploy her chute immediately. With one of her arms wrapped hard around Natalie's back, her other hand captured by the person doing his best to kill both of them, she had no hands free.

There was no wind resistance between the buildings, just dead air for the free fall drop. But then they rolled over and that quick moment threw Natalie full against her. Marguerite blessed gravity as the child wrapped her arms and legs around Marguerite's body. Not giving herself a moment to think about the fact she was relying totally on the little girl's survival instinct to hold on to her, she let go of her to release the chute.

The violent jerk upward yanked her father's weight against her. A scream tore from her as he broke two fingers of her left hand. Reaching across Natalie's back under her own arm, she pulled her rigging knife from its holster and flipped out the marlinspike with a touch of the spring. She saw a flash in her father's eye, his struggle to do something in the space of a heartbeat, but this was her element. She pulled, turning her body, praying for Natalie to hold on as she strained to reach him. She jammed the spike into his hand. Blood sprayed and she did it again. He let go of her with a feral snarl. The sudden loss of connection spun Natalie in the air as their struggle dislodged the child, but Marguerite let go of the knife, caught her forearm and yanked her back against her. Natalie regained her clutch on her with all four limbs, just as Marguerite had held on to David so many years ago.

She was too late to set them up for a good landing. The chute had twisted at the beginning, then righted itself out. That and her struggle with her father had wasted seconds they needed for Marguerite's skill to slow them down and save their lives. And the heading was taking them straight toward the opposite high-rise, a wall of glass and metal.

§

Tyler brought the car to a hundred and eighty degree stop next to Mac at the same moment Violet's husband shut down the motorcycle. Leaping out of the car, he looked up to see three figures go over the edge of the bank building, the child's thin screams reaching them like innocuous bird calls.

No, no, no. This wasn't happening. He saw the tumbling, watched Marguerite, saw...

"She's wearing her chute!" He looked around, his mind rapidly gauging their descent and bolted across the street. When he reached the storefront he found Mac beside him, already understanding. Tyler blessed the keen mind of a good cop.

This section of downtown Tampa was a ghost town on weekends, having no shopping or hotels in the immediate area. However, the nearby office building had an ice cream shop on the ground level that, when open for business, had an awning that covered the fifty-foot spread of sidewalk. Both men yanked on it, swearing against the mechanical lock. The clasps burst loose and they were backpedaling, taking it out, putting down the retractable poles, each man taking a corner to hold it steady against the impact that could quite conceivably split the fabric. But it was commercial-strength, heavy. If she could just slow them down... She had the skills, if she'd just look down and see the awning in time...

She got the chute open, yanking them back up. One figure broke away from the tangle. The sun emerged abruptly from the clouds, blinding Tyler a moment before he saw the twisted strands of the chute resolve themselves, the spread of nylon open up. They were coming down much too fast, with none of the steady control and direction he'd seen in that video. She was holding on to a frightened child and had wasted precious seconds dislodging her attacker. It was going to take a miracle to save her. Tyler started praying for one.

§

If you need me, want me, I'm there for you.

It was a ludicrous time to think of Tyler's promise, but there it was. Marguerite felt the chute start to slow their descent, but it was too late. They were going to land hard. She looked down again, trying to scope her best landing point for Natalie.

The blue and white stripes of an awning that she was sure had not been there a moment ago spread below her like a beacon. She angled her body, feeling the pull of the sheets, the air, the manner of their descent. Shutting out all else, she focused on just getting them to the ground, getting Natalie home. As the child's nervous gasping made her neck moist, she raised her legs, twisted, trying to position them as well as possible for the inevitable impact with the opposite building. Keeping tight hold of Natalie with one arm, she quickly snapped the buckles on the chute. The glass wall of the fourth-story level filled her vision. Curling her arm around Natalie's head and shoulders, she ducked her face into the child's hair.

The impact was like being thrown against the side of the SUV by the mugger, if his strength had been enhanced tenfold by steroids. She heard Natalie's scream, the thud of the glass, the chink of a crack. Felt bones break in her shoulder area, the area that had been weakened by a collarbone fracture so many years before.

But no pain, not the fires of hell itself, was going to loosen her grip on the precious bundle in her arms. Chute gone, momentum arrested, they dropped like a stone the last fifty feet into the cup of the awning. It bucked violently at the impact as they shot down it like rocks carried by the power of an avalanche. She wrapped both her arms around Natalie's back, her right hand and arm bent over the fragile skull. The wire frame jammed into her ribs, taking her breath before they went over.

Her gaze was suddenly filled with white, her parachute landing in the street, the cloud of nylon rolling over and over, bringing the first police car screaming up to the scene to an abrupt halt. Then she was falling. She closed her eyes, anticipating the pavement.

Instead, she collided with warm flesh, a sensation so startling for the sense of déjà vu, her eyes sprang open. It took her a moment to realize she was on the sidewalk with Tyler beneath her, his hard arms around her and the child, his amber eyes seeking hers. Mac had a firm grip on her legs.

They were on the ground. They'd made it. They...

Marguerite exploded off the ground, Natalie still in her arms. She staggered, fell to one knee, tried for her feet again.

"Angel, angel..." Tyler caught hold of her as she struggled.

"Where? Where is he?"

Mac stopped her forward progress, directed her attention with a nod. A bevy of police were now around the crumpled form of her father. As she looked, the officer on his knee next to the body raised his head, looked toward Mac and shook his head.

Her knees gave out but Tyler caught her, eased her to the ground. His strength was here, all around her and she pressed her face into his shoulder, inhaling him. She was beyond tears, beyond screaming, too overwhelmed to speak. As she held Natalie's shaking body, stroked her hand over her snarled hair, she felt the wetness on her legs where the child's bladder had let go and knew deep, shuddering joy at these signs of life. Natalie's mother would come and hold her through the nightmares, but they would fade in time. She wouldn't have to figure out how to do it alone. She raised her gaze to Tyler's face and realized this time she wouldn't either.

"You said you'd catch me if I fell." It was barely a whisper, but he heard it, she could tell from the emotion in his eyes. His body was shaking, his hands on her trembling.

"I didn't think I'd have to prove it quite so literally."

She drew deep breaths of him again, used her teeth on the pounding pulse in his throat. She suddenly, insanely wanted to devour him alive, to bring him into her body and never let go, always feel his strength and power, taking her over.

Saving her before the darkness could take her.

Chapter Seventeen

At length, he and Mac helped her to her feet and got her seated on the hood of his car, a necessity because Natalie refused to let Marguerite go. Tyler had to restrain the urge to physically separate them. While it was obvious that the child might be miraculously unharmed except for a couple scratches, the same could not be said for his angel. Her left hand was tucked around Natalie's waist, but two of the fingers were swelling, one at an odd angle, suggesting they were broken. Her struggle with her father had torn her shirt, allowing him to see that there was ugly bruising, blood and an alarming bump along the line of the shoulder where she'd taken the brunt of the impact against the building. They'd hit it at a speed that had managed to shatter the tempered glass and shards of it still clung to her side and back. Spots of blood clotted along her bare arm, staining her clothes. He was even more concerned about the matted area just above her left ear that had turned the blonde strands a pale crimson. She'd come down on the awning just as hard and he'd heard her involuntary grunt when she'd bounced over the metal frame. The stiff way she held herself suggested there might be rib damage involved.

He wanted to stay with her, but to keep her and Natalie from having to deal with anything else, he and Mac were drawn into the circle of cops to explain things. When the EMTs arrived, Tyler was relieved to see them immediately directed to Marguerite and her charge.

He kept his peripheral vision on them as he answered questions with brusque impatience. She made them look at

Natalie first, of course. As he listened with half an ear to
Mac and the other officers, he noted they had to examine
her in the protection of Marguerite's braced legs, because
the little girl simply wouldn't release her. She clung to
Marguerite's pants leg, standing between her knees, silent
tears running down her face while Marguerite stroked her.

"Hardly a scratch on you," the EMT confirmed, ruffling
the child's hair. "And you're sure she didn't experience any
head trauma? Not the pavement or the building?"

Marguerite shook her head. The EMT looked up. His
gaze covered the torn awning, the bent frame, shifted
upward to the shattered fourth-floor window and finally
moved all the way to the top of the Bank of Florida
building, tilting his head back to do so. "Christ, that's the
closest thing to an act of God I've seen all year, I can tell
you that. All right, then. She'll need to go to the hospital to
get a thorough looking-over, but I'm pretty sure all they're
going to find a few bruises. You're going to be okay,
honey." He gave Natalie a quick stroke as she buried her
face back into Marguerite's abdomen. As Marguerite's
arms closed around her, his gaze shifted to her. "Now
you're a different matter. Let's take a closer look at your
injuries."

She shook her head again. "I'll take care of it later.
We're waiting for her mother."

"Ma'am," he insisted. "I can see from here you've got
broken bones. The fingers," he nodded toward them, "and
most likely the clavicle—the collarbone. That blood over
your ear says you had a blow to the head, so you could have
a concussion. You just jumped off a building."

"I was there." The blue eyes fired, lips curling back in a
snarl. "I am not disoriented or confused. I said I'll take care
of it later. And I know what a fucking clavicle break is."

"Excuse me a sec," Tyler said firmly, leaving Mac with
the others to go to her side. "Angel." He drew her attention
away from the frustrated EMT. "They have to look you
over, make sure you're okay."

"Not yet. Not until it's over."

"Ma'am. Internal bleeding—"

"I said, *not until it's over*." She surged up from the

fender of the car, her expression so savage the man leaped back, startled. Natalie, holding on like a burr to her midriff, began to cry again. Marguerite bent over her and amazingly managed to lift her. When Natalie's arms and legs wrapped around her shoulders and hips, Tyler frowned at the sheen of perspiration that appeared on Marguerite's forehead. He assumed the only thing keeping her from screaming from the pain was her extraordinary discipline and residual adrenaline. Possibly the numbing effect of shock.

She sank back down to the hood holding the child and pinned the EMT with a glacial expression. "I didn't expect to live through today," she said. "You think whatever miracle saved her life is going to take mine in the next thirty minutes? I refuse medical treatment. I'll get it when I'm ready. Go. Away."

As the EMT shifted his gaze to Tyler, he put a light hand on her shoulder. When she turned her venomous look on him, he returned it with a hard, direct one of his own. "Think twice before using that tone on me," he suggested mildly.

He could have overruled her, forced her, for he could sense the fragility in her. The giddiness that she'd had when she first landed in his arms was fast slipping away. Something dangerous and dark was brewing just below the surface of those blue eyes, something unresolved, and he knew she had to be here to see whatever it was finished. So despite the roiling in his gut he allowed it, though every lover's instinct told him to simply dump her on a gurney, strap her in and send her out of harm's way.

"She'll be along to the hospital shortly," he said to the EMT. "I'll make certain of it. But leave her be for now." He laid a reassuring hand on Natalie's back, rubbing, feeling the tiny body shaking, knowing the only way they were going to separate them was with a pry bar anyway.

As if he'd reassured her with the same touch, Marguerite's tension visibly eased. The EMT gave him a short nod, not happy, but not much else he could do.

"I'll be right back," Tyler promised as Mac made an insistent gesture, calling him back to the huddle of cops.

When he reached them, a new police car arrived at the scene, lights going but siren off. Tina Moorefield exploded out of the backseat when the policewoman opened it. As her gaze darted around the crime scene, Marguerite straightened from the hood of the car, drawing her attention and just about everyone else's as only a nearly six-foot-tall blonde could, particularly one whose hands were stained with blood and who held a young child as if she weighed no more than an infant. Tina cried out and ran to them, her arms already out. Marguerite murmured to the little girl, lowered her painfully to her feet. Natalie turned, the brown eyes seeking, confused. When she found her mother, her face crumpled. She stumbled forward, choking sobs becoming wails.

"*Mommy...Mommy...Mommy...*"

Tina went to her knees when Natalie got to her, clasped the child to her almost violently, weeping. Natalie clung to her mother, wails escalating into screams. The terror that had been frozen for survival now found voice, because her mother's appearance said she was well and truly safe. She was okay.

Tyler saw Marguerite move stiffly toward them. She raised the right hand, whether to lay it on the woman or child, he didn't know. Lifting her head, Tina stared at the blood on Marguerite's fingers. Pulling Natalie's legs up around her waist, she staggered to her feet, backed away, her expression one of revulsion. She turned her back and let the policewoman guide them back to the car, away from all of this.

Leaving Marguerite standing there alone. As she'd always been. It made him want to snarl at the men asking him questions that didn't matter anymore. She was the only one that mattered. Mac's hand moved to his shoulder, the light pressure steadying him, telling him the man understood and was trying to get what needed to be done finished as quickly as possible.

When he'd caught her, Tyler had felt the warmth of her flesh against him, the beating of her heart. A shudder had racked him so that for a moment he hadn't known who was shaking worse, him or her. As he'd cradled her in his arms, with the child in hers, those blue eyes had looked up at him, humbling him by what he saw there. What he'd earned through patience and luck but would never deserve.

You said you'd catch me if I fell.

He understood that she'd always believed herself cursed, his angel. That she lived on stolen time. That she deserved nothing, even though she had clawed and scraped her way out of the dark morass of her memories by herself, a nightmare that would have made Sylvia Plath read like a Disney tale. But for a handspan of time, the few precious weeks they'd shared, he'd seen something come to life in her eyes, something that made him mad to protect her, to nurture that part of her, see it come to life permanently. Do as Natalie's mother had done, wrap himself around her and never let her from his side again, never let her experience harm.

He forced himself to focus when Mac repeated something to him. The sooner he got this out of the way, the sooner he could get her out of here. He'd get her somewhere she could receive the care she needed. He wouldn't let her be alone. Never again.

Marguerite watched Tina and Natalie leave, just shadows in the back of the police car. When the car turned onto a side street and disappeared from view, her gaze shifted. The coroner had pronounced her father dead, finished his on-scene paperwork and now they were preparing a body bag to transport him. Soon she knew she would be asked what she wanted to do with him. His only living relative.

A blackness rose up in her, foul and putrid, like rot that had festered in a wound for so long it was going to drive her mad. Maybe it already had.

She started walking toward that body. Tyler was nearby, talking to Mac. The moment she moved, both men's attention shifted to her. Since she had to move at a slow pace, they made it to her in several strides. She stopped, swaying, but when Tyler reached out she shook her head. "I'm fine. Your gun."

The syllables echoed strangely in her head, as if there were nothing else there. There was only this moment, just as all the philosophies she'd explored had taught her, the universal truths.

"What?"

"I want to borrow your gun." She managed it this time in her most polite tearoom voice. "The large one."

She couldn't form the words to explain, could only hope by the expression in her eyes she was conveying what she was after. That the unusual ability he had to understand the breadth and depth of her, places she'd been unable to go herself, would be there. Her gaze shifted to her father's body and then back to him.

"Mac." Tyler turned to the other man, who was frowning. "I think I understand what she wants. The coroner's already pronounced him dead and he's about to go to the morgue. Can you tell your men it's okay? Please?"

Mac's attention moved between them, to the dead man, back to Marguerite. She simply waited.

"You owe me for the paperwork," he muttered to Tyler. "Mountains of it. And a job if they fire me. Wait right here."

He turned, went to the other officers on scene, spoke to them. After a few moments of deliberation, of raised eyebrows and raised voices, he glanced over his shoulder, nodded.

Tyler gave her the Desert Eagle, butt first. "Do you remember how to use it?"

She nodded. She felt all their eyes on her as she turned, walked across the crime scene toward the being who had spawned her. Who had nearly destroyed her mind but not quite, thanks to good friends, the strength that she had found in herself and Tyler. Especially Tyler.

"It has a heavy kick," he reminded her. He'd stayed right with her, just a step behind, protecting her back. She closed her eyes a moment, then slowly opened them, fixed them on her father.

Impassively she observed how death had frozen the monstrous features into permanence. He'd soiled himself, a fragility even he had not been able to escape. It would have been her all those years ago if not for David's arms around her, his body beneath her to take the force of the concrete. Just as Tyler had done, he'd been there to catch her as she fell. David, Tyler and Mac. A monster of a father should have destroyed her faith in men according to any psychological textbook, but men like that had broken the theory, stole its power.

She felt Tyler's heat and presence, a comforting wall. Mac had moved to her peripheral vision. She understood he was trying not to hover, but was likely concerned about allowing a rather emotionally uncertain woman to handle a weapon.

The dark rage in her soul rose, screamed for this one last thing before she could go home. She lifted the gun from her side with her right hand, pointed it down at his body cavity. No. There was no heart there. The gun shifted and her finger squeezed the trigger.

He was right. The gun did have a kick. It put the bullet into the concrete, knocking a chunk loose, spraying rock. She almost lost her grip on the butt. Tyler grabbed her, spun her away to shield her as Mac backed up, cursing. The other officers moved closer, voices rising.

"Tyler, damn it..." Mac's voice, warning.

She sobbed in frustration but then Tyler was behind her, holding her, guiding her arms.

"Two-handed, baby."

She sucked in a breath as he began to guide her left arm up, pain radiating through her shoulder. Adrenaline had fled and now there was only pain. Tyler stopped, gently pressed her arm back down.

"I want to do it. His face. I want his face gone."

"Okay." His voice was soothing. Putting his right arm along the outside of hers, his chest against her shoulder blades, he covered her fingers on the butt. As she stared down the barrel, his left hand came into her vision, settling over the tips of her fingers and overlapping his own. She was holding the gun still, but his hands curled over her one in a two-handed grip that had become three-handed.

Holding her steady, just as he had done the day on his personal shooting range. It reminded her of the peace of that day and the other things she'd shared with him. The puddle stomping and the chapel. Those memories, as much as his touch, gave her the ability to steady herself.

"Go."

She fired and the bullet punched through the corpse's eye. The next took his cheek, his mouth. She turned his face into meat, shooting again and again while smoke filled her nostrils. Fire flashed before her eyes. She became aware of a rasping, sobbing sound coming from her, an animal in a trap. This wasn't making it better. She had to stop. Couldn't stop, not until...

She was clicking an empty chamber, trembling. Mac's hand came into view, carefully dislodged Tyler's gun from her fingers, for Tyler was busy holding her, turning her into his arms while she shook so hard she knew she would have shattered without his strength. She was cold, colder than she'd ever been, the fire of pain at the center of her chest so solidly contained by ice she would never be warm.

"It will be all right," he murmured against her hair. "You don't think it will, but it's going to be. Believe me. Trust me."

"Mac," she rasped.

"Yeah, sweetheart." His large hand touched her hair. She looked up into those silver eyes. The eyes of a good strong man, thank God and Goddess and everything in between for their existence. A man soon to be a father, who would deserve the title to be spoken with love and respect. She was sure of it, so much so that she knew what lay behind her could never have been called by the same title.

"What do they do with unclaimed bodies? Like homeless people?"

"Crematorium, I think."

"Tell the morgue...burn him. Let him burn forever."

Chapter Eighteen

Those were the last words she spoke. At first Tyler didn't realize anything was wrong. He took her to the hospital, had her checked out. The clavicle break was set, her upper body put in a figure eight brace, the left arm in a sling to limit the pain that mobility would create for the next few weeks. Her two broken fingers were bandaged and taped together. As she sat on the examining table waiting on doctors and nurses, she shook. He asked for blankets, wrapped her up, held her. At length, she laid her head on his shoulder and let oblivion take her, a result of the sedative the doctor gave her for the pain, he was sure. But when he roused her to go home, her eyes were blank. That distant look he knew had somehow expanded as if she was on another continent, abandoned, remote, uncharted like the Arctic. He knew the signs of shock, knew how to handle it. So despite the uneasiness that gripped him, he took her home to the Gulf. Put her to bed. Lay curled around her through the night, listening to the shallow breathing, stroking her hair, her shoulder, murmuring to her occasionally, giving her his body warmth, willing her skin to warm, her eyes to focus.

When she woke in the middle of the night, she rose and settled in his window seat, her legs drawn up as she stared up at the sky. Following her, he sat in a chair next to the window seat, his foot propped there, toes just touching her calf. She didn't speak and eventually dropped back off, her temple pressed to the glass. He picked her up and took her back to bed.

He let her sleep late. Sarah brought them up a breakfast.

When Tyler brought the tray to the bed, he noted Marguerite lay in the same position he'd put her when he'd retrieved her from the window. On her right side, only now her eyes were open. Putting down the tray, he helped her sit up and noticed he had to move her like a doll. When he spoke to her, her eyes followed him, but he might have been a distant seabird. He was giving her painkillers to minimize the agony of the collarbone break, but he knew what he was seeing was not the effect of the drugs.

"Marguerite, let's get you something to eat, all right? You need to eat."

And to his relief she did, but only when he put the spoon to her lips and applied pressure. She ate a few mouthfuls, took a drink of the juice as long as he was holding the cup. Several moments later she turned her face away. Turned away, period, curling back into the covers. Folding into herself, she drew her knees up so she was an outer shell, protecting the inner core.

He went to the intercom. "Sarah, will you come here a moment?"

The woman responded quickly, meeting him outside the bedroom door. "I'm going to call Komal Gupta. Can you sit with her? I don't want to leave her alone."

"Certainly." Sarah put a reassuring hand on his arm. "And Robert's gone to get our things. We'll stay in the guesthouse as long as you need us." When he started to object, she tightened her hold on him. "You're going to need to sleep and eat, shower, keep yourself up for her. We're here for both of you."

He nodded, reached out on impulse to hug her. Instantly Tyler realized it as a mistake, because it was the first time he'd allowed himself a gesture of comfort. All of a sudden it was back, the sight of her against the sky, leaping, the child in her arms, the few seconds when it could have all been over. Only a lifetime of training to think in the worst situations had compelled him to act.

Everything had stopped, had gotten quiet. That centering, that place of focus where he knew exactly where and who he needed to be at that precise second, had kicked in. Coordination, training and the total commitment of the mind to one thing came together for that all important life-and-death moment.

Now he was holding tight to Sarah and she was stroking his back, murmuring to him. He realized a good couple of minutes had passed. He eased back, embarrassed, but she reached up and cupped his face, her fingers touching the haggard lines.

Sarah thought he might have aged a decade since she saw him last. In his eyes she saw what was worrying him as clearly as if he'd shouted it. What was compelling him to call the counselor.

Not again. Not another one I've failed.

Tyler squeezed her hand. "Please keep her safe for me, Sarah. I'll be right back." He walked two steps down the stairs, turned back, his knuckles white on the rail, the harshness of his voice catching her attention. "If she stirs at all, Sarah, I don't care, to go to the bathroom, whatever, don't let her out of your sight. And call me immediately."

"Mr. Winterman, she wouldn't—"

He shook his head. "Nina's last performance, when I intended to go to her, there was a look in her eyes. And I knew it then, in my gut. It wasn't my fault, I know that, Sarah, but I know she did it because I couldn't be what she needed. Didn't matter if no one could or should have been asked to be so much, that's the simple fact of it. I can't lose Marguerite. And she's got that same look in her eyes right now. So be as dramatic as you need to be to get me back in the room if she gets off that bed."

He turned, continuing down the stairs, not able to bear the tears that sprang to Sarah's eyes.

He dialed Komal's number, explained the situation when the woman answered, was grateful when she said she'd leave now. He had the presence of mind to offer to send a cab for her, but was told she would drive her own vehicle because she could get to him faster.

He went back to Marguerite. When he relieved Sarah of her duty, he lay down on the bed, curled around Marguerite's cold body and put his arm over her, twining his fingers in her hands, clasped up against her chest. He rested his head just above hers, felt the signs of life and closed his eyes. *I don't deserve her, but she deserves to know there's more to life than this. Please bring her back to me and I'll never take her for granted. I'll make every day about loving her, pleasing her, being with her...* The ache was unbearable and he had to cut the prayer short. He pressed his lips to her ear. "Come back to your Master. He's going to fall apart without you in his life. Don't leave me, angel."

He tucked himself more closely around her, tried to give her his heat and everything she needed to crave life, hunger for it again. Though he despairingly wondered if it would not be "again", but for the very first time, if he succeeded at all.

§

Sarah's hand on his shoulder told him when Komal had arrived. Rising, he kissed Marguerite's temple and straightened his clothing. His hand lingered on her still hip. She didn't move and he had to force himself to turn away, to slide out the door where the quiet woman waited in the hall.

"I don't know what to do for her. I don't know what's best. Please help us. Help her."

Komal listened as he answered her questions, then she nodded. "Why don't you go eat the meal Sarah has laid out for you and I'll join you in a while? I'll send Sarah out. I need some time to observe her, check some things, focus on what's happening."

He couldn't quite make it down the stairs. He paced, ended up at last sitting on the landing, his feet through the slats, head against the rail, half dozing. Listening to Komal's murmuring voice, he strained to hear a response from Marguerite.

Sarah brought him out of his concentration with a touch on his elbow. She sat the tray containing a sandwich, iced tea and an attractive bowl of fruit salad next to him. It all looked fresh like summertime and it hurt him to look at it. It made him imagine walking down his back steps in the morning to see Marguerite in summer white cotton, her head bent in concentration over a book, considering her tea samples. He wanted her to move in with him. He wasn't so far from her business at his Tampa home and he could renovate it, make it more like the Gulf home if she liked it better. He'd hire security to keep an eye on her park twenty-four hours a day. He simply could not countenance being without her, not having her body next to him while she slept. She'd never wake alone from nightmares, never have to go to sleep worried or without someone to talk about those worries with. He was moving far too fast, he knew. He was scaring her with how quickly he was moving into her life. But she'd kept the ring. She had. No matter what else had happened, she'd kept it.

He put his hand into his pocket, felt the smooth touch of it there. The bastard had taken it off her finger, died with it clutched in his filthy hands. Mac had retrieved it for him. He'd have it cleaned, the prongs retightened, make sure it was perfect before he put it on her finger again. He pulled it out, stared at it.

"You should put it back on her."

"He's touched it."

"So have you." Sarah put the sandwich in his other hand. "Eat." She held up her ring hand. "It becomes a part of you and you feel its absence. Keenly. She'll feel better with it on."

Tyler swallowed a bite that he was sure was as delicious as anything Sarah made, but it had no taste. "I can't right now. He broke her fingers. The knuckle's all swollen."

She lifted her arms, unlatched the silver chain of the cross she always wore, held out her hand. Bemused, he put the ring in it and she strung it on the chain. Leaving the cross on the chain with it, she folded the necklace back in his hand. "Put that on her. She'll know it's there. It will make a difference."

"I don't know what religion she is. She's never said and getting information out of her is like pulling teeth. Contrary woman."

Sarah smiled. "It doesn't matter. The cross is a reminder of faith. We all have faith in something. Otherwise, we wouldn't go on living." She rose, ruffled his hair and went

Joey W. Hill

back down the stairs.

He held the necklace in his hand, closed his fingers on it as if it were her. With gentle possession, fierce need. All-consuming love. He was a man who'd lived enough years to know what love was and what it wasn't. He'd loved his wife. He loved the woman behind the door and would do all he could to keep her well and safe, if only she'd trust in him to do so and come from the place deep inside her where she now hid. Well, whether the damsel was by his side or inside a fortress with him outside, she was still his to defend and he couldn't let her down.

He made himself finish the meal, rose and splashed water on his face in the hall bathroom, got himself a clean shirt and was shrugging into it when Komal emerged.

"Let's go downstairs and talk." She gestured to the open sitting room, which was clearly visible from the bedroom door.

He nodded. "Let me call Sarah to sit with her."

"I was going to suggest the same."

When they faced each other in the sitting room, Komal began without preamble, apparently recognizing from his expression he had no patience for any other approach.

"Everything looks fine. Normal. Remarkable, considering the physical feat she pulled off. Her body temperature is somewhat low."

"She's always cold. Her skin's always cold."

Komal put out her hand, her dark eyes warm with understanding. "I'm not a doctor but my gut and experience say she's had a complete breakdown. She's drained, so tired there's nothing there. Exhaustion. Sheer and simple. She's out there floating in the wreckage, the post-flood. I think she just needs time for the water to wash out and to feel the people who love her around her. You need to keep a close eye on her right now. Very close."

He understood from the emphasis, the sudden sharpening of her eyes, what she meant. He'd known it, suspected it, but it was difficult to hear from someone who was trained to see it.

"But he's gone. She faced him, annihilated him."

"The man who haunted her life is gone, but the evil that

260

chose to manifest itself in the body of her father is not gone. It never is. Off to find another willing host, innocent prey. Will she ever annihilate the feeling of his hatred, his betrayal? His hands on her? See, that's the thing." Komal settled herself on the sectional sofa and drew him down next to her, giving him the seat that gave him a clear view to Marguerite's room. "The nightmare wasn't that he was still alive, but that he existed to begin with. With him gone, that hits all the harder, the truth of that. Will it ever be better? Will she ever not dream of the nightmare?

"Think of the Holocaust victims. Hitler's dead, the Third Reich is gone, but is it? When you've been touched by that kind of evil, you know that it doesn't have a specific face. It's an underground river in the subconscious of humanity, ready to rise up at the least crack in the soul of a willing host. And the only thing that makes life worth living when you really understand that is knowing there's someone out there worth living for."

"I'm here."

"Yes, you are." Komal smiled now, squeezed his arm. "It may take time, longer than you want or expect, but I think that's the key. Let her know she's not alone, that you're here. You're her raft. I'm just a phone call away if you need me for anything."

§

It was an easy task, physically. Staying with her, making sure she was always in his sight, talking to her, touching her. Caring for her bodily needs. Emotionally, he'd never done anything harder than watching those distant blue eyes refuse to focus on him, her lips refuse to speak, day after day, no matter what he did.

And he understood then how his wife had been unable to take those long, awful days when his detachment was absolute, his attentiveness apparently shattered beyond repair. He'd left her side in their bed night after night to sit on that landing, staring into the waters illuminated by moonlight. Too numb to search for answers, just going through the motions of living, too tired to talk to her, no emotions in him to respond to her.

He was gentle with Marguerite, spoke to her, cared for her, did everything necessary to keep the pain of her physical injuries to a minimum. Inside, his emotions ran the spectrum from fury with her for doing what she had done, to the terror of reliving the memory, to the frustration with her lack of response now when he had so much love he wanted to give her. He just had to keep offering comfort and reassurance with it, not knowing if it was disappearing into the black void of her mind that her blank expression seemed to indicate, or if deep inside that void somewhere his angel was receiving his love, using it to nourish herself and grow stronger, to take control back from the trauma that had seized her body.

Several days passed. Leila was glad to come every day in her capacity as nurse to check on Marguerite's physical state and Tyler stayed in touch with Komal. Marguerite would sit up if compelled to do so, allowed Tyler to bathe her without complaint and carry her into the bathroom for Sarah or Leila to care for more intimate requirements. Tyler would have willingly done it all, but he was overruled by the two women who agreed that Marguerite needed to be the one to give her permission for that. Otherwise, he never left her. He laid her on a blanket in the garden by the statue while he worked with his orchids. Let her sleep on the sofa in his office or gaze out the window from the recliner as he made phone calls. Put her next to him in a chair in the solar as he ate breakfast and coaxed her to take a few bites. She chewed and swallowed without interest as the sun shone through the paleness of her skin. He was beginning to feel like he had a mannequin he moved around the house with him. It was dark outside and dark in his heart.

When he watched Komal drive back down the driveway five days later, he fought a weariness that threatened to make him weak. Marguerite needed his strength, not his impotent rage at a man who was dead. She'd killed him, slain her own dragon so it seemed, but as Komal had said, she'd discovered the dragon lay not in the man, but the memories that would not let her go.

He turned, went back in and up to the bedroom. In the growing evening, Sarah had turned on the side lamp and he saw she was brushing Marguerite's hair, combing it out on the pillow, lifting her head as needed to straighten out the snarls.

"It's as lovely as the manes of those horses you see in the arenas, the Lizzie horses I always call them. I thought it would soothe her to have it brushed." She put it into a loose braid, bound it with a piece of ribbon she'd found somewhere in the nooks and crannies of domestic supplies he knew nothing about. "I gave her an extra pain pill while you were with Mrs. Gupta. She seemed a little more uncomfortable tonight, I suspect because of the rain we've been having. It should make her sleep more deeply." Her sharp eyes studied him. "Maybe you should take one, too."

Tyler shook his head. "Thank you, Sarah. I'm sure she'll thank you, too, when she's able. I'll sleep with her now, so go find yourself some rest. We'll take it slow in the morning. A late breakfast. If she's up to it I'll spend the day with her in the gardens."

"All right then. You just call us if you need anything." She slipped out, closing the door.

Tyler stripped out of his clothes, slipped in behind his unconscious angel. He touched the hollow of her neck, just above the cross and the ring strung on Sarah's necklace. The diamond sparkled at him. As he caressed her there, another thought occurred to him. When he settled in behind her, he laid the curve of his hand from thumb to the end of his forefinger around the matching curve of her throat, where the heel of his hand pressed on the ring and cross, making her feel their presence as well as his presence in the area where she'd always been most emotionally as well as physically responsive.

Her body trembled, a soft murmur, a quiet plea. "Ssshhh..." He wrapped his other arm around her waist, brought her in close to the heat of his body. "I'm here, Marguerite. Your Master is here."

§

He felt the touch on his shoulder, insistent, and then a sharp blow, almost as if he'd been shoved, hard. A brief flash of a face he'd seen before, but whose name he didn't know. He started awake, realized he was alone.

Years in military operations where he had to come awake with all his senses ready for battle kicked in. He understood in a blink the bedroom door was open and he was alone. He lunged out of the bed.

She stood on the railing of the landing, the marble foyer twenty feet below her. The sling on her arm had dropped on the floor. How she'd even gotten up there with the type of injuries she had he didn't know, but she was motionless on her perch, staring at something just above her through the arched window that availed him a sight of the night sky. She opened her arms, the white satin robe he'd left on her fluttering out on either side of her like angel wings.

There were ten yards and a corner from the hallway to the landing's catwalk. He covered the ground as if he had wings himself. As her body fell forward, he was already there, seizing her around the waist and spinning them, lifting clear of the rail and putting her on the carpet, pulling her off with enough force they both tumbled. He kept grim hold of her though, until he realized she wasn't fighting him. The glaze of sleep cleared from her eyes. She looked startled, then that distant look came back into her gaze. She'd been asleep. She'd been fucking sleepwalking, the extra dose of the strong painkillers apparently allowing her to perform a feat that would have been prohibitively excruciating if she'd been conscious.

He pressed his forehead down on hers as she lay beneath him, relaxed, her breathing already even again, while his heart raced so fast he thought he might be having a minor heart attack. Fortunately, he felt no numbness in his arms. Lifting her in them, he took her back to bed. This time he used her robe sash and bound their hands together so she couldn't leave again without his knowledge. He needn't have taken the extra precaution, however. He stayed awake until dawn brought light into the room again.

§

In the morning, he was able to get her to sit up so he could take her into the bathroom and let Sarah assist her there. He insisted on handling her bath himself so he could do a thorough inspection of her injuries and make sure there were no new swellings, heat or bruises. He remembered her first day here, when she'd turned over control to him. She'd discovered pleasure in the quiet darkness underwater, found that it wasn't empty and alone at all, but filled with the sensations he could provide and share with her. He recalled her apprehensive wonder, the incredible response of her lithe body. The assimilation of it all by her extraordinarily intelligent mind.

"How do women put up with all this?" He kept up a running dialogue as he washed her hair, made sure the thick length of it was rinsed clean, made sure he was doing nothing to aggravate her injuries. "I'm not saying I want you to cut it. I love your hair. I'm just appreciative and awestruck at all that's involved in keeping it beautiful. You know I'm going to mess it up. I'm going to put some man's shampoo on it that will make it dry and frizzy, not be the way you like it, so you're just going to have to tell me how to do it right before I turn you into Medusa." Putting the sponge down, he picked up a towel and raised her to her feet. And found himself looking into blue eyes that for the first time in days were focused on his face, his mouth. Somewhere deep she might be, but some part of her was listening, if only to his voice.

He managed, barely, to keep his voice steady, casual. "It's not possible, you know. You could never be anything but beautiful to me. I might not mind if you looked a little like Medusa to other men though. You get entirely too much attention for my peace of mind. You could have a bevy of Mariuses waiting on you hand and foot to satisfy your every desire, rather than having a cranky Master trying to tell you what to do all the time."

He pulled a robe over her shoulders, belted it and had to resist the urge to wrap his fingers in the ends, pull her to him and hold her tightly against his heart. "You're going to need to snap out of it soon, anyway. With Chloe and Gen running Tea Leaves, you know Chloe will be having topless male waiters serve the tea so she can sexually harass your employees."

Something stirred in her gaze and he picked up on it as if she'd spoken. His heart lifted at even this minimalist form of communication.

"Chloe is doing fine. I've had Mac and Violet checking on her daily. Her parents came into town as well. He broke her arm and leg, knocked a couple teeth out. She lost a good bit of blood from the stab wound in her side, but fortunately he didn't hit any vital organs."

He didn't want to tell her all that but knew he had to. She would want honesty, not vague generalities. "Most of her injuries were because she fought him like a Green Beret to keep him away from Natalie. I don't think her own mother would have fought any harder. He had to beat her unconscious to get away.

"Now, stop," he reproved, sliding the robe back off her shoulders and replacing it with a comfortable sundress that dropped over her hips easily. Too easily. She'd already been thin. Over a week without more than a few mouthfuls of food and enough water to keep her hydrated wasn't enough to keep her nourished. He knew it was past time to consider an IV and more in-depth psychiatric care. He couldn't help but remember Komal's reference during her last visit to those who never came out of a trauma or breakdown like this. People who were quietly cared for in expensive, private facilities where they received everything they could need and nothing they cared about, a lifetime as mannequins.

He pushed the thoughts away. It was too early to think like that. This was a woman who made subs long for the privilege of scarring them with permanent burns. Who had given him a run for his money in tennis. Had nearly put a fork through his fingers when he pushed her too far. Who had jumped off a building to save a child.

"Natalie's mother is going to blame you for a while. And the police department here, or the prison that was holding your father. Even Chloe. Anyone within range of her thoughts, because she almost lost her little girl. But it's not your fault, not any of it. I know you think if you'd died when you were fourteen, none of this would have happened." His throat closed at the flicker of acknowledgement, agreement even, in her face. "But that's total bullshit and I won't tolerate it." He closed his eyes, took a breath, resumed in a more even tone. "Let's look at it this way. Say you died with your mother and brother. Your dad might or might not have gone free without your testimony, but then or now he would be out there, his mind twisted. He would have struck again. Something would have snapped him. A waitress that looked like his mother, or the general humidity level or the Dow. And he would have killed or raped.

"But you stopped him. It began and ended with you. You ended it. And now you've earned the right to heal, love and live. You earned it a long time ago, a million times over. So I don't want to hear you worry about it any more." He arranged Sarah's necklace on her, straightening the interlocked ring and cross. "We have a wedding to plan and I'm not doing it all myself. In fact, I think there's a law that requires the woman to handle all of it. The man just shows up."

"Never said...I'd marry you."

The tone, sullen and faraway, made him want to turn cartwheels, but he took her hand as if they'd been carrying on a two-way conversation all along, his only reaction a tremor that ran through his fingers, which he covered by tightening his grip on her.

"But you will. Because you love me."

"Talk too much." She closed her eyes. "Never shut up. Tired. Sleep."

"Food first," he said firmly, then couldn't stop himself from holding her to him a moment. He kept his touch tender when he wanted to crush her, shake her. Beg her to talk some more.

He took her downstairs, coaxed her into an unsatisfying handful of bites. He was sure Sarah was cooking nine or ten different dishes for each meal, anything to coax out her appetite. Just nothing—

"Oh, holy Christ." He almost smacked himself in the head for his stupidity. "Marguerite?" He took her hand.

She was nodding off in the chair, inflicting sleep on herself to escape again. "Would you like a cup of tea?"

Her eyes opened, a glimmer of interest. After a quick call to Sarah he found that he had three types, all ones Marguerite had brought to his house for him to try. In short order, Sarah had steeped and brought him a cup of each. He spaced them before her as he'd seen her do at her own shop when she drank from several in succession, trying the different flavors on her tongue.

She studied them, reached out, touched them, moved them, changed their arrangement on the table, making their relationship a more widely spaced triangle. Picking up the middle one with her functioning right hand, she started to bring it to her lips. She hadn't eaten enough and she was normally left-handed. Her hand started to shake. Leaning forward, Tyler steadied it with his own and moved with her to bring it to her lips. It touched briefly, a quick sip. Her eyes looked up at him then down as she drank some more. He could tell her hand was tired, so he pulled over a chair and sat next to her. Slid his arm around her so she could lay her head carefully on his shoulder as she continued to take sips. Both his hands were clasped under hers, cupping them and the teacup, giving her the extra strength. He noticed the cup's heat and his heat were warming her fingers somewhat.

"Japanese tea ceremonies, *cha-no-yu*..."

Her voice drifted off, and he coaxed her back. "What about them? Talk to me, angel."

"During...the cha-no-yu... You do things a certain way, behave a certain way. Make the outside world quiet...contemplate... Stupid things. The way a flower grows." Her throat was rusty with disuse and she was quiet for another moment while he waited, trying not to press. "Only it's not stupid. It's beautiful. Simple and perfect. Why can't we be like that..."

"You're like that to me," he said at last. "I could sit and watch you do nothing for hours except sit in my garden. With the flowers. With that perfection." He fished out a handkerchief, took it to her eyes as he saw a tear fall into the bowl of the cup.

"Not." She sniffed. "Only if I was naked. You'd get bored otherwise."

"You being naked would be a lovely perk, but you're wrong. I would spend my entire life looking at you. Clothed or not clothed. I want to, remember?"

She closed her eyes, her face adjusting carefully to burrow into his neck. As her hand lowered, he helped her ease the cup back to the table. "You never give up."

"No. I don't. Not on you."

"You should. Just let me die, Tyler. I'm so tired."

Fear crawled inside him. The anger that was so close to the surface ripped at him with rabid teeth, but he managed to rein back the reaction. Lifting her from him, still supporting her, he curved his hand around her delicate jaw, his finger teasing her lips, bringing her eyes up to him. "Not going to happen. So stop pouting about it and get over it. I love you and you're stuck with me. You sleep as much as you need to, until you're no longer tired. Awake or asleep, I'm here with you."

A sigh went out of her. Her blue eyes drifted closed, the lids coming down over that distant, sad look, but he thought for a moment he saw a reaction of aggression. Defiance. But then she was gone, her breath even, telling him she'd left him again.

The desolation swept him, but he fought it. She'd spoken.

To tell him she wanted to die.

He lifted her, carried her to the sofa in the sunroom. He spent the rest of the afternoon watching over her slumber, doing paperwork, watching TV, reading. Trying not to lose his mind and roar his frustration.

Chapter Nineteen

"Mr. Winterman? There's a gentleman at the door for you. Well, actually he says he's here for Miss Marguerite."

Tyler left Robert watching over Marguerite and was surprised to find Brendan standing in his foyer. He wore jeans and a crisp shirt, his hair styled well. Every inch of him the late twenty-something professional, the pretty-boy type with a great body, the kind of looks that would make a woman run through a stoplight and create a four-car pile up to gawp at his ass if he was walking down the sidewalk.

He was a beautiful man, a man who carried Marguerite's brand. Tyler was all too cognizant of that as he turned from his contemplation of the vaulted ceiling, the artwork. "Master Tyler. You have a beautiful place here."

"Brendan. It's a long drive, unannounced."

"I thought I could make a better case in person. It's going around The Zone, what Mistress Marguerite did. I want to help. I thought I could help, in some way."

"How?" Tyler asked bluntly.

"Her name was on the news. Everyone knows she saved the little girl and the kidnapper was a man named Peninski, a released convict." Brendan met Tyler's gaze. "Do you believe in Fate?"

Tyler blinked, once. "I met Marguerite. So yes, I do. Not to be rude, Brendan, but..."

"You don't have time or patience for small talk." Relief crossed Brendan's his features. "It saves me from having to make it. Let me get to the point, then. When I was six years old, my parents were killed in a car wreck. I was placed in

270

an orphanage. There was a girl there named Marie Peninski."

Tyler stilled as Brendan inclined his head, acknowledging that he now had his unwilling host's full attention.

"I only knew her for six months before I was adopted." His lips twisted. "I was lucky. These looks of mine were from birth. And even more fortunate, it was a good family."

When he shifted, Tyler remembered his manners though it was an effort. "Let's sit down in here."

Brendan followed him to the sitting room, sat tensely on the edge of the sofa, leaning forward, his hands clasped together.

"In the orphanage, she was known as the girl that never talked to anyone, that looked through you. But she didn't look through me, though I don't know why. I guess I was lucky in a lot of ways. Maybe God decided a kid that had lost his parents deserved all the breaks he could get, though a lot of kids who deserve them don't get them. Like her." He shook his head. "When I was alone and frightened, crying into my pillow at night, she'd show up by my bed like this pale ghost. Scoot me over, play games with me, tell me stories. Always during the night. During the day she kept to herself. But if I got afraid or worried, or just needed her, I'd go stand by her, by this chair she sat in by the window. Eventually she'd just pull me into her lap. I didn't make her talk and she just held me."

His expression darkened. "I heard the whispers in the orphanage. In a way, it's like prison. You know everything about each other. I wasn't old enough to understand a lot of what I heard then, but I remembered. And I saw her scars when she came to my bed at night. She wore this oversized nightshirt and it would slip off her shoulder, so I could see. I touched them once and she just sat still, let me do it, but said I didn't need to know what they were.

"That same night, she curled up around me like she usually did, stroked my hair like my mother did until I fell asleep. But I woke up a little while later to find her holding me so tight, shaking, her face buried in my hair. She was crying for 'David'. I told her she could call me David if it made her feel better. In hindsight, I know she was sleeping in my bed as much for herself as for me."

Tyler could not speak, the images Brendan was creating too powerful for interruption. He waited silently as the man drew a deep breath, continued. "When I got a pair of potential parents interested in me, I decided I couldn't leave her. It felt wrong. So I asked them if they would adopt Marie, too. They were good people, as I said. They even talked to the director about it. But the court case was still going on and plus..." He lifted a shoulder. "They looked at the psychiatric report on her. They were good, kind people who wanted to adopt a little boy without complicated baggage. Even though you never get over the desperate fear of abandonment, I think..." His color rose, a muscle flexing in his jaw. "No, I *know* why I put up with Tim's bullshit as long as I did instead of knocking him on his ass as he deserved. But it wasn't near as severe as what she'd been through.

"I was going to refuse to go with them, but Marie told me it would make her happy to know I had a good home, people who loved me and that I needed to go. When I left, I offered her my teddy bear." The corner of his mouth twitched in a semi-embarrassed smile and he looked toward the Isis statue on Tyler's coffee table. "I know it sounds like a stupid, sentimental thing now..."

Tyler found it difficult to maintain any significant level of jealousy at the emotion in Brendan's voice, the honesty reflected in his tone. "It doesn't sound stupid in any way."

"But she wouldn't keep it." The man's face was a mixture of memory and regret, but admiration as well. "She was old enough to know that when I went to bed that night in my new home, with these two strangers who had become my new parents, I would desperately need something of my past to hold. She took a ribbon out of her hair and tied it around the bear's neck. Told me he'd watch over me for her. I've never met anyone like her, Master Tyler. Not even since. So damaged and yet she never stopped trying to protect someone who needed it.

"I didn't see her again for twenty years. Never expected to. And then my friends took me to The Zone and I knew her. Remembered the eyes, the hair. Even then, so young, she had a presence."

"Did she know you?"

"No. I think there's a big difference in the way you look at six versus twenty-six. And I never told her. I just...she was right. Tim was abusing me. I dumped him. At the moment I'm enjoying being on my own, thinking about what I really want. She came back into my life and gave me a gift. Again. I meant everything I said about the brand. I wanted her mark on the outside, because she'd already left it inside. She's my Mistress," he said determinedly, even as Tyler's expression became more forbidding. "Now and forever. And I love and honor her as such.

"I thought... Something told me to get in the car and come here and ask. I just had this feeling that she needs something from me and I swore to serve her. So with your permission, Master Tyler, I'd like to see her and talk to her, visit with her awhile. Today and maybe after that. And help you take care of her, if there's an appropriate way for me to do that. I'm available as long as you think I can be useful."

Tyler studied him. The story was remarkable. He knew as well as Brendan that there were few coincidences on that scale in life. And on top of that, there was nothing he wouldn't attempt to bring Marguerite back. To revive that ghost of a smile he'd started to see more often. To repeat that one miraculous burst of laughter he'd heard when she ran toward the chapel, her hair wet ropes of silk across her shoulders. Brendan might just be a stroke of fate sent to accomplish that. Hell, he was ready to shave his head and become a cult leader if it would work. Or worse, jump out of an airplane. The grim humor, offered to himself as if he could anticipate sharing it with her to coax out one of those smiles, gave him some hope, just as Brendan's presence did.

"All right." He rose, gestured. "She's out on the Gulf side lawn. Let's go find her. And Brendan?"

"Sir?" He kept the polite, formal address and Tyler didn't disabuse him of it, though he appreciated the man's sensitivity, underscoring his presence was not intended to usurp his host's.

"Follow that instinct that brought you here. Don't worry about territory and bullshit. I'll deal with whatever I have to deal with, but she's the most important thing."

Brendan nodded. Cleared his throat. "She loves you, Master Tyler. It was obvious to everyone the other night. Obvious to those who know how to really see. I have no intentions of pretending otherwise. You're right. She's the most important thing."

There was a hammock down near the water, strung between two of the live oaks. Sarah had gotten Marguerite ensconced in it, a glass of tea and a book of Japanese poetry Gen had brought over close at hand should she show interest in anything other than staring or sleeping. Marguerite's back was to them, her hair whispering back and forth over the curve of her shoulder as the breeze played off the water, rocked the hammock. Robert rose at their approach, nodded. At Tyler's glance, he left them. Resisting impulse, Tyler took his place in the chair, nodded at Brendan to go forward.

The man ducked under the hammock tie and knelt facing her. Taking the small duffel bag he'd brought off his shoulder, he put it on the ground next to him.

Her eyes were open and they shifted slowly to him. It startled Brendan, for he remembered the distance that had been in them when she was a teenager at the orphanage. When he'd met her again twenty years later, it had been much improved. The reserve had still been there, which was perhaps why he'd hesitated to identify himself to her, but she'd become more present in her own life. The eyes he looked into now were the eyes of that fourteen-year-old. Once again indifferent to life, careless of death, waiting for it. Maybe not even having the energy to embrace it. But he had to believe it was surface, a haven of retreat. Twenty years did not disappear in a day.

"Mistress." He said it with soft reverence. "Great lady. I understand you've been performing great deeds of late."

She blinked.

"I don't want to offend you by being here, but I felt I owe you a debt of gratitude," he pressed on. "One I can't ever repay, but I'm hoping you'll allow me one gesture at least." He opened the bag, removed a much worn and well-loved teddy bear from it. Around its neck was a faded ribbon that might have once been blue. Thinking of it clasped in a boy's arms, Tyler expected it to be bigger, rather than the small toy that Brendan held easily.

"You remember this?"

He took Marguerite's hand and laid it over the bear. When her fingers curled into it after a moment, Tyler leaned forward. She drew it out of Brendan's grasp, brought it in to her body where he could no longer see it from the back. He wished the chair were over where he could see her face, but he didn't want to move and interfere. From watching Brendan's changing expressions, he sensed that it would be beneficial for him to stay quiet, unobtrusive.

"I didn't think you remembered me. But I remembered you. I know you're tired of all the awfulness. I don't know why wonderful people sometimes have to deal with so much evil. But sometimes you meet a person who's gone through so much that she never forgets what's really important in this life. Who makes everyone around her feel privileged to know her. Who refuses to keep a little boy's teddy bear, even though he knows now she had more need of it than he did. Who made him take it because she thought he might suffer one less pang of fear or loneliness if he had it with him.

"Do you know the lone survivor syndrome? You're the only one who survives, so you wish you had died with your family. You know there's nothing you could have done or will do that will make their deaths worth it, that will explain why you survived and they didn't. As the years go on, you realize you won't be the person who finds the cure for cancer or ends poverty. But I want you to think about what you gave me. What you've given to Marius, all the subs at The Zone." He nodded, apparently responding to something he saw in her expression. "You look doubtful. But maybe it isn't important that you're saving masses or even saving one person. It's that you make the effort to save anyone, because when you reach out to save anyone, you're saying that person is important, worthwhile, they're needed. That they're an intrinsic part of all of us."

His eyes full of open, unconditional love for her, he reached out, apparently put his hands over hers on the bear.

"I want you to have this as a reminder of how you changed my life. There are reasons to stay here. Not just because we need you, but I think because you need us. I know you've been thinking about having another session with me." His tone changed, became teasing. He actually winked, his demeanor as comfortable as if she'd been fully herself. "Or at least, I hope you have. And Master Tyler, he's like a puppy around you. What other woman could beat him up and have him come back for more?

"Now there's a hint of a smile." Brendan glanced up, exchanged a look with Tyler. The man reached forward, uttered a quiet murmur that came to Tyler on the breeze.

"With your permission, lady."

Brendan stroked her hair from her temple, laid his palm against her cheek. "We love you, Mistress. Very much."

It got quiet, just the wind from the water and the cry of a heron drifting to them. Then Tyler heard Marguerite speak.

"Water."

Brendan leaned toward the iced tea, but he stopped as she spoke again. "Water."

Brendan glanced behind him, at the banks of the Gulf, then over at Tyler. Her right arm lifted, pointing.

Tyler rose, his concern propelling him to his feet. "Watch her collarbone and the left arm," he said. The other man inclined his head, put his arms into the hammock and lifted her out. Her arms were folded up against herself, her skirt fluttering over his tanned arm. Turning carefully, he moved toward the water's edge, Tyler right behind him.

"Down there... On the bank." Marguerite's voice again.

When Brendan set her down at the water's edge, Tyler stood within arm's reach behind her, Brendan in front of her, both men wary, protective. Tyler didn't have to convey his concern; he was sure it was obvious in his eyes. And perhaps because of Brendan's memories of her, he understood immediately where Sarah had not and stayed just as close to her.

Marguerite stood, looking out at the movement of the water, the blue sky, a formation of pelicans soaring above.

"Your adopted parents were good to you." She spoke as succinctly as if they'd been having an interactive conversation all along, though Tyler saw her lick her dry lips, swallow.

"Yes, Mistress. I love them."

"That doesn't matter. Children will love a monster if we think it's family. We love against everything that says don't love." She stared at the water moving around her ankles. "Did you know I've spent years donating my grandparents' inheritance to different charities, not in spite of, but for love of my family? I wanted to help pay their karmic debt, to hope they find healing and peace together sooner, become who they were...before. Even though I can't bear to look at a photo of them."

Her gaze turned to him briefly. "But your adopted parents were good to you. I'm glad. I was worried."

She nodded, as if settling something with herself, then began to unbutton the front of the dress clumsily with her right hand. She stopped, impatience in her gaze. Glanced toward Brendan. "I want this off."

The tone, so close to that of the imperious Mistress they knew she could be, startled both men. Brendan's gaze shifted to Tyler. "With your permission...?"

She looked at Tyler. "Will you trust me?"

He studied her quiet expression, the weak sway of her undernourished body. "To a point," he said at last. "My heart wants to trust you, but my fear for you..."

Breathing a sigh through his nose, he gave Brendan a curt nod. "She can't lift the left arm."

Brendan moved before her, unbuttoned each button carefully. She was completely naked under it except for the clavicle brace on her upper body and she lifted her chin as the dress fluttered back, showing that she was feeling the breeze on her skin, perhaps even enjoying it. Brendan eased her arm out of the sling so he could guide the dress off her entirely, as she'd demanded. He was as slow and patient as Tyler could wish, but Tyler saw the press of

Marguerite's lips, the tremor run through her. It made him wonder if he should have given her more pain medication this morning, since he'd been too shook up from last night to give her more than the bare minimum.

"My deepest apologies, Mistress," Brendan said. When he began to guide her arm back into the sling, she shook her head and moved forward, taking a step sideways to move around him. When she stumbled unsteadily, both men moved in, their hands brushing as they made sure she didn't fall. But she proceeded forward into the water. Wearing only the necklace and the brace, she took one step deeper, then another.

The men stayed right with her. Marguerite's eyes remained on the horizon, but she felt them around her, their concern and caring a bulwark on either side. She was absently surprised that Brendan hadn't backed away when Tyler had moved closer, but both were apparently determined to keep her safe. Her mind rolled the thought around, but was curiously blank, peaceful. The cool touch of the water on her skin soothed as she felt it slide over everything she was. Blood, muscle, sinew, scars, beliefs... Marie Peninski. Marguerite Perruquet. A trusting child, a scarred teenager and now a woman who had lived an interesting life, to say the least. As her mind moved over the memories Brendan had stirred, they brought her forward to more recent images.

Chloe's laughter, the children playing in her park. Tyler's amber eyes, his easy touch. Brendan's beauty. His devotion. The tea combination that Mr. Reynolds would bring in next. The embrace of the sky as she leaped out into the vastness of it. The impatiens she had decided to plant by the kitchen door in that bare shady spot that needed it, that was now only a mud puddle. A life without fear. A life filled with love and friendship. And suddenly, she found she wasn't quite so tired anymore. He was gone. And she was free. Perhaps always could have been free, the moment she decided she was.

She'd reached her waist now. Tyler's palpable apprehension was like a warm blanket that wrapped around her, making her feel safe, loved. She turned and reached out her uninjured hand. When he took it, she let her knees go and dropped below the water's surface, immersing herself, but keeping tight hold of his hand. Knowing that he would not have permitted it otherwise, but she didn't reach out to him only because of that. As she let the silent Gulf waters embrace her, she remembered.

Remembered her and David in that cocoon of warmth, the hold of their mother, perhaps *the* Mother, when all things were possible and perfect. Tyler's strong fingers reminded her that he'd filled the aching emptiness the loss of her brother had left her with for twenty long years.

His hand tightened on hers and she let him draw her toward him and up. She found the strength to push off the sand with her own feet. Surging out of the water into sunlight and the fire of his eyes, she felt it move in her, tears and happiness both.

Tyler caught her as she pressed against him, soaking what remained dry of his shirt. The water lapped at the hips of his jeans. She turned her head, her eyes reaching out to Brendan, bringing him to them. The man took her taped hand, his fingers holding hers gently as she pressed her face into Tyler's neck, breathed him in. Renewal. Rebirth. When there was love like this they were possible, no matter what the darkness.

Quiet determination rose in her to plant those impatiens, nurse the blooms and bring them to life. Giving them the chance to be as vibrant as they could, in whatever amount of time the world would give them. The fear she'd always felt in Tyler's arms was simply gone. Komal was right. Of all the things to fear in the world, the fear of being loved and loving back was the most absurd.

"Master, please forgive me," she murmured. "Forgive me for not being strong enough."

Tyler pressed his forehead to hers, a shuddering going through those lean muscles as he closed his eyes. "You tore my heart out, Marguerite."

"I know." She kissed his cheekbone, his closed eyes. "Thank you for loving me beyond your heart. Can you forgive me?"

"If you promise never to leave me. If you agree to marry

me."

She lifted her head then, felt joy flood her. "That's blackmail," she said, her voice not quite steady. "And you're as persistent as a terrier."

"Angel."

"Irritant."

He smiled then, caressed her wet hair. "Say yes, or I'll dunk you and hold you under until you agree."

"Brendan will protect me from your bullying."

Brendan chuckled, dared to run a hand down her back. "I think you should agree, Mistress. He looks determined to have his way."

That surge was the last of her strength. As her feet came back to rest on the sand, her knees buckled. It was Tyler who lifted her this time. Striding out of the water, he laid her down in the hammock again. "Brendan, will you go in and find Sarah, ask her for some towels?"

The man nodded and left them alone. Lying in the hammock, Marguerite could not take her gaze from Tyler's face. With her vision clear for the first time in days, she saw the deep lines of worry, the drawn tension of his mouth. The fierce resolve in him had been held in place past endurance so that the strain showed in every line. She remembered Sarah's words, how he sat on the landing, avoiding sleep so the vision of a dancer whose toes had given out on her, strangled her into a willful death, would not haunt him in dreams.

She'd asked for forgiveness, but only now did it hit her, the magnitude of the request. She could feel again, see everything clearly, the water's cleansing having loosened the guts and blood gumming up the dam to her emotions.

The things she had said and done on that building and since came back to her, not just from her own mind, but because she saw them buried in his expression where they could fester into a cancer if left untended.

She struggled up, despite her weakness. When he would have stopped her, she caught both his hands in her right one and dropped out of the hammock on her knees in the soft sand, bowing her head despite the pain that shuddered through her shoulder.

"Please forgive me, Master." She repeated it, lifted her gaze to meet his. He'd squatted down and was holding her upper arms, apparently thinking she needed his assistance.

"I can never forgive myself for saying and doing such things to you as I've done. I know how much it must have hurt you."

Her voice, low and broken, did something to Tyler. A wall shattered, behind which he'd stored his anger and worry, his gut wrenching, bowel-freezing fear. Because he heard her understanding of his pain, her knowledge of what she'd done, suddenly he didn't know if he wanted to kill her out of fury, keep her chained to him until he didn't feel the fury anymore, which might be by the time they were both well over a hundred, or hold her until every part of her was imprinted on him forever.

She sat on her knees, weak from physical and emotional stress and hunger, a woman willing to sacrifice life and more to save an innocent. A woman willing to sacrifice love. As he sat on his heels there long moments with her in her position of supplication before him, that thought repeated itself in his mind and love won out.

For he remembered the message she'd left for him. Chloe had insisted on calling and telling him as soon as they'd let her have a phone at the hospital. Sometimes it had been the only thing he'd been able to hold on to this past week, to believe somewhere deep inside her Marguerite was still there, wanting to be with him.

Marguerite had wanted him. Wanted to live with him. Which meant going onto that building had been even more difficult for her than most, because she'd just newly discovered the desire to live for love and she was about to go do something she'd been certain would obliterate that dream. He had been stupid to lose faith for even a moment. He thanked God that when he had, some other strength he could not name had kept him going.

All of that flooded in, intertwining with his harsher feelings, rational and irrational thought warring in an impossible conflict, until love touched him with insistent hands, recalling one other memory that made the conflict meaningless.

He knelt, lifting her chin. "Marguerite, when you jumped, do you remember anything that went right that should have gone all wrong?"

"You mean, other than us surviving that drop?" Her tone was dry, though her voice still shook with her emotions.

"It's important. Remember for me, if it's not too painful, angel."

Marguerite thought back to the dive off the building, the shock of the dead wind freefall, her father's abrupt release when she had expected more tenacity. The chute coming free...

"The whole jump was a miracle." She shook her head. "My best hope was to get Natalie to the ground in a way she had half a chance of surviving. BASE jumping, building jumping..." she amended the term for his understanding, "is very dangerous and very precise. Her additional weight, my father's interference, even when I released the chute. I should have been dead. Natalie might have lived, but likely with crippling injury. I didn't expect to make it."

"I know." And the anger and pain were in his voice. She reached up to him, aching, but he closed his hand on her wrist, preventing her from touching him.

"Did Chloe tell you?"

"She did. I understand. I do, angel. It's just...it's going to take me some time. Just let it go for now."

So she subsided, but it was difficult, for she needed his arms around her. "Why did you ask me that?"

"Because." He released her to run both hands over his face, a gesture so weary and un-Tyler-like that it almost frightened her. Then she squelched the fear. She would not be Nina. She realized now she relied on his strength, had become dependent on it in a frighteningly short time, but she would never let him think he could not rely on hers and he was due for some leaning. Some serious leaning.

It was a humbling thought, to realize the weight of the world could not break him, but the loss of her could have. The impact of that struck her hard yet it told her what he needed. What she needed to give him. But first she needed to be sure of her direction.

"Have I lost your love, Tyler?" She spoke the words softly, a gift she'd never asked for, never thought she wanted. Now her life seemed to hinge on it. There was an abyss moving inside her, frozen belief her only light. Her voice trembled like a sputtering flame, unable to let him finish whatever it was he was trying to find out because she needed to know right then.

Shock coursed over his features, but she continued on.

"You've cared for me, yes," she managed carefully. "As I'd expect you to do for me, or Leila, or Sarah or Violet, any woman you care about in similar circumstances. I just need to know." Her voice broke. "Have I hurt you past bearing?"

He pulled her into his arms and lay back, pulling her onto him so he held her firmly against his full length, her body wrapped in his arms, her head beneath his chin.

"When you jumped from that building, I died," he said simply, his voice a whisper in her ear. "I was so certain that I was going to lose you that I haven't known how to feel or think since, beyond the basic steps of caring for you. There's this rage in me, this anger. Every time I touch you, I want to hold you so tightly that I'll see pain in your face so it matches what's raging inside of me. So I'm afraid to let it show. I don't know what to do with it. I love you so much, Marguerite. There are no words for this kind of love. It's not pretty or romantic, it's as visceral as sex or breathing, something undeniable, necessary to go on living, for anything else to matter.

"I...God..." His hands clutched her. She felt it ripping at him, the memories of one love lost mingling with one almost lost. It was going to tear his mind in two, break a man who believed he was supposed to be unbreakable.

Marguerite lifted up, looked into his face, inches between them. Her skin was pale, face thin, but in her eyes Tyler saw that deep understanding she had of the world, its ugliness as well as its beauty, the temporal nature of it all. And something else. Her love for him riding all of it like a boat on rough seas, shining fiercely on her face like an angel's light fairly revealed to a mortal's fragile eyes. He blinked at the power of it as she held nothing back, showing him how important his answer was to her.

She needed him as much as he needed her. Whatever else had happened on her leap, she was no longer afraid to show it.

"Take me now, Master." Her fingers curled into his biceps. "Take me with your pain and rage, and your love. I'm yours to do with as you desire."

His gaze covered her face, the collarbone, still purple and bruised, the taped fingers. "Please." Her voice dropped to a savage whisper, seeing it. "Do it for both of us. You're my Master. It's as much a part of taking care of me as your gentleness. I want the pain. So I'll never forget, never abandon your love again."

In retrospect, he would wonder what compelled him more, the vulnerable submissive in her that made it a plea, or the fierce Mistress that made it a demand.

He turned them over, using his strength to overpower her as she desired, but also using it to roll her onto her back in a way that made sure no pressure was put on the shoulder. Even so, his gaze was burning on her as he rose up on his knees and took each of her hands in his, turned her palms so they were flat on the grass on either side of her hips.

"You keep your hands right there and don't move them." He lifted off her enough to get his jeans open, shoved them out of the way, revealing that her words had made him fully erect, large. Marguerite shuddered as he gripped her hips, lifted them slowly up, impaled her. He was strong, relentless, leaving her no doubt that this was punishment as well as pleasure, even as his actions showed her he was trying to minimize the pain that the act could not help but bring her. As she cried out, tears came to her eyes, but she embraced all of it, wanting to suffer it, wanting this punishment, the pummeling of his thickness and length inside her. The proof of his love in a way that the civilized world could never understand the way she did. His fingers dug into her thighs, bruising her. She tried to tilt herself up to him even more, proving to him she was his, all his.

Marguerite thought his eyes were fierce like a warrior in the midst of battle, almost a berserker's lust. Obeying instinct, she disobeyed, raising her hands enough to clamp down on his hands on her thighs, digging her nails in, drawing blood.

He snarled, caught her wrists and pinned them back down, using that grip and the force of his thighs between hers to keep her anchored at the right angle for his assault. A moment later, he let go of one wrist to put one hand high on her throat, making her undeniably helpless to him, to accept the mutual pain they both had roaring through them.

Thinking was hardly an option when her body and soul were so open and raw for him. She offered herself with the trust of a newborn. Since it was the first time since she'd been seven years old that she had trusted someone so much with her well-being, it was more fact than metaphor.

I'll take you at my pleasure, make you mine, but care for you no matter what... Every movement of him inside her, the expression on his face, sent the message clearly that she was his and only his. It brought her a sense of belonging that, up until now, she could only believe in extreme moments such as he'd brought to her since they'd started their journey together. In the fairy tale, when she emerged from sleep, Sleeping Beauty saw the man who promised happily ever after. But happily ever after was essentially irrelevant. Certain things bound people together forever and those things lay between the two of them. She would never doubt the message again, whether in peace or passion.

He came inside her then and her body wanted to rise up, seek the same fulfillment, but physically she was no match for him. He held her down, made her protect her ribs and shoulder and serve his lust and need. He let go of her wrist, reached between them and found her, stroked her, his eyes burning into hers. Within five powerful seconds she came, her body barely strong enough even with his restraint to withstand the physical wave, the tide of feeling that crashed into her. But like her trip into the water, she needed it desperately to find herself and begin again. But not alone this time.

His eyes, the set of his mouth, the implacable clamp of his hands, the force of his cock, made it an oath to her. She believed it more in this moment of primal anger and pain than she would have if it was delivered in flowers and poetry. The most momentous moments of her life had always been forged in pain and darkness. While there might not be light in darkness at times, there would be heat and safety with him, and love existed everywhere. She believed it now, not just because she had felt a moment of it when her father's expression shifted and she saw a memory of what he once was, but when she accepted the terrible pain she had inflicted on Tyler and saw and felt his love embrace her, a promise to always forgive. No matter what.

Desire. The joy of embracing it fully with body and mind rolled over her, left her quiet, at peace. For the very first time in her life.

He raised his body off hers at length, the harsh lines still cutting into his face. After he rearranged his clothes, he sat on his knees, gathered her up so she was straddling him, holding on to his shoulders with her one good arm as he buried his face in her neck. A shudder went through him, so strong it was almost like a seizure. His fingers dug into her back. He was shaking. And more.

She'd told him that he had to trust her the same way he wanted her to trust him. To give her his pain when it became too much to bear. Would she have gone to get Natalie if she'd understood how it would impact him? Yes, she had to, and Tyler had known that. But, oh, how sorry she was. How she wished she could have done something differently.

Her heart broke anew, yet it was a clean break, pouring out a wealth of poison and fear on the ground, giving it to the earth to absorb and cleanse as she held him to her. Held on as he did the one thing an intensely strong alpha man could do to bind a woman to him forever. Weep in her arms.

Her own tears bathed his temple. "Tyler." She whispered his name, whispered it to him as a promise. "Tyler Winterman, I am going to love you forever, I promise. I will never turn away from you again, not when I'm afraid or even angry. I'm yours and you're mine." Her arm tightened over his shoulders as she absorbed the amazing truth of that. This incredibly interesting, handsome, exciting and loving man was hers. All hers.

Brendan was coming across the lawn and she discreetly gestured with her hand, holding him off, not wanting to interrupt Tyler or embarrass him. Brendan assessed the situation, nodded and placed the towel on a bench before retracing his steps back to the house. Another good man. Also hers, in a way Tyler miraculously accepted and appreciated.

Despite the darkness, she'd always been surrounded by gentle flames, like candles in a room. Brendan, Natalie, Chloe, Gen... Tyler, coming in to bring more than light— heat, nourishment, warmth. She had been blessed, in so many ways.

"Please, Master." She held him close. "Let me have all of it. Let me take care of you. I'm not afraid of your pain. I love you. Nothing will make me stop."

Jesus wept. Those powerful two words from the Bible. How odd it was that chauvinistic, old-school men like Tyler and likely Violet's Mac thought it was shameful to cry in moments like this. When prophets could not help but weep at the folly and evil of men, knights of the round table wept at the loss of their king. Even Little John, a man as broad and strong as an oak, had wept when his great friend Robin had died in his arms. So the legend went. She thought the rare tears of a strong man might be a gift to angels and Divinity, proof that there was compassion and love in a world long ago gone mad and beyond repair.

At length he was still, just holding her. She rubbed him, rocked with him, silently gazed out at the water. She reflected she would have been content if Josh had come out and poured clay on them, forever immortalizing them here, a sculpture she would have chosen to call *No Matter What.*

"Tyler," she said at length.

"Angel."

She lifted her head and put her hand to his chin, brought his face up when he didn't want her to see the evidence of his tears. She leaned forward, kissed one eye, then the other, leaned back.

"What can I do to make you happy?"

Tyler's gaze coursed over her collarbone area, the bruising that had developed a greenish-black coloring this week. "Maybe punch me in the face. I was an animal."

"Don't apologize for it." She said it fiercely, surprising him with her passion. "We both know it's not needed. I want to make you happy. I want to love you. Tell me how to start, how to put my feet on the right road."

Despite the strength of her words, her voice was weak. Tyler knew she had to be fatigued in every limb. She was trembling as much from pain and exhaustion as from the late afternoon breeze coming in against her wet body and hair. His Ice Queen who always felt the cold. "Brendan's dragging his ass with those towels."

"No, he's not." She nodded. Holding on to her waist to keep her comfortably astride him, he turned to look toward the bench at the edge of the garden. There was a pile of terrycloth. "See? He even brought me one of your robes. He and Sarah both knew I'd want nothing clothing me but something of yours."

The simple assertion gripped his heart. "He came back a few moments ago," she continued. "He left them there to respect your privacy."

Tyler grimaced and she smiled. It entranced him, because for the first time since he'd known her, it came easily. It was not a broad grin but a serene curving of her lips, as if she'd given herself permission to use the gesture when she liked and was testing it out.

"I'm sure he's run off to tell everyone he knows that Master Tyler cried in the arms of a woman," she teased gently.

"Damn. I hate to have to hide another body on this property. I just buried the last person who aggravated me past endurance."

She tightened her hand in his hair, tugged. Catching her forearms, his smile became something else. "Marry me, angel. That's all I'll ever need. Your promise in front of God and everyone to be mine forever."

"And if I'm a terrible wife?"

"I won't complain a bit. After all, I did beg for the

privilege."

She swept her lashes down, casting a glance at him from beneath them in a way that made him want to fuck her all over again, this time with passion and laughter in the mix.

"You know a Mistress can't resist a man who begs."

Chapter Twenty

"In sickness and in health..."

Marguerite wondered if brides and grooms ever listened to their ceremony while it was happening. That magical moment of joining when the words held so much power. A power to last a lifetime, if the heart was open to claim their truth forever.

She understood now why knights did an overnight vigil on a stone chapel floor before taking an oath of fealty. She had, in a way. She'd sat in the little chapel on Tyler's property through the long hours of the night before their wedding, thinking over what those words meant, realizing how holy and sacred they were. Tyler had kept watch with her. He rarely let her out of his sight and she accepted that. In the quiet way she walked in his soul and he walked in hers now, knowing one another without words, she had understood that he had needed the time. After the honeymoon she would firmly insist on going back to work, but she'd given him the month before their wedding. They'd both needed it.

"Honor and obey..." She met his gaze as she said the words they'd specifically instructed left in the vows. Watched Tyler's eyes turn to burnished gold at the complex meaning of the phrase between them.

"Honor and cherish..." His voice was strong and tender both. Strong enough to be heard by all, tender for what could not help but be in his voice when he looked at her, bringing Chloe to sniffles just behind her. And he would cherish her. He already did. She felt it like a photo she'd once seen in a magazine of an Afghan hound, abandoned and left in a shed for forty days without food, the only water coming in from rain through a leaky roof. The dull coat, protruding bone, the nearly fatal dehydration, had shown a body close to death. But the eyes had lived. Tyler had told her that was what had frightened him so badly, to see that light almost gone from her eyes, rousing his fury and love to screaming pitch. Now she was feeling like that dog, the picture taken six months later. The shadows of fear and the nightmares were part of her forever, but she chose to brave standing out in the light of his love and dared them to follow, for he would protect her from all the fears that mattered.

Love nourished her, not just returning her to health but bringing her to a place she'd never been before. It shone in her eyes for everyone to see. She'd asked Chloe and Gen to serve as her maids of honor. Komal and Mr. Reynolds sat in the first row where her parents would have been. She'd wanted to honor the spirits of her parents, who they had been to her before tragedy had destroyed their family.

David would have walked her down the aisle, so bestowing that honor had been easy.

§

When she'd stepped out the back door of the Gulf house with Chloe and Gen, Brendan had waited for her.

Resplendent in black tie, his dark hair a silken fall to his shoulders, he had a sprig of lavender carefully pinned in his lapel that picked up the beautiful color of Gen's and Chloe's elegant sheath dresses.

He put his hand over his heart. "Ladies, I'm overwhelmed."

"I was about to say the same," Chloe responded, eyes merry. "Marguerite can walk herself down the lawn in that dress. It's my knees that are weak."

"Ignore her," Gen informed Brendan. "We all do."

He smiled, but turned his eyes to Marguerite, covered all of her, and apparently heedless of what her two friends would think, he went to one knee, bowed his head.

She cupped his jaw and he turned his head, kissed her

hand, placed his over it so he held on to it when he rose, stepping close enough so they would not hear how he chose to address her. "You honor me, Mistress."

"It's my pleasure," she replied softly, squeezing his hand. He gave her another lingering look then stepped back, withdrew an envelope from his jacket, offered it to her. "Tyler asked if you would read this before you came down to him."

He moved away, taking a step toward Chloe and Gen to give her privacy as she opened it. Marguerite noted that he put a hand beneath Chloe's elbow, proving he'd noticed as she had that Chloe was trying to shift all her weight onto one foot to relieve the ache in the still healing leg. She'd refused to use crutches or even the cane she'd brought and Gen had done a credible job of covering the lingering remnants of the bruises on her face. Tyler had paid for the cosmetic surgery that gave her back her two front teeth when insurance wouldn't and Chloe had regaled him with several renditions of the popular Christmas carol in joyous gratitude. Smiling a little, Marguerite opened the folded letter.

Dearest Marguerite:

You've taught me a great deal about stillness. About the many things that can drift into your mind and heart when you shut down the barricades created by noise. Unexpected gifts of insight, revelation and wisdom.

I wanted to teach you about love. Thinking it would be an easy lesson, because you already know the basics. You're right, it's a miracle. There are those who desperately seek it like a drug, an answer to problems, an aching need they cannot describe. But you taught me that love is found in stillness. It is the space between objects. It's the star you can't see if you look directly at it in the night sky, but if you look away, look forward, you see it in your peripheral vision, beside you, watching over you. If you lie down on the earth it's there, beneath you, cradling you.

You learned to create a stillness, a peace within

yourself, doing it with a very select filter. Together we found that love heals, it laughs, it cries, it feels. It is where truth begins and ends. It cannot be described or contained and it changes every moment. It has more faces and forms than we can count. Let me in, Marguerite. For once and for all, remove any and all filters between us. Let me in to share it with you, experience it with you. In this lifetime and however many after we're granted.

God is beyond our description, so we describe our ways of worshipping God instead. So it is with my love for you. I think of you sipping from a teacup, your pale blue eyes changing their expression every moment. I think of your tears on my neck, your trembling body in my arms. I think of you teaching me about tea, the importance of the rituals. Of you teaching a teenager how to be a woman. I think of your fury, like a storm goddess, taking you over the edge of that building, your hands reaching for that child as though she represented all that must be saved from the heartless evil in men's hearts. You're my angel, my tormentor, my woman, my love. I no longer draw breath without a part of you in the act. As I have said before, I will always be there for you, but now I want to take a chance and beg you to love me back, beautiful Mistress. To always be there for me as well. For I know you can take care of my heart like no other.

Your Master and slave both.
Tyler

She folded it back up, held it against her heart, her eyes closed, head bowed over it. Then a small smile crossed her face and she turned, looking toward Brendan.

"I'm ready."

She took his arm, felt the grip of his hand stay sure and steady over hers as he escorted her through the gardens, Gen and Chloe just ahead of them.

As they stepped into the arbor that would take them out of the garden, she could see down the slight incline to the wide expanse of lawn. Two hundred people in a wide crescent of white wooden folding chairs were arranged before a platform with a trellis. Their altar, all of it decorated with flowers and framed by the spreading branches of the two live oaks. Her gaze sought the figure of her groom, but a movement to her left caught her attention.

There were two people waiting for her at this exit from the gardens and Brendan had turned her to be sure she saw them.

Natalie carried a basket of flower petals. She was dressed in lavender silk and gauze, a lovely wide-brimmed hat on her small head. Shyly, she stood before her mother, who was dressed in pale green with tasteful amethyst jewelry, both of them looking like the promise of spring.

Natalie looked up at Marguerite, her brown eyes round. "You're so beautiful, Miss M. Mister Tyler said you needed a flower girl."

He had given her perfection. Every gift she could ever want that was within a man's power to give. Marguerite turned away, her hand going to her mouth as she saw Natalie's mother step out from behind the child. Brendan touched her bare nape. "Mistress?"

Just a murmured word and she nodded, acknowledging him, but the sobs had started and she couldn't stop them, not even in respect of the painstaking time that Gen had put into her makeup. Fortunately it had been lightly applied since Gen had pronounced, "Good Lord, you have eyelashes as thick and pretty as a baby's."

She felt other hands then. Raising her head, she saw Tina touching her shoulder and Natalie now in front of her, holding on to a small handful of her dress. Chloe and Gen stood back a respectful step but their eyes were already brimming.

"God, where's the photographer?" Chloe muttered, looking around, but Gen stayed her with a hand.

"Some moments you don't forget," she murmured.

"Oh, Marguerite." Tina wrapped her arms around her and Marguerite slipped her arms around her in return, feeling this new joy in reaching out. Touching, caring, letting pain go in the form of tears to wash it away and bring happiness, contentment. Natalie's little arms wrapped around her legs and she reached down with her other arm, held her close. Cupping that precious head, the little skull she covered as they hit the side of the building.

"Please don't cry on this wonderful day. I can't bear knowing I gave you one moment of guilt or unhappiness. I was so awful to you, so awful." Tina raised her face and made a noise of protest as Marguerite shook her head, still unable to talk through her tears. "No, don't you dare deny it. I help run a domestic abuse shelter, for God's sake... And yet, when I saw her there that day, I couldn't stop myself from blaming you and I knew—*knew*—what it is to run from someone. The damage they can wreak when all you're trying to do is care for those around you."

"It doesn't matter. Just...thank you. You've made this day so much more wonderful and I didn't think it could get any more wonderful." Marguerite at last let her go and turned to find Brendan there with a handkerchief, which he carefully applied to her eyes for her, being her mirror. With a smile, he even dabbed at her running nose.

"You're very handsome," Natalie stated, studying him. "Miss M, you should marry both Mr. Tyler and him."

Brendan chuckled and pocketed his handkerchief as Marguerite found a smile for the child. She discovered it wasn't so hard. In fact, it felt like the sun coming out after a cleansing rain. "But maybe he's waiting for you to grow up so he can marry you."

"I don't think so. He loves you."

There was an exaggerated bark of a cough from down below, wafting up from the trellis altar, a tone that sounded suspiciously like Josh, followed by a ripple of laughter from the audience.

"I guess we better go." Tina chuckled. She positioned Natalie ahead of Marguerite as Gen and Chloe took their rehearsed positions ahead of the little girl. "Now down you go, love. Just the way we practiced. Don't start scattering the petals until you reach the first row of people. I'll go sit in the audience."

Natalie nodded, gave Marguerite a small wave and started down the slope carefully in her shiny shoes, following the two women in lavender.

Brendan picked up her hand, fitted it into the crook of his arm, looked down at her with quiet adoration in his gaze. "Are you ready now, Mistress?"

Her hair had been dressed exquisitely by Gen, who revived her skills as a hairdresser from a previous life. It was piled high on her head with ringlets and a scattering of glittering pixie dust, an appropriate complement to the sleek evening gown of antique ivory she wore for the late afternoon wedding. She gave herself a once-over, took a breath.

"You've nothing to worry about. You're beautiful beyond words. If ever your husband forgets how lucky he is, Mistress, I trust you'll use me as necessary to remind him." Brendan gave her a wink, a wicked grin, making sure it was with laughter in her eyes that she came down the lawn to her waiting groom.

§

But she knew she was the lucky one. Lucky and blessed beyond anything she'd ever expected. It filled her heart, such that when she got to the altar, rather than reaching for Tyler's hand right away, she stopped several paces away. When Tyler started forward, she gave a short shake of her head and he came to a halt, studying her.

"What are you doing, angel?" he asked softly.

Marguerite glanced toward Mac who was sitting in the second row, then met Tyler's eyes. "Looking at who I really am. The mirror of my soul."

He swallowed, reached out and took her free hand, now outstretched. He drew her away from Brendan as the man let her go and discreetly withdrew.

She pressed her cheek up to his. "Thank you for your letter."

"Thank you for inspiring it." He held her close to him, prolonging the contact, a moment she wanted to last forever.

§

It was a day of memorable moments. When the minister pronounced them man and wife, Tyler raised his hands to her face, brought her onto her toes. He kissed her mouth, his arms sliding down and around her as he let go of his usual decorum before his friends and colleagues to simply crush her to him. She felt the hard promise of his body along the length of hers, hers to enjoy forever.

One of the tremendous perks of this whole forever thing, she reflected, her mind spinning, body rousing to his.

"Until death do us part," she breathed.

"No," he said against her mouth. "Forever, angel. You're who I want, forever."

§

The reception went on far into the night. The lawn had been strung with fairy lights and Chinese lanterns. Guests danced on the platform deck built for the DJ while others sat at the wide variety of tables, benches, hammocks and chairs. Neither she nor Tyler had intended a large affair, but in the end, exuberance had taken them. Since the wedding was a mere handful of weeks after the events on the Bank of Florida building, the response to their invitations was amazing and humbling. Her skydiving friends, submissives from the Zone, customers from Tea Leaves and of course Komal. All the candles kept multiplying until Marguerite couldn't imagine how she'd moved in darkness so long. She concluded that she must have had the eyes of her soul tightly closed, until Tyler forced them open with his Will and desire for her. Arrogant, wonderful man.

He had a wealth of friends as well, good friends. Violet, Mac and Josh she knew and now she got to meet Josh's wife, though she'd not had more than a moment to talk to the quietly confident Lauren. And of course Leila and a bevy of the women he'd shared time with at The Zone, making for an odd wedding guest list indeed. Their respective submissives hatched a playful conspiracy during the reception, joining forces to keep the bride and groom apart as each insisted on claiming a dance.

It was magic, she thought. The night was pure magic. Gen had been right. While there was a photographer moving around, snapping pictures, it wasn't necessary. She'd imprint every memory on her soul to view whenever she closed her eyes and remembered.

Brendan came for her last, when she thought her feet must surely fall off. Blissfully he took her hand on a slow song. She'd long ago kicked off her low heels and moved to the soft grass, so he was careful of her bare feet as he drew her into his arms and began to move in a semi-waltz sway. Laying her head on his shoulder, she found to her surprise that he was taller than she was, something she hadn't ever noticed before.

"You're tired, Mistress," he observed. "And the collarbone is still bothering you. I saw you massaging it a little while ago."

"It's a happy tired," she assured him. "Don't fuss. And Tyler's keeping as close an eye on me as you are." She smiled. "Marius wanted to grab my ass just to see if he would notice. As much of an urbanite as Marius is, I convinced him that out here in the backwoods, Tyler is more than willing to shoot people and feed them to the alligators."

Brendan laughed. "I'd beat him up for you, but we all know Marius would just take that as flirting."

Marguerite smiled again, but a more serious mood took her as she gazed at him. "Brendan, you asked me for something, that night at The Zone. Something I should have given you."

His gaze stilled on her face as he remembered, his body tensing beneath her hands. Marguerite stopped, looked toward her husband. Tyler stood talking to several of his male guests, but at her regard, he glanced toward her. She inclined her head, a warning of sorts, then turned her attention back to Brendan. She reached up, took hold of his head in both hands, brought him to her mouth. "You asked for a kiss."

Brendan had expected a tender press of lips. He was wrong. She opened her mouth to his, delved deep into him, pressing her body into his, letting him feel her fragility and strength together. Oddly, it brought the platonic memory of the teenager who curled around him, keeping his fears at bay. Just as it brought the memory of the woman who had given him emotional release through a storm of sexual sensation. Desire surged through him, tingling low in his back where her brand rested.

When she pulled back, she did so only several inches, those blue eyes a handspan from his. "Thank you for being the first boy to love me, Brendan. For loving me, period. And for reminding me why it's important to live."

"You could never have failed me in any way, Mistress," he managed, his voice thick. "There's nothing you owe me."

"I reserve the right to overrule you on the failure part." She framed his face in her hands so he could not look away, though he would never presume to disrespect her that way. "I love you, then and now," she said softly. "I should have told you that when you were six. And you are very important to me. I missed you very much when you left. I stole your sheets off the bed so I could smell your little boy smell for at least a week after. Thank you for being that important to me."

"Mistress," he said, low, his voice choked with emotion. She touched him, raised to her toes and laid her lips on his again. This time it was what he'd originally expected and more. Just the pressure, perhaps not even sexual in nature, just loving. Giving. Intimate in the ways she'd not allowed herself before. When she finally drew back, he pressed his cheek to her temple and they danced on while the fairy lights and laughter danced around them.

"Brendan," she said at last, quietly. "I have a favor to ask."

"Anything my Mistress desires."

"Can you go talk to the DJ for me?"

When the song ended, under a wealth of fascinated eyes, Marguerite turned and walked across the grass in her bare feet toward her groom, who left his friends to meet her halfway. She put her hands into his just as the DJ announced, "A special request, from the bride to the groom."

"Was that necessary?"

She smiled, remembering a different time when he'd asked the same question. A heartbeat later, he remembered as well and cocked his head, giving her a rueful smile. "And the same boy. Are you going to force me to kill this kid before he gets the chance to experience puberty?"

"Brendan is no younger proportionately to me than I am to you, old man." She moved into his arms, stroked his nape, her eyes glinting with mischief.

"Keep it up." He pursed his lips, smoothly moving her into a turn and then into an elegant dip that had her lips curving. He kept her there, traced a finger up her neck, holding her easily with one arm, letting her feel that strength that he could use for or against her. "We'll leave this party and I'll spend all night showing you just how old and doddering I am. This is nice, by the way." His expression got tender as she realized he was also listening to the words, acknowledging the careful choice she'd made.

The DJ had begun the soulful rendition of "Because You Loved Me", by Jo Dee Messina. As the female vocalist softly noted how she had survived the darkness of the world only because of one person's love, Tyler's heart was in his eyes. He turned her in the steps of a waltz, cradling her body, letting her lean into him. She recognized his attempts to give her some rest, his protective nature asserting itself.

"I suppose I'll have to suffer that kiss," he said at last. "Considering that the ladies I've had the pleasure to call my obedient submissives have been groping, fondling, kissing with tongue and otherwise doing everything they can to convince themselves I'm off the market."

She'd let her hair down after the ceremony. Now he gathered it up and held it to one side to place his lips on her neck, keeping them there while they were dancing.

"And don't think I didn't notice all of it."

"I was hoping you might. God, women are ten times more aggressive than men. If you want to instigate a catfight, I'd be happy to make sure the sprinklers turn on so it can become a mud wrestling contest. Clothes optional."

"Oh. I like that." It took him a startled moment to realize she wasn't talking about his suggestion, had ignored it with her endearing haughtiness. He followed her gaze to where Brendan had taken a seat next to Chloe. She was already engaged in conversation with him, looking beautiful with her short bob curling wildly around her face, despite the fading bruises that makeup couldn't quite hide and the cane next to the chair to support her when her leg tired.

"But I thought he was..."

"He's bi. And he's just looking for someone who speaks to his heart. He's very eclectic."

"And what about a Mistress?"

"He has one." She slanted him a glance up from beneath her lashes, teasing him. "Though I wouldn't be surprised if Chloe didn't have the makings of a Mistress when he has need of it. It's very empowering, the feeling of a man's submission to you. Addictive even."

"Hmmm." He drew her more firmly to him, loving this new side of her that had been emerging over the past several weeks. "You might just make me consider crossing over."

She locked her hands around his neck, her tone softening with affection. "I'm sure I won't live long enough to see that. You're a Master, through and through."

"Your Master. Yours only, tonight's liberties notwithstanding." His eyes sparkled, but the set of his mouth was serious, firm, making her want to bite at his lips and draw out his passion toward her. He noticed, because his grip tightened, putting the firm pressure of him against her loins. A promise of what he would give her later.

"Good to know," she murmured, running a finger just under the lobe of his ear, playing in his hair. She looked over, saw Chloe had captured Brendan's hand and was reading his palm. He studied the crown of her head, a bemused look on his face, that pleasant bewilderment that most people experienced when first exposed to Chloe's joyous nature. "Brendan just wants someone to take care of, someone whose heart answers his. Someone who will be loving and loyal, who will ease the little boy deep inside who's afraid he'll wake up and find everything he loves is taken away. For some men I think taking care of the woman they love is what matters most, whether they do it as a Master or as a submissive." Her gaze shifted briefly to Mac who was dancing with his wife now, his powerful arms holding her close to him. "And Brendan can teach Chloe how to lead the dance. It's not in her blood, but if they fall in love and she enjoys it, even just as role playing, it will be enough. It wouldn't be enough for every submissive, but it will be for him. He'll care for her as a cherished Mistress, even if she never takes the title."

"Because he has the Mistress of his heart already." Tyler pressed his hand low on the small of her back, making desire curl low in her stomach. "Like the knight who chooses his queen or another woman out of his reach as the lady who inspires him. She motivates him to be who he should be in this life, even when he gives his heart to a wife or lover." Before she could get flustered, as if he anticipated her discomfort, he changed gears. "Somehow, however, I don't think it will be difficult to talk Chloe into tying him up and having her way with him."

At the moment she slanted a teasing glance up at him, getting a bit lost in the sexy mischief evident in his amber eyes, a flashbulb popped. Marguerite saw Violet sitting back down with her camera. She and Mac had returned to their table and now Mac leaned back in his chair at the round table. He held on to the back slat of Josh's chair while Violet sat to his left. She was carrying on an animated discussion with Josh's wife Lauren and two others Marguerite didn't recognize.

Tyler followed her gaze and chuckled. "Oh, God save us, there's a couple you need to meet. Justin Herne and his wife, Sarah. A different Sarah from ours. Justin runs a women's erotica shop. Sarah is a police chief."

"I'm sure that was an interesting love story." She took in the dynamics at that table, two Mistresses with submissive males, though one always applied that term to Mac Nighthorse with some degree of astonishment. A man who ran a sex shop, who had a police chief as a wife. Then there was the potential of Chloe and Brendan nearby, obviously intrigued with each other. But how much less remarkable was her situation? A Mistress dancing with her new husband, also a Dominant.

"It really can't be predicted, can it? Relationships are more fluid than we think they are."

He picked up on her thought, brought her closer so he could brush his lips along her cheek. "There's no other option when you can't imagine being without someone."

She leaned further into him, feeling the music and the night surrounding them, the love of friends.

As the song came to a conclusion, she stepped back, but retained his hands. "I have a gift for you."

Tyler lifted a brow. "Angel, you never have to give me a gift again. You've given me what I want for every birthday and Christmas for the rest of my life."

Her blue eyes softened, her mouth trembling a little. He knew she was on emotional overload today, gripping every moment with both hands like that teddy bear that now held a place of honor on their bed. She wasn't afraid to savor it now and it made him want to kiss her again. And again.

But before he could act on it, she looked toward Josh. As if he was waiting for her signal, he reached over, tapped Justin Herne's arm. As Justin rose, Josh leaned over to Lauren, dressed in a strapless sequined gown, to kiss her bare shoulder. Reaching up, she cradled his face to press her own lips to his jaw.

"You are an extremely confident man," Marguerite observed, watching Justin Herne move toward them with the easy elegance of a wild creature. Looking deceptively civilized in black tie, he wore his dark brown hair pulled into a sleek tail at the nape, emphasizing the chiseled planes of his face, the dark eyes, the dangerously sensual set of his mouth.

"Admit it. You think I'm the handsomest man here."

She suppressed a chuckle, shot him an amused glance. "Those are wedding day blinders. Keep men like this around and see what happens."

Justin arrived before them then, so Tyler swallowed his threatening retort. The man withdrew a slim box from inside his jacket. "Per your specifications, Mrs.

Winterman."

The look on her face as the first of their friends called her by the title was worth everything to Tyler. Her wonder and delight was such that she didn't speak for a moment. Justin waited, a slight smile on his lips as if he knew the impact the words had had on her.

Tyler put his hand to the small of her back, touched her with simple intimacy. And not just to reassure her. Watching the close attention of the women clustered around the dance floor, he knew she was right. He really did have to cultivate some less distracting male friends.

"I'm sorry..." She cleared her throat. "I asked Josh—"

"Josh's contact for the jewelry maker was me. He's one of my specialty suppliers, an artist as great as Josh, only in the arena of gems and precious metals. I hope you like it." Justin turned, extended the slender box to Tyler. "Your bride had this ordered."

She reached out and covered Tyler's hand as he took it. Justin discreetly withdrew a couple steps so he was not blocking the view of their attentive audience. Tyler and Marguerite's pose had caught the attention of the other dancers, so the floor had cleared.

Tyler knew she'd never been shy under scrutiny. Even as a Mistress, she knew what was important was what was going on between her and the subject of her restraint. So he suspected the charming flush rising in her cheeks was for what she was about to give him.

"I willingly agreed to be your wife." A smile touched her mouth. "After your incessant whining." Laughter flitted through the crowd. Her eyes locked with his, all teasing melting away. "We took vows in the traditional way, but I also pledge myself to you in all the ways we know between us. And because of that, I want to give you this."

The conversation even at the outlying tables had stilled. Though she didn't state it blatantly, he supposed for the sake of the vanilla friends and family present, all understood that what was going on was important. He was riveted himself, caught by the intensity of those blue eyes and the significance of what she was saying to him. Words she'd obviously taken great time to think about and choose.

"When a child is brought into the world with loving parents, that child learns to smile, laugh, love, be stubborn. She learns to appreciate the reasons worth living. In that regard, you've been my parent over the past several months. I wasn't alive until I met you. You brought me into this world, delivered me here and helped me see that. You bound me to you, made me *want* to be bound to you. A parent is supposed to unconditionally love, protect against harm, care for the child, hold and shelter her. Lovers help each other discover passion and longing, understand that same type of love can be given without the binding of blood. You've been all those things to me."

She bowed her head. "I am a Mistress to others; you are the Master of me. Of my heart, mind and soul."

Tyler, too overcome to speak right away, followed the urging of her fingers and pulled the ribbon, opened the box. The choker was as he had described it to her that day by the tennis courts. A double helix of seed pearls, every third or fourth double row interrupted by a silver icicle. The main pendant was the frame of an angel's head and wings, the wings serrated delicately like the icicles, which would give tiny pricks to sensitive skin when they touched it with her movement.

He lifted it free to murmurs of approval and a smattering of applause from the entranced audience.

"I ask that you put it on me and accept me as yours forever, and know that all that I am, will ever be, ever was, belongs to you. I submit to your love and trust you to be my Master."

She said the words softly, but they carried easily to those nearby. It caused odd looks from those who were not cognizant of the underlying meanings, but it would be remembered by those who did not understand as simply an odd quirk to the day. Those like Mac and Violet, Brendan, Josh and Lauren, all watching, understood the impact of the moment.

As did he. Looking down into the face of her love and devotion, Tyler wondered for the thousandth of what was sure to be a million times what he might ever have done to deserve the gift. And what he could do to deserve keeping it for a lifetime and beyond.

"Whether it takes heaven or hell, I'll take care of you forever and never abuse the gift of your submission to me." He promised it, fiercely. She nodded and lifted her chin. Her neck was bare of jewelry, for she wore his ring on her healed finger and had given back the necklace to Sarah.

He locked the clasp around her throat. His groin tightened when gooseflesh rose on her skin, her eyes heating with arousal at the sensation of the restraint. He drew her to him with a hand on the side of her neck and brought her lips to his.

Chloe, overcome, reached out, covered Brendan's hand. "He loves her so much. You can see it. It's so...she so deserves it."

Brendan looked at her elfin face, bathed in the evening light. He had noted Chloe's slower movements down the aisle as she was obviously determined not to use the cane when she served as maid of honor. He'd had to tamp down the rage at the thought of someone harming her. He wondered if she had a lover. As she looked at their clasped hands, a bit of a flush rose in her cheeks. He discarded the idea of another man, and not just because of that flush. If he was the type of lover she deserved, he would have been by her side today, insisting on giving her an arm to lean on as she walked down that aisle.

Before she could draw away, he dared to turn her hand and enfold it in his, taking advantage of the excuse of mutual pleasure in the moment. He found he liked her small hand and hoped she wouldn't choose to move it away too soon.

When Tyler at last eased his grip, it was with no more than a breath between their parted lips. He gazed down into Marguerite's eyes, vibrant with their clarity and desire. For him.

"I can't wait to get you alone tonight," he muttered.

Marguerite had to tear her gaze away. As the applause faded, Justin stepped forward to take the box from Tyler and dancers resumed their movement on the floor. She gathered her scattered thoughts enough to take care of the final detail.

"It's exquisite and perfect. Thank you." She nodded to Justin. "To you both." She reached out and touched Josh's hand as well, for he had joined them.

Josh looked very sexy in Armani, a burgundy shirt under a tailored black coat, slacks, polished shoes, his hair a loose lion's mane of brown and black on his shoulders. Marguerite couldn't resist the urge to tease. "Did Tyler dress you?"

He clasped her hand with a smile. "He insisted, but I put my foot down at underwear."

Marguerite smiled, looked toward Justin. "I'm sure Josh gave you an address for the invoice?"

"And it better be mine, if he values his life." Tyler interjected. "I'll be paying for this debt, Justin."

"I expected nothing less," Justin said, unperturbed. "I've already mailed it to your home." Marguerite's surprised look became somewhat mutinous at being so smoothly handled by the two men and Justin and Josh wisely withdrew, deciding it was up to the groom to smooth any ruffled feathers.

Justin Herne reflected that smoothing Marguerite Winterman's feathers would be any man's pleasure. However, he had a lovely bird of his own. Sarah watched him, amused, as he pulled up his chair next to her.

"That looked like a strategic retreat. You two weren't trying to overwhelm her with testosterone, I hope?"

He slid his hand under Sarah's fall of white-gold hair, knowing her large gray-blue eyes, soft lips and the curve of her breasts outlined in the simple spaghetti strap black dress were enough to arouse his testosterone to alarming levels. He would have to think of ways to coax her into breaking a few public decency laws on the dark highways on the way home. In fact, he liked the idea of getting his hand under that short filmy skirt, past the thigh-high stockings, finding her pussy under the swatch of nearly nonexistent panties and bringing her to climax in the car. Several times.

"Justin." Her lips curved into a smile, her eyes heating, showing what he already knew and thanked the stars for. That he could arouse her with just a look. "Behave. There are people around. You're surrounded by cops."

"And not a single one of them carrying handcuffs. What earthly good are they?"

§

Marguerite and Tyler danced several more times before they were separated again. She did a three-woman dance with Gen and Chloe on the floor, enjoying quiet laughter with them as they coordinated feet and legs.

When Josh coaxed Mac out onto the floor with Violet and his own wife, she laughed, really laughed, so that she couldn't help the reflex to cover her mouth. Tyler drew her hand away as they watched Josh try to teach the big cop the first steps of a sexy Latin dance. Mac was not too enthused about gyrating his hips, even with his tiny Mistress laughing and pushing him from behind.

She and Tyler gave Natalie the honor of cutting the first piece of cake. They carried on conversations with almost every guest. Finally, in the early hours of the morning, they saw them off in cabs or their cars, depending on their level of inebriation. Marguerite held on to Komal a long moment before letting her into her car. She'd been unable to talk her into staying in a guestroom, but Tyler assured her several of the guests were headed back to Tampa. He quietly arranged for them to keep Komal's vehicle in their sights until they were sure she'd made it back to the turnoff to her suburb development.

She watched with quiet delight when Brendan walked Chloe to her car with his hand beneath her elbow. He even held on to it a few moments before leaving her, visibly reluctant to go. Marguerite didn't bother to hide her laughter this time when Chloe turned and mouthed *Oh. My. God.* across the driveway. Gen rolled her eyes and ordered her into their vehicle, then blew Marguerite a kiss. "See you back at the shop after the honeymoon!"

"Tired?" Tyler slid his arms around her waist as she watched them bump across the oyster shells down the driveway.

"In a way, yes. In another way, I feel like I could dance

308

under the stars forever."

"Well, we've one more group of guests to deal with. They're vowed to stay and mooch off our hospitality until the last bottle of champagne has been opened."

She chuckled as they strolled back to the party area. As she expected, she found the lone inhabited table was the one with Violet and Mac, Josh and Lauren, Justin and Sarah. Josh stood up and held out a chair for Marguerite while Mac pushed one out for Tyler beside it with his foot. Nearly half asleep, Violet blinked at them in benign pleasure, her body leaned into the curve of Mac's.

"Exhausting, isn't it?" Lauren, who looked like she should be a lifeguard on a Hollywood fluff drama rather than a doctor, crinkled her blue eyes in a smile at Marguerite. Josh's arm lay across the back of her chair, fingers playing with her bare shoulder. Sarah had her feet in Justin's lap. He was massaging them, his fingers occasionally drifting up her thighs so that she could slap at him like at a mosquito, making his dark eyes twinkle.

"Little Madonna." Tyler reached over, touched Violet's knee. "What a mother you're going to be. Watch, Mac. It will be a girl and you'll have two spoiled brats to care for."

"You're pregnant?! Oh my God, you didn't tell us!" Sarah jerked up, bringing her feet down so abruptly she managed to thump her heel into Justin's groin, then smacked her friend smartly in the arm as he winced good-naturedly.

"Hey, delicate condition here." Violet fended her off, laughing and shook a finger at Tyler. "You, I'm going to kill. And aren't you supposed to defend me?" She shot a glance at Mac.

Mac grinned at her. "Sugar, men never break up fights between women. It's the closest thing to watching them have sex with each other and we're always hopeful it will lead to that. Kind of like how it does between men and women on soaps."

"Yeah, like that happens," Lauren said dryly. "I *always* feel like having sex with Josh when I want to kill him."

"You always desire me," he said, unruffled. "You just pretend to be angry with me to make me work harder for it."

"Men. Pigs. The lot of you." She tugged his hair. Obligingly he tilted his head toward her, giving her an easy smile. Marguerite saw no shadows in his eyes tonight. There was too much love to light their way this evening, no room for nightmares.

"We're simple creatures, Mistress, when all's said and done."

"No. No, you're not." Marguerite was surprised when the words rose so strongly in her. She thought of what she knew of Josh, his artistic talent and those nightmares, his ability to give comfort with his easy manner. Mac's protective nature. And the small taste she'd had of Justin...it was obvious to her. And she wouldn't even begin on the man who sat next to her, his arm around her, holding her into his body, his warmth. His statement of perpetual protection and love on her throat. "You're so much more than that." She looked at each of them in turn. "You're our dreams come true. The dreams we all pretend we don't have until we meet you and then it all makes sense. From then on we know no matter what happens, it's going to be okay."

She raised the glass of wine Tyler had put before her. "To love. In all its forms. It gives us the ability to fly. To believe we can fly with the angels." She raised her gaze to Tyler and he met her look with warmth and all she'd just spoken reflecting back at her.

His attention went around the table, lingering on each woman as she'd done with the men, and then came back to his own.

"And to the angels themselves," he added. "Who make it worth taking that leap of faith."

"Hear, hear," Justin said. The glasses raised, catching the soft gleam of the fairy lights. Marguerite closed her eyes, thinking she felt the brush of wings against her hair a moment before Tyler's lips touched hers, sweeping all need for thought away.

Epilogue

"Can we make it happen that quickly?"

"Angel, we've got a whole month left before the carnival. A city can be built in a month."

"If you have more money than God."

"Well, aren't you fortunate to be married to me, then?" He grinned, slowed down to kiss her, but she spun away, pulling him onward.

"No time for your husband anymore?"

"Not a moment," she agreed. "He's kept me out of this part of the garden for two weeks. He told me today was the day I get to see what he and Josh have been doing. Our anniversary was yesterday, after all."

"More money than God doesn't faze an artist," Tyler grumbled. "I even tried threats of violence. He just waved his hand at me like he was swatting at an annoying fly. He's already made the damn thing. I didn't realize he would take half a week to determine how to set the base and arrange the area."

"Well, at least you tried. That's something." Showing a woman's proclivity for changing moods, now she stopped, turned full into him and rose onto her toes to wrap her arms around his neck and give him a heated, openmouthed kiss. Her body was soft and giving, making him groan and grip her hips, pull her hard against him.

"You sure you won't reconsider Jell-O?"

"No," he said decisively. "Sarah will not make enough Jell-O to fill a wading pool. She draws the line there. And I am not opening ten thousand of those little cups."

"Chloe will help."

He raised both brows. "She's..."

"Brendan told me he's bringing her. Or she's bringing him. It's unclear." Marguerite smiled. "But I suppose one of my employees is about to see a very different side of her boss."

"Baby oil." His eyes gleamed. "It's much easier to obtain by the gallon and it does lovely things to female skin."

"It's not too bad on males, either," she returned. "All right, then. We do wrestling contests in the baby oil pool and then the contestants can go to the open shower area. Only there's a cost. Men have to pay a donation to hold the detachable showerheads and the women can't leave the shower area until they've reached orgasm. And the couple that takes the longest to finish has to pay a bonus donation."

"I like that." He liked it a lot. Enough to want to whisk her away to their private bath area and practice.

"Oh, no." She disentangled herself and backed away, chuckling. "My gift. You promised."

He would promise her anything, his angel who had learned how to laugh and smile so much more easily this past year, who let him help her keep her lingering nightmares at bay with his arms safely around her through the night. And in that miraculous reciprocity that love had, she kept his at bay the same way.

"Why are you looking at me like that?" She caught everything, every change in his expression. It made it easy to learn to be open with her, in a way he hadn't ever trusted himself to be with a woman before.

"I was thinking how different you've become this year. The way you laugh and smile more." He reached out, touched the curve of her mouth, saw her quell the instinctive urge to cover the gesture, a gesture that had become instinctive of late only when pointed out, like now.

"Will you stop loving me if I become so different from the person you knew?"

"It has nothing to do with who you are today, tomorrow or yesterday, angel. It's about who your soul has always been, always will be."

When she took his hand, he saw her holding him in her

eyes, in her heart.

"Will Josh be waiting for us?"

"No. I wanted to give it to you when we were alone as man and wife."

Her expression always became tender, bemused when he referred to her that way, so he did it often. Now he squeezed her as they walked companionably through the trellis, the one under which they'd taken their vows. He'd moved it to the opening of this new part of his garden. It was a transition point for the area, which he knew she would understand, being a student of Japanese tea ceremonies. He'd become somewhat of one himself this past year, as well as an avid apprentice of Japanese gardening.

Marguerite noted this area was more intimate than her favored Aphrodite area. The vegetation here was all Japanese gardening style. Delicate maples, a rock garden with the tiny bamboo rake, the sand arranged in ripples to look like water. On the side of the clearing was a wisteria arbor, whose meaning she immediately recognized. Tyler had created an outdoor *machiai*, a waiting room for guests to cleanse and prepare themselves before entering the teahouse. Passing through the arbor, the circular area that followed contained a mat of greenery and soft low ground cover which could become a dew garden with the water mister, concealed as a tiny statue of a rabbit. Guests would stand there to clean their feet before they would turn to the stone basin on a pedestal next to it, a *tsukubai*, to wash their fingers and mouths, further purifying themselves before their host or hostess led them into the teahouse. A stone bench was here for them to seat themselves to wait for that host or hostess.

And the teahouse was perfect. Simple, natural materials. No nails, all peg construction. Small, intimate, for the preferred two to four guests.

"I thought you might finally decide to perform a Japanese ceremony for me. Inside, right now, there's a tea set with one cup. For us to share as the samurai did, to emphasize the bonds that exist between family. I thought we might go in there in a few minutes, share a cup together, make it official."

Family. She and Tyler were a family.

"I didn't know Josh was doing construction now."

"He isn't. Robert and I handled this part." He leaned forward to kiss her, holding his lips against hers in a quiet way as the cicadas buzzed and the breeze whispered through the garden area. Then he pulled back, turned her away from the teahouse, facing her toward an angle of the garden not visible until one stood here.

"This is what Josh was doing."

For a long moment she simply stood, staring at it. Not believing what she was seeing. Fragile dark green ferns clustered at the base of the sculpture that had been placed by a small waterfall crafted of round smooth stones. There was another rock garden here as well. Tyler released her hand, his fingers caressing hers a moment before he let her go. She felt him watching her as she went closer. A small bench was in front of the statue, a simple square wooden piece that could serve as a kneeling bench for prayer, a place to sit while one made designs in the rock garden, or a place for solitary contemplation. She stepped up onto it to bring herself closer to the statue's face, reach out to it with trembling fingers.

In the mortal world she'd never known him as an adult, but she knew this was how he would have looked. It was all there, the structure of his face, the intentness of his eyes, even the manner in which he stood. Alert, turning as if he was about to respond to her, a light smile on his lips.

She stepped down. When she turned to face her husband, the question was in her eyes, but she was unable to speak.

"I tried to tell you several times," he said. "But we'd get interrupted, or the timing would be wrong. There seemed no way to say it until I could show you, like this."

"H-How could you..."

"When I drove up that day..." Shadows gathered in his eyes. Because she knew the memory still haunted him, she reached out and he took her hand. Sitting down on the bench, he kissed her fingers. "When I jumped out of the car I looked up, looking for you. And I saw something."

Tyler turned his attention to the statue, remembering. "You leaped with Natalie in your arms, your father with you and then... It was like sunlight, only it was raining. Mac remembers it as the sun breaking through the clouds for just a moment, but I saw something else. Wings." He met her gaze. "A face, a length of leg. When your chute came out, he was all over it, pulling it out, open. He held on to it a moment, probably decelerating you a bit. Then he was gone as if that was all he was allowed to do. If I saw what I thought I saw, I'm sure he would have seen you all the way to the ground if he could have."

Marguerite stared at him. Her attention shifted back to the other prominent feature of the statue. She'd thought it had been Tyler's compliment to her brother's spirit, but she now recognized it as an attempt to reconstruct a memory. This older version of her brother had a pair of wings coming out of his back, all of it sculpted in bronze, every feather textured and separate. The smooth musculature of his arms and legs was defined well, though his body was clothed in a simple tunic. Marguerite was sure that was due to the fact he was her brother, since Josh's work rarely displayed clothing for the purpose of modesty. However, he had not hesitated to show in sensual detail what a beautiful mortal man David would have been. Making her heart hurt, wishing he had lived to enjoy the love of a woman, to give some woman the gift of himself.

"I thought about it a long time, not sure of my own mind on it," Tyler continued. "Then, the night you went sleepwalking in my house, when you got up on the balcony, I saw him again. He woke me up, saved your life. That time I got just a quick glimpse of his face. He has a hell of an arm. Just about knocked me out of the bed." Tyler smiled, though his eyes remained serious. "And I haven't seen him since. I guess he knew his work was done."

She nodded mutely, sinking down on his knee. Tyler put an arm around her waist, steadying her with a palm on her hip as they looked at the statue together.

"All those years in the field, remembering every detail of a person based on just a flash impression, paid off. I described him to Josh. Komal had pictures of your brother, so between that and my recollection he came up with his face, the body type and stance. I hope we did well."

"It's him." The words came out thickly. Tears began to fall, her expression torn between grief and joy. "Oh, God, Tyler. You..." She shook her head and he pressed his face to her throat, wrapping both arms around her.

"No, angel, I didn't want you to cry."

"Yes, you did. In a good way. And this is a good way, I promise. You just...you understand so much about me, more every day. And this...if you keep giving me gifts like this, I'll be the first person whose heart broke out of too much happiness."

"I'll be here to put it back together, angel. Every time. I promise."

§

Robert slipped into the garden as they strolled back up the path, smiling a little at their absorption in each other, remembering his and Sarah's days as newlyweds. He turned at a shadow, a rush of wings as if a heron had taken flight close by. Seeing nothing but the delicate pointed leaves of the Japanese maple quivering, he shrugged, bent to retrieve his garden tools and went to the statue to clip back some of the weeds trying to poke their heads out among the ferns at the base.

He discovered a feather there. Large enough to be a heron's, only herons didn't have feathers like this. Long and white with gilding on the tips like the touch of gold and silver mixed. Holding it in his hand, Robert felt a warmth sweep through him, a sense of peace, of the type of spiritual tranquility he often felt in his garden. He felt thanks sweep him. For the day, for Sarah. For Mr. and Mrs. Winterman. For the beauty of green things and flowers. For life.

Leaving his weeding tools for the moment, he went to find Sarah. He wanted to give her the feather, sensing that it was the perfect gift for the woman who'd agreed to be his for the rest of their lives.

The End

READY FOR MORE?

Check out Joey's website at storywitch.com where you'll find additional information, free excerpts, buy links and news about current and upcoming releases in the Nature of Desire series and for all of her other books and series.

You can find free vignettes and friends to share them with at the JWH Connection, a Joey W. Hill fan forum created by and operated for fans of Joey W. Hill. Sign up instructions are available at storywitch.com/community.

Finally, be sure to check out the latest newsletter for information on upcoming releases, book signing events, contests, and more. You can view current and past editions and subscribe to receive upcoming editions at storywitch.com/community or click the link under the Community menu.

About the Author

Joey W. Hill writes about vampires, mermaids, boardroom executives, cops, witches, angels, housemaids... She's penned over forty acclaimed titles and six award-winning series, and been awarded the RT Book Reviews Career Achievement Award for Erotica. But she's especially proud and humbled to have the support and enthusiasm of a wonderful, widely diverse readership.

So why erotic romance? "Writing great erotic romance is all about exploring the true face of who we are – the best and worst - which typically comes out in the most vulnerable moments of sexual intimacy." She has earned a reputation for writing BDSM romance that not only wins her fans of that genre, but readers who would "never" read BDSM romance. She believes that's because strong, compelling characters are the most important part of her books.

"Whatever genre you're writing, if the characters are captivating and sympathetic, the readers are going to want to see what happens to them. That was the defining element of the romances I loved most and which shaped my own writing. Bringing characters together who have numerous emotional obstacles standing in their way, watching them reach a soul-deep understanding of one another through the expression of their darkest sexual needs, and then growing from that understanding into love - that's the kind of story I love to write."

Take the plunge with her, and don't hesitate to let her know what you think of her work, good or bad. She thrives on feedback!

Find more of Joey's work by following her on Facebook and Twitter, and check out her website for more books by Joey W. Hill.

Twitter: @JoeyWHill

Facebook: JoeyWHillAuthor

On the Web: www.storywitch.com

Email: storywitch@storywitch.com

Also by Joey W. Hill

Arcane Shot Series

Something About Witches
In the Company of Witches

Daughters of Arianne Series

A Mermaid's Kiss
A Witch's Beauty
A Mermaid's Ransom

Knights of the Board Room Series

Board Resolution
Controlled Response
Honor Bound
Afterlife
Hostile Takeover
Willing Sacrifice
Soul Rest

Nature of Desire Series

Holding the Cards
Natural Law

Ice Queen
Mirror of My Soul
Mistress of Redemption
Rough Canvas
Branded Sanctuary
Divine Solace

Naughty Bits Series

The Lingerie Shop
Training Session
Bound To Please
The Highest Bid

Naughty Wishes Series

Part 1: Body
Part 2: Heart
Part 3: Mind
Part 4: Soul

Vampire Queen Series

Vampire Queen's Servant
Mark of the Vampire Queen
Vampire's Claim
Beloved Vampire
Vampire Mistress
Vampire Trinity
Vampire Instinct
Bound by the Vampire Queen
Taken by a Vampire
The Scientific Method

Nightfall
Elusive Hero
Night's Templar

Non-Series Titles

If Wishes Were Horses
Virtual Reality
Unrestrained

Novellas

Chance of a Lifetime
Choice of Masters
Make Her Dreams Come True
Threads of Faith
Submissive Angel

Short

Snow Angel